The Knife Sharpener's Bell

The Knife Sharpener's Bell

RHEA TREGEBOV

This is a work of fiction, and some liberties have been taken with time and space. The characters in the novel are products of the author's imagination, and do not refer to real people, living or dead.

Edited by Warren Cariou
Cover images: Arcangel
Cover and book design by Tania Craan
Printed and bound in Canada by Friesens
This book is printed on 100% recycled paper.

Library and Archives Canada Cataloguing in Publication

Tregebov, Rhea, 1953-
The knife sharpener's bell / Rhea Tregebov.

ISBN 978-1-55050-408-8

I. Title.

PS8589.R342K65 2009 C813'.54 C2009-903615-0

10 9 8 7 6 5 4 3 2 1

2517 Victoria Avenue
Regina, Saskatchewan
Canada S4P 0T2

Available in Canada from
Publishers Group Canada
9050 Shaughnessy Streeet
Vancouver, BC, V6P 6E5

The publisher gratefully acknowledges the financial support of its publishing program by: the Saskatchewan Arts Board, the Canada Council for the Arts, the Government of Canada through the Book Publishing Industry Development Program (BPIDP), Association for the Export of Canadian Books and the City of Regina Arts Commission.

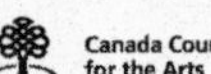

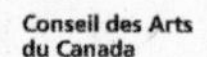

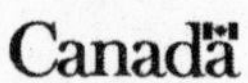

This book is dedicated to my mother, Jeanette Block,
and to the memory of Vladlen Furman.

Prologue

My father is wearing a heavy tweed overcoat and a brown wool suit, his best, as he boards the train. Brown tweed cap flecked with green, striped tie. He's smoking his pipe, a narrow tin of tobacco in his breast pocket: Prince Albert in a can. His white apron he's taken off and hung on the peg by the back door of the delicatessen. He's packed two small suitcases – white shirts, clean socks, long underwear.

The train hisses and snorts at the platform. Thirty people to see him off: neighbours, comrades, friends. I'm not yet nine years old. Winnipeg, February 1935. The station is splendid; I've never been in a room this big. I tip my head back and my mouth holds itself open, the vault of my palate repeating the vault above. But when my father moves towards the train, something shifts. I've been everywhere in the room but now I snap into myself. *Say goodbye*, my mother instructs. No. I won't let him go. *Poppa!* I'm taken up and smoke from his pipe wreathes my head. I nuzzle my face into the scratchy wool. There. That's what I want. But he puts me down, tries to settle me back onto the platform. My poppa – who has always found a way to fix things, has always found room for what I need – will not be moved.

I have to go, he says, his hands smoothing my hair back from my forehead. *You're a big girl now.* And he releases me, turns to the comrades, friends. No. The black body of the train shifts beside me. No. I concentrate. Somewhere above me, my mother is speaking, but I don't hear. In one slight movement I slip by, step up onto the train, over the frightening gap between the platform and the shifting metal body of the train, which will stir at any moment, which will move and sigh and take my father away.

I'm up over the gap, I'm in the strange air of the train. In the flurry of goodbyes, no one has noticed I'm gone. I'll find my poppa's seat. I want something of him – a last trace, a last place, a scent – before the train takes him. I slip along the aisles and spot his name on a paper tag. The car is empty; no one sees as I fit myself beneath his seat, between the two rows of back-to-back benches. It feels good. On the platform they've noticed that I've gone. I hear voices calling me. It doesn't matter. My heart is bumping inside me. It doesn't matter; I won't give up. *Make a wish.* All my body wants to keep my father home, and I will. It's with my body that I'll keep the train from leaving, from taking him away. The voices go by. I'm crouched against the rough fabric at the back of the bench. If they don't find me, the train won't go. My breath is scratchy in my chest, but it doesn't matter. My knees are dirty now from the floor of the train car. I think about dirt and bugs, brush my red plaid pleated skirt. Run my fingers, twisted, up and down, up and down the edges of my red suspenders, my heart getting quieter. There are more voices, but I'm concentrating; I concentrate, shrink into myself so that even I can't find me. Now it's my thumb that runs itself up and down the stiff elastic edge of the suspenders. The shuddering stops. The smoke from the stack diminishes, dies.

Chapter One

❄

Speak when illuminated. Good advice, even if it does come from a sign above a speaker on an elevator. I was taking it from the one level of the subway to the next, bent on some little chore. I doubt much of my mind was illuminated. I don't like the subway particularly; I walk whenever I can, but one knee was a bit stiff. When the doors opened to the platform, I saw that every surface – floor, stairs, columns, even the trash bins – was covered with words. At that moment, I went dark. I can't say I knew where I was, who I was. I didn't know why I had come into this forest of words and I couldn't understand any of them, couldn't understand the letters they were written in, as if it were some foreign alphabet. A stranger put his hand under my elbow – I must have looked as startled as I felt – and asked me if I was all right. With that touch at my coat sleeve, I understood. They were ads. The station had been papered in words that were intended to make us feel how empty we were so that we would want something. Is this the surface we've become, defaced, an illegible scrawl over everything? That solicitous stranger asking me if I was all right – I don't know.

I got myself home. Got past the beige cardboard packing cases that seem to be taking over my life bit by bit these days, snapped on the television. I do that a lot – leave the set on for company with the volume on mute. Let the images stutter by peripherally as I make dinner or tidy up. Usually I don't pay any mind to it, but this stopped me: their faces, again. As if they were in the very middle of inventing the world, standing on the edge of Eden. Such earnestness as they waved their resolute placards and chanted their chants, sang their songs. *No Blood for Oil.* Children, I thought. You are children. You believe in the world and you don't know what's waiting for you. You don't know what gate will swing shut on you, standing there hoping for Eden. I wasn't sure if I was cursing or blessing them.

So what could I do then but turn up the volume and sit on my bed and listen? Those bright faces, hope cupped in each one, they were ready to give up everything they didn't know they had – just as we had been when we were that ignorant, had that much hope. I say "we" when I shouldn't. I don't think I ever did hope that purely; maybe for myself, but not for the world. I was always standing at the edge of that heaven on earth holding myself back from it. I doubt I ever believed the way Vladimir did, or my parents.

I turned the television off. The room had gone dark, so I switched on the lights and I did what I do at the end of every working day – I went into the kitchen, turned on the radio and started making dinner. You have to eat. And you have to be glad to eat, to stand in your very own kitchen, in a light that's there when you touch a switch, and you've got food in the cupboards, in the refrigerator, and you can eat. I started slicing the beautiful brown mushrooms that I'd bought at the market just that day, but then the news came on the radio, and their voices, so fresh, and their faces came back to me. I told myself dinner could wait, even though the mushrooms were already loading the air with their fragrance.

I try not to be a coward more often than necessary. All I had to do was pick one more empty box, go into the spare room, open a drawer and take out the papers.

They were in crisp blue file folders, labelled, in order. My tidy daughter has taken care of that. My girl – my grown girl. They have a historical value, she tells me. I have to look after them, even if I can't stand to look *at* them. Some day her almost-grown son, my grandson, will want them. All right then, my dear. I will look after them. They'll go with me to the new apartment, to my new home where the snow will be shovelled by someone else and there will be no icy stairs for me to slip on. A crack in one little bone. It wasn't even a proper fracture, just a hairline crack in one minor ankle bone – I was out of the cast two weeks ahead of schedule! But that was the last straw. For her. For me too, I guess. Because of course she was right, as she usually is, though I'm not particularly fond of admitting it. Life will be a bit more simple for these bones, a bit easier, once I've left this house and am in the apartment. Once I've moved. This is the hard part. It's always been the hard part for the likes of me, the move from one thing to another, but then I get used to it. I always do.

So I took those folders in my hands. How could they hurt me, pieces of paper? I was about to put them in the box but then some of the pages slipped out from their crisp blue cage and words slipped out and I couldn't stop myself from reading them. Lecture notes from school, a newspaper article. A thin blue envelope with a square Canadian stamp, a sheet of paper in Manya's elegant hand, one in Lev's. And then an official document with its seals and signatures, its words and numbers. Article 58-1a. I stand accused.

I've kept myself busy, for years, for decades, so I won't have to stand accused. My mother wouldn't credit it, but I'm a practical person now, content as long as I'm at work. For the longest time work has been what's given me to myself. And what's kept me away from myself, I suppose. Maybe the only way to go on was not to look back. Or maybe the only way not to look back was to go on. Whichever was the case, that was how I managed.

It's not so foolish, not *so* cowardly, really, being afraid to go back. I know people, some of them dear friends, who live there. They're the faithful ones. They hold on and don't forsake the past, but I've watched what I think of as their real lives wane, their real children diminish, while they live amid ghosts or near-ghosts. I have a grown, healthy daughter to admonish me. A grandson who's almost grown. What good are memories? I've worked so hard for so long at not remembering. It has been a lot of work; it has been labour, keeping myself from the past. Hard work, not remembering. Somebody told me that once, in a dark room, the war just years, not decades, behind us. Somebody told me that, once, in a cold room.

But what yanked me into the past? Pieces of paper. Suddenly there I was, in the spare room. Kneeling, my heart yammering away in my chest. On my knees in the spare room, praying at the altar of my cardboard box, shovelling folders into it as if to keep some demon at bay. And remembering. I couldn't stop myself. Remembering, and wondering what got me here, to a house with a kitchen and light and food. What's getting me ready to leave.

We're in the kitchen. Poppa boosts me up onto a chair so I can reach, hands me an orange. "Here," he says. "Look, I'll start and then you can peel it yourself." His thumb gouges into the thick peel, then he hands it over, big and orange and not quite round, like a picture in a book. It smells like summer, smells bright even though it's almost always winter and dark. I put my small thumb in where Poppa's big thumb made a beginning, work the thick peel loose until it's all gone, every last nick of orange. Then with sharp little nails I peel off every scrap of white. The orange is still there, but it's different. I pile the peel and white in a little heap on the table, put both thumbs into the centre and break the orange apart. And now it's gone, no longer itself. Poppa's taken off his white apron; he's reading the newspaper. I can't think of what to say, don't want to spoil this present. I poke at a little segment with a finger, shiver. What was whole is broken. I don't know what to do.

I'm leaning my elbows on the table, leaning my whole body towards the bowl. I can smell the cocoa my mother has stirred into the flour, specks of it swimming in the air, a rich, steamy smell, the kitchen warm from the oven. In another bowl – heavy cream-coloured china – after the butter and sugar, go eggs. One tough rap as her fingers break the eggshell in two and the yellow spills out, the clear stuff around it. Five, six, seven eggs – seven eggs! A king's ransom, precious. Seven eggs are going into this cake because it's my brother Ben's birthday. Now the whoosh as she beats air into the eggs and the sugary, buttery pulp with the old wooden spoon, working round and round the bowl till everything is all of a piece. What was once eggs and sugar and vanilla and butter now are something altogether different, something rich and strange. The mix of flour and cocoa and salt goes in and stops being flour and cocoa and salt and becomes batter, which will become cake – but only if I remember not to slam doors, not to shout and wreck it all. My mother pours the batter from the big bowl into the cake tins, nudging each last lazy bit of batter out, to be sure that both tins are exactly the same. Then the best part happens. She takes the spoon and cleans the bowl, each round carefully overlapping until every last chocolate lick is cleaned off into the tins. Every last lick. Nothing precious is wasted.

That's why the work of memory is so perilous, why it hurts to do it. It gives you back what you had and with it what you've lost: my parents, my brother. Vladimir. I know them dead, now. Know them as I never knew them when they were alive, their lives complete, completed. Change is over; possibility's over. It's done. My father will never grow older; my mother will never soften. They never saw a grandchild, never knew my daughter or her son. What do I really know of them, with my child's perspective, afraid of who they were, what they meant to me, what I mean because of them? The day my aunt Manya told me the facts of life – I was thirteen and my mother had told me nothing – when she told me, I started to cry. Manya sat beside me on the bed, massaging a dab of lavender-scented cream into my palm, her small fingers tugging at each of mine, a firm pull, as she rubbed circles into each joint, the pink nails, white quarter moons at each base. My hands are just like Poppa's deft, compact hands. My mother's hands were narrow, the fingers long, elegant. When Manya was finished explaining, the calm, clear words of explanation – mother, father, egg, sperm – I took my hands back, chewed on a thumbnail, the tears starting in my eyes. Why, my aunt asked. Because until then, I didn't know I was my father's too. I thought I was just my mother's child, but with those words, for the first time, I knew I was half Poppa too.

Whose daughter am I? Why do I still need to know? If I am to remember properly, I should start where I started, in the apartment on Main Street near Selkirk Avenue, in Winnipeg, above the delicatessen. When I hear my parents' stories, I hear them told by others' voices. This is how children learn about their parents' mysterious lives before they were born: sitting under the table, at the foot of the stairs, listening while the grown-ups talk. We need to imagine our parents' lives before ours because we believe – foolishly, utterly – that they were born only to give birth to us. And maybe they were. Maybe our parents' lives came into being to generate ours, and ours for our children's.

I do know that I was the last, least, child Anne Gershon bore, the one she didn't want. I wonder if I ever had a home in my mother, who told everyone who would listen how she ran up and down the stairs in that first month of pregnancy, not caring if something bad happened? And then the child she didn't want turned out to be a girl.

What good is a girl? I have a fine son already.

The neighbour women don't like my mother should talk this way. *Pooh, pooh,* they spit, to keep away the evil eye. Not that anyone is superstitious, religious – *the opiate of the masses.*

The women know everyone and everything. They knew my father in the Old Country, grew up in the same courtyard in Simferopol. And they like to talk.

Avram Gershon came to Canada, they say, *after his first wife walked out on him.* Yes, he was married before: a wife and son he left in Russia. The first wife was a beauty – she was a seamstress maybe, maybe a nurse. One story is that she was a medical student, and the man she ran off with was the boarder they took on while she was in medical school. Though if you were to ask Anne, she'd tell you the first wife was nothing but a whore. So poor Avram, his heart was broken. The child was just a toddler when the wife ran away.

So Avram sells everything he has, buys a third-class ticket to Winnipeg. He steps out of the train station, 1914, the middle of nowhere! He could have gone to Chicago, or Buenos Aires, but he buys the ticket for Winnipeg. Doesn't know a single living soul in all of America, except for Sarah Katz, Hershel's wife. It's not that Avram and Sarah were sweethearts; she was married already to Hershel. Avram and Sarah weren't sweethearts, but they were like family: they grew up in the same courtyard in Simferopol. Sarah Katz. You won't find a better woman than Sarah Katz. All Avram had was a postcard with her address on it, and that was how he found her. Just walked into her kitchen. She had no idea. She's down on her knees, washing the linoleum. She hears someone at the door, and she thinks it's her husband come home early from work. There's Avram in the doorway, fresh off the boat. *Oy, Avram*, she says. Can't find another word in her mouth. *Oy, Avram*. She had no idea.

Poor Avram, his heart was broken.

The story is that when my mother and father met in Winnipeg, each had a story. Because my mother had a story too, another love story.

You want to know Anne's story? the women ask. Anne Gershon came from Odessa, one of four sisters, big-city girls. Odessa, it's all she'd talk about: the cherry orchards, the fountains, the beaches, the opera house. *Odessa.* She'd say it sweet like candy. *My city is the most beautiful city in the world.* That's what she'd say. *I never meant to leave.*

But she did leave, in 1914, just before the Great War. It all happened because, in Odessa, Anne had a boyfriend, a certain Lev Zvarensky. A fine-looking man: broad shoulders, more than six feet tall he was. Everybody said, now there's a match for Anne; *there's* a man who can handle her. They were talking marriage, Anne and Lev, when suddenly he falls for Manya, the little one, the youngest of Anne's sisters. Big brown eyes and a waist like a china doll. Suddenly it's Manya and Lev who are getting married.

What's the song about sisters? *A sister to hit you, and a sister to kiss you, and a sister to steal your love.* So for Anne, the taste of Odessa goes sour in her mouth. And she leaves, *for a little while*, she says. For a little while, till the taste improves.

And why doesn't she go back? Because of the war, and because she meets Avram. No, no, Sarah Katz didn't introduce them. Anne just went into Avram's store. She walks into the store like a queen, points to a can of tomatoes. Those green eyes, so proud she barely speaks a word to him. And Avram is smitten. He talks to her in his soft voice, trying to make her notice him. And meanwhile already she's decided he's the one.

Because Avram Gershon was a catch. You should have seen him in 1914: handsome, kind as could be. Such manners, such a gentle voice – one of those handlebar moustaches! Some people said he was no match for a woman like Anne, but Anne was the one he wanted. And *she* wanted *him*: a man she could handle. A man who had taught himself English by reading the newspapers, who was doing well enough with the store to send money home. It was not only that he was a handsome man and a capable man: it was politics too. Because they were both believers. You think *Avram* is a believer? Anne Gershon can talk politics till you're blue in the face. *Listen to me*, Yossel Zalinsky, the one with the store that sells artificial limbs, says to her one day, *the Union of Soviet Socialist Republics is no paradise. The Soviet Union is not a democracy, he says. It's been six whole years since the civil war there ended and still there hasn't been an election, not in the whole of the Soviet Union*. Anne takes a look at him. *Democracy?* Anne says. She tells him: *I'll tell you about democracy.* So Anne folds up her copy of the *Vestnik*; you'd think she was going to give him a good smack with it! *In the* democratic *United States of America*, she tells him, *they waited thirteen years after the War of Independence before they had elections*! And she looks round the room with those green eyes of hers. *Why should the Russian people jump right into a democracy?* she asks. *They've got better things to do*, she says. And you know there's no arguing with Anne Gershon. A real Bolshevik – she once threw a Menshevik right out of the apartment!

So it's a match. The neighbours warn her that Avram's a married man, but Anne says, *never mind, he'll divorce her*. And – that's the end of the story! He divorces the first wife. Don't think it was easy, but he does. And he marries Anne.

My parents' marriage was a marriage of believers. Like those young faces on the television, my father believed in possibility, in the future. *Make a wish*. He wanted his children with Anne to be born into a new world, a place where they'd have a chance to get an education. *For me it wasn't like that*, he'd say. *It's an old story*, he'd say. And we'd say, *tell us, tell*, and he would.

When I was ten years old, he'd say, *my father died*. We owed money, and because I was the oldest son it was my job to pay the debts. My mother had no choice: she apprenticed me to a shopkeeper. Twelve hours a day. Not much to eat. No shoes to wear either. The shopkeeper gave me cheap rubber boots that didn't fit. And so my feet got sores from them. No bed to sleep on either. I'd fold a blanket and sleep under the counter in the store. I was just a kid. Can you imagine? That was before the Revolution; that was the days of the tsar. My mother I'd see only for a few hours every week, when the shopkeeper could spare me and when my mother could get away from her own work. One night, I'm fast asleep under the counter at the shop but all of a sudden I open my eyes. Maybe I heard something or maybe it was just that I could feel someone in the room. I open my eyes and see my mother's face. She used to wear these long brown braids that she would twist around her head like a crown. I wake up and I see her face like that, with a crown of brown hair, and at first I think, *I'm dreaming, this is a dream*. But it isn't. She's really there. Not saying anything, just looking at me sleeping. And she's crying. Why is she crying? Because my father's dead and I'm sleeping under the counter and I have no shoes. Because she had to walk a mile in the dark in the middle of the night to see her child.

That's enough stories today, he'd say. *For you, things will be better.*

The stories come like fairy tales – my mother with her broken heart, my father with his, how they left and why and what they had and didn't. They preside over my birth. And there are other presences too: my brother Ben, standing over my crib. And on the bureau in our parents' bedroom, the photograph of my father in Russia wearing old-fashioned clothes. With him there's a very young boy, little more than a baby, a frilly lace collar around his neck. The boy is standing on a chair so that he and my father can shake hands: they're saying goodbye.

There should be two brothers standing over me like fairy godmothers in a story, watching the blanket rise and fall with each breath.

But it's Ben who watches over me, Ben who stares and stares at the photograph on the bureau. And he wants to ask, though he knows he never can, he wants to ask who the boy is.

The photo is gone. There was a day my mother tore it up, because it was unbearable to her, that other life my father had before her, any love that wasn't hers. She wanted him to have one life, his life with her, to have always been what he was to her. The one true love, the one true self. *Non sum qualis eram*: I am not who I was. When I first read Horace's *Odes*, just after the war, that line shook me; it seemed so true and terrifying. *All change is loss.* I read that in another poem once. Life changes us; we have no choice but to change. And sometimes we turn into a distorted version of what we could have been, what we were.

Much as I like to deny it, I'm an old woman. And I still don't know about love. My parents' story was a love story, but look what love did to my father. He let my mother drive him, take his life from him. The stories, films, the songs say *complete me with your love*. But maybe it's not that we're partial and looking to be whole. Maybe it's that we want to stay partial. We don't want to grow up, own our lives. So we hand over the keys of our lives, relinquish them to something that's not real . . . Poppa loved that first son just as much as he loved Ben and me. But he gave him up.

My father is standing in the kitchen, talking quietly to my mother. He's come up the stairs at the end of a day at the till, bone-tired, left the white apron on its hook. Later the farm girl who helps out in the store will take it away and scrub the heavy cotton clean. My mother sets a roast chicken, potato knishes, carrots on the table. Pumpernickel so dark it's almost black, her homemade dill pickles. *He's here*, she says. *That one, the boy.* Three months before, the family had written. My father's first wife was dead. My father's mother had also written to say that no matter what had happened between Poppa and his first wife, he should take his son in. Blood was blood. My father had sent the fare. And now the boy's here and Poppa has to make my mother believe that the little *mamser*, whose mother was a whore, shouldn't be left to sleep in the street.

We'll give the boy a chance, Poppa is saying. *We need an extra pair of hands. You have yours full with the little one.* His voice is soft, because there's no arguing with my mother. His voice is soft when he explains that it's not for himself that he's asking. He has his own son, a fine boy, and now the little one. Yes, the boy's a stranger to them, and at thirteen he's almost a man. All right so he's an orphan; we're all orphans someday and here he is, a stranger in a strange land. But it's not the boy who needs anything and it's not Poppa. It's my mother who needs the help. Work – the boy will learn to be a worker, not a hooligan, not an idle bourgeois. An extra pair of hands for my mother. Poppa's voice is soft, no arguing, so in the end my mother decides: they'll give the boy a chance. He'll work; he'll pay his way. And if he doesn't, he's out in the street.

And the boy is allowed to come into the house with his parcels, stand awkwardly in the room, the image of his father, though there's something different about the eyes.

He stands in the room as though rooms were alien to him. At eight, his mother already ill, he'd run away from home. In the chaos of those early years of the Revolution, the Civil War, there were gangs of street urchins, *besprizorny*. He'd gotten into trouble with the police, come into the custody of child welfare, been sent to a reformatory for street kids. Now he's in his father's house.

My mother tells him he's to share the room with Ben, who's been led to believe that the boy's a cousin, or adopted. The boy can go to Argyle School on Monday. Meanwhile, he can have some supper if he's hungry.

On Monday at Argyle School they put him in with the grade three class, so he can learn English. Small for his age at thirteen, he's still ridiculous. He says little, does what he's told. He tries out his new words of English on the customers at the store, twisting the sounds around his tongue. And he sweeps out the backroom, picks me up when nobody's looking, sings songs to me in Yiddish, plays peekaboo. I smile to see him, because he's there and because I am.

Annette, he says, giving me my name. The family calls me Baby or Monkey, but the boy gives me my name. It's the name my mother chose, a name that's almost hers. You don't name a child after a living person; it's bad luck. *I'll call her whatever I feel like calling her*, my mother says when the women shake their heads. *I don't believe in superstition*. My mother and Poppa don't believe in all that mumbo-jumbo, never go to shul. She'll call her daughter whatever she wants to call her. No arguing with my mother.

The boy doesn't argue; he keeps out of my mother's way. He knows a good thing when he sees it. In his first month in the apartment above the delicatessen on Main Street, he grows an inch, my mother setting the plates hard in front of him. Nobody's going to be able to say that Anne Gershon let a child, not even a *mamser* like him, go hungry from her table.

He sticks it out as best he can, listens, makes himself useful, fixes the wheels on Ben's wooden dog. Sings, on the sly, to me. He doesn't make any trouble. But even so, he doesn't last more than eight months in Anne Gershon's house.

When did the knife sharpener first come to me? I have to think back as far as memory goes, to the apartment on Main Street, to the crib whose wooden slats I believe I can remember. In this memory, the crib is empty. I've been taken from the apartment to the quarantine ward at King George Hospital with scarlet fever. Ben wants to know what happened, where Baby is. *She got sick from eating dirty things.* He goes into the bedroom where the crib is. Dull sunlight comes through the tall, narrow window. He'll be sick too. He runs his finger along the baseboards, puts it in his mouth, eats the dust. Nothing happens. It doesn't work. Only his sister is sick, gone.

The room is glowing a dark pink, as though a fire were burning at some distance. In hospital I turn and turn my head but the pillow is harsh against my cheek. Over and over again a sound sways in my head, two beats, light and then heavy. The first time I hear it. It won't let go. Something that's waiting for me, something that wants me, inevitable. I want to fight against it; I want to give in. That sound that is outside me, nothing of myself, and that is me. I want my mother but she isn't there. Someone takes my hand, puts something cold against my forehead. I have nothing but the sound and what it's telling me. Give up; don't give up. I want to fight against it; I want to give in. Something dark comes down on me and I close my eyes to everything. I have nothing but the swaying in my head, two beats, light and then heavy. I want it gone.

And then the sound does go away, and I'm better. I want my mother. The gown I'm wearing is too big, white, loose around the collar. But it's worn, clean; it's soft. The nurses take me to the window, hold me up against the glass. Far away in the hospital courtyard, I see my mother, dressed in black. Ben is waving with one hand, holding my mother's hand with the other. And far from the family, on the opposite side of the courtyard, I see the big boy. Just standing, not waving, but smiling up at me.

Ben's hand is hot in mine and he's tugging; my feet aren't fast enough. I'm eating an ice cream cone, but not fast enough, I can't keep up and pink cream is dripping onto the crook between my thumb and finger. I lick carefully, then I hear it again, the *dah-dong* of it. Two beats – light, then heavy. He's there, half-way down the block, bent over. One hand drags the grinding wheel while the other swings in an arc, and the sound sings out from his hand, two beats. My hand holding Ben's tenses, squeezes.

"Watcha doing?" Ben grimaces, working at the chocolate drips. "Let go!" He shakes his hand loose, then offers it. "Don't squeeze."

I nod, but I can't look at him, the sound puffed up tight

inside me. Something bad is going to happen. Fight it; give up. Be good and it'll go away.

"Be good. Eat your ice cream."

The sound comes in, fills me up. Something I should know, but don't. I start to cry. Ben yanks at my hand. "You stop it! Be good. Don't be a big dummy." I start to wail, the big balloon of sound filling my mouth letting go. On the sidewalk people turn to look at me. Ben's mouth goes hard. "Didn't Momma tell you to be good? Didn't she? Stop it." I can't. He leans over, whispers in my ear, "You stop it right now. Right this minute. If you don't, I'll tell the knife sharpener on you. He'll get you. If you're bad." He yanks at my hand again. "You shut up! Be good!"

I close my mouth. I'm bad. The bad man out there. I'm little and I can't do anything. Ben takes a handkerchief out of his pocket, spits on it, wipes my face. "C'mon. I'll take you home."

I was up visiting friends in the country last weekend, and I decided to go for a walk. It's one of the things that drives my daughter crazy, taking it into my head to go for a walk by myself along a country road at dawn. It was beautiful though, one of those narrow two-lane roads with tall firs on either side. Not much traffic. The mist was lifting off the paving as the sun touched it. I was walking along the edge on the left side of the highway, the way my father taught me, so I'd be facing the oncoming traffic. I was at a point where the road was quite narrow, no shoulders to speak of and rather steep ditches on either side. A large pickup was coming towards me, and he slowed, because there was no room for error, and I stopped. When he passed, there were two feet of air between us – two solemn feet between me and what would end me. Perfectly safe. I've known for a long time about that distance, that closeness.

"There," my mother says, straightening the frame. "See how nice that looks?"

My mother's bed has a fancy gold bedspread she pulls tight over the covers, and a mahogany headboard with little diamonds made out of lighter-coloured wood. Above the bed she's put a picture of an old-fashioned lady who's wearing a dress striped black with white. My mother cut it out of a magazine, and now she's put it into a frame she found for a nickel at the five-and-dime.

"She's watching the opera," my mother says. The lady in the dress has gold opera glasses in her hand, just like the ones my mother brought from Russia. My mother lets me hold them sometimes, though I have to be very careful not to break them because they're precious. Gold and a shiny glimmery something on the handle. Mother-of-pearl, she says. I don't understand how pearl can have a mother. You hold them up in front of your eyes and everything changes. Everything is closer to you or farther away. My mother used to work at the opera, in her country. In Odessa, where they don't need a wireless to listen to music, where there's real music on every corner. Where it's warm. Where my mother will go, if Poppa talks back to her. She'll start packing and go home to Odessa where it's warm. Farther and farther away.

I stand in front of the picture a long time, looking at the fancy lady. Closer and closer. She has pink on her cheeks. She has the opera glasses lazy in her gloved hand. Her dress is made out of something fancy, shiny. She doesn't lift her head, but I know she's looking at me. I think she wants something. My mother calls me for lunch, but I keep thinking about the lady, about what she wants, and I have to keep going back to the bedroom to look at her.

"You like the picture, Monkey?" Poppa rests his hands on my shoulders. "It looks nice above your momma's bed, no?"

"Yes," I whisper.

That evening at dinner I'm still wondering what I'm supposed to do. I'm supposed to do something for the lady, so that everything will be all right. If I don't do things the way she wants me to do them, something bad is going to happen. Everything will be wrecked. And then I figure it out. I have to sip my milk a special way, so it's not wrecked. I put my lips against the glass and take three sips and then wait, three sips and then wait. It slips down my throat fine. I finish the whole glass that way and I'm happy. Everything is good. When I go to bed that night I can feel the lady watching, but it's all right. I can't tell anyone: not Ben, he'd just make fun of me. And not Poppa and not my mother, because they'd just say *don't be silly*.

Poppa's smoking his pipe and reading the newspaper in the easy chair in the front room. I can only see the top of his head. "Be a good girl," he says, "and get me my slippers from the bedroom."

I want to be a good girl, but I don't want to go into the bedroom where the lady is. "I don't want to," I say.

"Annette," Poppa says, "be nice now and go and get me my slippers. Listen to your poppa. They're under the bed."

I go into the bedroom but I watch the floor all the way in and all the way out and I don't look up. There, I did it.

"That wasn't so hard," Poppa says, when I bring them to him. It was hard.

At dinner that night, I sip my milk the right way. I have to eat all my peas first and then my mashed potatoes. I can't eat my chicken until everything else is done, even the milk. Every last pea. My mother wants to know why I'm not eating my chicken but it's all right, I've finished the peas and the mashed potatoes so I swallow down every bite of chicken before she has to ask me again. Then everything's fine. It's all fine and when I go to bed I can feel that the lady's happy with me.

I keep thinking up better and better things to do. I put my clothes on from the bottom to the top one day – socks, underpants, skirt, undershirt, blouse – and from the top to the bottom – undershirt, blouse, skirt, underpants, socks – the next. When I feel the lady get mad at me, I think of something more to do. For a little while everything's good; nothing bad happens. But it gets harder and harder. I have to walk around the block three times one day. The next day I have to do it five times. Poppa doesn't like me going to the end of the block by myself. And I don't ever want to go into the big bedroom. Then no matter how carefully I drink my milk and eat my dinner, no matter how many dandelions I sink in a circle in the mud puddle, nothing seems to work any more, nothing's good enough. The lady's never pleased with me. I want it to stop.

Poppa comes out on the back porch and finds me playing with Blackie, my doll.

"Annette," he says, "your momma says you're all the time quiet. She thinks you're worrying about something."

I look up at him but he's so far away. The lady can see me wherever I go. She knows everything. Poppa picks me up and sits me on his lap. He pushes my hair back from my face. My poppa.

"I'm scared," I say and I can't help it; I start crying a little bit.

"Don't be scared," he says. "There's nothing to be scared about."

"I'm scared of the lady in the picture. In your room."

My mother comes in. "What's wrong with her?" my mother asks. "Why is she crying?"

"She's scared of the picture in the bedroom."

"Scared of a picture? Why should she be scared of a picture?"

It comes out; I have to let it out. "The lady makes me do things. I have to do things for her." I said it. Now what happens?

"Come here," my mother says, taking me by the hand. "Show me the picture."

We go into the bedroom. "That one. The lady."

"All right," my mother says, and she sits me on the bed. "This is what we'll do." And she goes over to the wall, takes it down, puts it face down in the bureau drawer. "There," she says. "It's gone. You don't have to do anything any more. You don't have to be scared."

I am not who I was. I was someone defined by what I obeyed, my mother and the laws that governed her, my sense of the world as ungovernable, my certainty of my own helplessness and its power. Didn't my mother, even then, offer me something else? Didn't she always offer me something else? One night in the apartment on Main Street the lights went out just after dinner. I reached for Poppa's hand in the darkness, felt it warm and solid in mine. But in the moment before I took his hand, that first moment of darkness, I called out *Momma*. I thought then, *why is it Momma I call when it's Poppa I love?* He was wearing the green sweater; even in the dark I could see it green. I pulled closer and we sat quietly together until the lights came on. When those days come back to me, the very earliest days I can remember, they're fixed, the family its own immutable constellation. My life was of a piece and then, when my father stepped onto that train, what was whole came to be broken and I fell into these fragmentary selves, this collection of beings. Sometimes I wonder who the girl on Main Street was. I was reading an article in the newspaper just the other day. It said that the self – which we have but animals don't – resides behind the right eye, a spot in the brain which, removed, or damaged, removes or damages who we are. And that who we are is defined by our memory of our life, but not by memory alone: by memory as it is imbued with emotion. Who we are. So if I remember your hand, Vladimir, but not the love that accompanied it, I am not who I was. I'm not. I have this other life now, the life that's not my old life. I've turned the corner from that old life, the one I won't talk about. Turning my back on the past, I haven't allowed myself to be that girl on Main Street any more, haven't even let myself remember all the separate people I've inhabited. And yet. Does *not who I was* mean *less than I was*? Could it not mean *other*, couldn't *different from* mean *more than*, mean gain, not just loss?

There he is, in the doorway of the delicatessen, the boy who's not supposed to be there. He's stopped in the doorway, watching his father. Avram looks up. "Come in, come in," Avram says. "It's good to see you. Have a bite to eat." He touches the boy's arm, then wipes his hands on the immaculate cotton of the apron, even though his hands are clean. The boy seats himself on one of the red stools at the counter, whirls slowly around once or twice. Avram's hands are quick making the sandwich, piling two inches of corned beef on the rye. He sets the plate down, sets himself down beside the boy, watches as he eats. "It's good?" he asks in Yiddish.

"Talk English, Pa," the boy says, his mouth full. "We should talk English."

"You talk good already." Avram pushes a plate of coleslaw towards him. "Anybody would think you were born right here in Canada."

"I need to practise. So how's by you, Pa?"

"You know, the usual," Avram says. "If I didn't have to give so much credit, we'd be sitting pretty. And you, *tateleh*? Is Sarah Katz looking after you? Still making those famous poppyseed cookies?"

The boy smiles. "I moved. I'm boarding with the Posens now; I've got enough cash for room and board. Bought myself a bicycle."

"Here," Avram says, "take a pickle with it."

"What's this you're reading, Pa?" the boy asks, picking up a thick hardcover.

"I got it out of the library, just published. About the Five Year Plan, what it's going to do for the Russian people."

The boy puts the book down.

"Listen to what they say here," Avram says, reading the English carefully aloud:

> *In the societies of the West the evolution of institutions proceeds for the most part without plan or design, as a sort of by-product of the selfish competition of individuals, groups and enterprises for private gain. In Russia, on the*

> *other hand, the Soviet government has sought to promote the rational and orderly development of the entire social economy. In the great Five Year Plan of Construction, which was launched in October of 1928, and which will run to October of 1933, a whole civilization is harnessing its energies and is on the march towards consciously determined goals.*

"*This* is interesting," Avram says. "*This* I make time to read."

"A lot of big words, Pa."

"And you," Avram gently closes the book, "how is your school?"

"I'm not going to school," the boy answers. "I got these odd jobs, and coming up in a month I got an apprenticeship with Cohen's Electric."

Avram sets his hands along the counter, runs his fingertips along the ribbed edge. "I wanted for you an education," he says.

"Tell me, Pa," the boy's voice goes sour, "what's the point, someone like me getting an education? I have no head for it."

"That's not true . . ." Avram says.

"I want to earn a living and pay for my keep," the boy says. "Don't offer me money, Pa." Avram's hands are on the till. "You know I won't take it. She'll say I stole it," he says. And before Avram can say anything more, he's gone.

The boy is as good with his hands as he is with his head, can make anything electrical work. *The electrician*, my mother calls him. Never uses his name. *Joseph*.

Joseph could fix anything. Every time he'd visit he would bring me a little treat: coloured pencils or a new eraser. And he'd help me draw: trees and suns, flowers. I could spend hours drawing, trying to put down on paper something that made a pattern, that had colour in it, a shape. When Joseph visited, we'd talk English to each other. He'd learned to speak good English, not my-country English like Poppa and my mother. He took me to see the fireworks once, gave me a piggyback ride all the way there. I wasn't scared because I was with Joseph. When the fireworks started, the sky was full of coloured bits of light, red and green and sparkly blue, some like flowers, some like pinwheels. And noises: pops like bubbles bursting for the little lights and a shaky boom for the bigger ones. Then a noise came that was so loud the ground shuddered and I shuddered with it and a big flower of light bloomed right on top of my head. It got bigger and bigger in the sky, came closer and closer till I felt the sky come down to touch me, till I felt the light inside my chest, breathed in light till I was full with it.

My mother is at the sink, washing dishes. "The *electrician* was here. He fixed the wireless," she says. Poppa is adding a column of numbers that's as long as the page. He can keep every one of those numbers in his head all the way down the line. He puts his pencil down.

"His name is Joseph."

The cat and I watch my mother's hands making circles with a soapy rag.

"I know his name," she says.

It's easy to read my mother's back. I always know when something bad is going to happen, like the day she tore up that old picture of the little boy shaking hands with Poppa.

When she gets mad, Poppa talks in his quiet voice. *There-there*, his voice says.

Poppa gets up, turns on the radio. "It's working good," he says, and goes downstairs.

My mother turns the radio off. "In Odessa, we didn't need a wireless. Every evening we could go to the park and listen to the orchestra in the bandstand."

They worked under the ground, my mother's family, in the mines, like ants. The whole city of Odessa sits on top of stone, she told me, limestone, and for hundreds of years my mother's family mined it. Hundreds of years and hundreds of miles of tunnels, a honeycomb of limestone tunnels. Maybe they're bees, not ants, my mother's family. A hive of relatives, her sisters and their families, still living in my mother's city, her country.

It's funny that Joseph has the same country as my mother – she wouldn't want to share anything with him.

I don't have a country. Or my country doesn't have a name. Maybe my country is the delicatessen: Poppa's white apron at night, the way it shines in the darkness hanging from its peg.

I've always lived in a forest of words, in a foreign language. On the first day of grade one at Aberdeen School on Selkirk Avenue, we walked to school, Poppa and me, his hand warm and quiet in mine. When we got to the doorway of the classroom, he said, *Come look and don't be scared. This is where all the little girls dance.* Aberdeen School was where I learned to be good. Reading the faces of the teachers was easy, and so was making my own face show them what they wanted to see: a serious little girl, a smiling little girl, a girl who does what she's told. And Aberdeen School was where I was told to speak only English: not Yiddish, which I spoke to my father, and not Russian, which I spoke to my mother. "We must all learn," Miss MacLeod explained, "to speak English so that everyone understands everyone else. Now if you speak Russian, and Darya speaks Ukrainian, and Nadya speaks Hungarian, how will we get by?" And though I knew the teacher was always right, I couldn't help thinking that I did understand Ukrainian, as much by the look on Darya's face as the sounds she made. And when Johannes, the little boy with the dull blond hair cut straight across in bangs, spoke Polish, it wasn't so hard either, especially if he had the ball in his hands and you knew he must mean ball. When I opened my mouth I didn't always know which language I was speaking, didn't know, really, that there *were* different languages, just different, familiar ways of settling into sound. Poppa had already taught me to read English. He read English just fine, though for my mother it was hard. *Russian is the only language worth knowing.* But I still had to sit and listen to the other children read *The Little Red Hen* and it would make me itchy, make me want to twist my toes and snap them against each other. Aberdeen School was where I learned to be good, but I knew I wasn't really good, that underneath being good was a bad girl. Poppa used to sing me the rhyme in English: *There was a little girl who had a little curl right in the middle of her forehead. And when she was good she was very very good, and when she was bad she was horrid.* The bad girl who can't sit still, who twists her toes and snaps them. The girl who wants what she wants. Who boxed Ben's ears once, because she was mad, even though he was bigger, even though he'd done nothing. Because she didn't get what she wanted, and she wants what she wants. She's horrid.

Miss MacLeod has told us to put our heads down because we were too noisy. I run my fingers along the smooth groove in the top of the desk where my pencil goes, round the opening for the inkwell. Bottles of ink are dangerous. Pupils are not allowed to use ink until grade three.

"All right," Miss MacLeod says, "time for Spelling."

I sit up straight and fold my hands in front of me on my desk, feet flat on the floor and knees together: Position One. It's so hard. And I don't want to, but I do.

"Now class," Miss MacLeod is saying, "what do you write in the right-hand corner of the page?" She turns to the blackboard and her black gabardine skirt swirls as she turns. "This is today's date," Miss MacLeod says, and she writes *October 18, 1932* on the board in her beautiful, clear printing.

I hold the pencil the way I've been taught, cradled against the second finger of my right hand. I'm getting a bump there from the pencil rubbing, my finger taking on the shape of what I do. *October 18, 1932*. It makes me shiver. I've never written the date before, never pencilled myself into time, but this is how time enters my life.

Time. I can stand in the spare room or I can walk back into my darkened kitchen and say, *it's Tuesday, it's six o'clock, it's time for dinner*. But time is slippery. If we let go that thread of the present, we're released into what gave us this moment, the darkness in it or the light. My father was a believer, a dreamer. His daylight dreams took him to what he thought of as his future in Canada, and then they made him get on that train. But he had nightmares too. Just like me. Sometimes I think even now I'm still dreaming his dreams. *Make a wish*. I want to remember.

In the dream of summer I used to play at my friend Cassie's house, a two-storey, white stucco with a picket gate painted green in the carragana hedge. *Picket, picket.* I liked that word. Cassie's mother fed us cinnamon buns hot from the oven. Her backyard was big and open: no trees or apartment buildings to make the sky small. They had a vegetable garden that took up most of it. Laundry flapped on the neighbour's line: sheets and pillowcases white against the blue sky. Once Cassie and I got to dig a new patch of garden. She showed me how to put my whole weight on the spade, and while we dug it was as if the soil got looser, deeper, as we worked it, sun hot on our shoulders. We were workers. The screen door squeaked. Good times.

But it wasn't good times; it was hard times. Kids came to school wearing clothes that were too big or too small, jackets made over from coats, patches on patches. Half the neighbours were on Relief. Because it was hard times, my mother would let me invite a friend over for lunch once a week, sometimes twice. *Nobody can say I let anyone go hungry from my table*, she'd say, setting the dishes down on the table, potatoes fried in lots of oil, salami sliced thick. *They can't say that about me. I'm not stingy like some people.*

Plenty did go hungry. Mrs. Goldbaum down the street's husband was a travelling salesman, no good, a gambler. Three kids to feed and nothing to feed them with. Poppa would leave bags of groceries on the back step and my mother wouldn't say not to. *They won't go calling me stingy.*

The boy from across the street showed off the new boots he got on Relief – soles *that* thick – and my brother Ben was jealous. But my mother made a face when he told her. *People should work.*

Some wouldn't take Relief, like Mr. Spratt, the lodger on the third floor above the store. He was thin, quiet. His footsteps overhead hardly made any noise.

The flowered apron covers my mother's knees. She's shelling peas.

"I'm worried about Mr. Spratt." Poppa sets his *Tribune* on the kitchen table.

"Worry about yourself, Avram." Each pod is unzipped, the peas stripped click click click into the enamel bowl. I want to eat one, just one.

"He's thinner every day." Poppa's hands rest on the newspaper.

"He dresses fancy, always in that dark grey suit, a white shirt, black shoes polished up. If he's under the weather again you can bring him a bowl of my chicken soup."

"God knows how the man lives."

"He gets odd jobs. He may have a bit of savings tucked away somewhere."

"Thirty-seven, and he looks like an old man. Look at the prices I'm charging here: fifty-two cents for a twenty-four-pound bag of flour. The farmers are getting nothing. Peanut butter nineteen cents a pound. He'd be better off."

"Better off how?"

"On Relief. If he was working for Relief at least he'd get a food voucher."

"People have no shame."

"Anne . . ."

"*No shame.*"

"Anne, people are hungry."

"They're lazy."

"Anne . . ."

"Just lazy."

"Hello there, Princess." Mr. Spratt comes down the stairs in his dark grey suit, white shirt and black shoes. He calls me Princess because I was born in the same year as Princess Elizabeth. "How are you?" His voice is softer even than Poppa's.

"Fine thank you, Mr. Spratt. And how are you?" Mr. Spratt talks so nice he makes me feel like I'm wearing little white gloves, all prim and proper.

"Dandy." He sits down beside me on the second from the bottom step, wipes his forehead with a very white handkerchief. The cat comes up and rubs against the dark wool of his pant leg.

"Mr. Spratt, how come you're wearing your suit on such a hot day?"

Mr. Spratt smiles a big smile. I hardly ever see him smile that big. Mostly his smile is quiet, like he doesn't want to bother anyone with it. He smiles big, and then the smile stops. "That's a good question. That's a question I should ask myself, I guess." He thinks a minute. "I like this suit."

"It's a nice suit."

"Thank you. But you make me wonder, Princess. It is an awfully hot day for a suit when you're not going anywhere special."

We're quiet for a moment.

"Did you used to work in a bank, Mr. Spratt?"

"No, I didn't work in a bank, Princess."

"Where did you work?"

Mr. Spratt takes his time before answering me. "In a big office. I had my own desk, a nice oak desk. And a secretary. There was a big fan on the ceiling that kept me cool. You would have liked that."

"Oh." I start to poke at a scab on my knee, then remember that I shouldn't.

"Did you read that book you borrowed from me about glaciers?"

"I'm about half-way through, Mr. Spratt. There are some big words."

"Just ask your poppa if there's anything you don't understand."

"Poppa doesn't always know the big words in English."

"Well, of course you're right. But your poppa will know how to look them up."

"All right." I start at my knee again, stop. "Mr. Spratt, can I ask you something? Do you ever hear something, like a bad sound?"

Mr. Spratt frowns. "What kind of sound do you mean?"

"I sometimes hear him," I whisper. "The old guy. Ringing the bell."

"You mean the knife sharpener, that old fellow? You don't have to be afraid of him, Princess."

I shiver. "But sometimes I hear that sound even when he's not there."

"When he's not there?"

"It's like the sound's inside me."

Mr. Spratt smoothes the crease in his trousers, wipes his forehead again. "Sometimes I think we're more afraid of what's inside us than what's outside us, Princess. Or maybe we're afraid that what's inside us isn't strong enough to fight what's outside us. Maybe that's why we hear something inside us that scares us. But don't be afraid of the knife sharpener. He's just an old man trying to make a living like everybody else. How about I take you to the library tomorrow, if it's all right with your poppa? We can ask him today."

"I'd like that a lot, Mr. Spratt."

"All right then. Well, if you'll excuse me, I've got to go meet someone."

"Is that why you're wearing your suit?"

"Guess so. See you later, Princess."

Princess. That was what he called me, Mr. Spratt. He always spoke to me as if I deserved some dignity, as though, given a little encouragement, I could think things through. But though he called me Princess, I knew I couldn't ever be a princess because the world was divided into kings and commoners, bosses and workers, fancy and plain, gentiles and Jews, and I always knew on which side I fell. *One person is just as good as another and workers are the best.* My family had always been working class: farmers and shopkeepers and tailors, they'd all made an honest living. My mother's family were miners in the limestone quarries in Odessa, nothing like the bosses, tycoons in shiny top hats who took money from honest people. Nor were they kings and queens shouting *off with their heads*! Nor soldiers; they'd never killed anybody, had never done anything bad. Never being able to do anything bad – that was what it meant to be good.

But I couldn't ever be a princess anyway because I didn't look like a princess, wasn't *the fairest of them all.* I was plain. I didn't even need to look in the mirror. All I had to do was look at my mother's face, her scowl when she said, *here, comb your hair already.* I couldn't even pretend to be a princess.

Except, when Mr. Spratt talked to me, that was how I felt.

Because of the heat wave, my mother wouldn't let us outside, not even to run down the street to Levin's store. She took a clean bedsheet and soaked it in cold water in the tub, then hung the damp, cool cloth against the window to keep the sunlight out. You're supposed to be afraid of sunstroke, heat prostration, but I was still afraid of other things: my mother, the artificial arms and legs hanging in the shop window of Zalinsky's store. The kids told stories about boys who hopped freight trains, about how, when they fell, they'd lose a leg or worse. But it was still my mother who scared me the most.

The air outside on Main Street was thick with smoke. They'd burn smudge fires of lilac branches in oil drums on the street corners to keep away the mosquitoes. The sidewalks were covered with empty sunflower seed shells that crackled when you walked. The trick was to stuff a handful of seeds into your mouth and one by one spit out the shells: *look ma, no hands*. The hulls crunched under people's feet, thousands and thousands crunching like the grasshoppers that came in July. Night didn't cool things any, but people still went out. Evenings were crowded with folks out for a walk, whole families on parade up and down the sidewalks on Main Street. Some even went out Old Country fashion in pyjamas and slippers; nobody said anything about it. Whole families out on the sidewalks, looking for a breeze, looking for a breath. The men would stroke their chins, talking, the way they did when they came out of synagogue. As though they were solving all the world's problems. The women talked too, one hand on a hip, but the kids stayed restless because it was hot; it was hot right through the night.

Ben wants a nickel for the movies, wants Poppa to ring in No Sale and take out a nickel for him and a nickel for me, but he won't – for a nickel, you can buy a loaf of bread.

My mother comes in, puts on her apron, tells Avram to

have his dinner break. He takes off the tired old apron, puts it on its peg and goes upstairs. Nine-thirty, and the sun still hasn't set. Light slants in the kitchen windows. My father sits at the table, spreads the newspaper out in front of him. *Cashier Robbed in Daring Daylight Holdup: $1,400 Stolen from Coca-Cola Company Clerk. Grace Church sermon on Sunday by the Reverend J. R. Mutchmore: "Can Capitalism Come Back?"*

Here's what he's looking for, another article about C. R. Cummings's trip to Soviet Russia. Must be a sharp fellow, this Cummings. He isn't taken in by all the anti-Soviet propaganda, that nonsense about labour camps, famines. Even in the *Winnipeg Tribune* sometimes they have to tell the Soviet side of the story. Cummings talked with a real worker there: *Here we produce cheaply because we have collectivized production. All the workers are working for themselves and not for employers and thus they have every inducement to keep down costs. It is true that we have a lower standard of living than in other countries, but it is still better now than it was before the Revolution.* A planned economy. And here, nothing but waste – farmers pouring milk into ditches to protest that the price is less than the cost. Here they waste everything.

It's hot in the kitchen. *The Grasshopper Armada: The Balance of Nature Must Be Restored.* These plagues of grasshoppers, dust storms, drought.

William Spratt comes down the stairs. Dark grey suit, white shirt, black shoes.

"How're you keeping, Mr. Spratt?"

"Fine, thank you," he answers, "and yourself?"

"Not so bad." My father shrugs, raises his eyebrows.

"And the news, Mr. Gershon?"

Avram shakes his head. "No good, no good. I keep thinking it can't get worse."

Spratt sighs. "That's what you'd think. People have to hope."

Avram looks up at him. "Have a seat, Mr. Spratt. Have a bite to eat."

"Thanks, but I've got an appointment. Tell Princess I said hello."

Something about the man's back as he walks off worries Avram. A man like Spratt out of work – it's not right that people should be denied an honest day's work. Anne's voice rises from downstairs. She's talking with Spratt. Maybe if business picks up a little Avram can talk her into taking the children to the beach on Sunday, taking the Moonlight Special home. He can manage by himself at the store.

He wants to telephone Joseph at his rooming house but the phone is downstairs and Anne gets upset. It's weeks since Joseph came by with his new girl. Daisy. Such a lovely child, such a silly name. A name for a flower, not a person. Joseph's not twenty years old – too young to be thinking about getting married. He's still struggling to make a living, still hasn't been able to go back to school. *The electrician.* He should get an education, a boy like that, with brains. Spending his days pedalling through the city on his bicycle, a ladder attached to one side, tool kit to the other, repairing light fixtures and radios, changing bulbs, for heaven's sakes, for the ones who are still afraid of electricity. Milk in the ditches and society types are still paying $189.00 for a radio-phonograph. It's right here in the paper – $189.00 for a Victor Radio Phonograph Combination. He'll call Joseph tomorrow.

That evening Avram is out on the back porch. Spratt comes quietly out. "I'm not disturbing you, Mr. Gershon? Annette's asleep?"

"Sit yourself down, Mr. Spratt. It's cooler out here. We were having a little talk but I put her to bed a minute ago."

Spratt laughs. "She's quite the conversationalist."

"She's shy, usually, Mr. Spratt. But with you she's a little chatterbox. With strangers she hardly says a word. Family is different. Me she has to ask about everything. Why hasn't Mrs. Andrychuk come to the store with the new baby. Why won't Ben let her ride his bicycle. How come Momma wouldn't let her friend Cassie stay for dinner. She got herself worked up into quite a state, wouldn't eat her food, because Cassie couldn't come. Tired her right out."

"I see Mrs. Gershon has a candle lit," Spratt says. "Is that for the Sabbath?"

"We don't light candles on Friday, Mr. Spratt," Avram tells him.

"I thought it was a Jewish tradition."

"It is for a lot of families. Annette's friend Cassie, they light candles every Friday night, say the blessing on them in Hebrew, the whole *schlimazel*. That one's a *yohrzheit* candle, in memory of Mrs. Gershon's mother's death. It has to burn all day and all night on the anniversary; you can't blow it out. Anya puts it in the sink overnight so the house shouldn't burn down."

"So you observe this tradition but you don't observe the Sabbath?"

"We just try to make ourselves comfortable without belief. Call it 'kitchen Judaism.'"

"Then you have dietary restrictions. I see Mrs. Gershon shops at the kosher butcher."

"Waldman's is the best butcher in town. We wouldn't eat pork chops, but we don't keep kosher, not according to anyone who's orthodox, that's for sure! All kinds of different Jews in this town, Mr. Spratt. And one half isn't talking to the other half because of it!" They laugh.

"I should check on Annette in a minute or so. I was telling her a story. *Tell me a story.* Every night I have to tell for her a story. *Tell me about the Old Country*, she says. And I have to tell her again about how my cousin was struck by lightning and for three days we had him buried in the ground till he came round. And I have to tell her again how after my father died they found for me a job with a shop-keeper, how I slept under the counter in the store . . . Everything for her is a story. . . "

"– I wonder sometimes what stories they'll tell about these times . . ."

Avram runs a hand over his bald pate. "Are you having any luck, Mr. Spratt?" he asks.

Spratt swallows. "I don't know if luck has anything to do with it, Mr. Gershon."

"You're right, Mr. Spratt. It's the government. Those people in Ottawa, the big shots, they don't care about the ordinary working man. And the bosses, the bosses only care about their profits . . ."

"You think so?"

"The breadlines, the soup kitchens – it's the government's fault. And the capitalists."

"Sometimes I think . . . I think it's just a question of character. A question of giving up or not giving up . . ."

"You've got a point there, Mr. Spratt. We have to keep trying, right?"

"I suppose we do."

"A bit cooler now that the sun's gone down, d'you think?"

"Not much of a breeze. I think I'll try a stroll down Main Street."

"Goodnight, Mr. Spratt."

"Goodnight, Mr. Gershon."

It's too hot to sleep, though Anne is fast asleep in her bed, exhausted. The bedroom is tense with heat. Avram tries not to toss and turn too much. It must be three o'clock in the morning when he hears someone walking quietly up the stairs. "Spratt?" he whispers.

"It's all right," Spratt whispers back. "It's just me." His footsteps go softly up to the third floor.

Next morning Avram's at the counter, wrapping up a package of corned beef for Mrs. Andrychuk. A man not from Selkirk Avenue walks into the delicatessen.

"A Mr. Spratt live here?" he asks, a powerful man, a wrestler's shoulders, the French accent strong in this throat: St. Boniface.

"Upstairs," Avram says. "Third floor."

"I leave this for him," the man answers, putting a crumpled suit jacket, dark grey, on the counter, and walking out.

Avram takes the jacket upstairs. "Mr. Spratt," he calls softly. "Mr. Spratt? A man left this for you."

The room is dark, but Avram sees a figure on the bed. The heat is already pushing down on the building, the third floor unbearable. Spratt seems to take a deep breath, then sits up as though the whole weight of the heat, the day, bore down on him. He gets up, walks to the door in shirt sleeves, in stocking feet. The first time Avram has seen him without the dark grey suit jacket, black shoes.

"Thank you, Mr. Gershon. I'm sorry to trouble you."

Avram hands him the jacket, doesn't leave.

He looks at Avram, and smiles, a thin smile. "I must have left it on shore. I went for a swim." He smiles again.

Andrychuk comes in. Avram looks up, smiles quietly. They must owe him close to $40.00.

"Mr. Andrychuk, how are you?"

"Mr. Gershon, I've been working two weeks now in Eaton's warehouse."

"That's good to hear, Mr. Andrychuk. It was three months you were looking, no?"

"Almost four. This is permanent. I got paid today. I'd like to settle something on my account."

"There's no hurry. Your credit is good."

"Please, Mr. Gershon." He puts two five-dollar bills down on the counter. Avram gets out the ledger. Andrychuk settles the cap on his head, adjusts his trousers.

"Can I get you anything?"

"The wife'll be in later in the week."

"Well, this is good news. It's good to hear good news."

"Mr. Gershon." The bell above the door jangles as he leaves.

Avram puts the two fives into the till. Almost everyone is paying on credit; business is thin. It's too hot to move. He can hear the children's voices upstairs in the bedroom, arguing and playing. They have to stay indoors. Anne won't let them outside in the heat. Today he will telephone Joseph. He won't let it wait any longer. Avram hears Spratt's gentle tones. The man has such patience for children. . . Maybe Ben can take everyone to Pritchard Pool. It'll be cooler beside the water. Such a shame Spratt doesn't have his own family, children.

Avram makes himself a salami sandwich, slices the rye thick. Heaps coleslaw into an oval dish. He hates to get the bread soggy with dressing. For dessert he'll have a taste of Anne's raspberry cordial. Nothing like it. He sits himself down on the red stool and opens the paper out on the counter, sets the funnies aside for the children. Ben loves *Buck Rogers. Two Dead, Scores Hurt in Political Riots in Berlin. Chinese Dies of Injuries in Traffic Mishap. Man Is Rescued After Jumping Into River.*

> *William Spratt, 390 Main Street, jumped from the Provencher Bridge. He was seen to strip off his coat and then jump by two bystanders who paddled out to save him. It was only after a struggle that they succeeded in bringing him to shore. Spratt was taken to the General Hospital by police ambulance.*

Avram sets the paper down, runs back up both sets of stairs like a much younger man. "Spratt?" he calls. "Mr. Spratt?" The children are playing on the stairs, but he runs right past.

William Spratt is bent over a piece of paper, creasing it into intricate folds. Somehow, his suit jacket has been pressed. Dark grey suit, white shirt, black shoes. Spratt looks up, shows Avram a little paper object folded like a sailor hat bent double.

"Annette asked me to make her and little Cassie one of these paper fortune tellers, Mr. Gershon." He slips his fingers into the folds, flips it idly back and forth.

"Thank you, Mr. Spratt; I'll give it to them. Mr. Spratt, maybe you would like to join us for dinner?" He's trying to look William Spratt in the eye, but Spratt's bent over another sheet of paper.

"Thank you," he says, head down, "but I've already got an invitation."

Avram jams his fists in his pockets, looks down at his shoes and then up again. "Are you sure?"

Spratt looks up from the paper, looks directly into Avram's face.

"Thank you so much. Perhaps tomorrow?"

"Tomorrow would be fine."

Avram stands in the doorway for a minute, then goes downstairs.

The next day Spratt is gone.

"You're worrying for nothing," Anne says. "He's hiding somewhere. It was in the papers; he was ashamed."

"Nobody knew him but us!" Avram answers. "Why should he be ashamed? He said he was coming for dinner . . ."

"He owed rent on the room," Anne says. "Our landlady told me. Almost two months already. She was going to throw him out, but he's such a nice quiet type. He kept trying to pay, a dollar here, a dollar there." She touches Avram's shoulder. "He was ashamed; he owed money. He ran away. Tomorrow's Sunday. Take the children to the beach for the afternoon. You need a rest. I'll mind the store. I'm not interested in swimming. Go. Take the Moonlight Special home. Listen to me."

"I'm going to visit Joseph," Avram says. "I'm going to spend tomorrow with Joseph."

She stands up and walks to the bedroom.

When Avram comes home Sunday evening, Anne won't talk to him. Monday it's busy. The Relief money is in and customers come into the delicatessen to pay something of what they owe. Anne still isn't talking; she keeps herself busy in the kitchen.

Avram puts two cheese blintzes on a plate and takes it out back, where he might be able to catch a breeze. He opens the paper. *Lux soap, 7¢ a bar. Jobless Conference Held in Edmonton. Tarzan, Lord of the Jungle.*

Unidentified Man Found Floating in Red River. Approximately forty years old, 130 pounds, five feet, ten inches. Dark grey suit, white shirt, black shoes.

He puts the paper down, picks it up. *Farmers' Army Gathers in Ottawa. Flit Kills Mosquitoes. Whose Problem Is It? Demoralizing dole-supported idleness.* And the *Society* page: *Printed Voile Frocks. White Softee Hats. Paris Falls for Five O'Clock Teas.* Society. He puts his head down on the paper, the cool newsprint against his cheek, the words pressing into him, the lies.

Hard times, hard winter. But walking down the street in Winnipeg, I don't think, *Winnipeg*, don't set myself in a particular place because in my life there is only one place, *here*. Five o'clock and it's already dark, the sky gone from royal blue to a velvety purple to black and the snow so white it seems to glow. Yesterday there was just a bit of snow and the snowbanks are still white, new with it. No wind tonight, so there's an extra stillness added onto the layer of stillness the snow seems to give.

A car is hunched at the traffic light and someone's inside, the person inside thinking his own thoughts just the way I'm thinking mine. We're each alone, looking out from behind our faces, seeing just the edges of cheek, nose, ridge of skin around the eyes, a kind of wavering shadow if I try to look down at my own face, but I don't like doing that, it's too scary. Though I do sometimes like the feeling of being alone, especially outside like this on the dark, familiar streets, the cold air against my face so that I feel the edges of myself, my skin, know where I end.

Winnipeg. Are there really other places? In the middle of

winter, in Winnipeg, it doesn't seem there are even other seasons. In school I've learned about the tropics – Tropic of Cancer, Tropic of Capricorn – but they sound frightening, not real: beasts, diseases. My school books say that in other places there is no winter. *No winter.* They can't put that one over on me. It can't be true. Nobody gets away without winter. The snow just comes and goes there, the cold not quite as cold. The snow, heavier, warmer, bends the feathery leaves of the palm trees till they almost touch the frozen sand. I like drawing palm trees, the sawtooth leaves, criss-cross of the trunks. Miss MacLeod says I'm the best drawer in the class.

It must get so cold in those thin grass huts. Here we have wooden houses, solid walls. I don't like the story about the three little pigs because nobody here uses brick for their houses. And wooden houses don't fall down, not in Winnipeg, no matter how hard the wind blows. Though lots of people are cold, even inside. And what about animals? I'm still not sure how animals get by in winter. Well, Nature takes care of everything, the balance of nature, Miss MacLeod called it. Mother Nature takes care of everything. Or maybe God. But Poppa and my mother don't believe in God. *Superstitious mumbo-jumbo.* It's Mother Nature who looks after the animals. Mother Nature and Poppa.

Poppa doesn't cut the bread under his arm, sawing away and letting the crumbs fall onto the kitchen floor, like my mother does. He sets the loaves on the counter and slices carefully. Then with the stiff flat edge of his hand he sweeps every single crumb into his other hand and then from his hand into a chipped bowl he keeps beside the sink. And when the bowl gets full enough, I'll wake up one morning and he'll be in his robe and slippers on the back porch, standing still as anything, his palms turned out and up, like a kind of a prayer. I wait without breathing, and then they come, the sparrows, and land on his shoulders, fingers, his head. They're not scared. What would it be like to be a sparrow? Or Poppa, who's nothing but good? *Make a wish.* I wish there was no stubborn knot of meanness to twist inside me. I wish I could be like Poppa.

Most days after school I go skating, even though it's dark by the time I get to the rink, and cold. My mother tells me how crazy I am to go skating in this cold but I want to; I don't listen. Fine, she says and she says I can't blame her if I get frostbite. I have to get out, so I sling my hand-me-down white figure skates over my shoulder by the laces. They're all scratched and a bit bulgy-looking at the ankles, but they fit if I wear two pairs of socks. When it's forty below, you can't even sit down in a snowbank to put on your skates – the snow pulls the heat right out of you. You have to keep skating, move. It doesn't matter how tired you get. If you stop, it won't take long for the cold to get you. The cold will climb inside you and then you won't be yourself any more. What will you be? *Something rich and strange.* Joseph read me the poem. Something rich and strange. No, you'd be dead. Dead, not yourself. That's the way it is. Even the air can be dangerous; not much between you and what wants to end you. Nothing's easy, not even dying.

I know about Mr. Spratt, the wreck, the waste.

I'm not supposed to know, but I do. What has he changed into now, Mr. Spratt, the grey, muddy water filling up his mouth?

We all go to the wedding, Ben all dressed up in his new suit, me in a brand-new party dress. Poppa makes even my mother go. But then, a few months later, Joseph stops coming by as often. It's because Joseph and Poppa have an argument about the Soviet Union, Poppa's trip. Poppa is planning to visit the Soviet Union to see our grandmother. Joseph says, *go, good. You need to see your mother.* That isn't what they argue about. What makes Joseph so mad is Poppa's plan to take us to Russia. He wants to see if he can get permission for all of us to go there. I've never heard Joseph talk to Poppa like that. *It's plain stupid; no, worse than stupid, criminal.* And Poppa says, *don't talk to your father like that.*

But I know why Poppa wants to take us to the Soviet Union. Because of Mr. Spratt, what happened to him. And because of what happens all over the capitalist world to ordinary workers who are just trying to make a decent life for themselves. And because Poppa is tired of the store, tired of giving kids loaves of bread when my mother isn't looking so they won't go hungry. And because of the future he wants for me and Ben. *In the capitalist world, there is no future.* No jobs, no chance of an education. That's why he wants us to leave.

I can't understand what's possessing you, why you'd even consider leaving! Joseph sounds so mad. And he keeps trying to tell Poppa what it's like in the Soviet Union, how things have changed since Poppa left twenty years ago.

Joseph doesn't understand, but my mother does. She wants her country back.

My father is upstairs in the bedroom, stretched out on his bed. The letter came yesterday. The room's warm, stuffy, the curtains closed. Anne's bed beside his is empty, the bed carefully made, the heavy gold bedspread pulled tight over the blankets. One hand holds the letter, the other lightly touches the nubby surface of the spread, gold, matching.

For eight months he's been planning, finding the money, arranging the paperwork, getting a good price on his ticket. Letters have been sent to offices in Ottawa and Moscow, to the family in Simferopol and in Odessa. Everything was falling into place. And now this letter.

> *With heavy hearts, we must write to tell you that your beloved mother, Sarah Chava Gershon, passed away November 15, 1934. She died quietly in her sleep. May she rest in peace.*

He's too late. He's missed his chance.

Anne comes quietly into the room, lays a hand on his arm. "Avram? You were sleeping?"

He shakes his head.

"Avram, listen to me. I've been thinking. The way things turned out, this maybe isn't the right thing for us. So much trouble to see your mother – *alevasholem*, may she rest in peace – and now everything is over and done with. Maybe, with your mother gone, we shouldn't bother . . ."

"Anya –"

"Listen to me, Avram: it's too much work for you. Why do we need to go and change everything? It's not like we're not eating, like we don't have work."

He sits up on the bed. "Anya, I've got the ticket. I'm going. We can't sit here and wait for the Messiah. Or Roosevelt, or Bennett."

She pats his hand. "See if you can sleep."

He turns over, closes his eyes. And then he's asleep, dreaming his mother's face, brown braids in a crown. Every night for the next ten weeks he dreams her face. Night after night he's the boy sleeping beneath the counter, the boy sleeping inconsolably beneath the counter.

Winnipeg, February 1935. My father wore his heavy tweed overcoat and brown wool suit when he boarded the train. I'd never been in a room that big. I tipped my head back to take it all in, my mouth holding itself open, the vault of my palate repeating the vault above. *Say goodbye*, my mother told me. *I have to go*, my father said. *You're a big girl now.* The black body of the train shifting beside me. I wouldn't let him go. In one slight movement I stepped up onto the train, slipping along the aisles until I spotted his name on a paper tag. I fit myself beneath his seat, between the two rows of back-to-back benches. *Make a wish.* All my body wanted to keep my father home. I thought with my body I could keep him from leaving.

And so the smoke diminished and died and the train stopped. I stopped the train because I want what I want. But after twenty minutes, the conductor swearing, the train delayed, they found me, and my father lifted me up, lifted me high and looked in my face, not saying anything. He held me hard against the tobacco-smelling jacket and then he set me down, where I kicked and screamed, almost nine years old, and my mother took me by the arm and onto the streetcar, and the train left, carrying my father away.

The train I failed to stop lifted my father out of his life, out of what had been, for me at least, a whole, and carried him east, from the Prairies to the Maritimes, Winnipeg to Halifax. In Halifax he boarded the *SS Montcalm*, which crossed the Atlantic to land in Liverpool. By train from Liverpool to Dover, by ferry to Calais and then on the long train to Moscow, my father was carried backwards from the New World to the Old, his life wound backwards into a possible future, into the country, the life he'd left.

All through the winter months I waited: for spring, for

Poppa to come back. All winter I walked the blocks to school in my heavy overshoes, in my heavy coat and double mittens, crunching the packed snow under my boots, watching the clean white snow dirty and then the dirt hide under a new layer of snow. What I wanted was my father, but what I had was my mother, who sat me down in a kitchen chair, got the tortoiseshell brush from the dressing table:

Sit still if you want me to fix your hair. Such a fidgety thing. I don't want you sulking all the time just because your poppa's not here to fuss over you. Hold your head still. When I worked in the orphanage in Odessa those orphans sat just so when we did their hair – no squirming and crying. All that work to do. Not that I was with the children often. I'll do anything but look after children. My job was in the dining room, laying the table, washing dishes. Hard work. You've never known that kind of work. And if I have anything to say about it you never will. That's why I don't like you hanging around my kitchen all the time. I'm not teaching you to be anyone's servant. Catch yourself a rich husband instead. Fourteen I was when I started with the job in the orphanage. Six days a week there and then three evenings a week at the opera house – during the season – as soon as I turned sixteen. We all had to find jobs; that was it. At the orphanage sometimes, after the dinner dishes were done, they'd ask me to check in on the dormitory. Those children were like wild animals, jumping, yelling, if you didn't know how to handle them. But they didn't dare act up with me. Stop crying, I'd say, and they'd stop, and without me laying a finger on them. These were orphans. You could have done anything with them. But I never needed to smack any child. Not like my mother, a hard woman.

She'd use her fists, the broomstick, whatever came to hand. And I always got the worst of it, even though my big sisters tried to keep her away from me. It was because I stood up to her. When I was twelve I got my arm broken. I still remember how it sounded when it broke, like a twig on a tree. And I remember my mother's face, like she knew she was doing just the right thing. No arguing with her. Nobody can say I ever laid a hand on any child, not even the electrician. Not me. Hold still. When I was your age, in Odessa, I had hair down to my waist. Every day I'd come home and one of my sisters would sit me down in front of the stove and brush my hair, a hundred strokes. And we'd walk, all us girls, along Nikolayevsky Boulevard, taking our time, and the boys would call out to me: hey, green eyes. I never even looked at a boy. My sisters taught me to respect myself. Here, we're almost done. I'm making you pigtails. So it pulled a little. Don't make a big to-do about every little thing. The orphanage was hard, but the opera I loved. That building – more beautiful than the opera in Paris, that's what they said. I worked out front, I told you, a cashier. Sure I watched! I never got to see the first act, but I saw the rest. *Che gelida manina*. Puccini, Verdi, Wagner. All the fancy big shots with their velvet evening cloaks and long white gloves. With my wages I bought those gold opera glasses trimmed in mother-of-pearl. If you're a good girl I'll let you play with them. Mother-of-pearl. Nobody was going to look down on me. Leave your hair alone already; it's done. Go. Go now and play.

It's spring. I'm tired of waiting for Poppa. I want what I want and I want Poppa, but I can't have him. There's nothing to do. I want to dig, but there's nothing to dig. I'm itchy from waiting. I've asked Cassie but the ground in her garden is still too wet from the thaw to work in, and below the wet part it's still too hard. So I'm out on the back porch, poking in the dirt of the flower box with an old bent fork, when I hear it, the *dah-dong*, full-bellied, swaying. The opening note light, and then the second note a gap in the heart, a falling. No way out. Ben's hunched over his arithmetic, but at the sound he looks up, looks at me. "Annette, cut it out. Don't start that stuff up again."

I can see the familiar look of irritation come over his face – see but don't see it because I'm so big with fear.

"Stop it," he says. "You're almost nine. You can't be scared of a stupid noise." But I can't do anything but feel this sound come into me: something bad.

"I'll show you, Annette. I'll show you there's nothing to be scared of." He sets his hands on my shoulders. "You can't be scared like this, understand?" Takes my hand. "C'mon. You come with me."

He's pulling me along the sidewalk by the hand. I can't see anything except my hand in his, breath a bubble in the mouth that keeps me from saying anything. The sound is coming closer, or we're coming closer to the sound, and I feel it pulling my chest tight.

"Annette, look up, will you? Just look up? See? See?" The sound has stopped. "Annette."

Ben's got me by the hand I can't get away can't do anything but what he tells me to do. I can't remember what I want. He's standing in front of me, looking into me so that I have to look at him, feel myself pulled out of my fear.

"Look up. Stop listening and look." He steps aside.

The sound stops inside me. I see an old man in a worn grey suit jacket, a navy turtleneck sweater under the jacket, the wheel for sharpening beside him, unmoving, the tarnished brass bell in his hand, silent, its grey wooden handle. Blue eyes looking at me without any malice, without any interest. He has no question for me, expects nothing from me, has nothing to say. Wants nothing. He turns away, walks on down the sidewalk and the sound begins. Outside me.

Ben takes my hand again. I'm shaking. "Let's go home," he says.

I can feel the sound outside me, far away, having nothing to do with me. Just an old man who wanted nothing. I looked him in the face.

How many times did Ben try to rescue me from myself? One day he took me down Main Street to Pollock's Hardware, past the little Ukrainian church, the one set back a bit from Main Street that's decorated with squat little swirly shaped towers – upside-down tops or right-side-up soft ice cream cones, onion domes. He'd worked all week clearing out the basement of Zalinsky's store and the dollar folded in his pocket was to buy me a birthday present, two days late. Pollock's smelled of sawdust and machine oil. It had shelves and shelves of cardboard boxes of nails and screws and loops and claws of black or grey metal that men in overalls pawed with grease-blackened hands. Girls didn't belong there, but Ben put something cool and oblong in my hand: a penknife, my very own penknife. Folded closed, it fit just right in my hand. All the way home I held it, ran my thumb along the flat, narrow edge. I had something dangerous: a weapon, a tool.

I had it for years, had comfort from it whenever it was in my hand. Ben's gift. Neither of us fortune tellers – we couldn't have known that nothing he could give me could carry me through what was to come. But that's not true. Haven't I always told myself that the self-pity of the old who have in fact survived their lives doesn't wash? I was carried through. And it was Ben's gifts, all of them, along with the others,' that kept me alive.

A whole crowd of us waited for Poppa's train – *a hero's welcome*, thirty people on the platform – but I wanted him the most. When he stepped down everybody shouted, everybody ran to him, my mother standing at the back, smiling. And then Poppa turned to me and picked me up. *Make a wish.* I put my nose into his jacket; he smelled different, distant. *Poppa*, I said, *you need to smoke your pipe.* He smiled into my face, not listening, and pulled me tighter to him. *You see, Monkey? I told you I'd be home before you knew it.* We bundled into the streetcar, got off at the Liberty Temple where the banquet table was set and the farm girl who helped at the delicatessen was bustling around, smiling, humming to herself. After we ate, Poppa gave his speech.

While I'd been waiting in Winnipeg, my father had waited in Moscow. After more than a month of paperwork, red tape, of waiting rooms, bureaucrats behind barred wickets, he finally got his appointment with Immigration. He'd stood in the high-ceilinged room and explained to the man behind the desk – a young man, younger than my father, his suit pressed, a good dark wool. My father had explained it all to the young man, but it wasn't easy. They don't let just anybody into the Union of Soviet Socialist Republics: My father had to talk the man into it; he had to explain. How capitalism was crumbling here, how the workers had been betrayed. About the strikes of the employed, the riots of the unemployed, the anarchy of capitalism, the corruption of government, of lives. *I'm forty-nine years old*, he told the man, *and my own hopes are rotting*. A planned economy, it was the only rational approach. Look at what had been accomplished in the Union of Soviet Socialist Republics: the Five Year Plan, the granaries full . . .

At first the man said nothing. My father thought it was all over, that he'd be refused. So he took out pictures of us, set them on the desk. Still the man said nothing. What is to be done? *Comrade. Comrade*, the man said, *this will not be easy, arranging the repatriation papers*. But my father wouldn't give up. Again he explained. It wasn't just him; there were so many back home who felt the way he did, who looked towards the Union of Soviet Socialist Republics for hope, who wanted only the chance to help give birth to some sort of a better world where the workers of the world could find a decent life for themselves, an honest living. *Comrade*, the man said, *do you not think that your first duty is to go home and make the Revolution in Canada?* The man handed back the photographs. *We need workers for the Revolution throughout the world*, he said. *You should go back to your family. Go home.*

But my father would not take no for an answer. No. He'd made his wish. And he would give my mother hers. He would at last make her happy, take her back to her family, her city. Had either of them ever really felt that Winnipeg was home? Coming back to Russia made sense in every way. It seemed to be the only thing that made sense. He had come to Canada at a loss, had come because he was so unhappy. He'd come to a place where he thought an ordinary man could make an honest living for his family. And they'd worked so hard to make a life here. They'd lived through the 1919 General Strike, when innocent men were shot dead in the street. All that work, all that belief, and then they had to watch that hard-earned life eaten up by hard times. Hard times. It wasn't hard times; it wasn't an act of nature! It was a government that didn't care about ordinary people, didn't give a damn about the workers. Finally my father told the man this, told him about William Spratt, about a fine man, a life thrown away because the government didn't give a damn . . .

He talked until there was no more to say, until the man behind the desk stopped offering other possibilities. *Very well then, Comrade*, the man said. *I'll see what I can do.*

So my father went back to Odessa, to wait again. Two weeks he waited, dreaming every night of family, Anne, Ben and me, Joseph; dreaming his mother's ghost, brown braids like a crown. In daylight, the Odessa faces crowded round him too, alive, wishing: Manya, the sister who stole my mother's boyfriend, Lev; my mother's two older sisters, Basya and Reva, and their families. Evenings they waited, the whole family around the table, all his favourite food, the lace tablecloth pressed, the samovar steaming hot, polished. Lev, a middle-aged man now, though handsome still, tall, took photographs of all of them. If we weren't allowed back, at least my mother would have photographs.

Sixteen days after his meeting in Moscow, a thick envelope arrived at the house in Odessa. My father opened it, his hands steady. Yes or no, he was ready. Yes. He closed his eyes, held his hands clasped in front of his face as though in prayer. Yes. Our repatriation papers were all in order: permission had been granted. He opened his eyes, ran into the front room to tell the Odessa family, my mother's family, the good news. We were going home. He could tell them he was at last bringing my mother home.

Home. In the Liberty Temple, everyone sighed. And my father told us what home was like: how everybody in the Soviet Union talked about the Five Year Plan, how every person felt that they had something to contribute to make the country better, how ordinary citizens in the Soviet Union knew that they could make a difference. Here's how it was: if the people living in an apartment building wanted to make a daycare centre in the building, or a reading room, what they did was call a meeting and talk it over. They worked together to make things happen – they didn't have to go begging to a landlord. And he told us about the beautiful apartment that Lev and Manya had in Odessa, and Lev had a very important job for the government. Things were good for them. Lev would be able to help us out.

But the thing that everybody was most interested in was when Poppa told us about how good a place the Soviet Union was for the Jews. It wasn't just that they had laws against the anti-Semites, he said, it was that the laws were being enforced. One of Reva's friends – Avram said the woman was from a very well-heeled Jewish family – told him a funny story: she and her husband had to go down to the police station to fetch their nanny, an old woman who had worked for them since before the Revolution. Why was the old woman arrested? For saying it was the Jews' fault that the lines at the grocery stores were so long! *The Jews' fault.* Three words and this harmless old woman had to sit for four hours in jail. That's how serious they were about the law, about justice for all the peoples of the Soviet Union.

And that wasn't all, my father said. They were very serious also about building a Jewish proletarian culture. They meant business. Lev had told him that in the Soviet Union in 1932 they'd sold more than two million books in Yiddish. And there was a Jewish State Theatre that did plays in Yiddish, and there were public schools for children where they taught in Yiddish, and magazines that published in Yiddish. And then my father told us about how much progress was being made in Birobidzhan, the special homeland that the Soviet government had set up for the Jews seven years ago. Basya gave him an article to read about the Jewish communal farms, about how they were turning rag men and tinkers into farmers, how they were making a *gan eyden*, a paradise, on earth! That's when everybody clapped and clapped. Then we gave Poppa the surprise: I stood up in the middle of the room and sang "The Internationale" in Russian. *Such a beautiful voice*, the ladies said.

And now we're home and the excitement's over. My mother's already in her bed, reading the *Vestnik* like she always does, her gold spectacles on her nose. Poppa's tucked me in (I wanted him the most) and turned out all the lights. But I'm not asleep. I'm listening for Poppa's voice.

"I talked myself hoarse," Poppa says.

"Should I make you some tea with honey in it? I have raspberry preserves."

"Never mind," he says. "You're in bed already; don't get up. Anya, I didn't tell you. There was a problem when I was leaving, at the border."

"What kind of a problem?" I hear the rustle of the newspaper as she sets it down.

"It's nothing really. Nothing. But, you know you wanted me to have photographs taken of the family in Odessa? Lev has his own camera and he took such nice ones, Manya and Lev, Basya and Reva – the whole family around the samovar.

Well, when I went through Customs, the Soviet authorities confiscated the film."

"What for? What do they want with pictures of my family?"

He sighs. "It doesn't make any sense. But I had to oblige them . . ."

"You let them take my photographs?"

"Anya, they must have a reason. They promised the film would be sent on to us as soon as it has been cleared."

"Cleared? Cleared of what?"

"I don't know, Anya. But don't worry. It's nothing."

It's nothing, Poppa says, and I hear the *there-there* in his voice, and then my mother's voice again, angry, and then less angry, and finally calm, because Poppa's spread his *there-there* over the room till everything's smooth, everything's good. Their voices go on into the night, and I keep listening, even in my dreams. I dream I'm on the shifting deck of a boat and I can still hear their voices talking about the new life we're going to have, and I think I can even hear Joseph's voice reading poetry, *o brave new world*, though his voice is sad, and then Poppa and my mother's again, talking about the good days and hours and Poppa always with me now, what I want, Poppa and me, so that nobody will ever take him away again.

What did I want? To be with my father. What did my father want? The future he thought he'd procured for his family when he first left Simferopol. When he left Joseph, his first-born. And now Joseph fought to keep us from leaving. He and my father talked spirals around each other. The talk, the arguments, stopped the day Joseph put his hand on my father's arm and asked him to leave us with him, me and

Ben. Joseph and Daisy would take care of us. If not Ben, then just me. I had been hiding on the back stairs, listening, and my breath stopped inside my chest. My father told Joseph he had to be crazy to think that he would ever leave one of his children behind. And then Joseph just looked at him, and my father covered his face. I wanted Poppa to apologize, to tell Joseph how much it had pained him to leave when he was hardly more than a baby, how terrible it had been for Joseph when his mother was sick and he had to go into the streets looking for food. Would my father have said something if my mother hadn't walked in just then? But she did, and Joseph walked out. I thought I'd never see him again.

But he came to the station to say goodbye. Everyone came, all the comrades, friends. I tipped my head back to look up, and so much space opened above my head. Anything could happen in that kind of space. And then I looked down, and there he was, Joseph, bundled so I hardly knew the shape of him. He looked at Ben and Ben looked at him, and then he picked me up and hugged me just before I got on the train. And it was as if my breath stopped again inside my chest, and I couldn't say anything and neither could he.

I know what Joseph wanted, what he would have said if he'd said anything. I know what he wished: *don't go*. But we didn't know what to say. Everyone was talking around us. Everyone was doing something. It was just Joseph and I who stood here, not knowing what to say or do. And then I was on the train, with Poppa and my mother and Ben, and it shuddered in the track and slowly dragged itself away, leaving everything behind. *You'll see*, Poppa said, *things will be different*. I didn't want things to be different. *Everything will be good*, he said. Things were good before. The train took us east, and then the ship took us further east, skimming along the surface of the earth as it turned away from us, whether I wanted it to or not. And I was transported, carried along on the current Poppa and my mother made for me, pulled by what they wanted. I wanted to go home.

Chapter Two

When I lived there, I never thought *Winnipeg*, didn't think I lived anywhere. But in Odessa, I found myself lost in someone else's country: felt scooped out, a space opening inside me. Nothing was right in my mother's country. The egg yolks were the wrong colour and the milk tasted wrong; things smelled wrong, looked wrong. Even winter wasn't really winter; the snow came and went. My uncle Lev was indeed a miracle worker. Through his connections, he had found us a good apartment, two spacious rooms with broad windows. But I missed Selkirk Avenue, where everybody knew everybody. I missed Joseph; I missed the store. I missed the movies every Saturday – the movies in Odessa were boring. Everything was boring and wrong. Nothing was right in my mother's country, not even the words in my mouth. *I told you not to speak English*, my mother said.

I won't wear the bow. We're in the new apartment, and my mother has spent ten minutes perfecting the angle of the white satin bow against my curls. I won't wear it. I've smiled and said hello, met the aunts and the uncles, the cousins and second cousins. But I won't wear the bow. I don't want to. I look ridiculous – girls in Canada don't wear things like that when they're almost ten.

"You're not in Canada," my mother says. "You're in *my* country."

I don't want to live in my mother's country. My hand goes to my head; I pull the bow off. It crumples in my fist and I feel the twist of anger inside me. Then I throw it, crushed, to the floor – the waste, the ruin of it – not caring what my mother will say, not caring what happens.

She takes a step back. "Where do you get such a temper?" Picks up the bow, straightens it. "Ten minutes I spent fixing it for you. Go. Be stubborn. Go to school already. You'll be late." I pick up my satchel and go.

In the new country, everything betrayed me, even the alphabet. I spoke just fine; I'd been speaking Russian since I was a baby, but the Cyrillic stumped me. I'd seen my mother's newspapers, the letters to and from the old country, but they made little more sense than the Hebrew characters of the Yiddish dailies my father read. My mother hadn't had the time to teach me before we left for her country. The characters were bewilderingly like and unlike English. *A* for example was still *a*. I was safe with *a*. And *t* was *t*; *o* was *o*. But *h* was *n* and *p* was *r*. Why? And then there was the backwards *r*, how wrong it was. My teacher, Comrade Ivanova, explained that the backwards *r* was a vowel: the "ya" sound. What was I to do with a letter for a sound that didn't need it? It was impossible. I'd gotten straight A's at Aberdeen School, but in Odessa I didn't even know how to read. I thought I'd get the strap, but the first day of school Comrade Ivanova had taken me to the front of the class and explained that, although in capitalist states teachers used corporal punishment to discipline students, in the Union of Soviet Socialist Republics, it was against Soviet law to punish children in such a cruel fashion.

They did their best with me. And I did my best, determined that Poppa wouldn't be ashamed of my bad marks. Raya, the Young Pioneer leader, assured me that it was easier to learn Russian than English, English being such an illogical language. She would stay late with me in the Young Pioneer room. The children had hung red banners in the corner with its little framed photograph of Lenin. Raya had the bluest eyes, kind eyes, and short curly hair so blonde it looked gold in the sunshine. She assured me also that in the Soviet Union they were *liquidating illiteracy* – ликвидируя неграмотность. It was a hard word, *liquidate*, but I knew what it meant – liquids, solids. Liquidating illiteracy was a good thing, even though it sounded bad, turning something that had its own shape into something that fit into a container.

Raya told me I would be able to join a Young Pioneer troop as soon as my marks improved. There were all sorts of clubs and activities, summer camp too. As I struggled with my new penmanship, Raya pulled her chair closer, brushed my hair out of my eyes. She told me that she understood that it was hard at first, coming to a new country. But wasn't it good to have to think about things? To know that things could change, that they could be very different from one country to another? In the Soviet Union, they were building a new world full of changes.

No. It wasn't good. I didn't like to have to think about things. I wanted everything to stay the same. I wanted to be with Joseph. I wanted to twirl around on a stool in the delicatessen, to see Poppa's apron hanging on its peg. I wanted to run upstairs and show Mr. Spratt my report card, all A's.

When Raya asked me to bring my mother in to speak to

the teacher about getting more help with my homework, I lied, told her it was my father who came for meetings because he worked closer to the school. I wanted Poppa, not my mother. I told her Poppa had just started work at the Centrosoyuz – at least that was the truth. Poppa would come; he'd make it better.

On Poppa and my mother's free day – they got the whole day off – we'd take the trolley to Manya and Lev's. The streetcars were never as crowded in Winnipeg. *We're jammed in like herrings in a barrel*, Poppa would say. My mother would get into an argument if someone bumped into her or poked her with their bag, and then Poppa would have to calm things down. Sometimes the whole trolley would get into the discussion – in Odessa everything was everybody's business. Poppa and my mother would talk about their work, about how happy they were to be workers, not bosses. It was good to have someone else the boss. What was even better was that they were working only five days a week, seven hours a day – if you could call that work, sitting in an office all day, Poppa said. He was a buyer, a manager at Centrosoyuz, a showplace department store. It was a step up for him, that was for sure. In the Union of Soviet Socialist Republics a person could do anything. My mother had a job she liked as well, at a nice, smaller-sized store. It was the meetings she didn't like. They had meetings, all the time, where everybody was supposed to criticize everybody else. A waste of time, people making a fuss over little things that could have been talked about over a glass of tea. Not that any of this could have happened in the old Russia, not for Jews. Nor in Winnipeg either – were they hiring Jews as managers at Timothy Eaton's department store? In the Union of Soviet

Socialist Republics, anti-Semitism was against the law. No such law in Canada. And child beating, wife beating; they were all against the law too. Because such things were *uncultured*, as they said. *Dark*, from the old days of the tsar. All the old darkness was gone.

That was why we were there: to live in a bright new world. My mother talked about our Uncle Pavel and Auntie Raisa, relatives in Moscow who had helped Poppa sort out the red tape when he first came to get permission for us to immigrate. Pavel and Raisa couldn't have been nicer to him when he was in Moscow; they'd helped out with all sorts of things. Under the tsar, Pavel and Raisa could never even have enrolled in university. And here Pavel was a full professor, of agronomy, at Moscow University, Raisa a medical doctor, a researcher. That was why they'd named their little boy Vladimir, after Lenin.

That was how they talked; that was what they believed, my parents, at least in those first weeks and months. To judge by Lev and Manya's apartment, my father *had* brought us to heaven on earth: four sunny rooms, high ceilings, big windows. In the twenties, under the NEP – Lenin's New Economic Plan – Lev had owned a few trucks, a small shipping business. He had a billiard hall too. Manya had sent us photographs – mahogany tables, stained-glass fixtures – beautiful. A *NEPman*, my mother said, a wheeler-dealer. Dirty money: he made it all in the black market. But my father told her that wasn't fair; it was all legal then. NEPman wasn't a dirty word then. Well, when Comrade Stalin threw out the New Economic Plan, my mother said, Lev was smart enough to know which way the wind was blowing. By 1931 he was a Party member – that was what landed him a job in Public Works. And it was a good thing for us he did, my father said, because that was how Lev could find us such a nice apartment so fast. Lev was the one who had pulled strings to get my father his job at Centrosoyuz.

What they couldn't stop talking about was how every single person in the Soviet Union had work. People back home wouldn't even be able to imagine it. People want to work. How can you respect yourself when you're out of work? Think of poor Spratt. But if it hadn't been for Manya and Lev, things wouldn't have been as easy for us. Whenever my father tried to thank them for all the help, Manya would just shake her head, wave her hand as if to clear the air of thank-yous. Manya and Lev didn't have any children. Barren, my mother said; Manya's completely barren. Just take one look at her. And it was true: Manya didn't look like anybody's mother, in her slim, neat dresses, her curly hair dark, no grey in it. I can't remember my mother with dark hair.

Whatever she thought, my mother said. But what did my father think? Was there any unease about the choice he'd made for us? He must have worried about Ben and me. He knew Ben's struggles learning Russian. At the Centrosoyuz, Avram had the "Western expertise" that in 1936 they still valued. Only weeks after he started working, there was talk of a bonus at the end of the year, of nominating Avram as a "shock-worker," someone who'd made a special contribution to the team, because he'd made some suggestions for administrative improvements that they were able to apply. Everybody seemed to want more efficiency, a less backward economy. All those years he and my mother were their own bosses – what really bossed them around was business: one day up, another day down. They could never count on anything. In Odessa, they had steady work, regular salaries. They were better off already. That's what he told my aunt Manya, as Manya fussed over him, brewing him glasses of tea, slicing extravagant cakes. There was construction everywhere in Odessa – the new Five Year Plan – and Uncle Lev was busy with all of it. The air was full of promises, full of the future. Could anything have been more different from Winnipeg?

But there was one thing, just a minor worry, that he couldn't hide his annoyance at: the bureaucracy. The country seemed knotted in red tape. It had taken my father forever to sort out the family's papers: residency permits, internal identification papers. What bothered him most, a knot he couldn't swallow, was that the identification papers had *Jew* as our nationality. Why should people still think that way? He hadn't been in synagogue since his father's funeral. He'd had enough of that mumbo-jumbo when he was a child. And then to see that here, in the homeland for workers, they marked down *Jew* . . .

Take care of your cousin Vladimir, they say. Vladimir and Auntie Raisa and Uncle Pavel – I never even heard about them in Winnipeg – are visiting from Moscow, so all the cousins are at our house. Pavel is Reva's husband's sister's son. Reva is my mother's oldest sister, so Pavel is fifteen years younger than Poppa. I'm to call Pavel and Raisa "auntie" and "uncle" when they aren't really my aunt and uncle. They're not blood relations at all – they're cousin's cousins. And I'm stuck inside looking after Vladimir because it's too cold for us to play outside. Ben and the other boys can play outside, but not us.

"Such important people, Pavel and Raisa," my mother

says. "Be nice to them. They've been very good to us. Important people: a professor, a doctor. You see? In *my* country you can do anything – it doesn't matter if you're a Jew."

I don't care. And I don't care about the Five Year Plan either, whatever it is, the adults blabbing on about it nonstop when they're not gossiping about each other. Auntie Basya and my mother can never get along. As soon as Basya leaves the room, before she even leaves the room, my mother's talking about her. Backstabbing. I chew the juicy English word, thinking in English English English. At least my mother can't come inside my head and pick what language I think in.

The big boys lumber around the apartment knocking things over and then running off. They're always bossing me around or running off to play without me. It's all right for Ben to go with them, but not me. As if I'm a baby. Vladimir's the stupid baby.

They want me to look after him, and I will. *Sit still*, I tell him. And he's so good, just like Poppa. He sits still while I fix his hair, tie the red satin bow. There! It's done. He looks ridiculous. *Ridiculous.* I say it to myself in English, take him to the mirror.

He looks at himself, the dark bangs cut straight across his forehead, the narrow hazel eyes, green mixed with brown, changeable eyes. He looks at himself and then me. The watery winter light on both of us, showing everything.

"I'm a girl," he says. "But I'm not." And turns to look at me again. "What are we going to do?"

I walk to the window, run my hand along the polished dark wood of the table, the lace tablecloth Manya crocheted for us. A pretty table, a pretty cloth. I feel the meanness in me, put a hand to my hot cheek. I'm ready to open my mouth, use my mother's voice, my mother's words. Wreck everything.

I look at Vladimir, who looks back at me, patient.

It's not fair.

I walk back, take the bow out of his hair.

"All right," I say, my face cooling. "Let's not play this game."

There. It's over. I can do what I want; I can be mean or fair. I run my hand through his soft hair, sorting it out. "What if I teach you how to read instead?" Raya, the Young Pioneer leader, was right when she said it would be easy to learn the Russian alphabet – it only took me two weeks. Now I don't need any help, I don't even think about reading. Spelling's a snap – it all makes sense.

I can teach Vladimir a few letters, give him a head start. Kids here don't go to school till they're eight.

"I already know how to read," he says. "My mother taught me."

Raisa and Pavel and Vladimir – they're a funny family, always so serious, always talking everything out. No one seems to shout in Vladimir's family.

I take down the *Red Fairy Book*, the one in English I brought from Canada. "I'll read you something new," I say. I translate as I read, the way I have to translate everything now.

My mother takes me through her city. "Now *this* is a city, Annette! Don't tell me you ever saw anything like this in Winnipeg. It makes me sick even remembering Winnipeg. I don't know how they ever fooled me into going there . . .

This is a city. *This* is what you call a street. I told Basya she should have taken you last week down Deribasovskaya

Street, but she never listens to me. I give her a few suggestions on what to do with those girls. She knows nothing about raising girls – her first three were boys – and does she listen to me? No. She's full of her own opinions. The girls are spoiled through and through, running around like wild animals. She's got to teach them how to behave. I've never seen such hooligans, not girls."

As my mother walks me through her city, I'm walking a different city, with Joseph. He's taking me to the Palace, where they're showing a Laurel and Hardy, and a cartoon, and a newsreel, and then we still get to see the feature talkie. Tallulah Bankhead is the star; we both like Tallulah Bankhead. Half a block from the house, we stop and Joseph kneels in the snow and wraps my scarf tighter around my face and then he tucks my mittens just so into the knitted cuffs of my coat. There, that's better.

"Such an ugly city, Winnipeg," my mother says, and we're walking down Deribasovskaya Street. Something in me agrees, though I don't want to. In Winnipeg, I'd take the long way home from St. John's Library at Salter and Machray, the wind sneaking up the sleeves of my coat. Church Avenue and Anderson Avenue, St. John's and then Mountain, College, Boyd, Redwood, Aberdeen. I'd look at the fronts of the buildings, wanting something. Most of the houses were of wood siding with little peaked roofs. But how the doors went with the windows, where the trees stood in the yards: it was wrong. There was always something missing. The only building I liked was the little ice-cream-cone-turreted Ukrainian church, a building with a sense of humour. It wasn't solemn and straight like other churches. But even it looked lonely, like it didn't belong. Nothing belonged, and it hurt, the way the furniture in the rooms in the apartment on Main Street hurt. And my clothes, the way they felt against my skin, the way they looked when I saw myself in the mirror. My own face made me sad, the eyes too big, nose crooked, nothing in the right place. In the picture books at Aberdeen School, the little girls' faces were right, the houses were right. The windows and doors were where they were supposed to be and trees shaded the houses. Rose bushes climbed up the walls. In Winnipeg I'd never seen a rose, except in a book. Something was wrong, something was missing on Main Street, on Selkirk Avenue, in Winnipeg.

My mother's hand pulls me along as we go window-shopping along the wide sidewalks of Deribasovskaya Street, the March sunlight warm, the brown knobs of buds on the trees splitting to a yellowy green. Soon there will be roses in Odessa. The wind is hurrying after dried-up bits of leaves left over from the fall and I'm being pulled along by my mother's talk, how beautiful Odessa is, how ugly Winnipeg. I don't want to agree with my mother, not even in my head. But I can't help remembering the sad buildings of Winnipeg. I turn my mother's voice down to a hum and look at the buildings: the doors and windows, the curlicues above the windows, the peaks above the doors. And I find a rhythm to them, a sense of being finished, right. Like faces with the features all in the right places. It's what I want. I stare at the faces of the buildings, trying to memorize them so I can draw them when I get home. Uncle Lev is teaching me to draw in perspective. The fronts are called *façades*, Poppa says, a French word.

All the nice words are French, my mother tells me. That's why they gave me a French name: Annette. Back in Winnipeg, and now in Odessa, when people ask where I got my name, my mother says, *I named her after me*. It's a good name, Annette. My auntie Manya, who likes French words too, says it's an elegant name. Manya herself is elegant, her clothes, the way the fabric lies on her shoulders, the little trim of lace. French lace, French words. *Façade.*

My mother talks quickly but her walk is slow. Her legs hurt all the time from when she had to stand fourteen hours a day at the store. We're at the Arcade, where a glass roof stretches between the buildings on each side of the street. Just like pictures she's seen of the Galleria in Milan, in Italy, my mother tells me. Italy's not that far away. Ben might travel there some day, to the *cosmopolitan* city of Milan, a sophisticated city, elegant. The Arcade is elegant too, as good as any store in Moscow, my mother tells me.

When I look hard at the shopfronts I can see that my mother's wrong: they're not elegant. There are too many curlicues and statues: they're showing off. The shopfronts aren't quite right; none of them is just right. My mother tells me we're not going to buy anything – it's too expensive. That's what she says, but it's clear she likes to look. Most of the clothes in the windows are too fancy too. I'd be embarrassed wearing them. Manya's clothes are simple. Does Manya sometimes shop here? My mother tells me that an honest worker can't afford the shops in the Arcade. Manya doesn't work at all.

I'm tired of walking, and I'm more tired of listening to my mother talk. She's scrubbing at my face with a damp handkerchief. *Stop slouching and stand straight or people will think you're uncultured.* I yank my face away and she stops. *Don't get yourself into another temper! Whether you're tired or not, we're going to see the opera house.* I haven't seen it yet, the famous Odessa Opera House where my mother worked as a cashier, where she looked through her opera glasses at all the ladies far away in their velvet evening cloaks and long white gloves. A different world. And now I'm here. We cross Theatre Square, under the curls of the lampposts. Fancy, but not too fancy: beautiful.

"Just like Venice," my mother says.

"Look," my mother says.

And, looking up, at last I see what I want, what's exactly right: the rows of windows set in half-circles and columns, the entrance with its two-storey porch, though it's too grand to be a porch, a tower almost. And the curve of the domed roof with a smaller dome on top of it, to finish it off, so that it's complete. Perfect. That sweet arc. I look and look and some of the sadness in me is taken away. When I get home, I'll put it down on paper, save it, have it for myself, forever.

It's my favourite skirt, plaid with red elastic suspenders. When I put it to my face I can smell Winnipeg: the delicatessen, the stiff smell of laundry puffing like sails on the line in the backyard. "Come here, Annette. Your suspenders are twisted." Poppa kneels to tug them straight. There's no hair whatsoever left on the top of his head. With all the blotchy shapes, the bumps, it's like a map of some country nobody's discovered yet. He smells different now; he's using a different tobacco.

"You're growing like a weed: last year the skirt is too long and today – look – it's just right."

"Poppa, will you be home late again today?"

He kisses me on the top of my head. "I'll try not to, Monkey. Go see how nice you look."

In the hall mirror the new white cotton blouse Poppa bought me looks altogether crisp. My mother has brushed my hair and tied a bow at the top. This time I didn't argue –

the bow's a perfect match for the red of the plaid. My winter coat is warmer than I really need for the make-believe Odessa winter. Though it's a hand-me-down from our next-door neighbour on Main Street, the navy blue wool is hardly worn and the brass buttons down the front shine. My friend Cassie told me it looked brand new. Cassie said she'd write, but I haven't had a letter from her. I didn't really believe she'd write, and now I'm not sure she even thinks about me, remembers me, though it's only been a couple of months. And I'm suddenly frightened that, if she doesn't remember me, it's as if I never was, as if we never spent all those hours playing hopscotch or digging in the garden. As if there never had been the smell of cinnamon buns or the wide blue Winnipeg sky open above the triangle of roof of her family's house.

But I remember. I remember everything.

I make a face in the mirror.

When I go down the stairs, I unbutton my coat, let the breeze lift the collar of my blouse.

My new friend Elena's waiting for me in the schoolyard. She's wearing two striped yellow bows in her hair. They perk up from either side of her head like the ears on a Scottish terrier. Elena has the eager, friendly look of a Scottish terrier: friendly but also calm. Nothing seems to bother her. When Raya asked her to help me with my school work, I thought Elena would make a face, stick her tongue out behind Raya's back. But she just smiled. Helping me was part of her volunteer "social work." All the students have to volunteer for at least two hours a week. But now I don't need any help with reading, and it's me who's helping Elena with arithmetic. Elena wears her little red Pioneer scarf tied under her collar or around her neck. Once she let me try it on.

"Luba just told me," Elena says, "her class is challenging our class to a socialist competition this term!" She's hopping up and down, balancing from one foot to the other.

I smile back at her smile. "What're we supposed to do?"

"Comrade Ivanova will help us draw up a socialist agreement between the two classes. This is how it goes. There are three points of competition: first, superior discipline during class; second, always being ready for lessons; and third, having the class's soap and towels always in order. So we elect two representatives from each class and it's their job to check on the class's progress. Maybe they'll elect you! And, best of all," she's so excited that the bows are vibrating, "we're going to draw a big poster to chart the contest: two railway trains, one for each class, racing from Odessa to Moscow. I'm going to draw the engine for our class!" Elena is the best drawer in the class, much better than I am. In Winnipeg I was the best. "We'll move the engine forward one space for each point we get."

"But what do we win?"

"Well, if our class does well enough, we get a red banner."

"Oh."

"If all the classes in the school are red-banner classes, then the school has a chance to compete in the district competitions."

"Oh."

"A red-banner class gets prizes, too, Annette. We get to go to the children's theatre and the museum."

"Oh! That's great."

A tall thin girl wearing glasses comes up to us.

"Luba, I'm explaining to Annette about the socialist competition."

"Don't you know what a socialist competition is, Annette?" Luba drawls out the words.

I look down at my shoes, the bump where my big toe sticks up. "Elena was just telling me."

Luba's playing with one of her braids. She doesn't have any bows in her hair, just elastics to keeping the braids tidy. "I guess they don't have socialist competitions in America, do they Annette?"

I'm not American. I'm from Canada. It's a different country.

"*Do* they have socialist competitions in America, Annette?" Elena's head is cocked to the side, making her look even more like a Scottie. I shake my head.

Luba's friend Sonya, a sturdy girl with bright button-blue eyes and masses of red curls, has come over too. She puts her hand on the sleeve of my coat, runs her fingers along the knitted wool cuffs.

"Did you bring this coat from America, Annette?"

I nod.

"My mother says you probably brought diamonds, too. And a whole trunkful of saucepans." Sonya tugs at the cuffs.

"Don't be silly, Sonya," Elena says. "Annette's father is an ordinary worker, a good Soviet citizen. How could he have diamonds?"

Sonya shrugs. "She dresses pretty fancy. Who knows what her father did in America?"

"Her father dresses real swell. I saw him. In a camel hair coat. He dresses like a real bourgeois." Luba gives me a little shove.

"That wasn't my father. He's my uncle Lev."

"Well your uncle's pretty fancy looking too." She gives me a second little shove.

"Leave her alone," Elena says. Both their chins are jutting out, about an inch from each other.

I want to tell them I'm not American.

"She's a show-off," Luba says.

"Is not."

"Is too."

Luba gives me another good shove, and then Sonya shoves from the other side.

"Cut it out," I tell them.

"Two against one isn't fair," Elena says.

They both smile. Sonya steps back, and then Luba suddenly rushes at me with a big shove and I'm sitting in the gravel on the playground, my elbow scraped red and full of little stones. Luba's standing above me, and suddenly everything's bright, white, and I can't see anything but her, can't see Elena, though I hear her yelling, can't see the sky. Luba's still smiling. I want that smile.

The brightness swallows everything but I want what I want, that smile, and then it's Luba on the ground beneath me, I don't know how, brightness pouring through me and I'm happy, so happy, and I'm sitting on her stomach and I can feel myself pounding my fists on her shoulders, my voice spilling out words in English, the language I'm not supposed to speak. *Leave me alone leave me alone leave me alone.* The soft give of her shoulder as my fists connect. I look at Luba's face and she's afraid. The whiteness recedes and colours come back. I can see that Sonya's gone and can hear Elena saying quietly, "Get up, Annette. Get off her. C'mon, the teacher's going to see."

I look again at Luba's face, her mouth open in surprise, the tears. That's what I wanted. I wanted her face to change. I changed it.

I get up.

"How'd you do that?" Elena asks. "How'd you throw her off you like that? She's so much bigger."

Luba's blubbering. "I'm going to tell," she says.

"You started it," Elena says. "We'll tell."

"You're both getting in trouble."

"You shoved her first." Elena says. Luba stares at Elena, but Elena stares right back. "And you know what? I'm going right now to tell Comrade Ivanova that you were intimidating a new classmate. And that you were making fun of her because she's American, when you should have been making her feel welcome in the Soviet Union. And that you shoved her right on the ground and she hurt her elbow and she had to defend herself."

Elena twirls around, takes hold of my good arm and starts pulling me towards the school. "Come on," she says, "we're reporting her to Comrade Ivanova. Luba's not allowed to taunt you and she shoved first – it's against the rules."

"No, Elena. We can't. We can't tell on her." My elbow smarts. I'm going to have to pick the stones out.

"Why not? She was pure mean."

"We can't be tattletales."

"Don't be silly. She's not supposed to make fun of you and she's not supposed to shove you. It's anti-social behaviour."

"But we'll get her into trouble!"

"She deserves to be in trouble. They might even expel her from her Young Pioneer troop. She started it – she knows the rules. Pushing other students around is definitely not allowed. And she's way taller than you, and stronger. And older. It isn't fair."

"Elena, please. I don't want to tell Comrade Ivanova."

Elena stops walking.

"Elena, I can't."

It was the first time I ever got in a fight. Something took over, and I found out that if you pushed me, I'd push back.

It was a surprise. Maybe my mother wouldn't have been surprised. I found out also that I wasn't outnumbered: Elena stayed. And Sonya vanished as soon as I pushed back. One of those people eager for a fight until it starts, ready to run. I wonder more about the likes of Sonya than I do about Luba. People recur. I met a Sonya much later, when there was nowhere for me to run. Tattletale button-blue eyes, a red curl straying over one eyebrow. Blue eyes with no specific malice, no interest. A guard by a door, a staircase, a locked gate. "Raise your hands," she told me, no expression on her face. "Turn around." That was years later.

In Odessa, my mother was getting very tired of me, my tempers, my moods. Nothing about her city pleased me, not Alexander Park, not the beautiful spring day, not the picnic she'd prepared. I hated Alexander Park and I hated Odessa, even in spring, even under the high blue skies, and I told my mother so, and I told Poppa he should never have brought me there. On this particular day the source of my outrage was that I hadn't been allowed to invite Elena to the picnic: it was too much trouble, my mother had enough children to look after already. Beside our picnic blanket was a little light building, a roof but no walls, and I walked around it, trying to make myself dizzy, refusing the sunlight. It was a *gazebo*, Poppa told me. Good for a party, nothing serious – a building that was hardly a building. Can a building have no walls? Beside the gazebo was the bronze statue of a monster, lion body, eagle's head and wings, claws. A *griffin*, Poppa told me, as if by offering me these new words, he could make up for taking me away from everything. A griffin with its monster head. I put my fingers in the open mouth, and when I closed my eyes I was back home, back in the front room in the apartment on Main Street, where it was always dusty, where the light always filtered through the yellowed Venetian blinds. I was standing beside the carved creature whose lion body made up the wooden armrest of the davenport, running my fingers around the open beak of its eagle head, the dark polished wood silky under my touch. Griffin. This was where I really lived, in a house with no walls, nothing to keep the outside out. In a park of monsters.

My heart hurts. I can't swallow because my mouth is so dry. Instead of the usual written exams we used to have in Winnipeg, for my Natural Sciences class I have to take an oral examination. I'm going to have to stand up in front of the whole class and give my answer.

I don't want to. I want Poppa to save me. Last week, he came for the meeting with Comrade Ivanova and she explained about the test. *Please make sure that Annette is not alarmed in any way about these tests*, she told him. Poppa just nodded. I couldn't say anything about how scared I was. I didn't want him to be ashamed of me.

The teacher nods at me to take my question. The tickets with the test questions are in a pile on Comrade Ivanova's desk. Two other teachers are helping, making notes on lined pieces of paper.

Elena's up next. Her marks are always "excellent"; she doesn't have to worry. *What is industrial dust and how is it harmful?* Elena stands straight in front of the teacher's desk and gives her answer. I can't hear what she says. There's a kind of roaring in my head, a buzz.

Two more students and then it's my turn. Elena sits down, tilts her head at me, smiles. *Don't worry*, she mouths. I have to look at the question, at the piece of paper in my hand that's crinkly and damp with sweat.

Why has a dog a muzzle and a man a face? Give three reasons.

What does it mean? All I can think of is a dog-face, a man-muzzle, a horrible man/dog face. Three reasons. I can't even understand the question.

That boy, Anatoly, is up next. He's running his hand through his curly hair, making it even more of a mess. Comrade Ivanova tells him to take his hands out of his pockets. He shrugs; one corner of his mouth goes up in half a smile. Even his half-smile is nice. He has green eyes, like my mother. And now he's answering but I can't hear his answer. All I can hear is a murmur, as if I didn't understand Russian any more, as if I were in a foreign country, and lost.

I am.

Why did Poppa bring me here? Why do I have to learn everything new? I want to be my old self, the one I knew, the one that never changed.

They're calling my name.

I hold on to the edge of the desk, haul myself up.

"Comrade Ivanova," I say, "I don't understand the question."

The teacher looks more surprised than stern, whispers something to the other teachers. "Annette, please take a seat again at the back of the room."

I go to the back of the class, put my head down on the desk.

The other teacher, Comrade Kazan, comes up and leaves a new ticket on my desk. "This is your new question, Annette. Please study it and we will ask you up again in a few minutes."

They're giving me another chance.

I have to give myself a chance. I have to stop being scared of everything, scared of nothing. What was I afraid of? The strap? There's no strap here.

So what can they do to me?

Send me home.

All right then, they'll send me home.

Tell my mother.

So what?

So what.

It doesn't matter what they do to me. It doesn't matter how I'm punished.

They can't make me do anything. Not if I'm not afraid.

I'm not afraid.

So much was taught in those classrooms. My teacher, Comrade Ivanova, Raya, the Young Pioneer leader with her kind blue eyes – they taught me, eventually, gently, with consideration, not to be afraid of oral examinations. Taught me this poem:

WORKERS
The snow is deep on the streets.
But see, the street workers sweep the snow from the streets.
We need not creep.
Our feet will not get wet.
Three cheers for the street workers.

I memorized the lines, and can still remember them. As in the poem, we were taught to cheer – to celebrate the workers, the genuine citizens, good comrades. To celebrate those who were us, who weren't the enemy. My mother was always talking about *enemies of the people*; so was Comrade Ivanova. People have to have an enemy so that they know who they are by knowing who they aren't. The young people I was watching today chanting on TV, they're as certain about their enemy as my mother was. *Enemy*: it's such a tidy category. But back then, it puzzled me. *Enemy of the people.* I was a literalist. Who would an enemy of the people be? If you were a person, how could you be an enemy of the people? Wouldn't you be an enemy of yourself? Sometimes I did believe myself to be the enemy. Because I was a foreigner, not really Russian, not born there, no matter how well I spoke, how good my marks became. And then there was the enemy within, that refusal, the hard twist inside me when I was pushed and didn't want to listen or to cheer or to be good: the monster.

The class newspaper, which we pinned to the classroom walls, was a good place to celebrate and denounce. My friend Elena drew wonderful satirical cartoons for it. I remember one about the story of the grasshopper and the ant. The grasshopper had a huge potbelly and wore a top hat and a watch on a gold chain. Anatoly, the green-eyed boy I was beginning to notice, liked to do Science reports, Michurin's latest achievements in horticulture. I thought he was terribly clever, Anatoly, always sure of himself in class, ready to answer the hardest questions. I particularly liked his hair: messy, but shiny clean. The boys usually either had their hair all plastered down or shaved off, and I didn't like either. We'd have regular reports on the results of the socialist competition between our class and Comrade Kazan's. Our class was winning, mostly because in Comrade Kazan's class gawky, spectacled Luba, my tormenter and victim, had received a "poor" in Science. At the end of the month, the checkup committee would decide which class would receive the red banner. I was only just beginning to perceive the thrill of red banners.

For Poppa, because I knew it would cheer him up, I copied out the article written for the wall newspaper by Marfusha, the woman who cleaned the corridors:

> *Illiteracy*
> *Even though I am over fifty and therefore do not have to study to overcome my semi-illiteracy, I did not want to be left out of the classes that were organized by the school committee. Now I can write a little and read the newspapers.*
>
> *On February 20 I received a bonus for my work and I am very proud of it. Therefore I made a pledge to write an article for the wall newspaper. Comrade Ivanova's class has kindly allowed me to use theirs.*
>
> *My life was dark before the Revolution, and I was always close to starvation. Now my children are doing well at school. Although I am an unskilled worker, my children will be qualified workers and will earn good salaries.*

It was Sonya of the disappearing act who had written the report on Comrade Ivanova's class, how well we were doing. Our pledge to have excellent discipline had succeeded thus far. We had all passed all our subjects. Elena's "excellent" grades were noted, as was Anatoly's need to work harder. Sonya took care to point out that I was the only student in our class to receive two "fairs." She cautioned me that, if I truly I wanted to be a Pioneer, my marks must improve. An excellent comrade, Sonya.

No more pencils, no more books: July. School was over. Uncle Lev would take us all down to the beach as often as he could get away from work. Uncle Pavel and Auntie Raisa and Vladimir were visiting from Moscow for the summer, and we all would go. I'd ask if Elena could come, but mostly my mother said no. My aunt Basya also rarely came because she and my mother were battling. My mother was always tussling with someone in the family or at work. She'd come along, though, having packed us a huge lunch, and then she'd stretch out on her side on the grassy part above the sand, legs straight, dress pulled down over her calves, head propped on one hand, her elbow digging into the ground. As if she ruled the earth. As if it were there to please her.

Sometimes, when Lev came for us, she wouldn't want me to go, claiming it was too hot out, or that I had chores at home. But she didn't need a reason; all she needed was a bad mood. It was easier and easier for us to find ourselves at loggerheads. Like the time I read through the pages of her new cookbook, quoting Comrade Mikoyan, the Food Commissar and book's purported author: *I once told Comrade Stalin I wanted to build up the production of sausages. Comrade Stalin approved, observing that in America, sausage manufacturers become rich, especially from the sale of hot dogs at stadiums, becoming millionaires, "sausage kings." Of course, Comrades, we need no kings, but we must make sausages at full swing.* Wasn't the idea that Comrade Stalin gave a hoot about sausages pretty amusing? My mother was bent over the table, tucking filling into the knishes she was making for dinner. She took the book from me, turned it in her hands. It had been published by the State Publishing House of the Food Industry. *You're quoting from a speech by Mikoyan. Are you saying Comrade Mikoyan is telling a lie – is that what you're saying!?* Yes. I was. But I told her no, I guessed not. *Well then, don't talk about things you know nothing about.* There were so many mornings my mother was angry, not only with me but with Ben or my father, or with something else. Who knows? I thought then that she should have been happy, because she was back in her country, in her city. But she wasn't happy. I don't know what capacity my mother had for happiness. I saw her satisfied. I saw her work herself into the ground. I saw her mind alive, saw her consume newspaper articles, argument. Maybe that was her happiness. I won't ever know.

Mornings when she didn't want to let me go, Uncle Lev would just look at her. *It's a beautiful day*, he'd say. *It'll be fine.* And my mother would let me go. It was as though there were more room for me in Odessa because of the space Lev and Manya made for me. Lev wasn't like Poppa; he didn't just give in. Mostly Poppa didn't come to the beach. Work tied him up. He was working longer hours and then there were so many meetings after work, so many committees. It seemed that he became quieter with every day, as though something in him was being silenced. Or maybe it was satisfaction, maybe he was settling into work he valued. At this distance, how can I know? I only know what came later.

At the beach, even without Poppa, we felt like a family, a different sort of family than the one we had in Winnipeg, especially because Pavel, Raisa and Vladimir were there. The three of them would cluster in the shade, Pavel in an old-fashioned straw boater that hid most of his handsome face. I didn't know he was handsome then, with his spectacles and thinning hair and elongated body. I'd never seen anyone so tall and thin. Pavel didn't smile a lot, but when he did, it was genuine. He always had a little sketch pad for drawing Fanchuk, a beetle with a friendly smile who stood on two legs. There was a Mrs. Fanchuk too, who was just like Fanchuk, except she had a big bow in her hair. Vladimir and

I loved these drawings. Pavel was so patient with his pencil, like Mr. Spratt with his paper fortune tellers. He showed me how to do them, let me copy from his drawings.

Lev, on the other hand, loved the sunshine, the water. His arms tanned and massive, he'd scoop huge waves at Ben, whose woollen bathing trunks sagged comically, practically drowning him. Though he wasn't as tall as Pavel, Lev was tall and much heavier. It would have taken two Pavels to make a Lev. In that powerful body, Lev moved as if he and the world were in it together, as if they were best friends, comrades. What did it feel like to have such confidence in one's body?

Ben and I couldn't stay out of the water, though we weren't used to the salt, which crusted in our hair if we didn't rinse it off. The sand there was a beautiful gold colour, much finer than the sand at Winnipeg Beach, which was all pebbles and stone. So much of Odessa that summer seemed to me perfect: beautiful, and warm, the way things were supposed to be. I'd never believed my mother when she told me how beautiful it was. The whole summer in Odessa felt like a holiday, the streets full of tourists. But I didn't want to love my mother's city. It made me feel like a traitor, an enemy of my own people, my real country. And I didn't want to hate Winnipeg. I wanted to remember good things, remember the columns at the Bank of Montreal. Because it wasn't true that all the buildings in Winnipeg were sad. The Bank of Montreal was the most beautiful building in Winnipeg, Joseph told me. It was designed by McKim, Mead and White, Joseph said, the best architects in America. He took me inside once to see the height of the ceiling, the marble columns, that hush inside, everyone sitting at their broad wooden desks. I used to imagine Mr. Spratt at one of those desks, like the lead in a movie; Mr. Spratt with his suit and tie, before he lost his job. When Joseph took me inside, shushing me, holding my hand, it was like being inside a movie. All the people who worked there looked like they were waiting for the clapperboard to bang, the cameras to roll – everything perfect.

I carried around like a talisman in my beach-jacket pocket all that summer the single scrunched sheet of paper, its blue ink smeared, of the letter Joseph had sent me. In the almost six months since we'd left, he'd written me twice. That sheet also has been preserved, amidst my papers, its blue scratches scarred by the salt spray and my hands.

> *No, Annette, I haven't been able to go to University. No dough. Mr. Pollock, who owns the hardware store – I was working for him for a while – he was real nice, though. Said he'd try and help me out with a loan for tuition, but I just couldn't make it work. So for now, evenings I'm going to Depression College. They give free classes, isn't that great? The teachers are the best, terrific guys. So I'm still learning. Tell Pa I'm not turning into a hooligan. Nope, not much in the way of work either. The last month has been really tough, so we're staying with Sarah Katz again. I think of you with every poppyseed cookie! Daisy sends her love.*

I would read and try to imagine Joseph hunched over a History essay in an upstairs room in Sarah Katz's apartment, wearing his sailor top, the navy blue and white striped jersey that I'd always loved. What if what I remembered had nothing to do with what was? What if Joseph didn't have that shirt any more, if he was thinner or stouter? If I never went back to Winnipeg all I'd have to hold onto of Joseph was what I could remember. And what if I remembered wrong?

Chapter Three

❄

That first year in Odessa, I clung to Winnipeg. Everything about Odessa reminded me of something else, as if I were living in two places at once, or no place. But bit by bit, the present overtook me. My life lost its strangeness, became ordinary to me. And since my parents had returned to their past, at least in some portion, it seemed to me they made their way more quickly, comfortably, through this new old life.

On their free days, my parents would get on the trolley to drink tea and eat at Manya and Lev's comfortable quarters, the samovar polished, hot, Manya catering to my mother with china cups of tea and exquisite purchased cakes. Sipping her tea, my mother read from the paper, lecturing Ben on the latest of what Comrade Stalin had said about education:

> *Only petit-bourgeois windbags could think that the elimination of the antithesis between mental labour and physical labour could be achieved by lowering the cultural and technical level of engineers and technicians to the level of average skilled workers. In reality, such equality could only be brought about by raising the cultural and technical level of the working class to the level of engineers*

and technical workers. Such achievements were entirely feasible under the Soviet system, where the productive forces of the country had been freed from the fetters of capitalism, where labour had been freed from the yoke of exploitation, where the working class was in power and where the younger generation of the working class had every opportunity of obtaining an adequate technical education.

Which meant, Poppa added, that Ben had to concentrate on his studies, and not spend so much time smoking cigarettes with his friends.

Because the Soviet people were united in solidarity with the struggle of the freedom fighters of Spain, at school we were collecting money for food and medicine for the people of Spain. What good did our solidarity do for the children and women and animals killed in the bombing of Guernica? Poppa didn't want me to see them, but the newspapers were filled with images of the Spanish Civil War. The photograph that frightened me most was the one of a boy whose eyes were open, even though he was dead. Dead, with his eyes open, he seemed more than himself; not lost or gone, but solid, permanent. Why did they call it liquidation?

Because it's a free day, everyone is at Auntie Manya's, Poppa with his feet up on the ottoman, reading the paper, my mother resting on the davenport with a damp cloth over her forehead. Lev takes a last sip of his tea and then, despite the mild weather, puts his suit jacket over his striped vest. Over the jacket, his camel hair coat and a burgundy paisley scarf. He wears shiny wingtip shoes, and a cream fedora.

Lev is going to the kiosk for a *Pravda*, and I'm going with him, despite my mother's objections, which by now, where Lev is concerned, have become perfunctory. The walk to the kiosk takes two minutes, but when we get there, there's the usual lineup for the paper. "Well, this isn't such a long line, is it?" Lev says. "Though it's good to have a sensible person like yourself to converse with while we wait."

"We never had to line up for a paper back home."

"I wouldn't think so. But it's a small sacrifice for living in the Union of Soviet Socialist Republics, isn't it?" I can tell by his voice that he's teasing. "Your school's going well? Your poppa says that your marks are all 'excellent' this term."

"Almost all of them. I only got a 'good' in Natural Science."

"Still, your poppa's very proud of you. And Auntie Manya and me too – we're all very proud of you." He tucks a curl behind my ear. "So what do you like best about school?"

"I liked it when our class decorated a tree for New Year's, like a Christmas tree. Poppa said it was fine for me to help decorate the tree and learn the song because New Year's here is not a religious holiday."

"You never had a Christmas tree at home?"

"Of course not. Jewish families don't have Christmas trees. But I always liked them. I always liked the way you could look at them and look at them and always keep seeing more, always have surprises."

"So if you didn't have a Christmas tree, did you light a menorah for Chanukah?"

"Uncle Lev, of course we never lit a menorah. My mother doesn't believe in superstition. All that –"

"– I know: all that mumbo-jumbo. Well, your mother's mother used to light a menorah."

"She did?"

"That's what Auntie Manya says. But your mother never got along with her."

I remember what my mother told me, how her mother would use her fists, the broomstick, how she broke my mother's arm once. *Like an animal.* That's what my mother said when she told me about her mother.

When we get home, I go to the mirror in the hallway of Manya and Lev's apartment to see if my face has changed, if it's any better. Lev has told me that I'm a nice-looking person. Manya comes up behind me, puts a hand on each shoulder. "You've got a heart-shaped face. See the way the hairline comes to a point? That's called a widow's peak."

"Manya, sh," my mother says. "It's bad luck. Don't make a widow of her when she's not yet eleven."

I shiver when she says it; I can't help it. Something bad is going to happen.

"Don't be silly," Manya says. "It's very attractive. Annette has such beautiful dark curls, such a lovely little face."

"Don't make her vain, Manya. She doesn't have anything to be vain about." And then my mother walks away.

At first neither of us says anything, then Manya pulls me into a hug. "It's just a superstition, Annette, not to give out compliments. She doesn't mean to hurt your feelings."

I can feel the lace on Manya's linen blouse pressing into my cheek.

Lev is in the front room talking to Poppa. "You should read this article. They're talking about closing down the Yiddish theatre in Moscow."

"What's this about the theatre in Moscow?" my mother asks.

"They might be closing it," Lev says. "I don't like this, Avram. It's not good."

"What are you worrying about, Lev?" My mother's face starts to go red. "You're worrying about anti-Semitism?"

"Exactly. That's exactly what I'm worrying about. It's an old habit that dies hard."

"This is the Union of Soviet Socialist Republics. There is no anti-Semitism. Closing the theatre isn't anti-Semitism."

Lev starts to go red too. "And what precisely is it, then?"

"Just like *Pravda* said," my mother says. "Yiddish theatre is a bourgeois nationalistic institution. We don't need petty nationalism in a Soviet society." Lev opens his mouth to answer, but my mother doesn't let him. "What are you making a fuss about? You hardly know what being a Jew is. You hardly understand a word of Yiddish. You've always spoken Russian, just like me until I went to Canada."

"That's scarcely the point." Lev's voice is very quiet, very calm. "The fact is – "

My mother doesn't let him finish. "You're a Party member, Lev. You should know you can't make an omelette without breaking eggs."

"But what if you're one of the eggs?" Lev looks furious now, all his plentiful good humour vanished.

"Annette." Till now, Poppa hasn't said a word. "This is not a conversation for children. Please go and play outside."

Go outside and play; this is not a conversation for children. They said it all the time, the grown-ups. All those conversations that were not for children – so many words, phrases, jokes, even (we heard them laughing, sometimes) that we weren't supposed to hear. But we knew what they were talking about: the show trials, the purges. And the Terror. Terror – an ordinary word until they started using it in frightened voices, in whispers. Something bad was happening. It was happening to someone else, not us, but what if were to happen to us? When the grown-ups told us to leave the room, we went. Because we didn't want to know, even though we did know. And then the day came when Poppa told us to go, and we knew that the something bad was happening to us.

> *Back of the head, a sound, metal clapper against the bronze mouth, tarnished brass, grey wooden handle. It fills me up. Blue eyes with no malice no interest no questions no expectations, the wheel for sharpening, circling, skating. It wouldn't take long. It comes swaying, bellying up to me. Worn grey suit jacket, navy turtleneck sweater, and the cold gnaws, comes to claw inside me. Dark grey suit white shirt black shoes. Rich, yes, rich and strange. Nothing's easy: I don't want to waste anything, the wooden spoon circling. The wind whirlpools and the grey, muddy water fills up my mouth.*

I sit up in bed screaming.

Poppa wraps the sheets around me. "Poppa's here, shush now, sha. She's having a nightmare," he tells my mother. "I can't wake her up."

"Annette!" My mother moves to slap me on the face. "Wake up!"

"Don't!" Poppa stops her hand before it touches me.

"Let go of my arm," my mother says. "I'm just trying to wake her."

"Don't."

The drama circle at school is going to be presenting a play of Pushkin's *The Fisherman and the Fish*. Elena and I are helping make the sets. Elena keeps telling me that I draw even better than her, but I don't believe her. I'm trying to read the poem again to get some ideas for my sketches, but I can't concentrate. Poppa's in the front room on the davenport. I sit down and snuggle in beside him. He's not even reading *Pravda*; he's just sitting there, staring at the wall, the light catching in the bevelled edge of the mirror.

"Poppa." I touch his shoulder. "I was talking to Elena."

"What? Elena?" His hands have been loose in his lap as if they were asleep. He opens them slightly now, as if he's suddenly remembered that they were there. "You were at Elena's today?" His voice is dull and worried at the same time.

I nod. Lots of days I go over to Elena's after school. Her mother works an early shift at the factory, so she's home when school finishes. "Elena was telling me about Young Pioneer camp. We have to sign me up soon, Poppa." He's not looking at me, not looking at anything at all, not even the light. "We get to wear our whole uniform every day, not just the red neckerchief." I've worked hard on my uniform, pressed it, sewed the detachment badge on the blouse myself. "And we get to sleep in these nice little wooden cabins, just like Switzerland, and we go hiking and swimming and Elena said the food's so good she gained five pounds last summer. Every single day you get up at seven o'clock for drill. At seven fifteen you wash and make the beds – Poppa, it would be a *shandeh* if I couldn't go . . ."

"Annette, your momma has told you that you're not supposed to use Yiddish all the time like that."

It's still difficult for me to distinguish which words are Yiddish and which are Russian – at home we mixed everything up together. "*Shandeh* is Yiddish?"

"A shame. Say 'a shame.'"

"But, Poppa? Uncle Lev *says* I should go to Young Pioneer camp; he says it's a good idea."

"Uncle Lev?" Poppa says.

"And I need shoes, Poppa. The ones Momma found in the market were no good, there were nails coming up right through the soles. The shoemaker said he couldn't fix them. Maybe Uncle Lev can find me new ones." Whatever it is we need – shoes, saucepans – Lev can always conjure up.

"Lev?" He says again, as if it's the only thing he can say.

"Don't talk to your father about your uncle Lev." My mother is standing in the doorway, watching us. "You'll just get him more upset."

"Why?" Ben asks, in the doorway behind her. "What's wrong?"

"Lev's in trouble," she says. " – in the middle of the night, in his dressing gown and slippers – didn't even have a chance to get dressed."

"What are you talking about, Ma? What happened in the middle of the night?" Ben asks.

"They took him away."

"Who took him away?"

"Who do you think?" she says.

And then I know.

We all know.

"It has to be a mistake," Poppa says.

"Avram. They don't make mistakes, the NKVD. They know what's what."

"Anya, what are you saying?"

"I told you he was a wheeler-dealer."

"He's a good man, Anya. What can he have done?"

"Whatever it was he did, it got him in trouble. The NKVD, they're looking out for the Soviet people. Everywhere you look – spies, traitors, enemies of the people. If they took him away, he must have done something . . ."

"How can you talk like that?"

"I'm not saying anything bad about Lev. But when wood is cut, the chips fly. That's how it is. Sometimes people – you wouldn't think they'd done anything so terrible – they end up in jail."

"He's an innocent man."

"If he was so innocent, how come he was arrested?"

It never happened. That's what my mother said. Lev wasn't arrested. It was a mistake, just like Poppa said. They took Lev in to ask him a few questions. A week he was gone and then everything was fine. He came home pale, a bit thinner, but he could lose a pound or two, his new suit jacket was getting tight. And they didn't take him away – they don't just take people away, my mother said, it wasn't like that. Everything was done according to regulations, it was all written down, you signed a piece of paper. They even had somebody who wasn't in trouble there to sign as a witness that everything had been done just right. Everything according to regulations. That was the law. If once in a while they make a little mistake, someone cools his heels for a week or so being questioned – it can't be helped. You can't make an omelette without breaking eggs. If you didn't do anything wrong, it'd all come out right. Everything was fine. It was nothing, my mother said afterwards. It never happened.

In April, the empty lot across the street from my school was always full of daffodils – hundreds of yellow cups open to the sun – and for my thirteenth birthday Manya and Lev had bought a cake with daffodil-yellow icing that could have come from a Paris pastry shop. But at the party at Manya and

Lev's, no one was paying attention to the cake, because that was the spring we could speak only of war. Though the loud-speakers that broadcast the news on every corner kept reminding us that the Soviet Union was a peace-loving nation, the Soviet people talked of the war they knew, but didn't want to know, was coming. And the enemies that we had felt like a vapour all around us – enemies of the people, enemies of the Revolution, foreign enemies, the enemy within – were beginning to condense. Our enemies were to shift swiftly in the war that was coming, but that spring we talked war and wanted peace.

What kind of peace did we want? The "peace" in Spain had begun: Franco had declared victory. The solidarity of the Soviet people with the struggle of the Spanish people had done nothing. My mother was certain of her peace. Comrade Stalin had been on the radio and had promised that Soviet citizens would never become cannon fodder in a capitalist war. And Molotov had written an article in *Izvestia*. All Soviet citizens could rest assured that Comrade Stalin would not let the USSR be pulled into another capitalist conflict by warmongers who were used to having others pull the chestnuts out of the fire for them. So there was no reason to worry. She was sure, my mother, as if she sat in Stalin's pocket. And in reply, Poppa would say nothing, as usual – *no arguing*. He seemed to be nurturing silence.

Lev was worried. Though it had been two years since that week of questioning, this was a new, a more careful, Lev. Nonetheless, when the talk of peace, of war, subsided, he nudged my mother, who finally instructed us to light the candles. Ben sang "Happy Birthday" to me in English, and then Manya, who didn't speak a word of English, joined in, making up nonsense words as she went along. After I blew out the candles, Ben handed me two thick notebooks with black covers and red binding, one lined and one blank so I could write in one and draw in the other. That would keep me from doodling all over Poppa's *Pravda*.

It was at that thirteenth-birthday party, after my mother had gone into Manya's bedroom to lie down with a headache, after the table was cleared, the cloth put in the bathtub to soak, that Manya sat me down on the davenport and did what she did every time I visited, got her little bottle of lavender hand cream and massaged it into my hands, so that I got to take the scent home with me, so that at night, in bed, I could smell lavender on my hands, Manya. That was the day Manya told me the facts of life and I learned that I belonged to my father too. That I belonged to both of them. But when, a few weeks later, I "became a woman," as the nurse at school phrased it, I didn't want to. Couldn't stand the feeling of the rags they'd given me. I felt more like a baby in a diaper than a woman. I didn't want to be a woman; I just wanted to be who I was. I said nothing to my mother, though I told Manya as soon as I saw her. My mother never asked, as though there were some understanding between us.

I was kept very busy with school that spring. They'd put me in an advanced Mathematics class, algebra and, though I liked algebra, it was a struggle. No Joseph to help me, and Ben had barely scraped through himself. My parents worried that Ben wouldn't do well in the university entrance exams. Ben didn't care. He'd be just as happy taking vocational training, doing something practical.

Poppa came home one day after work looking pleased for a change, a newspaper-wrapped parcel under his arm.

He'd been able to buy a bunch of bananas from a woman who was selling them on the street. We hardly ever saw them in the shops. But a far more precious trophy was the letter from Joseph that he'd collected with the mail. Mail was slow from Canada. The last time I'd gotten one of Joseph's rare letters it was only a page and half, and he'd spent two paragraphs talking about some movie he and Daisy had gone to. This time he'd written at length. Joseph still had his bicycle and ladder, was still repairing light fixtures and radios, but now he'd rented a little storefront, was selling a few small appliances, mostly used, some new. Business was getting better, but he was worried that it was because there was going to be a war. Nonetheless, business was better. But the best news of all was that Daisy was expecting. Poppa was going to be a grandfather. Before we could celebrate, my mother came home. Poppa slipped the letter into its envelope, put it into his jacket pocket.

My mother came home, as always, full of news. The cherry trees down the street were in bloom, further proof that her city was the most beautiful city in the world. Had we ever seen cherry trees in bloom in Winnipeg? Of course not. And the plum trees too. It was like summer already. Irena, the new woman at work, was nice and cosy with the boss. She had a mouth on her: her husband this, her daughter that. Irena's son had written a letter to *Pravda* demanding a larger room for his family. Meanwhile this same woman had been telling the whole shop that everybody in her family was such a big success. If he was such a success, why didn't he have a better room? What kind of success was that? Then the woman told her that Thursday night she had a dream about Comrade Stalin. She dreamt Comrade Stalin had visited the store, that he had made a speech standing right beside her. Imagine the nerve! And had we heard Comrade Stalin's speech on the radio broadcast at work this afternoon? They had it on at the store. It was a busy day, so she hadn't been able to pay attention to all of it. But she did catch one phrase: *uncommitted people are of no use to anyone.* We should all think about that. It was remarkable how Comrade Stalin spoke: very slowly and clearly, very simply. Anyone, even a simpleton, could understand what he said. Even a child. Comrade Stalin loved children, and he spoke so that even a child could understand.

The news continued as she prepared dinner. But when she took Poppa's jacket to give it a good brushing, going through the pockets she found Joseph's letter. *What's this?* she asked, knowing the answer. Poppa set down his paper. I had a pencil in my hand; I'd been making sketch after sketch of the cherry trees my mother so much admired, fretting over them, erasing, redrawing. At my mother's words, I didn't move; I could only look at Poppa. *Say something.* Poppa's hands sat quiet on his knees. *Joseph wrote.* Not a word to her about Daisy; not a word about the baby. My mother had the letter in her hands; it seemed suspended, expectant. He said nothing else, did nothing. Then I heard it before I saw it, paper tearing.

And my father said nothing.

How is it possible that he said nothing? How was it possible for my mother to tear up a letter from her husband's son? Joseph, my father's son, who was just a boy when he came to us. And all he had needed was kindness – where was it in my mother? I remember looking over at her, the sharp profile, green eyes. My mother. Couldn't she give Joseph anything, after all that time? And what was wrong with my father? He had let her turn Joseph away.

Because it was easier to let his son go than to fight. His own son.

And what was wrong with me, that I sat there, saying nothing?

I close my eyes, let myself feel Raisa's hands on my hair. She's making me a French braid. Raisa's the only one who can get my curls into a braid. It's a special occasion: Raisa is taking me and Ben and Vladimir on a tour of Odessa's famous catacombs. The Efrons are in town because Pavel's giving a speech for professors of agronomy. He's as skinny as ever, Pavel, but even I can see how handsome he looks in his suit and tie and starched white shirt. Although this is my first excursion to the catacombs, I've heard my mother's stories about them – how her family worked the mines, knew every nook and cranny, owned maps of the labyrinth – since I was a baby in Winnipeg.

"Only English today, Annette. We must be strict. I need to practise." Raisa likes reading books in English, poetry, stories. Her voice is low, almost like a man's. I like her no-nonsense voice. Last time she visited, I amused myself by teaching her to say "no-nonsense" in her throaty, no-nonsense voice. "You, Annette, are a very lucky girl to be speaking English and Russian so perfectly."

"To *speak* English and Russian . . ."

"Ah, yes. To speak English and Russian, to know so well grammar, to correct your aunt so conscientiously."

"And I can speak Yiddish too. Poppa and I used to speak Yiddish together."

"To know Yiddish also is very good. Don't pay attention when people say it is not good."

"Uncle Lev –"

"Uncle Lev is a very wise man. To Uncle Lev you must listen. Now allow me to concentrate on my very important work right now, which is making my niece presentable. Soon we must leave for our visit to the catacombs."

Although I'm eager for time with Raisa, the catacombs make me uneasy. Even the word sounds ominous, like a city for dead people, of the dead. I shudder.

"What is it, Annette?" Raisa stops brushing for a moment.

"Nothing." Underground. "Auntie Raisa, is the subway in Moscow finished yet?"

She nods. "They call it the Metro. The stations are like palaces. The tsar never had anything like it: chandeliers hanging from vaulted ceilings, marble floors. You come to Moscow some day to see it all finished."

Poppa has told me about the underground palaces for the workers. But I don't like the idea of going underground. Not to subways and not to the catacombs. I've heard too many fairy tales about the bad things that happen underground: witches and goblins who carry children away, never to return. I shudder again.

"Are you all right, my dear young lady?"

"I'm fine, really."

"You are still having those bad dreams?"

"The ones I couldn't wake up from? They stopped ages ago."

"Did I tell to you that Vladimir also would have that kind of nighthorse?"

"Nightmare."

"Nightmare. I did research. It is a phenomenon called 'night terrors.' The child cannot wake. Very normal."

"But Raisa . . ."

"There. You are now tidy and nice."

"Thanks, Auntie Raisa."

"All right. Your most beautiful hair is accomplished and now you must take your cousin Vladimir, as you promised, to the kiosk for a treat."

Vladimir's wearing his new sailor suit. He looks very serious in it. Vladimir and Raisa, they're good at looking serious. You never know what's going on inside Vladimir's head. Auntie Raisa calls him an old soul. I take him by the hand. "Thanks for the birthday card, Vladimir. And you wrote it in English!" Vladimir's note was written in cursive, in English. He hasn't even started school yet, but somehow Raisa has got him learning a bit of English.

"Annette, is Ben coming?"

"I think he's busy, Vladimir." Ben is probably smoking cheap cigarettes at the back doorway downstairs and teasing all the girls in the neighbourhood who just happen to walk by.

This time there's scarcely any wait at the kiosk, so we're soon back with our *Pravda* for Poppa and the treat. "Race you up the stairs," I tell him. And we come thundering up the stairs, Vladimir puffing behind me, trying to keep up. Yesterday he tried to make me run all the way up the Potemkin steps, but we were both breathless before we got a third of the way up.

"Momma," Vladimir says, "Annette bought me pumpkin seeds!" He runs over to her, hugs her legs so hard she almost tumbles over. I hand Raisa the seeds, wrapped in a twist of newspaper, then pick Vladimir up under the arms and start spinning him round and round and he's not serious any more. He's laughing until he starts to hiccup.

"Enough, Annette, enough! You'll choke the boy!" Raisa's laughing too. "And be careful of the new suit."

I set him down. "How about some of those pumpkin seeds?"

My mother comes to the door. "That's enough, children. Annette. Enough. Ben, get ready. Raisa is ready to take you. And you, Annette. That's enough foolishness."

I can feel myself beginning to fill up with anger, feel myself moving towards a collision. Why does my mother always have to stand that way, in doorways, her arms crossed as though she were the immovable object? And me the irresistible force. Stalemate. I can feel the air between us crackle. "I'll be ready in a minute," I say.

"Go already."

"I'm going."

Ben's standing in the hallway, watching, trying to keep the smirk off his face. Raisa's looking away, so careful with my mother – not to interfere, not to get too close. Raisa's smart.

Brimming, tragic, I stalk off to my room to get my sweater, walking in that funny stiff way I know I get when I'm angry. Where's my blasted sweater? I throw my blankets onto the floor, scatter my pillows. Vladimir comes into the room.

"Did you find your sweater?"

I scoop up the pillows, pull the blankets back up. I'm afraid to open my mouth.

"Annette? Can I help you?"

"It's fine, Vladimir. It's here somewhere. We've got plenty of time."

There was a little girl. . . . Straightening the blankets with meticulous fury I can see how idiotic I'm being over nothing, nothing, and I want to stop but I can't. Not with her, not with my mother. It keeps boiling inside me. I'm so tired of being caught in these eternal tempers, the tyranny of my mother's moods, my moods. Cartoon thunderclouds, bolts of lightning forming over her head and mine, between us. And the only thing to stop us is Poppa's *there-there.* Even his *there-there* doesn't work as well lately. And Poppa seems to get quieter every day, can't seem to get mad even when he should get mad. For Joseph, Poppa had no *there-there.*

All through the trolley ride I keep myself busy talking to Vladimir, trying to shake myself out of my mood. And now we're all walking down to the entrance, a breeze blowing the boys' shirts, Raisa's and my skirts. The air is fresh here, a bit cooler, but I can't smell the salty ocean smell of ships, of fish, of Odessa. It smells ferny here, green.

While we wait at the entrance of the catacombs for our turn Raisa explains, in her deep doctorly voice, how the limestone quarried here was used to build Odessa, to make the creamy façades I'm so fond of. Kilometres of limestone tunnels fifteen metres below the surface, a rabbit warren, a labyrinth. My mother was telling the truth. I never believe her, but the stories are true.

The guide takes us in. He's an older man, defeated looking, in a worn grey suit jacket, a navy turtleneck sweater under the jacket. It must be damp down there. He looks at me, smiles, his blue eyes crinkling. Then he turns and we follow him into the catacombs, going down the cool mouth of the tunnel. The daylight soon fades, but there are electric lamps along the walls. I take a deep breath. The air seems to cling to the inside of my throat, moist, almost sticky; cool but not fresh.

I'm still grumpy, still stiff. If I stay with Vladimir, it'll be better. I won't let myself take my mood out on him. He glances at me, twitches his nose. "Smells like a closet down here. Smells like dust." I nod. Cool, wet dust. Or moths. The taste of moths on my tongue – not that I've tasted moths – but a grey taste, stale and damp. Raisa and the guide are talking quietly now, politics, Hitler, the usual fear. The floor's smooth here, soft, almost polished, slippery with humidity. The cool down here is a different colour from the cool outside, grey, not green. I shiver. Ben sees me. "You done with your snit now, Annette? Busy being scared now? Scaredy-cat," he whispers in English.

"Don't talk English," I glower back, in English. "Momma says."

He switches into Russian: "*Momma says, Momma says.* Now you're Momma's little girl!"

I start to shake. I feel it, that twist of rage again; I can't help it. My mother in the doorway, blocking my way. Now the guide is explaining about how the limestone was formed, all sorts of scientific details that Raisa seems fascinated by.

"Do you ever get lost down here?" Vladimir asks.

"You have to know your way around," the man says. "If you know where you're going you can always find your way back."

"You have a background in science?" Raisa asks.

The man shrugs. "I used to teach in the university."

"Here in Odessa?"

"Moscow."

Raisa doesn't ask any more questions. The tunnel narrows and we have to go single file. Soon Ben and Raisa and the guide are way up ahead of us. I start shivering again.

"Are you scared, Annette?" Vladimir asks.

"I don't like being under the ground; it makes me feel boxed in." The air is even thicker.

"Momma says I shouldn't be scared, because if there's something bad that wants to get me I can fight it or I can run away. That's what animals do," Vladimir says. "We fight or else we run away."

"And you're an animal?" I ask.

"Of course I am. That's what people are."

"And what if you can't run fast enough to get away?"

"Well, then I have to fight. And even if I don't win, I did something." He pulls his hand out of mine. "I want Ben. I want to catch up with him."

I can hear the patter of his shoes, but he's turned a corner and I'm alone. Where's Raisa? There. Up ahead, still talking away with the guide, his worn grey jacket blending in with the gloom. I can barely see Raisa either, just the back of her cotton blouse, a pale blue that's almost white in this light. I lick my lips, swallow. My own blouse feels clammy against my back. The corridor narrows further. The top of my head brushes against the ceiling and I feel something fall onto my scalp. I run my hand through my hair: grit. Touch the ceiling; it crumbles when my fingers brush against the surface.

"Auntie Raisa," I call. Raisa doesn't turn. Nobody's paying any attention to me; nobody cares what I want. I feel the anger fold into the fear. And then the corridor gets wider, higher. It's a room more than a corridor, with much more light and benches set into the walls. Vladimir's sitting on Raisa's lap, chatting away. My legs are wobbly. Good. I can sit, calm myself down. But Ben has spotted me, can see how pale I've gone.

"What's wrong, Annette?" He starts to smile. I bite my lip, glare up at him. "You're pale as Momma's strudel dough." He pushes his mouth against my ear, says again in English, "*Scaredy-cat.*"

I'm sick of everything: me, Ben, my mother. Before I can think I give him a solid shove that lands him on his rear. I hear his shout explode in the chamber, but before he can get up I've taken off, running helter-skelter down a narrow corridor. My good shoes are slipping on the slick, smooth floor. I slow down, stop, sink down to crouch in the corridor. Hug my knees, close my eyes.

That sound. Maybe it's just my heart pounding away. No. It's there. Swaying, full bellied, below the drip-drip of water. Nearby. A knell. It's there, over again and over again, swaying in my head. Two beats, light and then heavy, and that gap in between. Stalemate. No way out. No way out of here; no way out of myself. I try to breathe it out, let it go. It comes up, into my throat. The knife sharpener. *He's not here.* All right, then. Ghosts. Goblins. The Minotaur of the deep. Half human, half beast. That's what makes it a monster.

Something bad. All right. But I looked him in the face, didn't I? And it wasn't me; it wasn't a monster either. Just an old man ringing a bell. I'm not so scared, not so angry. I open my eyes to the dim light, close them again. The air is a grey damp; my skirt's getting all crumpled in the humidity. And suddenly I remember the train car, the dry wooden floorboards of the train car, voices calling me. Sometimes it's right not to listen. *Be good. Be good.* No. I won't. I want what I want.

I hear footsteps coming down the corridor: the Minotaur, the bogeyman. I open my eyes. It's Raisa, her blue blouse pale, almost white. She doesn't say anything, just gives me her hand. "Come on," she says quietly. "The boys are worried." Back outside, in the sudden daylight, they're waiting in the shade of a chestnut, Ben's back to me. He hears us coming, but doesn't turn around. I can apologize later. We walk back up the ravine path in silence, the sun setting, flashes of light shifting, flickering between the trees with every step.

Chapter Four

As a child who had been transported by her parents' will from one life to another, I hadn't yet learned that other, larger forces could take all of us. In September 1939, Germany invaded Poland and the world was at war. My mother was right: if we had stayed in Canada we would have been caught in the capitalist war. But my mother's country was at peace, thanks to the non-aggression pact that Germany and the Soviet Union had signed in August. So it wasn't our war. Capitalist Canada was at war and capitalist Britain was at war but capitalist America was staying out. My mother didn't say anything about that. But she did keep saying that everything was fine. In fact, once the pact was signed, it became easier to get sugar, butter, meat – everything. But, though salaries had been cut, both my mother and Poppa were working longer hours. Everybody was. And unlike my mother, few were at ease. It was hard to believe in our peace. People wondered whether Stalin was just buying time to build up armaments. No one was sure that the Germans could be trusted. My father was particularly worried about Joseph. Despite Daisy, despite the new baby, he might have enlisted. Or perhaps he'd been drafted. We didn't know: when the war began, the letters stopped.

My father and Lev would meet in cafés and over tea, a delicate, delicious tea – we had everything in those days of Stalin's peace – they would discuss the situation. *What is to be done?* Lev would drape his camel hair coat onto a bentwood stand and they would sit at a table in a café in my mother's beautiful city and talk things over. The months of someone else's war went by and, over glasses of tea, they began to plan. In May and June of 1940, while my mother assured herself and everyone around her that, thanks to Comrade Stalin, her son – Ben was seventeen – would never be cannon fodder in a capitalist war, Germany took the Netherlands, Belgium and France. With no mail from Canada, we still didn't know whether Joseph had joined up, but my father was convinced that flat feet would keep him out of uniform. In the fall of 1940, as London was being bombed in the Blitz, Lev and my father's plans began to accelerate. Romania, whose border was only kilometres from Odessa, had joined the Axis powers. By early 1941, half the Jews of the city were leaving or preparing to leave. The difficulty was that my aunts Reva and Basya were as stubborn as my mother. Lev was at the end of his patience with them. It wasn't as if he wanted to shuttle people off to Uzbekistan. We would go to Moscow. But they wouldn't hear of Moscow. And Lev was determined that the family would all be together. What was rarely admitted in their café consultations was that Lev himself was finding it hard to extricate himself from the intricate web of business and work that he had created in Odessa. He had all sorts of irons in the fire, and there were all sorts of people who were depending on him. Besides, it took time to get the papers in order. He had to grease a few wheels. While Lev set his affairs in order, while my mother held onto her certainties, my father worried. Worrying was his specialty, he joked with Lev, even as Lev was arranging work for him at the Moscow Centrosoyuz, assuring him that, when the young men were mobilized, they'd need to keep the old dogs in harness.

By March, Lev had the papers in order. In eight weeks, ten weeks, they'd be set. He just had to get his work in Odessa settled. If Avram and the family got there a week or two ahead of Lev, it would be fine. And if Anne continued her resistance, they'd just present the move as a *fait accompli*. Reva and Basya would come to their senses. And once Anne knew that Manya and Lev were going, she'd come around, no matter how stubborn she was, no matter how irrational her sentimental attachment to Odessa. She wasn't a complete fool. If they kept the wheels quietly in motion, everything would be all right.

I knew nothing of my father's plans, though I saw his worry. I was caught up in my own private dreams. It was spring. The windows in our high-school classroom were tall and dusty, the sunlight tall on the wooden floors. The teacher's voice went on and on about geometry. I liked geometry – logic, Pythagoras, axioms, theorems, truth being divided into such tidy portions – but some days that voice just drilled into my head. I remember the teacher's suit as grey, dust grey, like chalk dust or the dust that coated the window ledges. He was old, hopelessly old, our teacher, the few hairs on his head white. He must have been forty, ancient. Sunlight hot and tall on the floor, on my shoulders, I'd drift, watching Anatoly, who sat in the row beside me, just ahead. We walked to the library together sometimes, talking. Elena never liked Anatoly. She said he sold cigarettes to the students, got them on the black market. I would see him in unsmiling conference with other boys behind the school. But Anatoly was the only one of my friends who showed any curiosity about my life before Odessa. There was a restlessness about him that drew me. And in this last year, he'd gotten so grown-up. He must have grown six inches. And though there was only a hint of fuzz on his upper lip, his face had changed, grown more angular, masculine. I'd study his profile, the tender curve of his eyelashes, the way his ears were set close to his skull, the untidy brown hair curling over his shirt collar – much more interesting than geometry. All I wanted was to soak up the gift of sunlight and think about Anatoly, about touching his face, feeling the flick of his eyelashes against my hand, his eyes green behind the silvery steel of the spectacles. Proofs, theorems. It was impossible.

Ben and I are at the kitchen table, doing our homework, trying not to hear. Our parents are in the bedroom.

"What are you saying?" I can see my mother through the doorway, the tension in her, can read how taut her mouth must be as she speaks each word.

"I've decided, Anya. I know it'll be hard for you, but we have to leave Odessa." All I can see of Poppa is his back. He's at the bureau, sorting through the family's papers: our passports, residency permits. I can make out the glossy leather.

"Have you gone crazy?" My mother's voice is sharp, frightened. "We have good jobs here. My whole family is here." She doesn't say that in the five years we've been here she has quarrelled with every member of the Odessa family except for Manya and Lev.

"Lev has things almost set up already to take the family to Moscow. All of us. And Pavel's working on it from his end in Moscow. We'll all leave together. And I've spoken with Reva. She and Basya are talking about moving east."

"Lev is going to Moscow too?" She sits on the bed; her face changes. Is it possible that she can be persuaded?

"Absolutely. There's no question about it."

"And Manya?"

"Manya agrees it's best."

"Manya and Lev . . ."

"And, Anya, listen. I was thinking about Winnipeg – " Poppa's so eager that he doesn't notice my mother's features changing again, going hard. If only I could tell him to stop, to go back, not to say Winnipeg, but he's not looking at me and it's already too late. "I was thinking – and this is only if we really feel that it's the right thing to do – there may be a way that we can go back, just for the duration . . . Maybe soon I'll be able to reach Joseph somehow, find out what he thinks."

"Back? Back where?"

"Winnipeg." Poppa looks up, but it's too late.

My mother's head is up, her jaw set. "I'm not leaving Odessa. No one is leaving."

Poppa settles the papers into the drawer, sits down on the bed. "Anya. Anya, listen, please." He's sitting straight, tall, even though he's not tall. "We won't talk about Winnipeg." His voice is calm. "Let's just talk about Moscow. We can't pick and choose now, not now. Try to listen. Me, I don't want to go back to Canada. Believe me, what I wanted was to come here. Just as much as you, maybe even more. But this war, Hitler – for him already Poland, Denmark, Norway, Belgium, France, they aren't enough. Hitler . . ."

"*My* country is not at war with Hitler. You're not making sense, Avram."

If only he hadn't said *Joseph*, hadn't said *Winnipeg* . . .

"Look around you." Her voice is grim with certainty, smug. "Are people running away like rabbits? No. Only my sisters would run! What are people thinking about? They're thinking about what they'll be doing for their summer holidays, about the beaches. Right this moment the workers are out planting the flower beds. *Planting flowers.* There is no war in my city. I don't want to hear any more about your bad dreams!"

"Anya, you have to listen to me. We're just kilometres from the Romanian border. Lev says plans are being made right now to evacuate the factories east. People have already left. Lots of Jewish families have left already. Odessa is not safe. If we go to Moscow – they'll never take Moscow. This peace . . . Lev and I, even Manya, we don't think it can last."

"So! You know better than Joseph Stalin what's best for *my* country?"

"Anya. I'm afraid for you, for the children. We'll just go for a little while, till things calm down. Pavel knows what's what. He's already finding work for us. Pavel and Raisa are good people. They'll help."

"*A little while*," my mother says. "When I left Odessa the first time I told myself I was going just for *a little while*. And look how long it took me to come home. Don't you ask me to leave again. Go. If you're afraid to stay in your own home, go. But you go without me. And without the children. Annette, Ben: they're staying with me."

June 22, 1941. Ben and I are arguing. Poppa's birthday is coming up, and Ben hasn't saved his share for the gift. He's smiling that smile he puts on whenever he knows he's in the wrong. As we turn the corner onto Deribasovskaya Street we're so busy being angry with each other that at first our words override the loudspeaker. A crowd has gathered on the sidewalk, everyone looking up to the loudspeaker, as though the words, with their weight, were forming themselves to be seen as well as heard. Every one of them listening, silent in the warm June day, listening with all of the body. I find a place in the tightly packed crowd, rest a hand on Ben's shoulder to steady myself. At first the Russian words won't form themselves into meaningful phrases. I look down at the shoulders in front of me. A brown sweater, on this warm day. It's an older woman wearing a babushka, white polka dots on navy blue cotton, small ones. In the bright sunlight, the dots dance. The woman's straw basket holds a bunch of onions, of carrots, their green tops still fresh. She must have picked her carrots carefully, bargained for every kopeck. I look up at the loudspeaker's open mouth, narrow throat. The broadcaster's words coalesce into meaning: Hitler's army has invaded the Soviet portion of Poland. Our peace is over.

Such a perfect day. The windows are open, a warm breeze blowing over the kitchen table, sun like a cloth over its surface. Poppa and Ben and I are at the table, listening to the radio. Poppa fiddles with the dial till the station comes in clearer, though it still crackles with some sort of interference. My mother is moving back and forth at the sink, noisily washing up, making a show of not listening.

> *The peace-loving peoples of the Union of Soviet Socialist Republics did not want to be drawn into capitalist conflicts. It was for this reason that the non-aggression pact was signed by our great nation and the German government.*

> *For more than two years, our nation enjoyed peace and prosperity, an interval in which our citizenry became stronger and more resolute, and in which our armed forces gathered strength and preparedness. In the face of this treacherous military aggression by Germany, the people have no choice. The German army has already dared to set foot on Soviet soil. They boast that they are unstoppable. The Germans will quickly find that Hitler's troops are no match for the unequalled courage of the Red Army soldiers. We are destined to win.*

Somebody else's war has become ours.

This sunlight.

"Maybe they are unstoppable."

My mother turns around. "What did you say?"

I didn't even know I'd spoken aloud. "Nothing. Nothing, Momma."

My mother turns back to her dishes.

"Well." Ben gets up. He's so tall. "We won't be sitting around like this much longer." He turns a dial; it's louder. The words crackle into the room – static.

"What do you mean?" I ask, my fingers moving along the edge of the wooden tabletop. I scratch at a crumb that's stuck.

"The caretaker says," Ben is watching my fingers, "that all civilian radios are going to have to be handed in to the local police. We're going to have to trade in Old Faithful here, our first contribution to the war effort."

I think about what else we'll have to contribute, how tall Ben has gotten, how he's filled out like a man. He *is* a man: the shoulders, arms, the moustache he's affecting. When I teased him that he was trying to look like Comrade Stalin, he just shrugged, snorted.

I look from Ben to the radio, Soviet-made, a present from Lev when we arrived, one of the many presents he "arranged" for us. Sort of a squared off beehive, about the size of a breadbox. There's a circle of bronze-coloured mesh for a speaker, an ivory dial for volume, one for tuning.

The old radio in Winnipeg was massive, its rounded mahogany back taller than I was. I'd be listening on the davenport, my legs tucked under me, my fingers going round and round the mouth of the wooden griffin head carved onto the arm as if they were weaving a charm, round and round the tame mouth of the beast. *Something bad.*

We gave it to Joseph when we left. Is he listening to it now?

I want to be home.

Poppa carefully stubs out his cigar, leaves the half-smoked length in the black glass ashtray.

He goes to the bedroom, opens the wardrobe, pulls down the suitcases.

"What are you doing?" My mother's in the doorway.

He walks over to the bureau, empties the drawers into a suitcase. "Lev has arranged everything. We can leave for Moscow as early as tomorrow; he'll meet us at the station. He's found train tickets, everything. We've got to pack. We'll stay with Pavel and Raisa in Moscow till we get housing straightened out. I've already written them. As soon as we get there I'll write Joseph."

"Joseph?" I've said his name before I can stop myself.

"We'll be able to write," Ben says. "Mail will get through now we're allies."

We're allies. We were enemies, and now we're allies.

My mother shifts in the doorway. "I told you before and I'm telling you now. I'm not leaving my city." Her face is in profile, the jaw working as if each word exhausts her.

Poppa's walking to the bureau. His hands are on the handle of the top drawer. They start to tremble.

"We're not going anywhere," she says. She's very straight in the doorway. No arguing.

In one motion Poppa pulls the drawer from the bureau, flings it across the room, into the corner opposite to where my mother is standing. It breaks; the fine dovetail edges split open. My mother's faded cotton nightdresses spill onto the floor.

His whole body is shaking.

"Tomorrow. I'm taking Ben and I'm taking Annette tomorrow on the train to Moscow. Come or don't come."

My mother has taken a step back. She takes another. "You're like an animal." She spits on the floor, takes her handbag, walks out the door.

Ben gets up from the table. "Annette? We have to help Poppa pack." He takes my hand. I'm trembling too.

Ben puts his arm around my shoulders. "Come on, Monkey. We've got to help Poppa with the suitcases."

The train hisses and snorts at the platform. I tip my head back, and my mouth holds itself open. The vault of ceiling is high, arched above my head. Poppa's face is suddenly in front of me. I snap back into myself. Poppa's here. It's all right. The station is chaos, the platform seething with people – baggage being navigated on the men's shoulders, women clasping babies against their light summer dresses, gripping the hands of their older children, holding on. But it's all right – Poppa's here. He's kneeling beside me, tugging at the knots of the ropes our bulging suitcases are tied with. He's here.

Where's Ben? Just behind us, his arms filled with bottled water, packages.

"Annette," Poppa says, "I've found our seats. Help me with the suitcases."

"We didn't say goodbye to Momma."

Poppa straightens, takes me in his arms. I nuzzle my face into the smoothness of his white cotton shirt. Poppa.

"I have to get you and Ben to Moscow." He kisses me on the forehead. "Raisa and Pavel will be at the station in Moscow. They know we're coming."

He pats me on the arm. "Look, there's your uncle." Lev is plunging, pushing through the frantic crowd. Lev the conjurer, a big basket of sandwiches, fresh fruit, biscuits in his hands. In seconds he's beside us.

"It's good you're leaving today," he says. "Manya and I will be joining you very soon." Lev is smiling, but he has to swallow before he speaks. "I need a couple more weeks – just a few things to finish up – and then we'll all be in Moscow together. Manya's fine; don't worry." His powerful arms swallow Poppa up in a bear hug. He whispers something into Poppa's ear. They mustn't have found her, mustn't have heard anything.

Lev turns to me. "You'd better hurry." Closes me in his arms, kisses the top of my head. He waves once more and then he's gone.

The black body of the train shifts beside me.

I concentrate. Somewhere. My mother is somewhere. *Momma.* Ben and Poppa are in our compartment, arranging the bags. I step up onto the train, step over the gap between the platform and the restless metal body of the train. And here's Poppa, and Ben, who's already rummaging through the basket Lev has left. I look out the window. Momma. That woman walking quickly, stiffly – no, it's not her. My mother isn't here; she's nowhere.

"Annette," Poppa says, "I have her ticket. I'll just take one more look . . ." I nod. Ben looks up, continues sorting out our baggage, fitting and refitting the boxes, suitcases around us. I look out the window.

Poppa.

He's so still on the platform. Everything else is moving, as the bags, baskets, packages are heaved through the train windows, as people shove their way onto the train, babies wailing, women shouting through the crowd, the train clearing its throat, anxious, ready. In all the noise, the smell of this hot, frantic day, Poppa is still, in his white shirt, his arms by his sides. The train shifts.

"Poppa?"

He turns around to face me, comes to the open window, moving towards me. "I'll find her, Annette, Ben."

"Poppa –"

"You two go ahead on this train. I'll find her and then we'll both come to Moscow on another train." He steps closer to the window, hands our tickets to Ben. "Ben, that green suitcase, hand it to me." Then he hands Ben a small packet in a brown paper wrapper. "Be careful with this." He lowers his voice. "Lev gave us some extra cash. Give it to Pavel and Raisa as soon as you get there. Everything will be fine. I'll see you in Moscow soon, soon . . ."

Poppa. I open my mouth, but not a sound comes out.

The engine takes a deep breath. Pumps like a slow heartbeat and the train pulls away.

I'm hot, my nightgown soaked in sweat, the thin cotton nightgown that Poppa packed for me, his brown hands on the white cloth, tucking in the folds, smoothing back my hair. *You're grown now.* No. I sit up, throw the sheets off, listen. Nothing. He went to my mother, and not with me. I hold my own two hands up to my face, feel the skin soft against my palms, my mouth open. Feel the loneliness slide down my throat, open a space in me. I'm porous, hollow, the night moving through me. If I start to cry, make noise, I'll wake Raisa and Pavel. I don't want anyone but Poppa. My face is wet, the tears slipping between my fingers, but I'm quiet. I should wash my face. I get up, don't turn on the light, feel my way with one hand skimming the wall to the washroom. The window is open, the room cooler. I stand at the basin and the breeze rinses my bare shoulders, arms, cools my face. Laps tenderly at my skin, touches me. *There.*

Fourteen days past summer solstice the light is everywhere, inescapable: Moscow's broad streets, tall buildings, are rinsed in light; every speck, corner, licked at. There's no place for me to hide from my father's choice. Even the nights are brief, barely any respite from the light. In that first confusing flurry of days I find myself walking unfamiliar Moscow streets as Raisa keeps me busy with one chore after another. The onion domes of Saint Basil's, the carnival shapes – ice cream cones, that little church on Main Street – are at home here at last. But not me. What am I doing here? Where am I? *Moscow, the capital city of the Union of Soviet Socialist Republics.* Fifty-six degrees north, farther north than I've ever been: six degrees of latitude north of Winnipeg, ten north of Odessa. Night brief. And twilight – that hour when darkness has taken over the eastern sky so that it's studded with hard cold points of stars that look artificial, as though Stalin himself has ordered them into being, that hour when the west is still light, still another world, the world of day – does twilight count as night or day? I don't know. I know nothing, lost as I am under the big M, the rings of arches that lead to the Metro stations. Under the vaults of the ceilings underground, the embrace of those arched walls closing over my head doesn't touch me. The escalators tunnelling down to the centre of the earth, step after step, lead me nowhere. I'm lost also on the sidewalks, among the proud stiff buildings, the streets wider than Main Street, wider than Portage Avenue: there's no place to hide.

Raisa takes a deep breath, spreads her short, neat fingers – so different from my mother's – across the table surface as if she's about to make an announcement. But she doesn't say anything. Didn't say anything at first when they met us at the station, believing that Poppa and my mother would be with us. The look on her face, though. Poor Raisa, she's stuck with us. We're sitting, stiff as puppets, at the table: Pavel and Raisa, Ben and me. Vladimir's roaming restlessly, touching the pictures on the walls, fingering the cushions on the davenport.

Then suddenly it joins us in the apartment – Stalin's voice, the first time he's been on the radio since the Germans invaded.

> *Comrades! Citizens! Brothers and sisters! Soldiers of our army and navy! My friends, I now speak to you in person. Since June 22 a perfidious military aggression by Hitler's Germany against our motherland has been under way. Despite the heroic resistance of the Red Army, despite the fact that the best enemy divisions and aviation units have already been destroyed, and that the battlefields are strewn with enemy graves, the enemy continues to thrust forward by sending fresh forces to the front . . .*

Despite the bad news, it's soothing to hear the familiar voice; it makes things feel more like home.

"Annette, sweetheart, can you stop humming?"

"Sorry, Raisa," I say. "It drives my mother crazy." Raisa flinches. Because I said the word *mother.* "It's just that I'm jumpy."

So jumpy that it's hard to pay attention to the speech. A few words filter through:

> *How has it happened that our glorious Red Army left the Fascists in control of a number of our cities and regions? . . . invincible . . . monsters and cannibals like Hitler and Ribbentrop . . . conditions favourable for German troops and unfavourable for Soviet troops . . . destined to win . . . bravery of our soldiers . . . abandon peacetime habits. . . .*

When the speech is over, Pavel switches off the radio, runs a hand through his pale, thinning hair. He's still handsome, Pavel, though his face seems thinner even than usual. He's so much younger than Poppa. I never really realized it before.

"Pavel?"

"Yes, Annette?"

"They're still safe, aren't they? My parents, Lev and Manya?"

"They're safe, Annette. It's just been hard for them to find a way to get here. But they're safe. You mustn't worry."

Raisa pours a glass of water, hands it to Ben. "Ben, do you have Joseph's address? We have to send a letter to your brother, tell him he can write to you here."

Ben nods, puts his hands around the water glass, clenching and unclenching.

We have to write and tell Joseph that Poppa didn't come . . . *Full fathom five thy father lies*. I hear Joseph's voice again, reading me Shakespeare poems back on Main Street. Poppa left us just the way he left Joseph. No, I can't think that way. And what if Poppa's lost to us now, gone? And Joseph so far away. Nobody to help me. But it's not true. I have Ben. Ben's here. And Raisa and Pavel and Vladimir.

"Poppa," Vladimir says, frowning. "What Comrade Stalin said . . ."

"What is it, Vladimir?"

"There was a part in Comrade Stalin's speech that didn't make sense."

Pavel pulls Vladimir onto his lap. He looks small there. Is he small for nine? Pavel's so gentle with him, like Poppa. He frowns through his gold spectacles, though his hand continues to sift through Vladimir's hair. "What part, Vladimir?"

"Well, he said that it was because our troops weren't ready for war that the Germans had been able to take over so much of our land so fast. And that the reason that we weren't ready for war was because we'd trusted the peace. But then Comrade Stalin said that the peace with Germany had given us a year and a half to get ready for war."

Earlier in the year, Vladimir had sent a letter to Comrade Stalin. Raisa had written us about it, amused and moved at the same time. Vladimir was worried about the beggars that he'd seen in the streets of Moscow. He thought Comrade Stalin should know, that he should do something about them.

Not fair. That's what Vladimir would have been thinking: *not fair. Mean.* I remember thinking that way myself, believing the world was supposed to be fair.

So Vladimir had written to Comrade Stalin, and then been upset when nothing had changed, when he'd kept seeing the same beggars in the same streets.

"And also," Vladimir goes on, "at the end of the speech, Comrade Stalin said that our army was invincible. But at the beginning of the speech, when he was talking about Germany, he said that history shows us that no army is invincible."

Pavel pulls Vladimir tighter to him. *Not fair*, that's what we're all thinking. "It's rhetoric, Vladimir. Under these circumstances, I suppose rhetoric is excusable."

"What circumstances, Poppa? What Comrade Stalin said?"

"What did he say?"

"That we're fighting for our lives."

Pavel goes pale, doesn't answer for a moment. Vladimir wriggles in his lap. "Poppa . . ."

Pavel kisses the top of his head. "It's not something for you to worry about, *tateleh*. We're here, in Moscow; we're safe."

In one of the labelled, orderly blue file folders, I have it still – miraculously – the letter on thin paper, in Lev's elegant scrawl. The only letter we received from Odessa that summer. But I don't have to look for it: that summer Raisa let me read it and I pored over it; I read it until I'd memorized it, wanting Lev's promises to come true. Wanting us all to be together, to be safe.

July 10, 1941
Odessa

My Dear Pavel and Raisa,
I write not knowing whether you'll receive this letter – we're not sure what's getting through. Avram has sent the children three letters already, but no mail has come from Moscow. I'm sure you're concerned about us, but you needn't be. You'd be surprised how little has changed here. Odessa is still Odessa, and summer still summer. The municipal flowers are obediently in bloom and the cinemas advertise the latest movies. Shops and cafés have their doors open to catch a breeze. It's been very warm.

All this despite the fact that, two weeks ago, martial law was declared – at least the Odessa version of martial law: curfew from midnight to four thirty am. Shops to remain open no later than ten o'clock at night. Theatres, cinemas and cultural establishments to close no later than eleven. Scarcely a strict regime.

But despite appearances, and despite the carefully modulated constant good news Pravda *keeps offering us, if one observes closely enough, there are changes. The sidewalks, with many more women than men, aren't nearly as crowded. And people don't stroll these days – they walk quickly, preoccupied. I think even the citizenry of Odessa is beginning to understand that the party's over: it's our war now.*

And there are more obvious signs of the preparations for war. On every major artery of the city there are work crews, mostly women, building barricades of timbers and sandbags across the streets. A portal is left for the trolleys and for the truckloads of women volunteers who are digging the anti-tank ditches on the outskirts of town.

Thank God Avram got Ben and Annette off safely to Moscow.

I know that you'll be troubled that we haven't left ourselves. I want to assure you that I'm at this very moment tying up the last loose ends, dealing with a few more obligations. Shipping has been paralyzed and there are some crucial shipments stalled, some delays. As soon as I have these last things settled we'll pack up the family and leave. Manya has her own concerns about this delay, but refuses to leave without me. We haven't been able to do anything about persuading Reva and Basya to take their families east. And dear Anya remains difficult as always. I'm sure in the end we'll pry her loose of her beloved city. We'll get everyone safely out.

I have to trust my instincts here. It's a question of timing. And you do know that my timing, so far, has been mostly good. The paperwork for our evacuation to Moscow has been in order for weeks. I just need another week, another two.

Your loving cousin,
Lev

The July evenings were unexpectedly cool, good sleeping weather. But sleep didn't come easy for me in that first month of separation. Raisa had made the davenport in the front room up as a bed for me. We had to move it away from the window. A few bombs had fallen in June, and Raisa was worried. I would lie sleepless in the dark, hanging on to my family, their faces – Poppa, my mother, Manya, Lev – remembering the sound of Poppa's voice: *there-there.* And when I did dream, I dreamt in English, dreamt that I was back in the store.

> *The shelves go up high, high. I'm little again. The store's full of customers; everyone's talking English. And there's Vladimir making milkshakes. "One for each of you," he says. It's the old family: Poppa, my mother, Joseph, Ben. I'm counting us. I keep counting, but one of us is missing, and I don't know which one.*

For now they were safe. The rumours about the Germans bombing Odessa were just that, rumours. And we were safe. They had not bombed Moscow since those strays in June. Though blackout curtains shielded Pavel and Raisa's apartment from the half-light of night beyond them, they were just a precaution. *Preparedness, preparedness and resolution are the keys* – the voices on the loudspeakers blared it all the time. And Joseph too was safe. We received a brief letter from Winnipeg; he was still in Winnipeg, had tried to enlist but been turned down, just as Poppa thought, because of his flat feet. And they'd had a little boy, and his name was Nathan. Poppa had a grandson whose name he didn't know. Joseph was writing to Odessa as well – he'd let us know if he received any news.

Ben joined a People's Army unit. The men couldn't be processed fast enough to get them into the real army, so People's Army units were formed. Vladimir and I would watch Ben's unit drill, the slightly uneven rows of young men moving up and down in front of the apartment building, people waving from the windows. Such young faces, trying to look stern, trying to look older. The sound of their marching wavered because they were in shoes – they hadn't got any boots as yet, no uniforms either. The boys were all eager to stand beside each other, move into line, into formation; so eager to give up their individual lives. Their voices – I didn't recognize the patriotic songs they sang – and their footsteps would echo against the walls of the buildings, the sound moving through the open windows, out of the public space and into the private spaces of people's rooms.

The days and sleepless nights ran into one another. At night, as I drifted towards dreams, English words would wash through my mind, funny bits about English. Miss MacLeod, the comfort sounds she used to make when one of her pupils scraped a knee: *Now-now. There-there.* Poppa's sounds, the sound of soothing. *There-there; go to sleep. Now-now; don't cry.* English in my head. It should have been *then-then*, really, to go with *there-there*. I think in those first weeks of shock I lived nowhere but inside my own head, my good-for-nothing head. What I wanted was to sleep through the night with no dreams and to wake up and be in one place, be where I was: Moscow. I was in Moscow because of my father. He dreamt Moscow into being for me, because of what he wanted for me and couldn't give himself. Who dreamt Moscow first, who dreamt Moscow into being? Some tsar back in the fourteenth, fifteenth century? At first there was nothing and then there was this city. People wish for things, dream them into being, good or bad. And not just buildings, or roads. The Revolution, the Union of

Soviet Socialist Republics. Marx, Lenin. Stalin. But not just them. People like my mother, and Poppa, and everyone else who believed in the Revolution, in a Soviet Russia.

And the war. Hitler dreamt it. It's all desire: cities and streets and governments and wars, anything built by people. Hitler wanted his *living space*. Germany wasn't enough for him. He willed a war. No, that's not true either. It wasn't Hitler alone; it wasn't one man. Not Hitler and not Lenin and not Stalin. Someone wished them into being, dreamt along with them. Whole peoples, nations, believers who dreamt them into power. Awake and dreaming, they'd made it all.

And what about me, what have I dreamt into being? Or have I let myself be dreamt by someone else? What about me?

> *Joseph's head is bumpy; my knees bang against his shoulders. He's giving me a piggyback ride. It's dark and very late. The air smells of the sharp, sweet scent of grass. The sky is full of coloured bits of light, red and green and blue – blossoms and pinwheels of light. "Did you like that, Annette? Do you like Firecracker Day?" I can hear pops like bubbles bursting and then a shaky boom. That flower of light, right on top of my head, inside me. I'm big with light. Then it fades. How can Joseph carry me like this? I'm too big for a piggyback ride. He's walking away from the fireworks, but the noise is getting louder. Someone's banging on the door. I can smell the sulphur from the matches. I'm pounding Joseph on the shoulders. He has to stop. It's too noisy; I don't want to go.*

"Annette," Raisa's voice is in my ear, "Annette, get up."

I'm too tired to get up. I try to pull the covers back on.

"Annette, we've got to hurry."

"Where's Poppa?" That howling, sirens. Is there a fire?

"Annette, wake up. You're in Moscow. It's Raisa. We have to go down to the Metro station; we'll be safe there. Come, Annette. We have to go."

Underground? I won't go. Pavel's in the room. He has Vladimir in his arms, half-asleep. Ben's beside me on the davenport, pulling on his sandals.

"Ben, what is it?"

"An air raid. We'll be safe in the Metro station. Get up."

Ben takes my arm and I'm outside, part of a river of people pouring out of the apartment buildings that moves for me, carrying me away into the night, the cool July air. The people in the crowd have no faces, only shoulders and backs, pyjamas and robes, some with their day clothes hastily put on. Just the determined set of those shoulders and backs as they move towards safety. Then I see that there *are* faces, a few, children like Vladimir still little enough to be carried, their small tousled heads bobbing on their parents' shoulders, sleepy, pale. And the roar, the wailing of the air-raid siren as it moves through the night and through it the noise of the German bombers above us. The streets are dark but the sky is criss-crossed by the light of the searchlights.

Then we hear a noise so loud the ground shudders and I shudder with it, and suddenly the sky is full of coloured bits of light. I stop, feel the current of people flow past me, and I become myself again, someone. Ben grabs me from the centre of the street, holds me against the warm brick wall of a building, presses me against it, his body between me and whatever is out there. I can feel the concussion from the bomb reverberating in the wall.

"We're all right," he says. "Let's keep going. It's not that close." And he's pulling me back into the street. We're propelled along with the crowd. I twist around: Raisa's right behind us, Pavel with Vladimir just ahead. We cross the street.

Another explosion. I stop again, feeling myself separate out once more from the crowd. I want to look up: only a few stars. Then the whine. The notes diminish and suddenly there are more stars, a huge blossom of light right on top of me. The light expands from its centre, coming closer and closer till I feel the sky coming down to touch me, till I feel the light inside my own chest –

"Annette!" Ben grabs me again, this time by the scruff of my nightgown, pulls me into the safety of a doorway. "Are you nuts?" He's speaking English. "Why do you keep stopping in the middle of the street?"

There's no point answering because the roaring has grown louder, not just the sirens but the sound of bombs, of falling, of everything collapsing. Just across the street one of the walls of a building abruptly sags, then the whole structure crumples, falls in on itself. The dust immediately layers my face, my throat. I'm coughing, choking.

Then Ben is pulling me along again, silent. We're safe; we can see the mouth of the Metro opening for us all, the big M. Vladimir's pale face over Pavel's shoulder is about half a block ahead, and beside him what must be the back of Raisa's head. I don't have to decide anything: the crowd courses down the steep polished steps and I'm part of it, going into the Metro station, down to the workers' palace underground. The bad things are happening up on the streets now; it's the streets of Moscow which may become the city of the dead. And underground is where the living are kept safe.

Summer's gone. The September sky bears down on us. It's a steady rain, untiring. My clothes are heavy with it. The truck takes a corner and the woman I'm sitting beside is flung against me, a warm solid body. I shiver, and the woman, her smile glinting silver, puts an arm across my shoulder. "Not as good as your boyfriend, but I'll do for now. I'm Katya."

"Annette."

"The work will soon warm you."

An older woman on the bench across from me offers her flask of vodka, but I shake my head. The girl beside her looks no older than me but she's stocky, bundled in so many layers she's almost egg shaped. *Humpty Dumpty sat on a wall* . . . the words run through my head in English. The rocking of the truck lulls me. My eyes close and I lean against my neighbour's solid shoulder, still foggy with the bad dreams of the night before.

Raisa and Pavel got up before dawn, making me breakfast and layering me in old sweaters, a jacket Ben's outgrown, mittens over gloves. I'd been afraid that Pavel wouldn't let me volunteer for the women's brigade, tens of thousands of them digging immense anti-tank trenches at the outskirts of the city. But he said yes right off. He'd been on the streets himself every day, filling sandbags for hours. Everyone with a free day volunteered. All the shops and monuments and public buildings were being barricaded. School had been suspended. When I got to the square, I worried again that they wouldn't take me. But there were other volunteers just as young, and none of us were told to leave. We piled into the trucks, handed up with a few words of encouragement. And now the truck is carrying us beyond the edges of the city to where the anti-tank ditches are being dug.

When I open my eyes – it can't have been more than a minute – the egg-shaped girl is munching on a piece of bread, the kind of black rye Poppa used to eat. The kind he eats, would eat, will eat. Poppa. Think of something else. Food. I'm still full from breakfast, but I feel in my pocket for the fat lunch Raisa packed, three thick sandwiches of bread and cheese. "You'll be surprised how hungry you get," she'd said, stuffing them in my pocket. "You haven't ever done physical work before."

Never worked. It's true. What use have I been, what have I ever done with my body? Hide. Listen. Watch. I'm not a worker. And something in me believes that if I'm not a worker, I'm not real. I want to do something hard.

I must have dozed again because the truck has jerked to a stop and Katya, the silver-toothed woman, is shaking me. We scramble out of the truck and over to the crest of a low hill. In the cold rain, a bit lighter now, rank upon rank of earlier shifts of women are already at work with shovels and wheelbarrows. It's the measured, even pace of work I've seen before: the girl plucking a chicken back in Winnipeg, scrubbing the back stairs on her hands and knees; my father unpacking cans in the delicatessen. And in Odessa, women sweeping the streets with their twig brooms, construction workers gnawing at the streets with pickaxes. Here there are hundreds, maybe thousands, of women.

The immense ditch seems to deepen as I watch, the work taking on an intricate pattern communicated from body to body as each row of women fills the wheelbarrows and baskets of those above them, who in turn lug the loose earth away. It's as if their bodies were of one mind, each individual woman's will blended to become a single will that is both hers and that of all the others around her, their lives belonging to each other now. Just beyond the horizon, invisible still, there's the greater army against which this inverse dike is being built, a presence these women already feel. The hard lean male bodies in their steel boxes have also left their individual, their private lives to join into a single will.

We're called to a makeshift shack where we're given our shovels. The egg-shaped girl and I are led along one of the muddy paths, our boots slipping on the soggy ground, and assigned to a section of the trench that's no more than rain-sodden string sagging from stakes. The rain has become a fine mist dampening the back of my neck. I set my foot on the flat of the shovel. Dig. That's what I'm here for. I step down on it, wait for the bite into firm soil. But the ground here is saturated, and I have to lean hard into it as the blade skips along the slippery mud.

Damn, damn. On a second try, I manage a half load but can barely lift it, my boots sliding in the muck. I can't get a solid enough grip with my feet to fling it off, and the mud clings to the blade. I slide a half-hearted cupful off with my boot, feel the emptiness open inside me. The girl in the layers is working steadily beside me, her feet planted wide, a shallow ditch already forming at her feet.

A fury rushes into me, flooding the empty space. I lean into the shovel, manage a half load, whack it against the ground behind me so that it loosens and falls. Dig in again, get another half load, and this time I fling so hard the handle slips from my hands. I lose my balance, my feet sliding out so that I fall heavily, though my long jacket cushions me, the back of it coated with mud. Stumbling to my feet, I find Katya beside me.

"Come this way; we need you over here."

Shouldering my shovel, head down, I run a quick mitten across my cheeks that doubtless leaves a smear of mud. I don't deserve to be with these people – my useless body, useless ideas. Katya leads me to a corrugated tin roof sheltering a pile of sand, empty burlap bags stacked to one side.

"We need you to fill the bags. See?" She points to the end of the trench that's completed, the wall of sandbags above it.

The tears still in my throat, I can't say anything; nod, wipe again at my face. Her hand rests for a moment on my shoulder, then she turns back to where the trench is taking shape. The roof has kept the sand mostly dry. I start with small loads, holding the bag open with one hand and the shovel in the other. Do something hard. By the third bag I'm working smoothly, filling bags and then dragging them to the side. The work has warmed me so that I'm damp with sweat. Got to slow down a bit, or I won't be able to keep it up all day. As the minutes pass, sand filling the rough burlap bags, I feel myself fall into that even rhythm of work.

A hand on my shoulder again. Katya. I didn't even hear her come up. "Annette, come. It's time for lunch."

I must have been working three, no, four hours. The stack of filled sandbags marks my labour. I've done something.

The women are gathered at an improvised kitchen, drawn by the smell of soup. I peer into the pot: beef and barley. Not a shred of meat, but there must have been bones; I can smell it, and there are bits of fat at the surface. I take my tin bowl and spoon and eat. It's so good. Katya and I sit on a couple of filled sandbags where we're out of the rain and soon we're joined by other women. I take out my sandwiches, offer some to Katya, who refuses and pulls her own lunch, bread and sausage, from her pocket. The woman from the truck offers me vodka again and this time I take a sip, choke as it burns down my throat. The women laugh, pat me on the back. I feel the delicious heat run through me.

A hand shakes me awake. I've fallen asleep on the truck ride home – most of the women have. We're back in the city. My legs tremble as I climb down. Pavel's waiting, soaked through. How long has he been waiting?

"How'd it go?"

I grimace. "I was no good at shovelling. But they had me filling sandbags."

"I'm proud of you." He squeezes me, hard. The rain has plastered his thin blond hair against his skull. He must be losing weight; he looks skinnier than ever. "Come on, let's get you home. You must be freezing."

We walk home in silence.

The apartment's cold and I'm shivering even more. Raisa wipes her hands on a tea towel. "I want you in the bath right now. The water is already heated. And when you get out, you're eating soup."

"Yes, Comrade Doctor!"

She smiles. "You have to forgive the military tone. But I don't want you sick."

"Yes, Captain."

I strip off the sodden, filthy clothes – so many layers I'm almost clean beneath them. Slip into the tub. The sand got inside my work gloves and the skin on my hands feels raw. My arms are tingling. They don't belong to me. I float them on the water. Somebody else's arms.

September faded. Moscow itself was fading, being beaten into the ground by the bombing, and by rain. As the Moscow River curved its wide grey road through the city, rain battered the last leaves from the trees. It was a season nothing like the crisp, dry autumns in Winnipeg, their spicy smell of fallen leaves – cinnamon, nutmeg – the smell of beginnings. In Moscow the days dissolved in freezing rain; rain bleached the city of colour, bleached it grey. I hadn't seen my parents in three months.

The streets of Moscow were full of foreigners, people who were once the enemy – British, Australians, Canadians. Some Americans as well, though America still hadn't entered the war. And not just military personnel: diplomats, officials, journalists, other undefined civilians, their faces both familiar and unfamiliar, their voices, clothes. English, the forbidden language, was spoken casually on the sidewalks, as if my old life had come back, translated, mine and not mine, just as these strangers were and were not the enemy. Every night we'd close the blackout curtains, locking out the night, locking in the light. Locking out the enemy, locking in the family, though it was hard for me, in those days, to tell one from the other.

Pavel and Raisa kept Vladimir close by them. Evenings, often as not, he'd be sitting on Pavel's lap in the armchair as Pavel read him a story, but the words sounded sluggish, exhausted, as though there were a shortage of language, oxygen, along with all the other shortages. Vladimir in turn kept close to me whenever I was home, seemed never to be more than a few feet away from me. Since early August Odessa also had been under siege, cut off, and Vladimir was always bringing me good news, the good news the papers insisted on printing. He'd point to a headline: *The Triumph of Odessa*. Pavel had told him that we could hold Odessa indefinitely. We were still getting supplies through the Black Sea, and the wounded could be evacuated by ship. The shelling hadn't been that bad. Though we'd gotten two more letters from Joseph in Winnipeg, even a snapshot of Daisy and their son, we'd heard nothing more from Odessa, no letters since July. But Vladimir pored over the newspapers, eagerly reading us stories of Red Army soldiers, of Partisans behind the German lines. Fairy tales where the princess divided gold dust from flax seed, and the hero lived, or died a good death.

In Moscow, where we could see through the newspapers' fairy tales, death was everywhere. The bombs had begun falling again. Nights were the worst, the air raids almost continuous, the darkness broken by searchlights, filled with the noise of fire engines, the shuddering rumble of the big black bombers overhead, the air-raid sirens. Countering this was the comforting pattern of our own anti-aircraft guns – four staccato booms, then a pause, then another series of four deep booms. Every night buildings fell to the bombs that did make it through, and every day work crews cleared the rubble, trying to keep pace with the damage, to keep up appearances. Mostly I was numb, unbelieving, though my nights were torn by nightmares, new ones this time. It was the shelter of Pavel and Raisa's care, as much as the bomb shelters, that kept me from coming apart with fear.

But soon we didn't bother going into the Metro stations any more, though others would line up early in the evening, blankets and pillows under their arms, waiting quietly to settle in for the night. But after a bomb fell right into the mouth of one of the Metro escalators, Pavel said there wasn't much point in going out onto the street where we had no protection at all. Our chances were just as good at home. It was only when I was at work on the women's brigades that I felt good about our chances. Three days a week I reached into the open truck, took the others' hands and was hauled up onto the wooden benches and driven to the outskirts where the trenches were expanding, growing deeper. Raisa didn't want me working that much, said I'd wear myself out, especially with food rationing becoming more and more stringent. But I wouldn't listen. I could feel myself growing stronger, felt my body changing because of the work, my clothes fitting differently, my arms, which had been like sticks, becoming rounder, muscled.

When I was with the others, I believed we couldn't be beaten, would never be beaten. But when the truck dropped me off in the city square, I was afraid again. Afraid for Odessa, though Odessa still held. And afraid for myself, for Moscow, as the Wehrmacht moved steadily towards us. And although in *Pravda* and *Izvestia* there was nothing but good news, though there was no shortage of proud headlines, no shortage of official broadcasts from the loudspeakers on every corner, the voices permanently cheerful, confident, no one could keep the rumours in check. Moscow seethed with them.

I lug my parcels up the stairs to the apartment. Raisa gave me the family's ration books to take to the Central Market. The caretaker's wife is on the landing, deep in conversation with Pavel.

"I'm sure it's nothing, Comrade Polankova." Pavel's almost on tiptoe, poised to escape, but round little Comrade Polankova is leaning into him, willing him to stay. It would be comical if they didn't both look so wretched.

"That Olga Moiseyevna, from the fourth floor, she told

me they've taken Lenin's body on a special train all the way east to Tyumen! How could they?"

I've seen Olga Moiseyevna on the landing, deep in discussion with the other tenants. A solid, sturdy-looking woman, despite her bright red nail polish, her heavy earrings and elaborately tailored suits.

"They've taken Lenin's body east?" Pavel says. "Well, if it is true, it may be a necessary precaution . . ."

"It's nonsense! It's not true, it can't be! The sentries are still posted at the Mausoleum, just as they always are."

"Well, then – "

"And then she says that Comrade Stalin has sent his daughter where it's safe. She says that Svetlana has been sent all the way east to Kuybyshev, while the people of Moscow are left dodging bombs!"

"Oh, I'd very much doubt that – "

"They say even Comrade Stalin himself has left Moscow!"

"Now, I really can't believe – "

"Lies, all lies." Her face is contorted with terror. "Comrade Stalin will never abandon Moscow." The colour rises into her face.

Pavel pats her hand. "It's all right," he says. "I'm sure it can't be true."

There-there, I think. *There-there.*

When we finally get in the door, Raisa is sitting leaden at the table, her coat still on. "The water's boiling for tea," she says.

"Raisa," Pavel asks, "is something wrong?"

"I'm fine. I'm just tired, so I came home early."

She's silent again, so Pavel makes the tea, sets a glass in front of her. "There was a woman at the clinic," she says. "A Jewish woman, a refugee. I was treating her for shock. She kept telling this far-fetched story over and over again. The same story in the same words in the same wooden fashion. She claimed she'd been living in a village that the Germans had occupied." Raisa stops.

"And the story?" Pavel asks.

"The story? The story was that the entire Jewish population of the town had been rounded up and taken to the countryside, told to undress, lined up and shot – old women, children, babies. Her own two children had been shot in her arms, she said, but the bullets had somehow missed her. When night came she'd crawled naked out of the mound of bodies. She somehow made it to Moscow, babbling her story all the way."

"What did you do?" I ask.

"What could I do? I sent her to the psychiatric ward."

Though it's been another day of brilliantly blue sky, the room filled with sunlight, it's freezing, inside and out, and we're bundled in sweaters, Pavel and Vladimir in fingerless gloves. Pavel says he can't remember an October this cold. Till this freeze, the German trucks and tanks were mired in the mud from the endless rain. But the frost has made the roads easier for them, and the Germans are moving quickly. There are rumours that stray troops have been seen right at the outskirts of the city.

"But if it stays cold like this, the weather is on our side," Vladimir is saying. *The Russian winter. Napoleon. The best ally of the Russian people* – it's as if the loudspeaker were blaring inside Vladimir's head, inside mine. Rubbish. But Vladimir goes on, his childish voice vehement. "And Hitler was so sure they'd take Moscow in a few days that he only gave the troops their light summer uniforms – "

"And I heard that the Tsar's ghost was seen in the

Kremlin," I say, "but we mustn't pay any attention to this nonsense."

"– and their hobnailed boots are freezing to the ice. So they're throwing them away and making shoes out of straw. And when we capture them, we're going to feed their shoes to the horses because they're so hungry! And we'll make the German soldiers walk barefoot!"

"Vladimir, stop it!"

"What?"

"It's cruel talking like that, even about the enemy."

Vladimir just looks at me. Pavel doesn't say anything. He's at the table, his papers scattered over the polished surface. Though the university is closed, he's still working, making notes for the research paper he's been writing all fall.

My pencil traces Poppa's face over and over. I can't draw my mother, can never get her right. My head's aching – more bad dreams. Last night I dreamt we'd all gone down into the catacombs again, me and Ben and Poppa and my mother, Manya and Lev. Joseph and Daisy and their little Nathan were somehow there too, though Nathan looked like Vladimir, was and wasn't Vladimir. I'd felt the air clinging to the inside of my throat, the smell of dust and moths.

Someone's at the door. Pavel and I look up.

Another knock, heavier. Vladimir starts to get up, but I put my hand on his shoulder. I hear it, full bellied, swaying. Two beats. The sound again coming into me, tight. Right there on the other side of the door, what I've been of afraid of, what I've been waiting for. I can't. I can't look it in the face.

"Don't answer it."

"What is it, Annette?" Pavel's still at the table.

I drop my voice to a whisper. "Pavel, they say German troops are within twenty miles of the city . . ."

"Annette." Pavel is quiet at the table. "Annette, dear, we don't want to alarm Vladimir . . ."

"Should I open the door, Poppa?" Vladimir asks.

The knocking has become banging; whoever is at the door is frantic. It's a solid door, oak panelling. The brass doorknob is battered, but recently polished. Right here.

"Poppa?"

"It's all right, Vladimir." Pavel gets up. "I'll get it."

Pavel crosses the room and reaches for the knob, and Vladimir is suddenly at his side. Pavel gestures for him to step back, but Vladimir stands his ground, takes Pavel's free hand.

It's Olga Moiseyevna, our neighbour, leaning in the doorway, blood coursing down the side of her face.

"Olga Moiseyevna, come in. Let me help you . . ."

"I was so afraid you'd gone, Comrade Efron. So many families have been evacuated. I've knocked on six doors and no one answered."

"You're bleeding . . . What happened? Annette, please get a wet washcloth from the kitchen."

"Those hooligans! Cannibals! Fascists!"

Vladimir is beside me. He takes my hand. "It's all right, Annette. Don't be afraid."

"Comrade Efron, they were taking everything, everything!" She looks around. "What's the boy doing here? Hasn't your son been sent east? Didn't they give him a ticket? They've organized special trains. Surely you know that?"

"My wife persuaded the authorities to let her keep the clinic open. And we want Vladimir to stay with us."

"Good for her. Well, I wasn't leaving either. I'm sixty-two years old but I'm still strong and I know how to shoot a rifle!"

Vladimir squeezes my hand. I can't move, can't take my eyes off of Olga Moiseyevna who, despite the cut on her forehead, the blood, is standing upright as a little soldier in the middle of the room.

"What happened?" Pavel asks. "How were you hurt?"

"I'm telling you! I won't leave my home to be ransacked by those criminals! I'm gone for maybe an hour, and they think I've left with all the other dirty cowards. I come back and they have my phonograph in their grubby hands, every drawer in the apartment turned upside down . . ."

"Poppa, Poppa, I'd *heard* there was looting all over the city!"

"But surely not in our building . . . Where was Polankov?"

"Polankov? That mouse? Hiding in his apartment. I knocked on his door first. Those imbeciles, I shouted at them to stop and look what they did –"

"Please, sit down. Let me have a better look at your head." Pavel puts his hands on her shoulders, leads her to the davenport.

I hand him the washcloth.

"Thank you, dear. Can you pour a small glass of brandy for Olga Moiseyevna? There's some at the back of the cupboard."

I'm shivering all over; I can't move.

"I'll get it, Poppa."

"No, it's all right, Vladimir," I say. "I can reach it easier."

"It's still bleeding," Pavel says. "We'll have to go find Raisa. I'm sure this needs stitches. It's too bad Ben isn't here . . ."

"I can go, Pavel," I say. "It's only fifteen minutes from here." And before he can say anything, I've got my coat on, am out the door.

My hands steady now, I button my coat, then find myself

stopped, stalled on the staircase down to the street. It's a vault of ice – the sun never gets in here.

I'm not afraid.

Now that there's something to do, I'm all right.

When I reach the sidewalk, I have to wrap my scarf around my mouth and nose: the air's choked with the smoke from bonfires. The government departments and all the foreign embassies have been ordered to burn their archives. They're all packing up, withdrawing east to safety in Kuybyshev, the temporary capital. Fifteen hundred miles between the bureaucrats and the front.

Briefly, I smell another smoke, the green smoke of lilac branches, the smudge fires that were set to counter the mosquito plagues of Winnipeg; the sultry sidewalks of Selkirk Avenue, the crackle of sunflower seed shells.

But it's cold. I'm walking on glass from smashed shop windows. I'm alone. I can't remember ever being alone in the street in Moscow before. The road is empty of traffic, the normal, everyday traffic of life. The broad sidewalk is all mine; Moscow's mine.

And then a truck hurtles by, inches from me. I step back, catch a glimpse of blurred faces in the open back, panicked, stricken. The roads out of town are clogged with evacuees.

There's a little cluster of people at the corner, whispering. Across the street three men, no, four, are hauling furniture onto laden trucks. Are they owners or thieves? I walk more quickly.

Half a block down there's another knot of men standing in the arched entrance to an apartment block: two of them in worn caps, and then an older gentleman with an old-fashioned moustache. Something glitters in his hand. A necklace? Diamonds? One of the men wearing a cap pockets it, hands the older man some kind of paper . . . I must be staring, because they turn my way. I walk quickly ahead.

There's a man with a rifle standing in a doorway across the street. He's not in uniform. Must be from one of the People's Army units . . . Ben reported to his unit early in the morning. He's probably at the station, helping load the trains.

A shopkeeper is standing in the middle of the street in a white apron. *Poppa.* He looks at me, puts something in my hands.

"Here."

What is it?

"Here, take it."

A saucepan. Better than gold. I see his wares are at his feet – that shop window with the broken glass, does he work there?

"Here, better you have it than the Germans."

I hug it against my chest, walk blindly. Stop. A log in the middle of the street; someone has left a log – no. A body, a man, an older man with white hair, lying quietly in the middle of the street. A fat little determined current of blood running from his head.

Dead.

I've never seen a dead body before.

Why do they call that colour red? It's black against the grey pavement. Everything around me is black and grey, no colour anywhere. Just the black blood. It's not a colour, black; it's the absence of light. Absence flooding from his body.

A woman's voice whispers in my ear: "He was looting. They shot him."

"Who? He . . ."

"A looter. Don't stop. Just walk on."

I turn round. A stranger, her red hair tucked into a babushka.

"Don't turn around. Don't stop. Just walk on."

I feel a hand grasp my elbow.

"Just keep walking."

A breathless, wordless block and the hand is gone. I turn, see her disappearing around a corner.

The saucepan in my hands – will they think I'm a looter too?

Everything is very bright, very clear and still. Am I alone again? No. Up ahead, there's a man in a worn grey overcoat, something familiar about him, though I can only see his back.

There's a faint popping noise somewhere to the south of us. Pop, pop. So far away. The man turns, and I recognize him. "Comrade Polankov!" I call.

"You, girl, what are you doing here? Where did you get that?" He points to the saucepan. "You shouldn't be here." He grabs me roughly by the shoulders. People keep telling me what to do.

I shrug off his hands. "I have to go."

"Didn't you hear the shots?" His sour breath is in my face. I hear the popping noise again, faint, harmless. I'm used to the firecracker whiz of the shells.

"Shots? The Germans? They're here?"

He laughs. "No, not those sons of bitches. The NKVD. They're shooting prisoners in Lubyanka . . ."

Lubyanka – the prison's only a block away.

"Shooting prisoners . . . ?"

"They're less trouble that way. I told you, girl: go home."

"I can't. I have to fetch Raisa . . . Comrade Efron. There

were people in the building, stealing things, looting, and Olga Moiseyevna from the fourth floor, she's been hurt. My uncle Pavel thinks she needs stitches."

"Olga Moiseyevna hurt?"

"They were stealing her phonograph."

His face changes. "You go home now, child." His voice is oily, solicitous. Now he wants to seem obliging, helpful. He knows he'll be held responsible for any looting in the building. "Don't you worry; I'll go and fetch Comrade Efron."

I hesitate.

"My dear child. I'll go straight to the clinic. We'll be back in your apartment before you know it." He smiles hard, pats me on the shoulder. "You go home."

I come quietly into the apartment, set the saucepan on the table. Pavel comes in from the bedroom. "I'm so glad you're back. It really wasn't wise, letting you go out . . ."

"I met Polankov in the street. He said he'd get Raisa. They should be back soon."

"Very good. Excellent."

"A shopkeeper gave me a saucepan."

"He did?"

"How is Olga Moiseyevna?"

"The brandy seems to have calmed her." Pavel's face breaks into a quiet smile. "I think she may even be dozing. And Vladimir's keeping an eye on her. But she will need those stitches." He puts his arm around me. "You're white. Maybe you should have a sip of brandy yourself?"

"Pavel, I saw a body in the street."

"You did?"

"And I heard shots."

"Shots? Surely the Germans can't be here in the city – "

"No, Pavel. It wasn't the Germans. Polankov said the NKVD were shooting prisoners in Lubyanka to get them out of the way."

Pavel swallows, turns from me. "Annette . . ."

The door opens. It's Ben; he's flushed from running. "I met Raisa and Polankov at the corner. I ran. They'll be here in a minute."

"Shouldn't you be with your unit?"

"They sent us home, Pavel. I need Annette to help me. We're supposed to go to the *gastronom*. They're distributing all the food to local families."

"Distributing food?"

Ben stuffs his hands in his pockets, mutters something.

"What did you say?" Pavel asks.

"So it doesn't . . ."

"Doesn't what?"

Ben looks up. "Doesn't fall into enemy hands."

The sun's so bright that Raisa's kitchen is almost warm. I'm chewing on a heel of rye, daydreaming Winnipeg, food, my mother's roast chicken, the potatoes and carrots braised in the chicken juices, cream soda in the fancy stemmed goblets from the delicatessen, the bubbles lazing their way to the surface.

A week ago, during the panic, when I was lugging bags of flour home with Ben, stacking tinned goods in the cupboards, it all seemed hopeless.

On one of our treks, we stopped to watch an apartment building burn down. It had been hit by a stray bomb. Some of those who stood were just passersby, but there were also families from the building, a few belongings at their feet: an album of photographs, a tin bucket, a pair of battered, leather-bound books. Even they stood dully, as though what was happening had nothing to do with them. Nothing to do but watch as it all went down.

But Moscow still hasn't been taken. Five armies are defending the city, the Siberian troops in their white padded uniforms immune to the cold. Comrade Stalin has been on the radio again, vowing Moscow will stand, refusing to leave. Everybody says that he'll be at Red Square, no matter what, for the November 7 celebrations.

So we've gone on, made our way through each day listening for the sound of the shells, the gunfire, waiting for the sky to fall.

But it hasn't, not yet.

A key at the door. Vladimir, his cheeks bitten bright pink by the cold, runs over to kiss me. "Are you working with the women's brigade tomorrow?"

I nod.

"Poppa doesn't want you to go. It's dangerous. Some of the women ended up behind the lines and saw the German troops go by."

"He's your father, not mine. He can't tell me what to do."

Vladimir loosens his scarf. "I stayed most of the afternoon at Momma's clinic; it's warmer there. Look what I brought you – an Englishman gave it to me!" He hands me what at first seems a misshapen apple. A pomegranate. I set the lumpy, ruddy globe on the table. It's the first time I've ever seen one. An *Englishman* has given Vladimir a *pomegranate*. Before the war, one was as improbable as the other. And now these foreigners are on the streets of Moscow, neither enemies nor spies nor saboteurs, but our allies. A couple of weeks ago, before the panic, I'd seen a man and woman, stylishly dressed, standing at the doorway of one of the cinemas where a British film was being shown, speaking in strong English accents. I touched the woman's sleeve, but she looked me up and down with such a detached gaze that I just shook my head and walked away. What would I have said?

I cut the pomegranate carefully in two, break one of the halves into pieces. The honeycomb of waxy white skin wraps seeds bright as rubies. The taste is tart and sweet in my mouth. Vladimir takes a section, licks the clear red juice from his fingers. The more I break it open, the more I find.

Late in the afternoon the electricity, which has been off all morning, comes back on. Though we're not supposed to use it for cooking, Raisa has made an illicit borscht of beets, cabbage, onion – no meat of course. Pavel's late for dinner, so we wait. Raisa gives Vladimir a piece of bread to hold him off. At last we hear slow footsteps on the stairs.

"Pavel, come in. What is it? Is something wrong?" Raisa asks. Pavel sits at the table. Raisa ladles the borscht into bowls, sets one at each place, resting a hand briefly on the nape of Pavel's neck. She leaves just enough for Ben, who's out with his unit.

"Pavel. Please tell us."

"Let's eat our dinner. We'll talk later."

Vladimir is at the soup. Raisa tears him off another piece of bread. Pavel sips, swallows, keeping his eyes on the bowl. Another sip, another swallow. Raisa hasn't touched hers. I've been watching them, but find that I've eaten most of the borscht, am chasing the last shreds of cabbage across the bowl with my spoon.

"This is delicious, Raisa." Pavel sets his spoon down. "But I'll finish it later. I'm going to lie down for a while." He walks into the bedroom.

Raisa watches Vladimir finish his soup, carefully pours her own into his bowl. He doesn't seem to notice, just keeps eating. I should have saved him some of mine . . .

She goes to the bedroom; I follow. Pavel is sitting on the bed, his head in his hands, face wet with tears.

"They took Odessa, the Germans and the Romanians."

"Are you sure?" Raisa's voice is sharp. "It isn't just another rumour?"

"I heard on a street loudspeaker. It's official. On October 16, the Red Army, the Navy, withdrew. The Romanian army just walked in."

"The Navy withdrew? They withdrew?"

"Without a fight. Comrade Stalin ordered the withdrawal." He's crying still, the tears running down his face.

"It's not true," I say. "Comrade Stalin wouldn't let them go without even putting up a fight."

"I'm sorry, Annette. Raisa – "

"What is it?"

"Raisa, Annette can help us." He looks up at me, his eyes searching mine as though he will find in them something incalculably precious he has lost. He doesn't seem to notice the handkerchief Raisa is offering him.

"She can help us what, Pavel? Please, try to calm yourself. I'll get you a small glass of brandy." She turns quickly, goes to the cupboard.

Pavel looks up. "We have to pack our bags."

"Our bags?" I ask.

"We have to pack our bags." But he sits on the bed, only his long tapered fingers moving, fidgeting with the bedspread.

"Why, Pavel?" It doesn't make any sense – Raisa has always refused even to contemplate being evacuated . . .

"We have to go there. To Odessa. We have to find them."

"Pavel . . . Uncle Pavel . . ."

"Your mother, your father." His voice is so low I can barely hear.

Raisa's back, a small tumbler of brandy in her hand.

"Lev, Manya . . ." The words are dry; he licks his lips. "We have to pack and go to Odessa and save them all."

"Save them?" Raisa asks.

"We have to bring them home."

Home. I'm looking down on the top of his head, the thinning blond hair, the thin gold frames of his spectacles. My uncle Pavel. Lost. Gone, vanished into grief. Collapsed, his whole self sagged.

I sit. Home. Winnipeg. Odessa. Moscow. It doesn't matter what city I've dreamt myself into or what someone else has dreamt for me. "Pavel." I take his hands. They're smooth, dry, uncallused. Raisa stands in the doorway. Two grown-ups helpless. I put my hand on his. "Pavel, we're Jews. There is no home."

Then, suddenly, I can't look at them. I pull my hand away, walk out of the room, away from their helplessness, uselessness. Walk past Vladimir, out of the apartment, down the stairs, into the street. If I don't stop, if I keep walking, if I can keep my mind at bay, I won't have to think about Poppa, my mother, what these useless grown-ups have done to me.

Some things elude me, even now as the memories invade. I can't remember where or how I heard exactly what happened in Odessa. I do remember needing to be alone, seem to remember walking along the river, finding a park whose name I didn't know. Do I remember brushing aside the snow, sitting on a park bench? Have I invented this memory, transposed it from something else? There was, somewhere, the darkness of early evening in Moscow and the silent branches of a tree. Was it oak, chestnut? That evening, if it was that evening, the streets were crowded with rubble from a recent bombing. How the details came is lost to me, rubble, but I remember that they came in pieces, and more in numbers than words.

Today I can sit at my desk and turn my laptop on; I can go to a search engine and type in the words "Odessa massacre" and in .32 seconds, 306 hits will display. If I scrolled through them all, would I have the story of Odessa? Would I find my parents' story? If I read every fact, every eyewitness account, would I know anything more than I know now? Today we collect facts on an invisible network of electronic signals that burn like the neurons of the brain, a network that is both permanent and ephemeral. Point and click. And despite this, who knows about Odessa? The people of Odessa, certainly. But in the larger world, which holds its convenient or inconvenient stories, its myths and legends, truths and facts about that curious marriage of industry and slaughter, the story of what happened in Odessa is muted. "Less known than some other massacres," to quote my Internet source. The numbers themselves are contested. But let me offer a few.

October 16. Time staggered that day, got cut up into minutes, days, numbers. On October 16, the Red Navy abandoned Odessa. The Fourth Romanian Army under General Ciuperca assisted by German units occupied the city. Though these forces met no resistance, on the first day of occupation, the German Einsatzkommando 11B, with the help of a division of the Romanian intelligence service, went into the city shooting any civilians they happened upon. It is estimated that 8,000 people died like this, mostly Jews. Almost a week later, on October 22, at 17:35 hours, Russian Partisans blew up the Romanian military headquarters. The Romanian commander, 16 officers, 9 non-commissioned officers and public servants, and 35 soldiers were killed. From Bucharest, General Ion Antonescu mandated the quota for reprisals: for every Romanian and German officer who died, 200 Communists were to be killed. For every soldier, 100 were to be executed. At first, the soldiers shot at random. But the next day, the reprisal began in earnest at 12:00.

So the next number is 12. No, that's not right; the next number is 23, because it was October 23. The important number is 5,000. At 12:00 on October 23, 5,000 civilians, mostly Jews, were hanged or shot. Five thousand. Even today, I find no refuge in numbers, because to count them right, you'd need to give each number a face. It would take me a lifetime to count to 5,000.

It was easy, on October 23, for the Romanian soldiers to pick out the Jews. The Soviet state had made it simple: it was marked on our identity papers. But the numbers don't stop at 23. They get bigger. The same day, October 23, in the afternoon, 19,000 unarmed civilians, mostly Jews, were gathered and penned behind a wooden fence in a square near the harbour. They were sprayed with gasoline and set on fire.

Pick a number. You have 5,000, and then you have 19,000. Add 34,000 killed later in October; add 10,000 taken on a death march in November. Add 20,000 transported in cattle wagons to the death camps of Domanevka and Bogdanovka. By the end of February, through fire, bullets, starvation, deportation, they had almost cleaned the city of Jews. Almost.

Because the figures can't be exact. Who was hidden by a neighbour, colleague, friend; given new papers, life? Who slipped into the forests? Five thousand; nineteen thousand; thirty-four thousand. The numbers have been rounded off. What I wanted was the right number. Nineteen thousand might have been 18,929; twenty-five thousand might have been 25,034. I wanted more than arithmetic; I wanted mathematical possibility.

I wanted to take one away.

And let that one be – Poppa. No, Manya. Momma. Why should Manya die . . . why should my mother?

Take one away, or take twenty.

Why not? Take twenty, all of them; put them some place safe. Subtract one living. Then you're not taking away, you're adding. One. Any one.

Though there are places the mind stops, in those long days, the months, of not knowing, I imagined, and I still imagine, my parents in the Odessa apartment just at that moment before things ended and began: Poppa woken from his dream by my mother pulling at his shoulder, telling him she heard shooting, him telling her it was just a dream, that it was nothing – though it wasn't, it was at their door. I imagine them hearing trucks grunting up and down the street, voices, and then, at a distance, the quiet popping of gunfire. Did they argue about Lev's plans, how they were all of them, Manya and Lev, Poppa and my mother, my aunts Reva's and Basya's families, they were all supposed to go into hiding? Because Lev, as always, had his plans. Did my mother lament that her city, her beautiful city with its wide sunlit streets, its beaches and orchards, her city had been abandoned, given over, without a fight? Did Poppa tell her that there was still time, that Lev's plan was their best choice, their best, their only chance? Did my mother listen or refuse to listen? Did they hear, as they argued, the burden of something large crashing to the street, the sound of it breaking, scattering across the pavement? The shots becoming constant, regular; something falling, crashing, just below their window. Did they hear the voices broken against the walls of buildings, shouts, the barking of dogs? Did Poppa ask her one more time to go with him, to look for Lev, to find where he was hiding? By then was the sound – shouting, crashes – seeping through the closed window, did glass break in the window beside theirs and for that room was there then no barrier from what was going on outside? The street then flooded with sound, motors and trucks and the awful barking of dogs, voices screaming: women's, children's. Men's. Was my mother's back to Poppa, saying neither go nor stay? Did boots come up the stairs before they could move; were people shouting in German, Romanian? Did someone pound on their door, shouting orders? Or did they, at the last possible moment, leave; did they hide?

If you don't dare imagine, or remember, or think, the thing to do is to keep yourself busy, work till you're numb. There's a dull ringing in my head; I can't make it stop. The apartment is freezing. You'd think that would help me stay numb, but it doesn't. The problem is that I'm standing at the window, doing nothing, watching Moscow bury itself in snow. Busy snowflakes covering everything, making a new, smooth surface on the surfaces out there. Busy wind tormenting the odd, stubborn dry leaf still holding to a tree. It's just as cold inside as out and I have to get out of this apartment, do something, walk at the very least. I can't be with anyone, can't look at anyone. So I put on my coat, leave, though I won't get away from myself no matter how far I walk. Five o'clock and it's dark already, the sky gone from blue to purple to black. No wind tonight. I walk until I find, in one of the bomb-damaged buildings they haven't managed to repair yet, part of a room that's still intact. My place, my very own three-walled room. There's an upholstered armchair no one has found and hauled away yet, an oval wooden table beside it, a doily, clogged with plaster dust, still protecting the finish. Lace curtains drift against a window that might have looked out on what – a lilac tree, a cobblestone yard with flowerpots, garbage bins – but now looks out on nothing, on a heap of rubble higher than the ceiling.

I sit in the chair and close my eyes. Try to trace the outlines of Poppa's face, my mother's, but I can't bring their faces into my mind, can't bring them to me. I open my eyes.

Someone's here. Someone's here with me in this empty, furnished, broken room.

A soldier. He's stepped inside, out of the wind, to light his cigarette. I can smell sulphur, see the flare of the match as he lights it, the outline of the rifle slung over his shoulder. He's in uniform. A smile, the glint of teeth. He's seen me. He looks young in the darkness. He smiles, takes a step towards me. I smell the harsh smoke from the cheap cigarette.

"Hello there, sweetheart – what are *you* doing here?"

I stand up.

He's just a few feet away, smiling, pulling on the cigarette. "You want a cigarette? Look here." He flashes something white. "I've got a whole package. See? Don't look so worried. What's your name, doll?" He stands quietly, pulling on his cigarette, smiling at me.

But I'm not here. I'm in Odessa, burning. No. Underwater, water like blue air drowning the city. I look him in the face. Take one step, then another. When I'm by him, I start to run. I can hear him laughing behind me. "You don't have to run so fast, little girl. I'm not chasing you!"

I'm caged again, back in the apartment, looking out the same window, watching the same snow. Just me and Ben and Pavel home. I need to work. But sometimes even work fails me. Two days ago I was out with the brigade, inside the city this time, clearing rubble, cutting firewood, the steadiness of the work warming me, though it was snowing yesterday too. Two other girls and I were digging to clear around a sewer pipe. One of them stopped, reached into her pocket for a cigarette, struck a match to light it. That bitter, sour smell of sulphur again; it rasped at my nose, throat. Then I looked down at the shovel in my mittened hands, and there I was again: Odessa. The frozen mud at my feet was Odessa soil, and I was digging my mother's grave. I saw first the coffin, smelt its raw unfinished pine – such a hopeful smell. Then the coffin was replaced by bones – clavicle, ribs, pelvis, femur, the long elegant finger bones of my mother's hands – white and dry as a Hallowe'en skeleton. And then the bones were covered not by snow but ashes, heavy, sooty, dark. My mother's hands. I covered my eyes with my own hands not to see it, felt my knees go, felt the scream come up in my throat, some word I spoke but couldn't understand. And then someone picked me up out of the mud; someone brought me a flask of vodka. I swallowed till I was dizzy. Numb. They sent me home.

A clattering. Ben's puttering uncertainly by the hot plate, layered in sweaters, his fur cap on his head, a cigarette jutting from between his lips. I want to slap it from his mouth. Doesn't he feel anything?

We don't know.

We don't know whether Poppa and our mother died. They can't all be dead. So there are moments when I can hope, pretend.

But it's no good; it's not enough. Because even if they *were* saved – if it wasn't Poppa, wasn't my mother or Manya – it was someone else. Someone else with their arms useless to protect their wife, their father, their child.

You have to try not to think about it, have to let yourself go dead around the hard bits that won't go away. But too much dead weighs you down.

"Annette?" Ben's still clattering about. "Is there any tea left?"

"I told you there was tea. Raisa saved it for you. Put it in the saucepan and heat it up." He's making a lot of noise, then fumbling with a match. "Don't!" I grab it from his hands.

"What's the matter with you?"

I put my hand on his arm. "Just use your cigarette, Ben. Don't waste a match. We don't have that many left."

"Forget it. I don't want stale tea." He stalks into the bedroom he and Vladimir share. He's rarely home, wrapped up in his People's Army unit duties. He's moving away from family and towards something else: his life. His life or his death.

A minute later he comes back into the kitchen. "Any cheese left?"

"In the blue dish."

He pokes at it. "It's mouldy." Flips it into the garbage pail.

"Ben!" I fish it out, wash it furiously under the tap. "What's wrong with you? You think we have food to waste? You can still eat it – all you have to do is trim the bad part off." Damn him, I am not going to cry.

He looks straight at me, but his eyes are masked; nothing, he'll give me nothing. "You eat it." He makes a disgusted face, turns away.

I grab his arm. "Don't talk to me like that!"

"Ben?" Pavel's taken off his glasses and is rubbing his eyes. He's hunched, as always, over his research papers. "Ben, have you finished that letter to Joseph you were writing? I just wanted to add a note."

"Not yet, Pavel. Is there any point in writing?"

"I think the mail will be getting back to normal soon . . . Well, then, I wonder if you could run out and get me a copy of today's *Pravda*?"

"I'm going out to meet a friend. I can't."

"I'll go, Pavel," I say. I'll go before I haul off and slug Ben. "I need the air."

"Thank you, dear." The door bangs. Ben's gone before I am.

I bundle myself up, head downstairs, fuming. I can't be bothered to pick my way through the drifts on the sidewalk and before I know it I've lost my footing and tumbled into a snowbank. That cools me down some. No one has shovelled the snow; there's no one to shovel it. The city feels empty, hollowed. Like me. They've moved Raisa's clinic into one of the vacant schools – most of the children have been evacuated. Only a few people are in line at the cinema and there's no lineup at all at the newspaper kiosk.

By the time I get back to the apartment building, my mind has gone into neutral. It's good to get out, even though my hands are going numb with cold.

A big black car is parked in front of the entry.

I can hear some sort of racket upstairs, then light steps running down the stairs: it's Vladimir. The back of his hand is against his mouth, the corner torn and bleeding, his face dark with anger.

"Vladimir, what is it?"

"Comrade Polankov . . ."

"Polankov hit you?"

"No, no. He was screaming, so I went to help. These big men were hitting him."

"Hitting him?"

"I tried to stop them and one of them slapped me."

"He what?" I take the steps two at a time, all my fury returned, walk through the open doorway of Polankov's apartment. "Who are you? What are you doing here?"

There are three large men in overcoats, fashionable,

good quality. They look at me, smile at one another. I don't care who they are; I hardly know who I am. I'm shaking with rage. Polankov is on the worn davenport, head in his hands, sobbing. I don't give a damn about Polankov.

"You go to your own apartment, missy," one of the men says. "This is none of your business."

I close my hands into fists, unclose them. "You slapped my cousin. That's my business."

"Look, missy – nobody meant to hurt the boy. He bit my friend over there, and he got a little smack for it. No harm done. And you tell your little cousin –" the man is inches away from me, "– he shouldn't be defending enemies of the Revolution." The sweet smell of candy on his breath.

NKVD. They must be NKVD. Polankov has done something wrong and the NKVD have come to arrest him.

The men are so calm, so amused by me. Because they know they can do anything, and I can do nothing. I must be nuts – what've I done, barging in here, shouting at NKVD?

Vladimir's still in the doorway. "Vladimir," I say quietly, "listen to the comrade. Go upstairs to your father." He vanishes.

Polankov is weeping so dramatically that it's impossible to feel sorry for him. The arrest documentation is on the table, proof that everything is official, everything has been approved. Proof that the men who are quietly, methodically going through the apartment are just doing their job, guarding the Soviet state from enemies of the people. They've beaten Polankov, but he must have been resisting arrest. As long as you cooperate, everything will go smoothly. It's not their fault Polankov made a fuss, made this unpleasantness necessary . . .

"You're not needed here, missy," the man says.

I meet Pavel on the stairs. "Go see to Vladimir," he says. Then I hear his voice in Polankov's apartment. "What's the problem, Comrades?"

"No problem at all, Comrade," one of the men says.

"Pavel Efron, Professor of Agronomy at Moscow University. I live on the third floor."

"Your papers, Comrade."

I run to our apartment. Vladimir meets me at the door, his hand against the injured mouth. "Where's Poppa?"

"Talking with those men."

He goes pale.

"It's all right, Vladimir. Don't worry." We hear the murmur of voices downstairs, Pavel and the men. What if they take him too? What if Pavel doesn't ever come back up the stairs? What will I do; what will Vladimir do? I pull him to me, hold him against me, feeling something move through me and into him. "Vladimir, it'll be all right."

"Promise?" he says, speaking into my body.

"Promise, Vladimir. I promise. He'll be fine."

I make the promise knowing I have no right to, that they may take Pavel, bundle him along with Polankov into a Black Raven paddy wagon, and that will be the end. My words do nothing. I can no more stop the men from taking Pavel than I could stop my father's train, and where it took us all. Than I can keep my parents safe from whatever has taken them in Odessa. We're specks spun along this current; we count for nothing.

And yet, that shock of love still moving through me, I promise myself, Vladimir, that, wherever *my* father is gone to, his will come back. Knowing, certain, that I will, if I have to, put my body between this boy and any harm, will do all the nothing I can do for him.

"Annette?" It's as though he can feel what I'm thinking.

My hand goes to the sore cheek. "This doesn't look too bad. I'll put a cold cloth on it."

"He'll come back?"

"He's just talking with the men; he'll be right back." And it's true: we can hear voices in the hall, the regular rhythm of conversation, Pavel's tenor steady against the men's bass. Maybe this promise will be kept. "See. He'll be upstairs in just a minute."

"Annette, they called Comrade Polankov an enemy of the Revolution." Vladimir's mouth is trembling, with indignation now, not fear.

"I heard."

"They said he'd 'abandoned his duties.' I guess because he didn't do anything to stop the looting."

"Olga Moiseyevna's apartment . . ." I dab at his lip with the cloth. He flinches, and tears start in the hazel eyes, the colour almost transparent now. It'll be all right. We'll be all right. "Did you really bite one of them?"

He flushes red, nods.

"Vladimir – what were you thinking?"

"I wasn't thinking. I was just mad. Like you when you yelled at them."

Neither of us was thinking. How valiant we are when we don't think. "Mouths heal quickly. It won't be too bad." I can hear the convincing calmness of my voice.

"Annette?" Pavel's voice calls softly. "Can you come downstairs for a moment?"

I touch Vladimir's shoulder, whisper to him that I'll be right back, believing it. When I get downstairs, Polankov is gone. Pavel is there, composed, talking with the smallest man, who's shorter than Pavel but twice as broad. His voice sounds even and I feel my jaw unclench, my heartbeat steady.

"My wife and I will vouch for Polankov. He rushed to the clinic to get my wife when our neighbour was attacked. My wife will verify that." He's speaking very quietly, standing very straight.

"We'll take that into consideration, Comrade."

"Here's my niece. You wanted to see her papers?"

The man waves his hand tolerantly, sucks his teeth. "It's all right, Comrade."

"I can come down to your bureau and make my statement as soon as my wife is back from the clinic."

"Very well, Comrade." He looks me up and down. I straighten, try to look at him directly but can't quite. "You keep an eye on these youngsters."

Pavel's mouth tightens; he nods.

And the man is gone. Pavel too, gone – to check on Vladimir.

For the first time I notice the smell of cabbage cooking. A few potatoes have been left half-peeled beside the white enamel pot. The lacey bedspread on the brass bed is rumpled. I turn off the hot plate, close the door carefully behind me.

I wonder if that winter of 1942 was the worst. Every night had its own nightmare. I would dream about my parents, the delicatessen. I'd be back in Winnipeg, smelling pickle brine, smelling the dust on the tins of fruit, the vinegar my father used to clean the counter. Everything completely real, but backwards, the counter on the wrong side of the room, the stools green instead of red. Sometimes I'd discover the building was on fire, sometimes that I had gone into the backroom to find Poppa, but the backroom wasn't the backroom any more, there was another room behind it, and yet another room after the second room. Or I'd be trying to lock the front door against something terrible, but the bolt wouldn't latch, the workings coming apart in my hands.

I would dream hunger dreams, too: my mother cooking chicken soup. I'd be able to smell the clingy, rich smell of it, a tang of garlic. I could feel the smooth wooden boards of the kitchen floor under my bare feet. My mother would have her back to me, skimming the scum off the top of the soup. She never noticed me, and I knew in every dream that I mustn't ever disturb her, mustn't get her upset or – or what? Or she'd pack her bags and go. Home. Home to Odessa. I'd lean my elbows on the table, lean my whole body towards her, but I could only watch as she sorted with her fingers through the chicken bones, pulling the meat away. Her fingers quick, busy but calm, she'd strip off every bit of meat. I was hungry, but not allowed to eat. Her long elegant fingers would pick up the bones, put them in her mouth, cracking them carefully, sucking out the marrow, taking everything good.

That hungry winter we brewed dried pumpkin peel for tea. Raisa would hunt and hunt and come home from the market with the trophy of an onion. I felt the emptiness, the cold crouching inside me like it had made itself a home in me. It wasn't just Poppa, my mother. Ben was gone. Not long after the news about Odessa he enlisted. For a day he just vanished, and when he came back, he was in uniform. What could we say? For me he was gone but not gone because he was somewhere; he was at war. I would try to imagine that somewhere, and then stop myself, because what I imagined scared me.

I comforted myself with writing to him, though I was

careful about what I wrote. The letters have their own folder. Of all that didn't come back to me, they did come back to me, bringing their own news.

January 23, 1942
Dear Ben,
I'm writing to let you know we're well here. Please don't worry about us. Since early December, when Germany abandoned the attack, the city has been secure. After all those months of noise – the air-raid sirens and fire engines, the slow screams of bombs and shells, the rumble and grind of truck engines – it seems strangely quiet here. Things are getting back to normal. The civilians who were evacuated are slowly coming home, the bureaucrats too.

I worry about you all the time. The newspapers are reporting such terrible losses, so many dead.

We have our own small battles. Winter has been hard. We're short of oil, coal for heating, for cooking. Clothes, shoes, tobacco, matches, eggs. No gasoline for civilian cars, so horse-drawn sleds are back in the streets. Pots, pans, chinaware, hairpins, combs, brushes, soap, razor blades – they're all but impossible to find. No toys. No boots, no overshoes for sale. You see people patching their shoes on the curb so they'll hold together for the walk home. Don't think we've given up, though. The opera and the ballet are still on, the ballerinas performing Swan Lake by night and cutting firewood by day. We all cut wood, loading it onto trucks or trains and then delivering it all through Moscow, stacking it roof high in the city's squares.

And of course, now that the Americans are in the war, everyone is more hopeful.

Since you enlisted I've gotten two of your letters. They take months to get to me. Please write more often. And write more. You tell me what you're eating, what you're reading – those war thrillers sound pretty dumb, but I'm glad you've got your hands on the Pushkin – but you don't say anything about how you are.

I've started helping Raisa at the clinic. The workload's too much for her. The clinic is to serve civilian war workers, but it's very hard for Raisa to turn anyone away. It's tough finding the most basic supplies: Aspirin, bandages, adhesive tape.

And then we're still doing the paperwork for this business with Polankov. Pavel and Raisa have to file affidavits, give statements, all in defense of that horrible little man. The thing is, we heard that after the looting house managers – "lickspittle remnants of the defeated classes," according to the newspapers – were being shot to restore public order.

At least his wife makes it seem worthwhile. "We're so obliged," she keeps saying, "so obliged." She's brokenhearted that she can't make us one of her famous apple cakes – but butter, sugar, eggs, where would you find them now? There are hungry faces all over the city, people with their clothes hanging off them. At the brigades, people work as if they were under water. They're so ground down by the shortage of food they can barely lift a shovel.

Just writing about food makes my mouth water. But don't worry. We're having bread and cheese and soup for dinner. Raisa makes sure there's always something. And because there are three of us working now, since I started helping most days at the clinic, our ration allowance is good.

I do have Raisa and Pavel, and Vladimir. We all look at Vladimir and thank our lucky stars he's still a kid. Those stories in the papers about mothers giving up their sons gladly – I don't buy it. Who could be glad?

Yesterday Raisa told me more of the story about why they named Vladimir after Lenin. She was pregnant with him in 1932, just eight years after Lenin's death, in the middle of the first Five Year Plan. She was on a trolley listening to two women grumble, the usual complaints about the food shortages, the lineups, all the hard times of those early years. And then – a minute later – they were talking about their factories' goals for the Five Year Plan, the figures, strategies. There was such determination in their faces, she said, such optimism that the sacrifices that they were making would bring better times for their children . . .

That's what made her want to name him after Lenin. The Revolution was young then, fifteen years old. In those days, she said, they were all living in, for, the future. All that sacrifice was going to pay off. I'll write down the lines from this Mayakovsky poem that she recited – she still remembered it:

> *Later*
> *we will drink*
> *all the juices of the earth,*
> *tilting the world*
> *like a cup.*

I know you're not big on poetry, but isn't it beautiful? And it makes me sad. All that sacrifice. And now more. It helps me understand why you had to sign up. It's not that I'm glad. But I understand.
Write soon.
Love,
Annette

That long winter, it seemed we'd never see another season. But winter leaked into spring, and Pavel found full-time work for me at the Mostorg, one of Moscow's biggest department stores. By the spring of 1942, the Mostorg was five floors of mostly bare counters, because every button factory was putting out bullets, so customers had to fight over the little merchandise that was left to sell. My days were filled with typing and filing. At the end of the day I'd look up and there'd be a stack of papers beside me that meant I'd been useful. Like the brigade work, it made me feel real, kept me from thinking. How many decades now have I used work as an anesthetic?

After a couple of months, I started interpreting for customers, snooty American women mostly. Whenever I heard the loudspeakers talk about how we were fighting "shoulder-to-shoulder" with the Americans, all I could think of was the padded jackets of those society ladies. After so many years of making sure I never let a word of English slip in public, I was being asked to translate. And then they seconded me into a job translating Lend-Lease purchase orders and invoices. So I paid out my days moving from English to Russian and Russian to English, my old life seeping into the new. Beside the little plaster bust of Lenin on my desk, I had a vintage English typewriter from the days when the Mostorg was Muir and Merrilees, back before the Revolution. The *e* on it was broken, I remember, the tail of the bottom curve missing. Poor old *e*, the most common letter in English, the proletarian vowel – it'd been worn out with work. There were other relics too, bone-china teacups, saucers. It's strange, what lasts, the past surviving inside certain stubborn objects, certain stubborn heads. You find pools of the past in the present, currents of the future. After the Revolution, people were so sure they could sweep the old away – tearing down buildings, churches; renaming the streets. But within people's heads, within china teacups so thin the light came through, the past persisted. While out there, in the world, in time, things stopped, ended. People still called it Muir and Merrilees. Some of the customers must have still remembered those times. Those who, like Joseph, had been kids during the Revolution were only in their thirties during the war, young. Now and again I'd find myself imagining Joseph as a little boy in the store with Poppa or his mother. But of course they'd never been to Moscow.

Sometimes it felt as though I lived from one of Joseph's letters to the next, that taste of home, the knowledge that at least one part of my family was safe. He didn't write long letters, but he wrote often, sent us pictures of Nathan, a dark, sweet-eyed boy. Everything changed once the war began, so business was good for Joseph. He kept busy repairing radios. People were glued to their radios for war news. And he was selling plenty of new ones too, though the government was threatening to stop civilian production. To Joseph's tender, hasty letters, Daisy would add a note, a funny little sentence or two about her spindly Victory Garden or the lopsided socks she tried knitting for the troops. Even Nathan would add a scrawled little drawing in crayon.

Beyond the letters from Joseph, I think it was Vladimir who kept us all – me, Raisa, Pavel – able to hope in those months, as we ploughed through long days of work, Raisa at the clinic, Pavel back at the university. As we waited for word from Ben, thought and didn't think about what had happened in Odessa. Every time I looked at Vladimir it seemed he'd grown. He had those knobs of elbows, long fingers, broad palms; an elongated creature. On one of those endless July days, he dragged me to the Park of Culture and Rest, Gorky Park, to see an exhibit of captured German equipment: parachutes and uniforms and shoes. They even had downed planes. The Germans put cutters on the front wings of the planes to slice into the metal cables that held the barrage balloons to the ground, those huge lolling inflatables that were set up to protect us from low-flying planes. Vladimir was eager to get close enough to see the planes, even though they were scarcely more than wrecks.

We walked out into our sunlight and waited for a trolley to the park. Even though we were the only ones getting on the trolley, I had to follow Vladimir to the back because the rule was that only pregnant women were allowed to get on at the front. It offended Vladimir's sense of fairness ever to bend the rules. There were, in fact, two pregnant women seated at the front, the worn flowers on their cotton dresses stretched tight, distorted, over their bellies. War or no war, women still got pregnant. Vladimir, in the meantime, was chattering on about the People's Army squad he'd seen pulling an enormous barrage balloon across the square like a pet whale on a leash. Then he was on to one of the fantastical but accurate stories he loved to collect. This time it was spiders: the British used spiders' silk for the crosshairs on gunsights. They'd found that the common British spider had the strongest silk. But even spider silk wasn't fine enough, so each strand was sliced in half with a razor blade. And then they let the spiders go, not wanting to hurt them, because these patriotic spiders were helping the war effort.

When we got to the park, the sun beat down on my head, burned into the skin of my forearms. We walked under the tall cool shade of the chestnuts, their candelabra blossoms long gone. Along the path were families picnicking, blankets and tablecloths spread out on the grass, and suddenly I was crowded again with the absences I could never fend off, no matter how busy I kept myself: Poppa and Momma, Manya and Lev. Ben, who was somewhere fighting. Ben, who had told me over and over again that it was foolish to hope. And though hope was useless, I couldn't stop.

Vladimir and I went down into a stream bed. The path was overgrown and still damp with rain from the day before. By the edge of the path we found patches of tiny wild strawberries. I popped a few in my mouth, despite Vladimir's cautions about cobwebs, bird spit, beetle footprints. Down an even smaller path right along the edge of the stream we found a clump of tiny blue flowers: forget-me-nots. They should have been blooming in May, not July: spring flowers in the middle of summer. The wind shifted a branch and we were outlined in sunlight, then the light shifted again into shadow. It was as if, in that spot, it was still spring, while all around us was summer.

Place is time. How can that be? But it is. Somewhere else there was peace, while in Moscow there was war. Just as now, in this city, we are at peace while all around – Israel, Chechnya, Afghanistan – there is war. In that moment in the shade beside that stream, all I wanted was not to be where I was. I wanted my father never to have brought us to Russia. I wanted never to have left Winnipeg, because if we hadn't left, we might have all been together on that hot day of summer. I wanted it never to have happened. I wanted us never to have come.

But there was something I wanted that I could have: I wanted Ben, and Ben was coming home on leave.

I can't find my brother anywhere among the uniforms. I try to make out faces, features, but the boys are lost to the stiff brown sameness of their woollen jackets, the peaked angle of their single-starred caps. Clothed in the State.

A fresh wind blows, swelling the cotton shirts where the jackets are unbuttoned, lifting the cigarette smoke, the smell of male bodies.

The press of palms over my eyes. My brother's found me because I'm still me, Annette.

"Knock-knock," he says in English, his hands warm, light over my face.

"Who's there?" I whisper.

"Me," he says, and the hands are released. He pulls me into his arms, holds me. And then lets me go.

He's thinner, much thinner. And taller. Can he be taller or is it just because he's so thin? His head is shaved; most of them have their heads shaved beneath the caps. After he enlisted I saw him twice in uniform, but I've been remembering wrong, I remembered the old Ben, not this new self that has swallowed the old.

"Look at you," he says. "You scrawny thing, there's nothing to you – you eating okay?" He works his mouth, rumples my hair.

We stand a foot apart, looking at each other. Then I'm shoved up against him again as a florid-faced woman in a beret steams by, using her massive cardboard suitcase to carve out a path.

"Just give me a sec," he says. "I have to check where I put my papers." He sets down his duffel bag, sorts through his pockets.

Another boy in uniform stops in the little island of stillness Ben has made, puts his head down, the peaked cap shielding his eyes. He's lighting a cigarette. He scratches at a match with his fingernail and a flame blossoms.

The whiff of sulphur catches me and I'm down again, underground, the grief shovel in my hands, a crowd beside me digging too, all of us. But I'm not with the anti-tank brigade – it's graves we're digging, deep as they're wide. A grave for Poppa, and I can see the tanned skin of his bald head, the blotchy shapes and bumps on it, that map of an undiscovered country. A grave for my mother, ruling nothing now, stretched out on her side, legs straight, an elbow digging itself into the ground, into dirt. Others now too; I can feel but not see them all around me, the bodies in their soft fall . . .

I reach out.

Ben looks up, puts his hand to my shoulder. "You okay?"

I lean my forehead against his shoulder, feel the muscle against the bone, the lack of give. Ben; flesh and blood. "It's just the crowd. I was dizzy for a second. I'm all right now." Close my eyes, let the images scatter.

"Let's get out of here," he says. "I've had enough of this mob too." We snake our way down the platform, Ben steering me by the elbow. When we get out onto the sidewalk, the crowd thins. Outside the station the air is fresh, the day sunny and cool. We wait at the curbside, watching the wash of traffic go by: cars, trucks – mostly military vehicles – bicycles, pedestrians. A rhythm here, as though the random comings and goings all were purposeful, orchestrated. And they are, despite each driver's plans, the decisions he makes: the whole country an intricate symphony of activity conducted by the war effort. Inside this consonance there's a separate rhythm, slightly off-kilter – the thwap thwap of a skipping rope, two little girls turning the rope for a third, who can't seem to miss. Her feet on the pavement lift and return. They have those damned eternal bows in their hair, all three of them – floppy ones, so bedraggled you wonder what the point is. The girls are wrapped up in their play, oblivious to the tanks and army trucks that pass by, dwarfing them.

A thin man in a grey suit stops briefly to watch. Who does he remind me of? Mr. Spratt. Except that he wears spectacles, which he takes off and angles to the sunlight to focus the rays so that he can light up his Kazbek. The strong scent of the cheap tobacco drifts towards me. Just smoke, not sulphur.

I touch Ben's shoulder. "How are you . . ."

"I'm okay, Monkey. I'm fine." He bites his lip, won't say more. Won't say anything. A space opens between us, no man's land. His arm goes around my shoulder. "Don't worry so much."

"Raisa's turned herself inside out making you dinner."

"Can't wait to taste it. So," he lets go my shoulder, "I got that last letter just days ago – you still working the brigades?"

I nod. "About four evenings a week."

"No wonder you're skin and bones. And the job at Mostorg?" He's walking fast, despite the heavy bag over his shoulder. I have to quicken my step to keep up but it feels good, moving out of the bad dream and through the sunlight, Ben, however briefly, beside me. "Don't you get bored with it, typing, filing, totting numbers up on that stupid abacus the whole day?"

"They changed the job. I'm translating now; it's not as bad. The place is full of Brits and Americans."

"You're just a kid. You should be back at school. You're not planning on spending your life typing . . ." The schools have reopened, the city gone back to much of its routine. Ben's mouth is closed against what he doesn't say: that Poppa would have wanted me to go back to school.

"I'll take my university entrance exams once things are back to normal." I won't say *when the war ends*, won't jinx things. After the bravado of loudspeakers, I stay away from the word *victory*.

"Ma and Pa – still no news?"

I shake my head.

"And Joseph, you've heard from him?"

"Lots. Short little letters, but they're funny and sweet. Daisy writes me too. It's so strange that we've never met Nathan . . ."

"You okay?" He's speaking English. "You okay here on your own?"

"Raisa and Pavel are so good to me. And Vladimir's a pet."

"They're good people, Monkey." We stop on the sidewalk. "I've got three days," he says, "and then I have to go back."

The tide is turning, our day has come, there's light at the end of the tunnel – in February of 1943, every cliché felt true. In early February, we'd beaten the Germans at Stalingrad, and the victory felt real. It was impossible not to feel hopeful. But there'd been no letters from Ben, not since his brief visit, those three days of leave. We knew that he'd likely been stationed at Stalingrad. We were winning the war, but what did winning mean if I lost Ben? I kept writing so that I could keep hoping.

February 18, 1943
Dear Ben,
I've got the apartment to myself for once, my free day. I spent half of it standing in line to get a paper. At least the weather was mild again today. The whole winter here's been mild, which is more than lucky, since we still have hardly any heat in the apartment. The only time I feel warm is at the parties I go to at the British Embassy.

Yes, parties. I met some English boys, press attachés with the embassy, when I was asked to translate for them at the Mostorg. It was February 2, the day of the victory at Stalingrad, and when we got the news the boys asked me to the party.

I know you're going to tease me about the boys, but I don't care. We all felt like celebrating. I like the dancing, and I like flirting, and it feels so good to be able to speak English! I met a lot of nice boys there. They take me to the movies, or the theatre. They all have very English names – Christopher and Clarence and Oliver – and English manners, and they're all perfect English gentlemen. Your English beaux, Raisa calls them. They act more like brothers than beaux, so don't get all knotted up about this. They make me miss you.

No news, Ben. We haven't had a letter from you in ages.

That's where the letter ends. I don't know if I've lost the rest of it, or if I never finished it. There's a newspaper clipping too. I keep these clippings as if they keep the truth. Poppa was like that. He'd spread out the newsprint sheets as if, reading, knowing, he somehow owned it all.

The clipping is of an illustration, a soft pencil drawing of the winning submission to an architectural competition. I remember, when I first saw it, admiring the pencil technique. Concrete walls curved like the sides of a malting mill or silo, like the rollers of a printing press, a conveyor belt. To the left a "Greek" statue, toga and sword and all – why did everything have to be fake Greek? And then, stuck in the middle of the façade, a tiny ridiculous dollhouse door. A door for whom? The caption reads: "Winning Project Proposal by Georgii Golts: Monument to the Fallen in the Struggle for Stalingrad."

The fallen.

How did those boys, flesh and blood, the strong young bodies I danced with, become *the fallen*? Why do these stale words take the place of emotion? Genuine suffering is taken and puffed up at the same time as it's turned into nothing. Using words to make the pain, the people, these boys, both less and more. Rhetoric. That's what Pavel always said. Necessary in war. But I hated it, hate it still. Ben. I can see the stammer of a body, the long slow tumble off a tank, off some muddy hill. I can see, in slow motion, that body's fall into nothingness, into decay, its chemical elements going back to soil. *No.*

The blue folder is beside me on the bed, and there it is, the scrap of paper that ended one stage of my waiting. The paper is yellowed now with age, the letters of Pavel's name and address in white on the red strip along the top. It was clean and white that day, the government telegram:

> *Comrade Efron. We regret to inform you that your cousin, Benjamin Gershon, has fallen in the line of duty . . .*

Weeks later we got a box of Ben's "personal effects": snapshots of me and our parents, a crumpled paperback copy of Pushkin's short stories, the jacket of his uniform. I still have the brass buttons from that uniform somewhere in my sewing basket. And my letters, carefully folded and bundled with string.

I get up, wash my face. I'm letting myself drift here, letting myself drown in old griefs when I have things to do, boxes to pack. I go back into the spare room, take my black woollen coat from the closet, run my hands absentmindedly along a sleeve. There's a rim of grey dirt crusted along several inches of the hem. We were at the cemetery, my daughter and I, my grandson too, some colleagues from the office. An old friend, poor Oscar Rheinhold, had finally passed away. Before the funeral it had been raining, but as I stood among the mourners, the rain stopped. The wind was bad and there was no shelter there among the headstones; trees a fringe at the edges of the cemetery, but none among the aisles.

At the graveside my legs suddenly went rubbery and I began to sink to my knees. My daughter was right beside me, and she gripped me by the elbow to help me stay upright. "What is it?" she asked. "What's wrong?"

"Nothing . . ." I whispered. "I'm all right."

"I'm right here," she said, her hands strong at my elbow.

The wool is soft in my hands, but the dried mud is coarse. I rub at it with my fingers. It's grey, though the earth was black, heavy, for the mourners as we stood in the wind, each with a shovelful for the grave till it was almost filled in. A crust of dried mud under my nails now. My fingers stop. I don't want it cleaned up. Let it stay.

We got no funeral for Ben.

Chapter Seven

Poppa's thumb presses tenderly into the thickness of the peel to make a beginning. "Here," he says, handing me the orange. "Look: I've given you the world." But he's mistaken: it's the sun he's given me. I sniff the bright smell of summer and when I break the not-quite-round globe open, it is the world that spills out: Selkirk Avenue, Main Street, the delicatessen, all miniature, all perfect, preserved. And then it's Deribasovskaya Street, its creamy façades; the Opera House and Theatre Square, the curved iron of its lampposts. I bite in and it's not just place, it's time, all my days, on my tongue: midnight on the train from the beach; four o'clock walking in darkness from Aberdeen School; noon at the Odessa beach; the white dawn of Moscow in June. Each day, each moment, repeats itself and is unmoved, eternal. "Here," Poppa says, "take it now. It's yours."

In the spring of 1944 I was given another number: April 10, the day Odessa was liberated by Allied troops. By then we could all sense it coming, the end of the war. The Allied armies were recapturing more and more occupied territory.

The Americans were fighting their way north through Italy. Though we'd heard nothing from Odessa, in the spring of 1944 I didn't know how not to hope. Something in me whispered, *if they took Ben, they'll give you something back*. As if I'd somehow made a pact, a bargain with fate.

Through the trolley window I'm watching the spring snow gather. Though the winter snow had all gone and the early tulips were coming out, the crocuses and snowdrops already in bloom, today we had a sudden cold snap. The rain hesitated for a moment and then turned to snow, that ripe, heavy snow. On the sidewalks it's melting, but on the leaves of the iris, three inches into their new growth already, it's collecting. And on the grass, still brown from winter; on the branches of the trees, still bare, though the nodes of leaves have swollen, though the willow branches have gone yellow, the dogwood red.

A long day. I'm glad it's over, glad to be going home. I settle my handbag into my lap, close my eyes, then open them when two young men board, speaking English. They're not in uniform – they must be with the American Embassy. Two more stops. I almost nodded off. I rub the heel of my hand into my eye –

I see him.

A man's back, brown wool overcoat, sloping shoulders. He's stopped in the street, absorbed in something. The snow in a halo around him.

Poppa.

I push my way through to the door, pound on it and I'm out into the unexpected cold, the fragile snow.

Poppa.

I'm a block away but I see the brown coat, walking now,

turning the corner. *Run*. Full out, my coat flapping behind me, scarf loosening. I catch sight of him as I turn the corner, scream, can't help myself, scream as I see him: "*Poppa!*"

The man turns – sees me. "Annette?"

I throw myself into him, feel the strength of his hug: Poppa, Poppa.

But something's wrong; there's too much strength in the embrace.

I look into his face, touch it.

It's not Poppa.

"It's me, Annette." He hides his face in my hair.

My legs buckle and he puts his arm around my waist, holding me up.

"I thought you were Poppa . . ."

"It's me, Joseph."

I test my palm against the saucepan; it's warming. The water stirs, comes to life under the heat. Joseph has brought us packets of black tea. I feel the slight tremor as the water heats up, remember Science class: the excitation of molecules, transfer of energy. Joseph is here. For the two blocks home I could hardly speak, hardly walk, but I kept touching his sleeve, his face. Little fat snowflakes melting on his eyebrows, his moustache. He's come back to me, my Joseph. And if he's come back, can't anyone? Can't anything happen now that Joseph is here? And now that he's older, he looks so much like Poppa. What's the phrase in English – *the spitting image*. The spitting image, except for the eyes. I know Ben's gone, but if Joseph can cross an ocean, if Joseph can be here in Moscow, can't I believe in anything? Should I?

But no; Joseph may be my only miracle. Because he's come bearing news. I know it. And I've read his face, his eyes. It's no good, the news. He's hardly touched me since that moment in the street when I thought he was Poppa; he's scarcely been able to look at me. He's talking quietly to Pavel and Raisa. His face, he looks old, old. And he's what – thirty-one? The water's rumbling now. Is it now that I have to stop hoping?

"Annette?" Raisa touches my face lightly. And hers is so sad. "Come, dear. Sit down next to your brother. You don't need to do this." Her palm rests, for a moment, on my cheek.

Joseph's still talking in low tones to Pavel, his body contained, as though he wants to withhold what he knows.

Pavel comes up to us. "Here, let me take that." He takes the tray, sets it on the table. Raisa is pleating a cloth napkin between her fingers.

"Annette . . ." Joseph says. I hear the plea in his voice. No, please Joseph. Don't say anything; just be here with me. Let me rest in this moment when you're here, but I don't know anything. Don't know it, your news. The teapot's in my hand. Pour the tea. I pour: Joseph, Pavel, Raisa, Vladimir, myself. Count. Five glasses of tea. The number seems wrong.

"Annette, come sit down." Pavel says, making room on the davenport. Vladimir squeezes in, sitting awkwardly on Pavel's lap; so tall and only twelve. He's shivering. Raisa rests a hand, heavy, solid, on my knee.

"Joseph, tell us." Pavel's hands are on his knees. All we can do is listen. "Tell us what you know," Pavel says, "what you learned in Odessa."

Joseph studies the curtained windows, swallows. My brother, here with us, sitting beside me. I could touch his hand if I wanted to. He's completely familiar, and yet he's been changed into someone else by the burden of news that he carries. He moves a hand thoughtfully over his jaw, the old gesture – the sage in front of the synagogue, the businessman contemplating a deal, the farmer eyeing his crops. But it's a diversion, a way of not saying, for just one moment more.

Vladimir wriggles on Pavel's lap. Pavel whispers in his ear and he settles down.

"Raisa, Pavel – you should've seen Annette when she was a toddler. She was such a sweet little thing."

"Joseph," Pavel says, "we have to know."

Raisa's holding my hand, which is cold and damp. I can see Joseph's mouth moving, but it takes a moment before I can focus on the words.

" . . . so as soon as I heard that Odessa was liberated, I caught a liner in New York. I didn't bother writing; the mails are too slow. I had to find things out." He stops, licks his lips. "I couldn't just sit there not knowing," he says in English, looking at me, though I won't look back. And then he switches back into Russian. "I was ten days in Odessa. And there's good news." He takes a breath. "I've seen Manya."

"Manya!" Raisa's hand goes to her mouth. "Manya is alive!"

Joseph nods.

"Did she tell you about the others?" Pavel asks. "She's all right?"

"She's in hospital," Joseph says. "She's weak, but she'll be all right in time."

"What did she say? Lev? Avram?" Pavel asks.

"Pavel," Raisa says, "let him talk."

"Lev," Joseph says, "joined the Partisans. He had valuables – jewellery, ammunition, weapons – so he bought a place with the Partisans for him and Manya. They went into hiding with a group, about eighty of them altogether, in the catacombs."

" – the catacombs?" Pavel asks.

"Poppa." Vladimir's voice is still childish; it hasn't broken yet. "Don't you remember seeing the picture in the papers the day Odessa was liberated? All the Partisans in the square coming up from underground?" There must have been at least fifty of them in the photograph, the men in patched padded jackets and felt boots, the women in babushkas and shawls. And they'd looked solid, triumphant, as though the months and years in darkness, below ground, hadn't touched them.

"Annette," Joseph says, turning to me again. Now he's going to tell me. He holds himself tight though his voice is gentle, tender. "Manya told me that Poppa and your mother didn't want to join them. Lev had arranged for them to come too, but they refused to go into hiding."

I want to stop his mouth. For a moment, I want to choke the words from his throat, anything, any violence to prevent the violence of what I know he is going to say. But I do nothing, wait for the words I know are coming, the rage freezing over inside me into something else, numbness, till I feel I can hardly make the effort to breathe, to let my heart beat.

I'm watching his face. His hand goes over his chin again. "They died," he says, "with all the others, in October, in the first few days of the occupation. Basya and Reva and their families must have gone then too."

Poppa and my mother. Both gone.

I'm not crying. *Gone.* First Ben and now Poppa and my mother. I'm alone. They're gone. Gone to bones. Shot. Or worse, not bones: gasoline and a high wooden fence, the fire that day, ash. The fire would have made a fine, sooty layer on the Odessa sidewalks, that people would have swept, the next morning, trying not to think.

Vladimir's crouched beside me on the floor, his head on my lap, his arms wrapped around me. He's crying quietly. "Don't be sad," he whispers. "You're ours. You have us. We'll look after you, Momma and Poppa and me. We'll take care of you."

I put my face in his hair, breathe. They're dead and I'm still alive.

"Annette?" It's Joseph, the delicate weight of his hand on my arm. Relieved of his news, he can bear to touch me. He's handing me something. "Take a sip of tea." Vladimir lets go of me, walks to his father. Now I'm so light. If it weren't for the weight of Joseph's hand, there'd be nothing to keep me to the ground. "Annette," he says again.

I put the rim of the glass to my mouth.

He goes back to his chair. "The Partisans were well organized, Manya said. They had supplies, arms, provisions; even an infirmary. Lev and Manya both survived underground for two full years."

Underground. I close my eyes and see the guide opening the steel gate, letting us all down into the cool mouth of the tunnel, daylight fading. Two years. How many days without daylight? Dense air clinging to the inside of my throat and that sound at the back of my head, two beats, the knife sharpener, his bell, metal clapper against bronze mouth, the second note utter, final. Vladimir beside me. *Don't be afraid*, he said, squeezing my hand. The taste of moths on my tongue, stale and damp. The floor's smooth, soft, almost polished. The top of my head brushes the ceiling and the grit falls onto my scalp. The second note final. It's final now.

Nothing left to do but look it in the face. You go down to live. Manya lived. And my mother and Poppa died.

"Annette?"

They keep repeating my name. Who's calling me? They keep calling and calling, but not one of them is Poppa. Raisa's arm is around me.

" . . . then Manya got typhus," Joseph says. "Lev managed to nurse her through it and then got sick himself. He died within a week." Big strong Lev. And Manya is alive.

Raisa's pacing the room. "Do you think Manya will want to come here?"

Joseph shakes his head. "I don't think so. She's still not well."

Lev is dead, my uncle Lev. Poppa. My mother. Gone. Like Ben.

"Annette?" They're calling me again. I open my eyes: Joseph.

"Are you all right?" he asks.

"No."

I'm in the kitchen, toasting a piece of bread over the burner, a dishtowel over my arm. Since Joseph's news, I've been sleepwalking through days, work, meals, sleepwalking through sleep, no dreams, no thoughts, nothing to feel. But now something wakes me. This merciless sunshine is spreading itself across the room, blue sky, sunshine, why? Thinks it can go anywhere, take anything, barging into this kitchen. I don't want it. Not sunshine, not toast. I don't want bread in my mouth, don't want to eat. I want nothing. Want the night rising up in me to take everything, want night in my throat. Why did they? How could they bring me here, why? Why did they come, why did they stay, why did they take me, why did they leave me? In the train station, why did he get down? And leave me. What did she need? Why didn't she need me? I need them and they're gone.

Something dark and burning in my eyes, my throat. Good.

"Annette!"

The dishtowel's yanked from my hands.

"Annette, for God's sake!"

Pulls me. Grabs my arm, takes me from the room.

"Are you crazy? Are you trying to burn the place down?"

Burn me down. Burn me with them.

Hands shoving me onto the davenport, a cloth on my face. I have a glass of water.

"Drink this."

I drink it down, cool rage down my throat. Rub my eyes; my hands come away black.

"You're all right."

I can hear him now, Joseph, pulling me against his shoulder.

"It's just smoke. The toast caught fire, and the dishtowel. But it's nothing. I'll clean up later. You're all right. It's fine."

And now I can hear him crying, feel him shaking with anger, sorrow. I set my face against his sleeve. I can feel it; I can feel everything. I want them back.

My head aches, bulges with it. I've been at my desk all day but I can't work, haven't gotten anything done. Not all week, not since Joseph. I put my hands against my temples, rub. The cold feels good. I have to work on little bites of it, nibbles: they were shot with the others. Or in the square by the port, burned. It would have been the smoke that killed them first . . . I have to stop thinking about this. My arm hurts. Yesterday I almost set the apartment on fire making toast. I wanted to burn. A little bit of my arm did. Joseph ran and got Raisa; she bandaged me up. I have to stop thinking about how they died, have to.

Someone's standing at the door to the office, a man in a tailored overcoat. A foreigner.

Joseph, my brother.

"Joseph . . ."

He smiles, comes towards me.

I have him. I still have Joseph and in him I have Winnipeg and the delicatessen and Poppa and Ben. Have even my mother. So much to carry inside me, to remember. With Joseph here, at least there's someone to share the cargo.

He's standing by my desk, hands at his sides as if he's still afraid to touch me. "Did I startle you?"

"I'm just surprised. I wasn't expecting you." The good cloth of his overcoat, the sturdy leather shoes – everything about him is new, good quality. This is how foreigners look. This is how my brother looks.

"I was running a few chores for Raisa, but I'm all done now." He's talking English, his eyes gentle on me. "Stuffy in here." He takes off his fedora, loosens his tie – every little gesture so like Poppa. "How's your arm?"

"My arm?"

"The burn." He points to the bandage.

"It's nothing. I don't even notice it."

"You sleep okay? You look worn out."

"I'm fine, Joseph. I mean . . . I'm all right."

"How about coming to dinner with me, Sis – what do you say?"

"I thought the restaurants were all closed for the duration . . ." I've never seen the inside of a restaurant in Moscow.

"A couple have opened lately. Come on, kiddo."

"Sure," I say. "Sure, let's go." And it's as if, speaking English to him, I've fallen into some self that never was: the girl who grew up in Winnipeg, who went to St. John's High. Whose brother Joseph helped her with her algebra problems. Whose parents are alive.

He takes my coat down from the bentwood rack. "Or we could stand in line for drinks at the *kokteil-kholl* on Gorky Street . . ."

I shake my head. They haven't turned me into a drinker yet. "No cocktails, thanks. But dinner, that would be great." I can't help it; my mouth starts to water at the thought of a restaurant meal.

He helps me on with my coat, turns the collar down, rests a hand briefly on my shoulder. The first time he's touched me. "Good. It's just a couple of blocks to the Metropol; we can eat at the restaurant there. I plan to fatten you up some."

As we leave the building, the wind comes up. It's still chilly today. Joseph's walking fast – I have to quicken my pace to keep up. It's always better when I'm moving, when I'm outside.

"Hey, button your coat up. That wind's cold."

He wants to look after me. I remember him kneeling in the snow, tucking my mittens into the sleeves of my jacket. He wants to look after me but no one can. I slip each button into its slot. From where I'm standing I can see the heavy bronze doors of the GUM, the walls of the Kremlin, still camouflaged.

Joseph touches my elbow, another tentative touch.

"When you wrote me about Pa putting you on that train without him, staying behind in Odessa, you know, it didn't surprise me. Your mother, she had such a hold on him."

Had. I have a new tense for my parents now. I had parents. I had a mother and father.

I can't say anything, just nod.

"We don't – Annette – we don't know if anything would have turned out differently if they'd left Odessa with you. We can't know. There's no saying . . . there's no saying they would have survived anyway. You know how hard it was even here in Moscow." He touches my elbow again, squeezes my arm, his hand firm now, as if he wants to make sure I'm really here. "Are you mad?"

"At who?"

"Them. Are you mad at them for staying?"

For dying. I'm mad at them for dying. I can't say that out loud. "And what about you?" I ask. "Aren't you mad? All those years ago, he left you here, left you and your mother . . ."

"My mother left him."

We've never spoken about this.

"But then when you came to Canada, and he let my mother treat you like that, kick you out of the house – "

Now it's Joseph who's silent.

"It wasn't right, Joseph. I always knew it wasn't right."

"I did fine, Annette. I *am* fine. I knew Pa loved me, even if, even though she put up all these obstacles. And I had you. I remember the first time I saw you, how you took me in with that look little kids have. How you made me yours. And now I have Daisy, and Nathan. More than I ever thought I'd have. I have the business too." He smiles quietly. "I'm doing really well now. Putting money aside, saving." The smile broadens. "See? I can even take you out to dinner at the fanciest restaurant in town."

We're here. We stop in the middle of the sidewalk, take in the hotel's winsome little turrets, the mural in watery blue mosaics arched above the entrance.

"That figure in the centre, Joseph? She's called *The Princess of Dreams*."

"Some building." He chews at his moustache.

"The height of art nouveau."

"*The Princess of Dreams*. Hey, Annette, what was the name of that guy who used to call you 'princess'? The lodger?"

"Mr. Spratt. He used to call me princess because Princess Elizabeth and I were born the same year."

"Spratt? He's the skinny one, the one – "

"The one who drowned. Who killed himself."

Joseph nods. "Poor guy. Listen, we can't stand out here forever. You're shivering." He takes my elbow again, nudges me through the door into the lobby, then into the dining room. "So what do you think?" I've never been in a room like this. I tip my head back and space opens above us, a vault with stained-glass lozenges and medallions.

"Smart place, isn't it?" He's almost grinning again. Nothing better for Joseph than giving me one of his treats.

I nod. "Pavel told me the façade used to be full of bullet holes. It was damaged during the Revolution."

We both look up again, follow the shadows of clouds moving over the vault.

"Hey, Annette, you wrote me once that you were thinking about studying architecture . . ."

I nod again. "It was Lev got me interested. You know how I'm always drawing, sketching stuff? When I was just a kid, Lev taught me two-point perspective. And he has . . . he had . . . all these great books with illustrations of buildings. Even when I was little he'd let me look at them. I remember he told me to make sure I just touched the edges of the paper when I turned the pages. Otherwise the oil from my fingertips would stain the illustrations. He used to wear white cotton gloves – " I stop. I can't stand remembering. The waiter comes to my rescue, escorts us through the maze of tables to a small one at the back of the room.

"Order whatever you want. Sky's the limit. You need some meat on your bones," Joseph says as the waiter hands over the menus.

I pretend to read it over, swipe furtively at my eyes.

"Annette." Joseph puts his hand on mine. "Everything you've written me about them – I'm so glad you had Lev and Manya in Odessa. It sounds like they, Lev especially, like Lev could take some of the pressure off with your mother."

"He did. Manya too. I always felt they were on my side. Do you think I'll be able to get to see Manya soon?"

"It'll probably be awhile. Did you read the letter?" Joseph brought me a letter from Manya.

"Not yet." I've been afraid to look at it, to know more than I already know.

"So it was Lev got you thinking about studying architecture?"

"He always said it suited me to a T. He even knew some bigwigs who taught here in Moscow. I remember him talking to Poppa about pulling strings for me."

"You know Poppa would want you to go to university."

I shake my head. "I can't think about it now."

"A girl like you, with your brains."

"You never got to go."

"That doesn't mean you shouldn't."

"I know."

"Listen. I have to talk to you, Annette." He puts the menu down. "I have to check with you before I start making any arrangements."

"Arrangements for what?"

"I want you to come back with me."

"Back?"

"To Canada. I want you to come home. As an orphan, it looks like you might be eligible for emigration papers."

I'm an orphan.

"We can look after you, Daisy and me. Daisy would love to have you. You've never even met our Nathan." His face is bright. He's got another treat for me, the very best one this time, the prize in the Cracker Jack box. "You could live with us. You could go to university in Winnipeg –"

I can see that alternate self again, can picture United College, the lawns of the campus a green dream, the traffic on Portage Avenue.

"Before I do anything more, Annette, I want you to tell me: do you want to come home?"

I take Joseph's hand in both of mine – a small hand, not that much bigger than mine, the fingers intelligent. No wonder he's so good at his work. I could live with Joseph.

"Annette?"

I turn it over, palm up, pat it.

Home.

I have everything. Even Manya's letter, the one Joseph brought from Odessa for me. I take it out of its folder, put the paper to my face – is it possible that it still smells of lavender?

May 15, 1944
My Dearest Annette,

Joseph will bring you this letter. I know you will want me to come and visit the family in Moscow, but I will have to wait some time before I'm strong enough to travel and, as you're no doubt aware, travel is still difficult.

I know also that you'll want to hear more about your mother and father. I've picked up my pen many times and then put it away. I'm sure you understand how difficult it is to turn to those events.

There was something unreal about the first days of the occupation. Even Lev seemed paralyzed at first, I think because he felt so bad that he hadn't gotten us out of Odessa in time. And he'd failed to convince Basya and Reva and their families to leave, as well as your mother and father.

Lev had had contacts all along with the groups that were forming into the Resistance. I guess he knew the occupation was inevitable. He'd arranged for all of us to join the Partisan cells that were planning to operate from the catacombs.

You have to understand that Anya, your father, me, your aunts and uncles – we weren't of any value as fighters. So we wouldn't have been welcome. That's the way it is with the Partisan groups. But Lev had it all worked out. Joseph has probably told you about the cache of guns, ammunition? And Lev had valuables too: some jewellery, other things. All of this was our "ticket" into the protection the Partisans offered.

And there was something else. Do you remember your mother's stories? About the family, generations of us, working in the catacombs, the mines? I know Anya didn't have the greatest credibility with you . . . You might have thought these were fairy tales, but it was all true. Your grandfather, great-uncles had all kept detailed maps, plans of the catacombs, as souvenirs after they'd retired. They'd tell endless stories, argue about the various tunnels, paths. Lev had been the keeper of this archive, and the maps were invaluable to the Partisans.

And this is how we were all to stay together. It was our best chance.

Your mother refused to go. She said Lev wanted us all buried alive. You know how she could be when she got her back up. "I won't live in a sewer," she said. "I'm not going to live like a mole, like an animal, underground."

It did seem like madness, going into the catacombs. Reva and Basya also refused to join us. Maybe if they had agreed, your mother could have been persuaded. I tried to convince her that it was the only choice we had. I even – you'll laugh at this (you know I'm not in the least religious) – I even asked her to pray before she decided.

"I don't talk to God any more," she said.

You must realize, though, that even if your father had been able to persuade her, there's no telling if it would have saved them. It didn't save Lev. We were all so frightened – it was hard to know what was right. Your mother was always so certain, and your father's tendency was just to go along. It was as if his last act was to put you and Ben on that train.

I'll write more later, my darling girl. And hope to see you before too long.

Your devoted aunt,
Manya

How is anyone in our shiny new century to understand the choice I made then? How am I to understand it myself? It seems so foolish, from a distance; worse than foolish. I was eighteen and an orphan. I was my own worst enemy. I was my truest self.

I'm beside the creek in Gorky Park, sitting on the bank, the ground still breathing damp from yesterday's rain. Tentative spikes of forget-me-nots are pushing up through the earth. Soon all the undergrowth here will be starred with their flowers, a blue haze, as though the earth were full of possibilities.

I've come to think. Here, in this little crevice in time. I'll float here, drift, till I've figured it out. So many voices in my head – Raisa, Pavel, Joseph – all telling me: *Go. Go home.*

I pull my knees to my chest, rub my chin against the soft cotton skirt. What would Poppa want me to do? I could live with Joseph, who loves me, who I've loved since I was a baby. Joseph, who first called me by my real name, who gave me myself. The Joseph I was taken from could take me back. I could have my own family again, a bit of it.

Who do I belong to, whose am I now? I have to decide, like Poppa, who chose to come here, wanting to make us a life.

If we hadn't come we'd be alive, together.

But he did choose.

When I think Winnipeg, I think delicatessen: Poppa behind the counter, his white apron tied round his waist. But there is no Poppa, no delicatessen.

I take out Manya's letter, sniff at the lavender. Read it again; read and reread it. Touch the inked letters with my fingers.

I can feel the damp seeping through the cotton of my skirt, the May air, mild today, stroking my forearms, sun filtering through the branches of the trees, the complex shift of pattern on my skin.

Pavel, Raisa, Vladimir. Do they belong to me? Are they borrowed?

I don't own anything.

I put Manya's letter back in my pocket, twist my head to ease the ache in my shoulders and suddenly, with that single gesture, I'm back in Odessa, at Manya's, the samovar steaming, agleam, Manya offering poppyseed cake warm from the oven. I can smell the sugar-and-butter smell of it. Done to a turn, like everything Manya made. A friend of Manya's is over with her new baby – we're celebrating. Real French champagne for a toast. The grown-ups have wineglasses in their hands, so they give the baby to me to hold. He's a pretty baby, a head full of black hair, a newborn, just days old. You can see his newness; the little body is still used to the underwater world of his mother's belly, still adjusting to gravity, the neck barely strong enough to turn his head. I have him on a pillow in my arms and as I watch, he turns his head weakly, the pillow cushioning it as it wobbles. And suddenly I remember, fully, in my body, remember.

I remember the world receiving me, how good it felt to be *not able* and to have the world make up for it, to have the world come to me without my having to go to it.

I'm not some helpless infant.

I'd been thinking that someone else would decide, that I could just drift. That what I *didn't* do would give me a life. If I wasn't greedy, if I wasn't rude. If I wasn't too full of myself. If I sat tight, if I didn't ask for too much, if I didn't try too hard, if I didn't presume. If I held back what I wanted. Held it back until it was unrecognizable to me.

As if my deference, my meekness, could appease the gods. What gods – the lady in the picture? My mother? My mother, of course. It took so much to appease my mother. And now my mother and all she was is gone, except for how she lives inside of me. I look at my hands. Poppa's hands. I'm not Poppa's any more. I'm no one's daughter now.

I can't keep waiting for my life to happen, to be loved, to grow up. I can't wait for someone else to take me into his arms and carry me into the future, into life. I have to make a life for myself, wish it into being.

I hear it now, the sound, but differently from the way it has rung in my mind before. The sound comes, swaying, full bellied. Two beats, light and then heavy, and a gap in between. Nearby. But it's not a knell; it's a call, and I'm not afraid. I'll stay. I won't leave Moscow. I won't leave Pavel and Raisa and Vladimir.

I was my own worst enemy and my truest self. At eighteen, in the wake of all my dead, maybe it was loyalty that made me decide to stay. I told myself I wouldn't betray my parents' decision to believe in the workers' paradise. I couldn't bring myself to give up on their version of goodness, the golden promise at the core of their lives – despite the many things about Comrade Stalin's country that I already knew. The many things I knew and tried not to know. If I had been allowed to know nothing of the greater horrors of the Terror, didn't I at least know our own little corner, Lev's arrest? Polankov had told me about the execution of the prisoners at Lubyanka during those days of anarchy when the Germans were so close – hadn't I heard the shots myself? Weren't these clues, crumbs that should have led me somewhere near the truth? But we were just coming out of an even greater terror, out of a time when the enemy was clear, when that dream of the triumph of the Russian people, of their heroism, was much more than a dream.

And then again, maybe it wasn't loyalty to my parents, but loyalty to Vladimir, the promise that I made him that day they took Polankov away. And loyalty to all the borrowed family – Pavel, Raisa, Vladimir – that the war had constructed for me. Maybe I was afraid to lose the tentative new self that the war, and my parents' absence, had given me, that Pavel and Raisa's less complicated, less painful love had given me. Their love felt – still feels – absolute, even though we weren't blood. They were the family I chose that day, rather than the flawed one given me. Given and then taken.

I told myself I wasn't afraid, but maybe I acted only out of fear, maybe one more change, one more translation, was more than I could bear.

Or maybe it was that I wanted to make any decision. Anything to break that passivity that had been cultivated in me. Maybe it was that deep stubborn streak, the perverse need to want what I wanted, however arbitrary.

I look back and want to grab that girl by the shoulders and shake her, tell her she's a fool. I wish I could shake her from her stubbornness, her certainty; give her the foreknowledge to make a better choice. But I can't unwish any of those false steps, because each one of them took me to my daughter, and I can't unwish her. Wouldn't unpick a single stitch that gave me her.

Chapter Eight

❄

I put the receiver down, decide not to dial. Why do we call it "dialing" still? I don't know when I last saw a rotary phone. I was about to call my daughter. My grandson volunteers weekends for a children's theatre company. They're putting on a puppet show. My daughter left a message to say she has tickets for the opening. I was about to call, to say I was coming, but the puppets intervened. Now I have puppets in my head and I'm remembering Vladimir, in Moscow, when he was just about my grandson's age.

I was in my third year of architecture, working very hard, evenings, weekends, but with the energy of the young. Despite the two perspective drawings and two elevations that I needed to finish, Vladimir had cajoled me into going with him to the puppet show at the Obraztsov Theatre. What a combination of adoration and condescension boys that age feel for their female relations. All he had to do was loom over me – how quickly he grew, after the war, to loom over me – and smile. And of course, as always, I let him talk me into going along.

When we first arrived in the theatre, it seemed like just the antidote to my long week of work. The theatre was warm, crowded – a full house – and it was good just to sit, to close my eyes and feel all that space above me open.

The Obraztsov Theatre was remarkable. I didn't think much of the building itself, but the performances were extraordinary. They still are. The concert that night began with a series of satirical sketches. The cunning faces of the puppets were caricatures of stock Russian types: stuffy bureaucrats; buxom, meddlesome housewives; nervous scholars. There was a gypsy chorus of fifteen puppet dancers, each an individual in miniature. One little fellow kept hitching up his jacket as it slipped off his shoulder – a virtuoso performance, the puppeteers invisible, the little characters fluent, as though they were willing their own actions.

And then, about the fifth skit, four figures appeared on stage in loud checked suits, their features grotesque: exaggerated hook noses, cruel, thin mouths; their chins weak, eyes sly. They capered around the stage to a parody of American jazz played against a background of English-sounding gibberish. The sketch was titled "Cosmopolitan Chorus."

Rootless cosmopolitan: the new code for "Jew."

I closed my eyes against it and saw my father's lost face – first whole, as I remembered it, then distorted, garbled by the hate that killed him. A second later, Vladimir grabbed my hand and pulled me from my seat and past the insulted knees of our neighbours, who sat and watched and laughed.

That wild decision I made during the war to let Joseph go home without me, it came, at least in part, from what I felt those days, that my life belonged to the lives of the others fighting alongside me. And then at last the war was over. I was alive. I held firm to my choice, happy that I was alive, and that I was at last in school, as Poppa would have wanted. I wanted my life. And even if, because of my alien background, my Jewishness, I didn't exactly fit the image of the good Soviet citizen, I could follow Pavel and Raisa's path. Educate myself, contribute. Belong. Or think that I belonged. Although around us the evidence was gathering – the arrests, the purges – we kept our heads down. Believing that work, that good intentions, that patience, would all pay off. Hadn't we, after all, survived the greatest evil? Surely now we deserved a life. We told ourselves that ugly little incidents like the one at the puppet theatre were just surface disturbances. But as the evidence gathered, it began to shake even the sturdy belief of people like Pavel and Raisa, whose lives had as their foundation the gifts, and the purpose, the Revolution had given them. Even they began, inwardly, to question.

The night after the puppet show I come home from school to a quiet apartment. Instead of being in the midst of her usual cheerful and efficient dinner preparations, Raisa is sitting, listless, on the davenport. As always, Pavel's at the table, reading. He picks up a copy of *The Lives of the Saints*, a little volume the size of a hand – Raisa's, not Pavel's – the cover a moss green buckram with gilt lettering. Pavel never can resist a bookstall. But there's something in his face that worries me, that reminds me of the afternoon when we heard about the occupation of Odessa, that collapse. We talk of how buildings fail, as if volition were involved, as if there were a choice. I saw that collapse, once, in Pavel's face, I saw the structure fail. I'm afraid of seeing it in his face again. I lean over his shoulder to read:

> *His limbs, torn and mangled by many cutting blows, are commanded to be broiled upon the fire in an iron*

> *framework which was of itself already hot enough to burn him and on which his limbs were turned from time to time, to make the torment fiercer, and the death more lingering . . .*

A description of the martyrdom of Saint Lawrence.

"Pavel?" I ask. "Pavel, it's kind of awful, isn't it? Grotesque?"

"I suppose so." He turns to me, gripping the book on a slight twist, the cover askew. "But what's intriguing to me is not that these people's suffering was grotesque. It's that they themselves are sublime."

At the tone in his voice, Raisa sits up. "Pavel, dear, you're bending the pages." Raisa can never bear seeing someone mishandle a book.

"Sublime, really, the human spirit. Even in pursuit of a false god." He looks at his hands, sets the book carefully beside him. "These people believed in something you and I consider absurd. And yet this belief, it enraptured them." He pauses, looks up at me again, again that look on his face. "It was a belief in goodness. At least that's how it started."

Raisa frowns, gets up to sit across from him. "Pavel . . ."

"The State," his voice is soft now, "why is it that we accept the State as though it were a natural phenomenon? We believed . . ."

"Pavel, please. This is not a conversation for children . . ." Raisa takes the book from his hand. "Annette, I should be making us dinner. Can you help me?"

After dinner, I find her sitting on their bed, the book closed on her lap.

"Raisa," I ask, "are you all right? Pavel doesn't seem himself tonight."

"We've just, we've been worried lately. It's work, Pavel's and mine."

"You work too hard, both of you."

She looks up and past me. "Sometimes it feels as though I've just put my head down for thirty years and worked and never looked up, never checked which way the wind was blowing. It's a mistake, Annette. It's a mistake to play the innocent, use work like a drug."

"Raisa?"

She gets up. "But the work has been good. I've done good. I have nothing to be ashamed of. Pavel has nothing to be ashamed of either. We've always done our work as it had to be done, and up to now that's been enough. Hasn't it? I see how we are, Annette. Exempt; privileged. And now, now when I hear about others suffering, about this suffering that we have allowed, somehow, to be invisible to us . . . How is it possible that I didn't see, that there's been a hidden suffering behind all the visible suffering I've tried to heal? I want to see myself as innocent, Annette."

"Raisa, I don't understand."

"Of course you don't. We don't want you to."

I rub my hands over my face to push away the image of Raisa's face when she said that, of the puppets, the invisible puppeteers. Not a conversation for children. They didn't want us to understand. Because knowledge was dangerous. But by then I wasn't a child. Or I didn't think I was. I was twenty-four.

Because there's a rumour of chickens, I'm standing in line in front of the store, in the cold, the grey dark of Moscow in winter, hoping to bring a trophy home for Raisa, to divert us, to cheer us all up.

How long have I been waiting here in line? And for what? I stare at the plastic displays of food in the windows of the shop – ham, chicken, sausages, cheese, fruit – a relic from the days when few could read. *We're liquidating illiteracy.* I feel a nudge behind me, inadvertent.

"Excuse me, Comrade. Pardon." A man's voice. A string bag has bumped my knee, a grey overcoat brushed against mine. I put my hands back in my pockets to warm them, look down at the stooped shoulders of the older woman in front of me.

The man behind me touches my shoulder. "Annette? Annette Gershon?" His face is narrow, grey. "It's me. Anatoly Trubashnik. We were in school together in Odessa."

I suddenly see, through the man, the boy I knew: the brown hair, steel-rim glasses; the soft, clever mouth, warm and hard at the same time, the residual faint irony in the smile. And those green eyes, so like my mother's. It's been nine years, nine and a half. How did he know me?

"Anatoly. What are you doing here?"

"I'm in science at the university. What about you? How is it that you're in Moscow?"

"I got out of Odessa in '41, just before the siege. I have relatives here."

He hears it in my voice. "Your family . . . ?"

I shake my head.

"I'm sorry."

I can't look at him.

"Sorry," he says.

"And you?" I draw in a breath. There's a greyness about him.

He shrugs. "Me? I'm fine, what's left of me. Didn't finish my hitch in the army until a year and a half ago. Just before the war ended I caught some shrapnel when the guy beside me got blown to bits."

I flinch.

"It's fine," he says, some sort of smile working along his face. "None of the essentials got clipped."

"My brother was killed at Stalingrad. Were you –?"

"Stalingrad? I was too young."

Of course he was; we're the same age.

"I enlisted when I was eighteen; it was '44."

"Where were you, then? Where were you stationed?"

"We were moving back into Poland." He leans in close to me, whispers. "*Liberating* Warsaw."

I hear the disgust in his voice. "What . . . ?"

"Warsaw." His mouth against my ear. "We stood by the river, did nothing. Let the Germans grind them up."

I reach up, whisper back, "I, I heard . . ."

"A pack of lies."

I look around. No one's paying attention to us, a thin young man in civilian clothes, a slight, attentive young woman.

He presses his lips together. "I must be crazy talking to you like this. Annette?"

"What?"

"Annette, come to my place; come for dinner." He takes my hand. "Let's go."

"Right now? I wanted to get a chicken . . ."

"Aren't you sick of this? How much of your life have you spent standing in line? Come on. I'll find us something in the cupboard."

For a block we say nothing. He's let go of my hand. Maybe he's regretting his chicken. Or his words.

"Freezing out here," I say at last.

"Comrade, as a daughter of the working class, you must be stalwart!" He takes my hand again, squeezes it. "It's not far. Remember we used to walk to the library to study together? Did you have a crush on me?"

"It was brotherly love, Anatoly. Respect for a comrade. Besides, you were a bad influence."

"Me? I was a mamma's boy!"

"The girls used to say you sold stuff on the black market."

He laughs. "Somewhat of an embellishment of the facts. I was a teenager. I retailed a few cigarettes from wholesalers. Hey, remember Comrade Lozovsky, that sanctimonious physics teacher? The one who only had one arm – he kept the empty sleeve tucked into the pocket of his suit jacket?"

I start to laugh. "And I was so immersed in my studies, and adolescence, that I never even noticed the missing arm?"

He laughs again. "That adolescent hormonal fog. No wonder they keep the boys and girls separate these days. Hey, can we just stop for a minute?" He leans against me, catches his breath. We're passing a vast construction site surrounded by high board fences. Anatoly's face sharpens. He leans towards me, whispers again in my ear. "The fence means they're using forced labour. See the guard towers at each corner, the armed sentries?"

We walk a half block in silence again, then stop in front of a narrow stone building. "This is us," Anatoly says. "Fifth floor."

In the entrance he presses a switch and a dim yellow light floods the vestibule. His eyes are the way I remember them, those light green eyes. "Annette, do you ever feel . . . It's just, sometimes it's hard to feel that I'm the same person I was back then, that Odessa schoolboy." His voice resonates in the bare vestibule. "It, it scares me, how things change. How easy it is for people to change." He leans towards me, touching my shoulder. How did he know me?

I am not who I was. Are we still young, Anatoly and me? There's something in his face, in the way that he holds himself, that argues against it. Are we who we were, who we should be? For a moment we're quiet in the quiet building.

"Do you want to go? You can go. You don't have to come in."

"No, no. I can visit for a bit."

"Then come on up," he says. "I bet you're starving."

The elevator's not working. By the time we get to the top of the stairs, Anatoly's out of breath. He fits the key into the lock, calls out, "Misha? You here?" Picks up a scrap of paper from the table. "Lucky boy: my roommate's at his uncle's for dinner. The aunt's a fabulous cook. And the people you're staying with, Annette?"

"Cousins. Not real cousins, not blood relations, but our families were close. I've lived with them since I got here. They're good people."

"I have to scrounge in the cupboard. I'll be right back."

I undo my coat, run my fingers along the books on Anatoly's shelves. A wall of shelves. The window in the room is large, and because the building's on a rise, I can see grey black bits of the river, its broad, careful, elegant curves. Except for the books, the furnishings are sparse: a davenport they must use as a bed at night, a cot tucked underneath it, an armchair.

"We take turns: one week Misha gets the davenport and I get the cot, and the next week we switch." Anatoly has come back into the room, half a loaf of dark rye in his hand, some cheese, a bottle of vodka. He holds them up. "Provisions. Take off your coat; have a seat."

"It's chilly in here. I'll keep it on for now." I sit down in the armchair. It's leather – must be of pre-war, probably pre-Revolutionary, vintage, the red of its leather darkening to crimson with wear in places, fading to pink where the sun has taken the colour.

"Bread's fresh." Anatoly hands me a sandwich. "I haven't even asked what your work is."

"I'm taking architecture at the Mossovet Workshops here."

"You must be a good student."

"I don't know. Too good, maybe. *Do what the teacher says.* Deferential. And the head of the school, Chernikhov – he has this rigid, elaborate system of pedagogy. I sometimes wonder what I'm learning; *whether* I'm learning or just acquiescing."

"Do I detect anti-social tendencies in that statement?"

I smile, not sure whether it's all right to laugh.

Anatoly smiles stiffly, walks over to the window. "Your cousins, what do they do?"

"Pavel teaches agronomy at the university; Raisa's a doctor. She used to work in a clinic but after the war she was promoted to health officer at the Machine Tool Factory. She's doing a study on health hazards there. She's probably up for a commendation for it. And their son Vladimir just got into medical school."

"Genuine Soviet citizens all," Anatoly says.

I hear the acid in his voice, the sneer at my family, at what they've been able to make of their lives. He's still facing the window. I study his back, the tense shoulders. What am I doing here with him?

"The reason that we're so happy about Vladimir getting into medical school is because there's a quota for Jews. Maybe you didn't know." I button my coat again, reach for my gloves.

He turns from the window. "You going?"

"Yes."

He stands there. I'm on the landing when I hear him call me. "Annette, please? I'm sorry. Please come back. You don't want me drinking all this vodka myself, do you?" I turn around. "I'm sorry, Annette. I don't know what gets into me sometimes; I just get sour. Please don't go." He takes my gloves from me, smoothes them. "Just stay for a bit."

Go. Stay. Go. I follow him back into the apartment. He hands me a glass. "Sit, please. I really am sorry. Tell me about your family. Your cousin got in, then, despite the quota? Must be a smart kid."

"He is; he's brilliant."

"Please sit down. You're not drinking. Do you want a glass of tea? It'll warm you up. I can put on the samovar. Please, finish your sandwich." He's still playing with the gloves.

I put my hand out for them.

"What's going on," Anatoly says, his voice angry again, "it's disgusting. But your family, they're managing?"

"Anatoly? Can I have my gloves?"

He smiles, puts them in the pocket of his jacket. "I'm holding them hostage. Take your coat off. I'll put the samovar on."

I put my hands in my pockets. Go. Stay. Go. I can hear Anatoly clattering china. I should go. He comes back with two glasses of tea, sugar, sits on the davenport, pats the cushion beside him. I sit down.

"So your family's doing all right?"

"Pretty much. May I please have my gloves back?" He takes them from his pocket, hands them to me. I see a scar across his palm, something dark lodged against one knuckle. He puts a hand to my cheek, just touches it with cold fingertips.

"How can you stand it?" he asks.

Those puppets prancing. "It's not a surprise, Anatoly. It's always been there, the anti-Semitism. It's always there. It was there in Canada. We're used to it."

"But here there are explicit laws against it, Annette. Isn't that why your family came here? And the law hasn't changed."

Such innocence; such outrage. "Look – Pavel, my uncle, he says we have to try to see it in perspective. Culture doesn't change as quickly as economics. In time, maybe the next generation, maybe the one after that, the tendency towards prejudice will diminish. Some day it may even be eradicated. But till then, it'll flare up and then fade. Pavel thinks Comrade Stalin must be unaware, somehow, or it wouldn't be happening."

Anatoly shrugs, makes a face. "But in the meantime, it must be tough for you."

"I think it's harder on Pavel and Raisa than it is on me. They were here at the beginning. They've spent their whole lives working for this, this future."

"But for you?"

"I'm here and not here, Russian and not Russian. But I'm not a cynic either."

"Not like me," he says.

"Are you a cynic?"

"Maybe. What I am is tired. The war made me tired." His face has gone grey again. "And it makes me impatient. And mean, sometimes." He looks at me. "Maybe being tired like this makes it hard for me to stay in this future we're supposed to be living for. I have trouble even staying in the *now*, standing in line for my possible chicken. The war keeps coming at me. I want to *be* in this room with you, be *here*. Not in some dugout, waiting for a grenade to take me apart. I have to work at not remembering." He shifts on the davenport, and I can feel the shape of the air between us shift. "Sometimes takes my whole day just to expend all this willpower in not remembering." He's back on his feet, pacing the small room. "So you like it, living in Moscow with these cousins?"

"I feel lucky I have them. Lucky I still have a family, even if I've had to more or less make it up. Mostly I'm pretty happy here."

"Are you?" The words come out hard.

"Yes." I touch the armrest. "I am. Getting into the Mossovet – it feels like I've got my bearings now."

"What's it like – *being happy*?" That anger again, saturating the room.

"Don't." Suddenly I'm just as angry. I don't need this man and his wounds, the bile in his voice. "You've no right to tell me I shouldn't be as happy as I can manage." What does he know about me? I walk to the window, away from him. Stare out, the river so calm, iced over. Stand and stare and feel, for some reason, the anger drain away.

He comes up, puts his arms around me, leans his head against mine. It's heavy. He leans against me and I can't bear it; I'm going to fall.

I'd seen those copies of Greek statues, the young men's bodies slender but strong, the line of hip bone clear above the thighs. His body was like that, muscle rounded over the shoulders and that notch above the breastbone, tender, female. The skin there was soft, untouched, except that you wanted to touch it, rest a forefinger where it fit. I would run my fingers along the lines of bone, lightly touching the dark places, black nodes on the forearm, calf, where the shrapnel was still buried.

Misha, the roommate, soon realized that Anatoly and I

were lovers without our having to say anything. And from then on, solid, cheerful Misha went to dinner at his uncle's a bit more often, leaving Anatoly a casual, detailed note about exactly when he could be expected back. And he'd clear his throat, rattle the doorknob, take a long time fitting his key in the lock before he did come in.

Which was good, because we lost time in bed, let it loose in the bedclothes, in the touch of skin, mouth, tongue. Mostly we were silent, or not silent but without words, because words felt wrong, inappropriate, as though we were suddenly clothed in some outmoded attire. Words would bring us back into particular being. And I wanted to be, for once, in a place without words. A place where I got to rest from being human, sentient, myself – no flattening things out with words. I don't know whether in these moments I was animal or divine, but they gave me back myself.

I didn't know either what all this was for Anatoly, though I could feel how much he needed me. Though he was careful of me, gentle, when we were in bed his face would darken, the light went from his eyes. And I could feel him starving, his mouth against my neck or on my breast, his chest against mine. He buried himself in me, wanted to vanish; needed to feel whatever it was he was feeling, reconstitute himself. He didn't talk much about the war. I couldn't imagine that place in him, where it took him. But it didn't matter. I wanted him. Wanted this: to let my grief go.

And so for weeks after that first lovemaking, we let ourselves get lost in one another, stayed in bed as much as we could. We made love, and we talked. With Anatoly, I could talk about Odessa, my lost family, Ben, Poppa, my mother. He'd met them all, however glancingly. I even told him snippets about Winnipeg, my long-ago life there, about Joseph. Though he told me my infatuation with architecture was "lacking in theoretical rigour," he let me go on about it. He even let me drag him out of bed to stand in front of my favourite buildings, freezing, while I rhapsodized about my beloved façades. And I loved our talk.

But then, about a month after we met, Anatoly vanished for three days. He'd already dropped hints about little side deals he had, small-time black market adventures. I didn't like it, didn't like any of it. He teased me about being a prig, then said nothing more to me about it. I'd gotten used to his erratic schedule, gotten used to him showing up hours late or not at all when we were supposed to be meeting friends for a movie. But this three-day absence was different. When he finally turned up at the apartment it was three o'clock in the morning, and he was haggard, drunk. He wouldn't say where he'd been or what he'd been doing. I told him to leave and not come back, told him I couldn't be with someone so irresponsible. The next day he was back, sober, his arms full of flowers. Wrapped in brown paper was an expensive architectural book I had been coveting for months in a bookstore window. I didn't know what to do. Go. Stay. Go. I couldn't give up on him. Not then. But I told myself I'd taken a step back, that I didn't love him, not yet. Told myself I wanted him, but didn't need him.

I've been pacing the apartment for two hours. We were supposed to be going to the opera. Some pal of Anatoly's was going to get him a pair of tickets to *Prince Igor*. I hear voices in the corridor, Polankov laughing, Anatoly. When I open the door Polankov gives me a guilty grin. "So next week, then, my friend?" Anatoly says.

"Next week, maybe the week after. Evening, Comrade," Polankov says, and heads down the stairs.

"Hey," Anatoly says, kissing me hard on the mouth.

I push him away.

"What's wrong? I've just got a little business arrangement going with your caretaker. Nice fellow, Polankov."

Black market. He's making more of his little deals on the black market. "No he's not a nice fellow."

"Clever fellow, then. Look, I brought you a present. Two presents."

"I don't want your presents."

"Not these?" He waves the tickets at me. "Two tickets, row 15. For once we don't have to sit in the gods."

"It's too late. It's nine thirty. Curtain was at eight o'clock."

"Damn me. I got waylaid. Well, before you reject number one present, let me sweeten the deal with number two present." He pulls a bottle out of his jacket. It's vermouth-vodka, a bright green mixture of wormwood and vodka. The one time I tried it, it tasted like ink mixed with furniture polish. "No dice? You won't drink with me? You're mad."

"What did you expect?"

"Tell you what," he says. "Forget about the opera. We'll go dancing. What do you say?" He takes two glasses from the sideboard, fills both. "Have a drink – great stuff."

I shake my head.

"You're right: it's not a lady's drink, vodka-vermouth." He finishes his glass, raises the second in a toast. "To my dear departed Annette. I mean, departing. We're off, aren't we? We can still see the second act. Or, if the lady prefers, we can go dancing."

"Do you dance better when you're drunk?"

"I'm drinking; I'm not drunk. It'll take at least three more shots before I even begin to be drunk. And yes, I am a better dancer when I'm drunk. It de-inhibits one's inhibitions." He takes another long swallow.

"Why don't you take your bottle home with you? It's all the company you need."

"Better company than what I've got here. You're a cold fish, Annette – anybody ever tell you that?"

"Go home and get drunk. Take your bottle."

I'm reading in the front room when I hear something at the door: the doorknob's twisting back and forth. "Who is it? Who's there?"

"Me. Anatoly."

"Go away. It's after midnight."

"Please, Annette. I need to see you."

"Go away."

He starts pounding on the door.

"Be quiet! Everyone's asleep."

"Just let me in . . . I have to talk with you."

"All right, but be quiet."

His voice drops to a whisper. "I'll be very quiet. Silent as the grave."

"Good."

He's leaning in the doorway, grinning. "You should have come dancing. We would have had fun."

"I'll get you a coffee."

"I brought my own beverage." This time it's a bottle of vodka, half drunk. "I met some friends. You should have come."

"I have school tomorrow."

"Such a hard worker. Well, I'll have a little slug for the both of us." He sits at the table, takes a long swallow and another, closes his eyes. His head nods.

"Anatoly." I set my hands on his shoulders. "You should sleep it off."

He opens his eyes, leans his head against me. "Annette, Annette. You're not mad."

"Not now."

"But I like it when you're mad; that's when you're you. But you don't like it, do you? You don't like yourself when you're angry. I'm going to have one hell of a hangover tomorrow." He kisses my arm. "I'm mad all the time, you know. Did you know that about me?"

"There's lots I don't know about you."

"If you knew more, maybe you wouldn't like me so much."

I stroke his head, heavy against me. "Who says I like you?"

"That's right. I shouldn't make assumptions. It's dangerous. It's a dangerous life. Hey, Annette, do you remember how people used to talk during the war? *When this war's over, we're gonna get married, you just wait and see.* All sorts of promises. Everybody talked like that – *just wait till the war's over.* Bet you said that, didn't you, Annette?" He doesn't wait for an answer. "But what if it's never over? In here?" He taps his head. "What if it doesn't want to go away?" He reaches for the bottle again, takes another swig. "But you did what you wanted to do, didn't you? Architecture school. Just like you said you would."

"That's right. Maybe we should put the bottle away now, no?"

"An architect. Good for you." He sits up suddenly, twists around to face me. "You want to know about architecture? I can tell you all about architecture. You ever heard of a *zemlyanka*? No? A *zemlyanka*, now there's ideal Soviet architecture for you. Genuine folk art. You know how we build them? No? You never learned? We built lots of them, lots of them."

"Anatoly, maybe I should put you to bed. You can sleep here tonight. Raisa won't mind."

"No no no no no. I shouldn't go to bed, Annette, because I got to explain to you how we built a *zemlyanka*. Listen and you'll learn. You dig a pit about two metres deep, right into the ground. No matter how frozen the ground is, you dig right in. And then you line the pit with nice fat logs. And then, then, you make a roof and a floor and you find a stove – see? See? That's how we stayed warm during the war. Five months. Five months like a worm under the ground. One day they had to pull me out of the mud, did I tell you that? I went outside naked and stretched myself out in the mud because I knew what I was. A worm. I tried to dig myself a grave with my fingernails. They had to pull me out. Did I tell you that? Did I tell you about that, about my home in the *zemlyanka*, my life as a worm? Did you know that about me? Did you know that about architecture? Soviet architecture?" He slumps back into the chair. "You just ask me if you want to know anything about architecture."

His head sinks onto the table and he's asleep.

The next afternoon the door to the apartment opens; it's Raisa, her arms full of packages. "Anatoly gone home?" she asks.

"Vladimir walked him to his apartment about an hour ago. He was still feeling sick."

"It's the wormwood," Raisa says. "They shouldn't be allowed to use it." She pushes my papers to the side, sets her packages down. "That was quite the performance again last night."

"I'm sorry, Raisa. He gets like that sometimes."

"Are you serious about this boy?" She starts drumming her fingers on the table, and before I can answer, she continues. "It must be a comfort that he knew you in Odessa, no? What was he like then?"

I shrug. "The same and not the same. He was different from the other boys. He always seemed to be in charge, somehow, always knew what he was doing." I haven't said anything to Raisa about Anatoly's extracurricular activities making little deals on the black market.

"The drinking, does it affect his school?"

"School's fine, Raisa. He doesn't drink that often."

"And this sour little edge?"

"He's not really like that, Raisa. It just comes out –"

" – when he drinks."

"What are you saying, Raisa?"

"I just want to know if you're in love with this boy."

"Love. Do you believe in love, Raisa?"

"You're annoyed with me."

"I'm asking."

"Do I believe in love? Do I believe in chemistry? That's what all this adolescent infatuation is about, Annette. Propagating the species. If you want an opinion on love you should ask Vladimir. He's the expert on love."

Vladimir's in love: some girl at the university.

"Falling in love is a fad with these kids Vladimir's age. They're so starved for contact with the opposite sex that as soon as they get to coed classes at university, they're obliged to declare themselves madly in love. It's an adolescent epidemic. But you're too old for infatuation. You need to think carefully about what you want. About this boy." She sits down. "Can we deal with love some other time? I should get going on supper. And you need to finish your work." She picks up my textbook, Chernikhov's *Architectural Fictions*.

"You sound tired," I say.

"A long day. It's all this worry at work."

They've finally told me about the trouble at work. The union office had asked Raisa to sign a letter accusing the chief engineer at the plant of being an "enemy of the people." They were claiming that he had tried to obstruct the doctors' efforts to improve working conditions.

Raisa hasn't decided what to do yet. If she doesn't sign, she's almost sure to lose her position. She's never liked the man, an officious stuffed shirt who's been impossible to get along with. But he's thoroughly competent.

And, more to the point, he's a Jew.

I still have it, my copy of Chernikhov's *Architectural Fictions* with its fawn and pigeon green cover. The fine binding seems to carry something of Lev. It belonged to him – he must have bought it just after it was published in '33. He had a whole collection of architectural books, pamphlets and photographs too, that he would sort through wearing his white cotton gloves. He'd invite me in, explain what I was looking at. He'd puff on his cigar and talk about how he and Chernikhov knew each other way back when, before the Revolution, when Chernikhov was studying in Odessa. They used to drink in the same cafés, talk politics, art. By the time I was admitted to the Mossovet Workshops, Chernikhov's ideas, his elaborate, overly systematic methodology, had fallen out of favour, but he was still head of the school. Lev's stories, these beautiful illustrations, were what got me seriously thinking about studying architecture. I didn't know how to read the axonometric perspectives until Lev explained them. And I remember, as a kid, fretting to myself about the title, *Architectural Fictions*. It should have been "architectural facts": something as solid as a building couldn't be a fiction.

There's a glossy coloured plate for Fiction 51. Looks more like a mechanical spider than a building. *An idealized industrial complex distributed on a road system.* That disc or spool in the middle must be the complex, but because of the axonometric it looks like it's exploding in place. And the spokes that are the roads look like they're either floating or sinking. The colours are beautiful: that flat red for the disc, a gorgeous yellow flowering at the right hand as background. 1933.

Even today, in the twenty-first century, it still looks like the future, what the future was supposed to be.

How is it that I am what I am? Why have I sunk myself in my work the way Raisa did in hers? This fascination with architecture, the obsession with sorting out what's wrong or right about a building, finding a way of shaping things in the world so that they fit – I want a world where things fit. At one time the playfulness, hopefulness, of these drawings was enough to make me believe in the future.

It's a miracle, having something of Lev's. Manya had a few things from the apartment, odds and sods, that one of the neighbours managed to save for her. She sent me the book when I started university. Something from Lev.

And I have, as well, a few of my lecture notes, the handwriting tidy, dutiful:

> *– the new architecture a rejection of outdated canons and of the idealistic aestheticism that considers art an end in itself*
> *– the machine the source of a new aesthetic of asymmetries, dynamism and functionality*

– fundamental laws governing the relationships of bodies in plane and space

The words don't make as much sense as the illustrations. Those broken, beautiful forms – is that what the Revolution was supposed to have done? Break things to make them better? When this book was published everything was new; everything was possible. The old smashed up to create the new, and beautiful.

Chernikhov was so quickly out of fashion, his Constructivism declared "bourgeois aestheticism," a throwback to conventional standards of beauty.

But I wanted beauty. Still do.

And what about love? I don't know if I understand any better now than I did then. How do I weigh and measure my love for Anatoly, if it was love; for Vladimir, Raisa, Pavel, Ben, my parents? I don't think we even have the right vocabulary. Plato's parable about each person being half of a whole, each incomplete – it doesn't give me anything now. Why do we need to make ourselves complete in someone else? Why do we think individuals are essentially incomplete? It's an infantile fantasy, a yearning to go back to the womb.

What I need to understand is the durable kind of love built on want, not need. It's a structure, as much as any of the buildings I've made. You build it out of days. I've had my own taste of it, though it came late. Sometimes what I've felt for others has seemed to me indelible, like my love for my parents and Ben, which has lasted longer than the individuals that generated it. For my daughter, my grandson. Blood love. And for Joseph, my brother, whose offer I refused. I have his letters too. I have to squint to read his faded scrawl, though by now the words feel almost a part of me.

September 14, 1944
Dear Annette,
Sorry I didn't send this sooner, but we both know I'm not much of a writer. And mail to the USSR hasn't exactly been "express" most of the time . . .

Wish you had decided that you wanted to come back here, but it was up to you.

About Poppa. I never really thought he could have made it, but there was always this kind of wish that somehow he had. I guess you know what I mean. Hard to give up on that. I'm sorry we had to.

It was good to meet Pavel and Raisa. I'm glad it's them you're bunking with, even if you are camping out on their davenport still. They're sweet people; you deserve sweet.

Like I said, things are good for Daisy and Nathan and me. Feels like I'm making myself a real life here. Daisy and me, we've already saved for a down payment on a house. If I ever do get you back here, you know you can always move in with us.

I'm showing all the folks from Selkirk Avenue the snapshots I took in Moscow. Everybody says you're a real looker now . . . Tell Vladimir to keep an eye on you for me.

Your brother,
Joseph
PS I hope you do go into architecture. At least one of us will get an education. You always were the smart one.

After the war, Joseph's letters stopped, the way the letters from Odessa stopped in September 1941. I found out later that at first he'd written, but when we didn't reply, he knew the letters never reached us. And then, as the Cold War became worse, he stopped writing, knowing that letters from a capitalist state, contact with enemy foreigners, would only mean trouble for us. In those years, I also wrote letters to him that I never mailed. About my trip back to Odessa. Raisa and I went back, once. She and Manya and I went to the port, the square where it happened, where Poppa and Momma were killed with the others. We stood on the pavement beside the water. But we didn't find anything. No blood, no cries, no smell of smoke. There was no dark mark of burning along the stone walls that lined the square, no gauge of how high the flames went, how thick the smoke rose, no memory. Just people going about their business. As if nothing had happened. Or as if what had happened were nothing.

Chapter Nine

❄

As 1950 ended, the country fell into a frenzy over Stalin's seventieth birthday. The Museum of the Revolution was crammed with gifts, letters, telegrams. The ovation for Stalin on the radio was endless – shrill, strained voices chanting slogans. It must have been hard even for the staunchest of believers not to be taken aback. It was whispered that Stalin couldn't have known the scope of the adulation; if he had, he would have been mortified.

I tried, as had become – and has remained – my habit, to hide in my work. I'd broken away somewhat from the rigours of Chernikhov's convoluted pedagogy. That December the instructor for my studio was Mikhailov, a brilliant, genial fellow I had a slight crush on. I was chumming with another female student, Polina, and we'd decided, perhaps to impress Mikhailov, to work as a team on a study of the Rusakov Workers' Club, a building on Strominka Street by the Constructivist architect Konstantin Melnikov. The boxes he'd set jutting out of the third storey of the building always seemed to me ready for flight. I still love Melnikov's work; love his vision of the "force of maximal possibilities." Maximal possibilities! What an absurd concept then, in 1950.

What an absurd concept now . . . I'm not sure even now why we were allowed, in Chernikhov's school, to study this champion of intuition over method. I'm even less certain of how the buildings of this visionary of individualist space survived Stalin, though they did, more or less. Today the Rusakov Club is on the "endangered heritage" list; even in 1950 it was beginning to decay. But Polina and I had copies of the original plans and sections. We were doing measured drawings, perspectives, everything. Anatoly disapproved of the Rusakov and continued to plague me about "ideal Soviet architecture."

I think he was drinking less in those days, though perhaps I'd just gotten used to the drinking. He'd still disappear for a day or two, wheeling and dealing in the black market no doubt, shady activities that I chose to ignore. There was much I chose to ignore because I liked being in bed with him so much. His stolid pragmatist of a roommate, the kindly Misha, had fallen absurdly in love with an exquisite young woman named Nadya. Nadya was a serious Komsomol classmate of Misha's who lectured him on his obligations as a citizen. And Misha solemnly accepted these lectures, lapping it up so long as he could remain in the company of the exquisite Nadya. But Misha's infatuation with Nadya gave us more privacy, more time with each other, and we made the best of it.

I hid any uneasiness in work, in the intensity of my attachment to Anatoly. We were all caught up in our private lives. Vladimir was at the top of his class in medical school; Pavel was hard at his research at the university. But Raisa was in trouble, still battling the situation at her plant. Things were coming to a head: she was almost sure to lose her job. We all thought the worst that could happen, though it would have meant that she'd have had to put her research on hold, was that they'd demote her back to a job at a community clinic. Pavel told us there was nothing to do but be patient; these things would blow over eventually. We kept thinking rational thoughts about the worst that could happen. How was it that I still believed that my life, at some final moment, would simply fall into place? But I did, and so these disruptions surprised me. I hadn't yet learned that our lives get to float along the surface of events only briefly. We never know whether this is the moment before things settle at last, the moment we're about to come home, or the moment before everything's shaken apart. But I thought then that everything bad had already happened. The war was over. We were alive.

Anatoly and I are at a retrospective of Eisenstein films. I haven't seen *Potemkin* since I was a little girl in Odessa and I want to watch it again, find the edits, see how the story was constructed. And I need the distraction. I can't stop worrying about Raisa. We're holding hands in the theatre, and when the lights go down Anatoly's comes to rest, light and alive, on my thigh. I can feel his warmth through the smooth wool of my skirt. We'll have the apartment to ourselves this evening. I look at Anatoly, smile. Then a peripheral flicker tells me the film has started. Shots of Stalin's birthday celebrations: the mountains of gifts. The camera zooms in on a hand-knitted child's bonnet, given, the announcer booms, by a French woman – all she has left of her child who died during the occupation. All she has.

And then they're showing an old newsreel about the American bombing of Hiroshima, more evidence of capitalist atrocity and American imperialism according to the

Russian subtitles. *The people of the Soviet Union will not be deterred by these images of horror. We will match American technology rocket for rocket and bomb for bomb. Despite America's adventurism in Asia, the Chinese people have stood up, winning their own civil war and establishing the People's Republic. And now the flames of revolution have spread to Korea, breaking the chains of European colonialism. The peoples of the Soviet Union will not hesitate to stand up themselves against the threats of the imperialists, now led by the United States.*

The film is all scratchy. It's only been five and a half years; seems odd that the film would be in such bad shape. The voice-over is the original English, and the announcer's voice is terrified and smug at the same time. *A pillar of smoke*, he says. *The mushroom cloud fearsome proof of American know-how.* It reminds me of something. *A column of fire.* Year and years ago, before we left Winnipeg. I must have been eight, or nine. Ben and I were invited over to my friend Cassie's for Passover, and they read the story of Exodus: *With a mighty hand and an outstretched arm and with signs and with wonders.* And then President Truman's voice comes on, and he is saying, *we wished in this first attack to avoid, insofar as possible, the killing of civilians.* The Russian subtitles are indifferent to the English words. I might well be the only one in the room who understands them. And then another voice comes in on the newsreel, the translated voice of a witness, a hibakusha: *There was a bluish white light that flashed like an electric welding spark. The world went white.* The slow menacing blossom of the cloud, then shaky, ragged shots of the pulverized landscape; the odd anomalous chimney left standing like a burnt matchstick; a building or two still upright but awry, as if looking askance at its own survival. Then a network of steel girders, the structure whole but askew, a cobweb some hand has brushed aside. And the crisp, agonized postures of the corpses. *And he saw our suffering.*

Everything bad has already happened.

He was always heavy in me, Anatoly. Maybe I still carried too much grief to have found someone lighter. If he hadn't been so beautiful, the line of hip bone clear above his thigh, those green eyes, that notch above the breastbone, tender, female, that I needed so badly to touch. If he hadn't been hurt, hadn't been taken apart in his war. I loved him hard. It was Anatoly who had told me how much work it was, not remembering, in that cold room, the war just years behind us.

He's been gone again, for four days this time; no messages. I've been to the apartment but Misha can't tell me anything. I'm at the studio, fussing over an elevation. We're a hard-working little bunch – quiet conversations here and there, the squeak of parallel rules along their wires, the shush of soft brushes cleaning off erasings. A dull light comes in the dirty windows. There's a layer of grime over the entire studio. No one ever seems to clean, though I've seen the caretaker hauling a mop and bucket up the stairs. When I look up, Anatoly's there. Grinning.

"You look good," he says, leaning over to kiss my neck. "I like watching you work."

I stand up. It's as if I've gone over a cliff and into the deep and am slowly filling with water. An interior scream rising in me, an animal grammar. If I open my mouth, the whole studio will be drowned in one scream. "Go away. Leave me alone."

The grin's still there; pure innocence. "What's wrong?"

"Where were you? You were coming over to Raisa's for dinner four days ago and you never showed and you never came by. Misha didn't know where you were. No one knew."

It's gone now, the grin. "Does everything have to be so dramatic, Annette? I was tied up for a few days. I was out of town."

"Where? Why?"

"I don't have to explain myself to you. I had business. I told Misha."

"You didn't tell Misha. He had no idea where you were."

"He forgot. He's too busy screwing Nadya to remember what I tell him."

"What about school?"

"School is fine. I got suspended. Just for a week. It doesn't matter."

"I want you to go." If one more syllable drops from his mouth, the scream will come up. I have nothing but the scream. Because that's all I can do with Anatoly. Not let go. Not hold on.

He puts an arm around me, leans into my ear. "Please. Please. Don't say that. Annette, I'm sorry. Misha just forgot. He's like that. Don't be mad. Don't be mad at me. I can't stand it." His lips brush against my ear. "Please." He puts his arms around me, leans his heavy head against mine. And I know I'm going to fall. I let go: I hold on.

It's not the usual raw weather. The day is mild, so Anatoly and I are walking across the river on our way to Novodevichy Cemetery, where we're to meet Vladimir. The walk is part of our truce. I can't stop forgiving him. Anatoly's back at school, doing well, contrite. He's been promising to go with me to

Novodevichy since August. In summer Novodevichy is beautiful. Gorky's buried there, and Chekhov, in a cherry orchard no less. But today despite the mildness it's hard even to imagine summer. Though the sun is out, it's still a chill brightness.

Suddenly Anatoly sets his hand on my arm, grimaces. "Another cramp," he says after a bit. It's the shrapnel in his calf. It can take years, decades even, to work its way out of the body. So we rest a bit, leaning against a railing looking down on the stretch of frozen water, the wide sidewalks lining the embankment, snow-filled now. Raisa says the embankments of the Seine are like this, though the Seine is much narrower. On the sidewalks above, vendors sell old books, prints from battered wooden stalls. I won't ever see Paris. "I'm all right now," Anatoly tells me. We start up again, and soon Novodevichy Convent is just ahead with its wedding-cake layers of windows, its bright red brick, its gilded domes, its towers and turrets and battlements. The domes repeat themselves, squat, heaped like toadstools, disorganized – more fairy tale than real, more imagined than constructed, as if only too much were enough. At the entry the gatekeeper is sipping his glass of tea, his breath fogging in the air. He nods us on. We pass through the high arch into the cemetery and head down a winding, meticulously shovelled path. Two tidy rows of small firs, their boughs laden with new snow, meet at right angles. On the third side there's the high red brick of the convent wall. Vladimir's standing in front of an immense white marble tomb, a book in one mittened hand, the other tucked into his pocket.

"Vladimir," I call.

He looks up, puts the book into his satchel. He looks

small beside the white marble column of the tomb, which must be close to seven feet high. The lower portion is square cut, but from the top, the head of a woman and one helpless-looking hand abruptly emerge: Nadezhda Sergeevna Alliluyeva, Stalin's second wife. She looks cold, a coldness not marble, but snow.

"See that searchlight mounted on the wall, Annette?" Anatoly points to the red brick. He leans towards me, whispers dramatically, "They say it's for Comrade Stalin's midnight visits."

They also say that Alliluyeva was poisoned by Stalin. I glance over at the two police patrolling nearby. They're not paying us any attention. I can't keep myself from shivering. Vladimir puts his arm around my shoulders.

We pause as Anatoly stops to stretch his sore leg, then takes out a pack of Belomorkanal. He offers one to Vladimir, who shakes his head. "Saint Annette doesn't smoke, or I'd offer her one," Anatoly says as he lights up, drawing the smoke in deeply. Then we continue down the path, the sunlight cold on the gravel.

"Annette says you've joined a literary club." Anatoly squints through the smoke at Vladimir.

"It's not a club, so much. More a reading circle. We've been meeting for a while now. A bunch of kids I knew from Pioneers. I told you about Solly, didn't I, Annette? Really interesting fellow. Solly and some younger guys."

"Guys? What's the point of a literary circle without pretty girls?"

"We have our share. A couple of very pretty girls. They like poetry."

"Of course. Reading anything good?"

"Esenin. Blok. He's interesting."

Anatoly raises an eyebrow. "Interesting indeed."

Vladimir shrugs. "The thrill of the forbidden. We have as much fun hanging about afterwards, walking around the streets of the Arbat, fancying ourselves literary critics."

"And school?" Anatoly asks.

Vladimir grimaces. "I wish we could just concentrate on our coursework. It seems like we spent half the fall on the November 7 festivities, and then all this nonsense for Comrade Stalin's seventieth birthday. And the next thing you know, we'll be working on our May Day celebrations. It's a bloody waste of time."

"Commemorating joyous national holidays like genuine Soviet people is a waste of time, Comrade?" Anatoly takes on the loudspeaker voice.

"Can I have a puff?" I ask.

Anatoly flicks the ash from the cigarette, adjusts the cardboard holder, offers it to me. "You've decided to join us sinners?"

I shake my head. "I just want a puff." The raw smoke scratches at my throat. I hand it back. "Why do you do that?"

"What, smoke?"

"No. Make fun of everything."

"Your little cousin Vladimir's right – this enforced celebration is a waste of time. Don't tell me you enjoy all these parades and banners?"

Vladimir grins. "You haven't seen her on May Day, Anatoly. On May Day Annette takes her vodka like a man. It fuels her dancing, increases her appreciation of the street music and the fireworks and acrobats . . ."

"I've always liked parades. In Winnipeg Poppa would take us to the Santa Claus parade every single year." The past catches me in a wave and I have to stop on the path.

"Are you cold?" Vladimir asks. "Should we go in?"

"Why would the army celebrate the Saviour's birth?" Anatoly asks.

"I'm fine, Vladimir. It wasn't a military parade, Anatoly." How can I even begin to tell them? "No army. There were floats, and clowns, and Santa Claus in his reindeer sleigh."

"Do you remember much about Winnipeg?" Vladimir asks.

We sit on a stone bench under the bare branches of an immense elm, the stone faintly warmed by the sun.

I remember everything.

"Ben took me to the circus one time. We rode our bikes down Main Street right past the edge of town. If we'd gone a few blocks further, past Kildonan Park, we'd have been completely in the country. It felt like the city was just barely perched on the surface of the land. It could blow away any time, leave the prairies exactly the way they were before all those buildings with their false fronts were built. We could stand at the edge of town, and the prairie would just open out. It was like *we* were the ghosts – the landscape was more real than we were." That emptiness that had no need for me.

"Do you ever feel like that here?" Vladimir asks.

"Here? Not really. I guess the closest I ever felt to it was at Pioneer camp. When I was a kid, Pioneer camp was heaven."

"Saint Annette at peace in the workers' paradise . . ." Anatoly says.

But it was lovely, the woods round the campsite thick, dense – so different from the thin birches and scrawny elms scattered along Lake Winnipeg at the beach. These Old World woods are soaked with history, wise. And exhausted.

What I had really wanted there, and found, was to have

every day shaped for me. Every day had a form. And I felt part of something. I felt that I had a purpose beyond the small purpose of my life.

Anatoly takes out another cigarette. "God, those ditties we learned in Pioneers!:

How wonderful to live in the Soviet land!
How wonderful to be beloved of the land!
How wonderful to be useful,
and wear the red tie with pride!"

He minces his way through the lyrics. "We lived in 'the very best country in the world.' Such patriotic fervour, but we knew nothing about any other country." His face has darkened. I reach for his hand, but he puts both fists in his pockets, looks out over the snow-covered clearing. "Just look at them," he says, gesturing to the tombstones, monuments. "All the lovely dead. The best of Russia, dead." There's a cold fury in his voice.

The police pass by, talking to each other, casual. Guarding the dead. "Anatoly," I say at last.

He swallows, sighs. "What?"

"Were we better off serfs?"

"Of course not. But I'm not convinced we're living in the promised land. Maybe the promise has been broken." His eyes trail the police, who are at the far end of the clearing, who can't possibly hear us.

Vladimir, who has been quiet, looks up at Anatoly. "We spent four years fighting fascism, Anatoly."

"Then why did our army sit and watch while the fascists burned Warsaw?"

"Anatoly." I put my hand on his arm.

"Are we supposed to give up believing that we can make something better here just because it's a mix of bad and good?" Vladimir asks.

"Of course not," Anatoly says. "Look, Vladimir. It's not useful to see things as *either* socialism *or* fascism. Do you think socialism had reached perfection here? Do you think that the way things are right now, here, is the fulfilment of what Lenin, or Marx, had in mind? Look around you; look at where the power lies. Party bureaucrats. Apparatchiks. Petty officials."

He puts his arm around Vladimir, his voice gone suddenly brotherly, though I hear an echo of the loudspeaker in his voice. "There are people who would say that what we have now is nothing more than state capitalism. You should read Lenin; read Marx, Hegel. Start with Lenin's *The State and Revolution*."

"Anatoly, Vladimir's got more than enough work already . . ."

"No, Annette, he's right," Vladimir interrupts. "I should know more, read more."

"I'm just saying that if we do know more, we'll do a better job of understanding what we have, what we want changed. Anyway, it's not going to be up to old folks like you and me, Annette. We're worn out. The war did us in." Anatoly's smiling now, his voice light. "It'll be the kids Vladimir's age who'll be the vanguard of real socialist progress. Right Vladimir?" He punches him lightly in the shoulder. "Come on, it's freezing. I'll buy us all roasted chestnuts."

You don't get close to it in winter – the smell of earth. My schoolmate Polina has given me a pot of basil to keep on the windowsill beside my drafting board. The little plant looks cramped, so I'm moving it to a bigger pot. Have to water it first, and when I do, that earth smell is released. I lift the plant out gingerly, tenderly, from the damp soil, both hands cupped around the root system, then set it in the new pot, tamp the soil home. There. A bruised leaf gives off its own fresh, peppery smell. Makes me suddenly, briefly, homesick. Everything comes back to me in smell.

Homesick for what? For my life, which I'm nothing if not in the middle of.

I lean over my drafting board, studying the façade that I'm working on. It's complex, and I can't quite get it right. I want to try changing the proportions of the windows just a bit, realigning them to see how it looks. Mikhailov, our handsome studio instructor, is a couple of tables over. He sees me looking at him, nods, then strolls over.

"Gardening in the studio is strictly prohibited." He mock frowns at the basil plant. "But I see it's not primarily your agricultural concerns that are weighing heavily on you . . . You have a problem?"

"Comrade Mikhailov, it's this façade. I can't quite get it right."

"Can you articulate your problem here a bit more clearly?" He pushes back a strand of thick black hair, frowns for real, in concentration, though one eyebrow goes up quizzically. "Usually I can count on you to be a bit more coherent . . ."

"It needs a better balance of elements. Those windows look too heavy in the wall, too big."

"Well, how about something like this?" He draws a couple of sketches, doodles almost, in the corner of the drawing, then heads off without waiting for a reply. I study his sketch, such light, deft strokes. But it's what I want. This small change in proportion and it's settled into beauty. There.

There.

The murmur of student voices in the studio rises, dims, but I'm not listening, I'm elsewhere: walking the long bare sidewalks of Selkirk Avenue, of Main Street, following my mother reluctantly down Deribasovskaya Street, wandering the streets of Moscow. Since I was small, I've been hunting something in buildings: rightness, wholeness. In the ungainly faces of the Winnipeg houses, in those dislocated façades, everything out of place, there was always something missing, something that left me steeped in sadness.

I can hear Anatoly, his familiar, confident cadences: *aesthetics aren't universals; they're merely subject to the current ideological fashion*. But I don't believe it's just petit-bourgeois aestheticism, this craving for beauty, for integrity. If these human structures are made carelessly, made ugly, how do they honour the people who live among them? Why shouldn't we love what we've made, why shouldn't we take care making it?

I need wholeness. I need things to be right.

That's how I'm home.

I've found it in my work.

I have to stop myself from laughing out loud: I sound like a good Komsomol. But this is what gives me to myself, this work.

I start the drawing again. The classroom noises fade. Polina asks if I want a break but I shake my head, scarcely look up. There. There. That's what I want. I rub my eyes. The studio's almost empty. Mikhailov must have gone home already. I'll have to show him the new drawing tomorrow. Polina is still working away a few desks from me, her blonde curls hanging into her face, and Olga, one of the older students, is slumped across her drafting board, fast asleep. It's so quiet that I can hear her breathe. Down the hallway the caretaker sweeps his mop doggedly backwards and forwards across the black and white tiles.

I'm happy. It comes to me that I'm happy.

Have I come to the end of grief? That was where I was living. It inhabited me, was me.

What I'd been all that time, knowing and not knowing whether Ben or my parents were alive, was grief; what I'd been was the past. Wrapping myself around that loss, holding it tight so that it didn't escape. So that the loss hadn't really been a loss – it had been a presence. Because if I let the grief go – who would I be?

And now, after the months, years – six years since I learned of their deaths, six and a half – I want to extricate myself, to take the memories, emotions, the grief, outside of me, so that I can feel something else. To have room for something else.

For myself, my work.

For Anatoly, maybe.

So have I, then, come to the end of grief? This morning, and other mornings like this one, I've woken and thought merely of the day, what I have to do, whether I'll be ready for class; thought with pleasure of this drafting board.

And, in that moment, Poppa, Ben, my mother – they're gone. They're not with me and neither is my grief.

I don't know what to do with this. Even the loss of grief is a loss. I'm afraid of it. But want to come to an end.

Because I am not just my love for Poppa, for Ben, my botched love for my mother. I'm also their love for me, and Raisa's love, Pavel's – who are still alive. Vladimir's, Manya's. Joseph, Anatoly.

And more than that, I am – myself. This wash of thought, emotion, impulse, perception. The eye squinting this very moment in the late sun, the hand drawing the façade, toes cramped in their worn shoes. Something mutable and transient but, nonetheless, finally, there.

It has stayed with me, that antidote to grief. The drug of work, as Raisa said. And the self it gave me. It still cures. At this very moment, when I should put the boxes, the folders away, when I should go back to the dinner I'm still grateful for, my kitchen steeped in the fragrance of mushrooms, all I want is to go to the office, sit at my desk. The desk is very beautiful. I'm inordinately proud of it, designed it myself. I'm proud of my office too, which is, of course, both spare and elegant. Populated with "pedigree furniture" as my daughter calls it, her proletarian sensibilities somewhat offended: the standard architect's office fare, Barcelona chair, Corbu chaise longue. I like his Basculant chair best. Despite my "semiretirement," I still come in three or four times a week, drink coffee, fuss over sketches, bother everyone. I'm proud too (the sin of pride following directly on the sin of humility) of what I have managed to build here – a few schools, many homes, one art gallery I'm altogether too pleased with, a clinic. I think my mother would have liked my buildings. My father too. They aren't tall or grand: no palaces for the workers . . . But they are beautiful, I believe, and they're whole. It's hard to be whole.

I should eat. Or turn the television back on and listen to what those children have to say. But I'm hungry. My body still has its appetites, still communicates these things quite nicely: *You're hungry: make a snack. You're tired: take a nap.* There are days when I wake up feeling so strong that I can delude myself that I'm still thirty – on the inside, at least.

When everything still seems possible, even love. I'm thinking about my old friend Oscar Rheinhold again. He was eighty-seven when he died, ripe, as they say. I'd rather die ripe than rotten. Margaret, his wife, had died four years earlier. I couldn't stand Margaret, a sour, pinched little soul perpetually disappointed in Oscar. I put up with her for twenty years only for Oscar's sake. Everybody did. And then she died, and Oscar was released from his fidelity, and took up with the woman who'd been his next-door neighbour for thirty-five years, also widowed. It sounds like the punchline to a joke, but I think it was the first time he was happy with a woman. And it moves me. It moves me.

I should be making dinner, tasting my mushrooms, but instead I've gone and picked up a snapshot I still have of Vladimir, sere old woman that I am. I haven't been able to pack it away in a box; it'll go last. It used to sit on the bookshelf at Pavel and Raisa's. It was taken on one of his last summers at Young Pioneer camp. He looks about fourteen. He's leaning over a heap of firewood, holding one end of a double-handled saw, his thick hair brushed back from his forehead. He's got one skinny, sinewy arm resting for balance on a log. The smile on his face is quizzical, hesitant, as if he were caught at the very moment at which he was about to grow up – as though he'd made up his mind about it.

But that winter of conversations, of intrigue, he wasn't smiling much, Vladimir. He'd lean in his chair at the table, an arm draped over the back, the casual stance contradicted by his face as he talked to Anatoly. The two of them would be sunk into another intense political conversation. At first I hovered at the edge of that talk, fielding questions from Anatoly that felt more like interrogations: didn't Vladimir and I know that Lenin had left a will warning against Stalin? Were we not aware that there were unnumbered camps across the country holding millions of prisoners, most of them unjustly condemned?

I never was the kind of believer that my parents, or even Pavel and Raisa, were. I'd always felt that, under that surface of belief, there were things that were wrong. So Anatoly's information and the propositions that it offered were seductive. It made me feel there was some way of breaking the code, of seeing beyond the official story. I wanted to know. But mostly the talk made me miserable. Anatoly's theories were ungiving, unforgiving. And his immense certainty – socialism is this and not that; Lenin meant this and nothing more or less – there was something wrong with it. The loudspeaker voice. My mother's certainties, though Anatoly's certainties took a different tangent from hers. Swallowing my anger, I would pick up my class notes or my textbooks and pretend to read them while the sparring continued.

Because it was really Vladimir that Anatoly was talking to; it was Vladimir that he needed to taunt, to challenge. The two boys, men, wrangled over everything, so that everything was a showdown, hands at their six-guns. And Vladimir, who was reading Marx and Lenin now as often as he was reading poetry or his medical texts, seemed to be enjoying it. He'd always rise to the bait, try to measure himself against Anatoly.

They didn't argue when Pavel or Raisa were around, though. We hid our talk from Pavel and Raisa just the way the adults had once protected us. *This is not a conversation for children.* In those days, we grown children were the ones who needed to hide what we knew, or thought we knew, or were afraid to know. I quickly tired of those boys and their talk. I wanted it to stop. Because it exhausted me. And because it was dangerous. Much as we were our own closed circle – or so I thought – we were putting ourselves at risk with every word.

Anatoly and I had another one of our fights about it. One evening when he turned up late to meet me, he claimed that he hadn't been drinking, that he'd been out talking with Vladimir. I told him he was a bad influence. These conversations were damaging. Vladimir was being distracted from his school work. Anatoly was an idiot to think that such topics were harmless, without consequences. And he had no right to draw Vladimir into his idiocy. This analysis of the Soviet state, it wasn't idle conversation. It was tinder. If anyone overheard, we might all get into trouble. NKVD, informants, you didn't know who was standing beside you in the Metro station, who was reading next to you on a park bench. And the NKVD had listening devices; we'd all heard about them. Anatoly was silent for a moment and then launched into me, ridiculing my bourgeois concerns, circling me with his disdain, his certainties. He told me I was a coward and stalked out. Two hours later he was at the apartment door, drunk but contrite. It was his pattern: leaving, coming back, apologizing. Always coming back.

Chernikhov is giving a lecture at three o'clock. I've come early to the lecture hall to make sure I get a good seat. I take the stairs two at a time, though they're grooved with wear, each step a little concave hazard. At the top of the stairs there's a tight cluster of students. But instead of the usual casual buzz of conversation, gossip, their faces are taut.

Mikhailov, our studio instructor, has been arrested.

One of the things I liked most about Mikhailov was his sense of humour, how he was a bit outspoken, not as eternally careful as the other profs. He'd say things, joke.

It's a political charge – Mikhailov has been declared a *socially dangerous element. An admirer of American democracy.* Enemy of the people.

Then the talk stops because one of the professors opens the double doors to the lecture hall. We all file silently in. Polina has saved me a seat. We always sit beside each other at lectures; we share each others' notes too. So we sit and listen, as if nothing has happened. After the lecture, I ask Polina whether she's heard about Mikhailov. She nods, makes a face. "He's not the only Jewish faculty member to get in trouble."

"He was Jewish?"

"Of course he was," Polina says. "Couldn't you tell?"

Tell.

What tells Polina this? Some mark, some stain or word or scent gives her this certainty that she asserts so easily.

Polina's not Jewish. I've never thought about this before. It didn't matter.

"Mikhailov's real name was Mordukhov," she says.

A name, then, or a feature. A smudge that distinguishes him and at the same time makes him indistinguishable from others of his kind. My kind.

Polina's face is furrowed with concern. Mikhailov is one of her favourite teachers too.

Polina's face is innocent.

When I get home, Vladimir's at the table as usual, reading.

"Pavel and Raisa still at work?"

He nods. "We're supposed to eat without them."

"What's today's organ – the intestines? The reproductive system?" I lean over the table: Stalin's *Issues of Leninism*. "Are you reading that article Anatoly recommended?" The page he's reading has phrases underlined, the pencil marks of Vladimir's tight, meticulous handwriting crowding all the margins.

Vladimir nods, but his mouth goes tight. "I read everything Anatoly recommends."

For the past week or so, Vladimir and Anatoly have been circling each other, alternately locked in talk and aloof from each other.

Vladimir gets up from the table, goes to the samovar. He comes back with two glasses, passes me one. His hands are big, now; broad across the palm but the fingers are slender, supple. He settles down beside me on the davenport. "Did you see this?" he asks, picking up a candy-red cardboard cylinder from the end table and twisting it against one eye. A kaleidoscope. "Solly gave it to me."

"Solly Koznitsky? The fellow who's studying philosophy? The one in your literary circle?"

"Yup."

"I still haven't met him. You should bring him over for dinner."

"I will," he says. "Promise. It's just we study mostly at his house or his girlfriend Lena's . . ."

"Vladimir, you're not, you're not being indiscreet, are you?"

He looks at me, laughs. I can't laugh back. "You know what I mean. You're not talking about anything . . . about the stuff you and Anatoly talk about. It's a bad idea."

"I am a doctor in training. I intend to be the soul of discretion." Not an answer, really. He passes me the little cylinder. "Want to have a look?"

"Sure." I had a kaleidoscope back in Winnipeg. Pale bits of paper in it that the mirrors inside would pull into patterns. This one's better than my old one – no paper bits. Much more satisfying because there are infinite combinations. You can look at anything, change anything, even the least little chunk of a windowsill, corner of a room. Change anything through looking, though nothing really changes.

I turn to pick out the pattern on the davenport fabric, then to Vladimir's open book: Stalin's text taken apart, reorganized. An ordered distortion. I move to the margins of the page, play with Vladimir's pencilled notes; they look like a musical score. Then I focus it on Vladimir's face. I can see only a fragment – the diminutive topography where jaw meets ear – repeated and inverted so that it's unrecognizable as Vladimir. He's not closer or farther away; he's just not Vladimir.

"Annette, you all right?"

My face always gives me away. "A bad day," I say. "Another faculty arrest: Mikhailov. Turns out he's Jewish too."

Vladimir's face goes grim. "Our department has had two Jewish faculty fired. *Zionism in the service of American imperialism.*" His long fingers tap against the fabric of the davenport; he takes a sip of the honeyed tea.

"Annette," he says. I focus the kaleidoscope on his mouth, teeth. "Annette, I get scared."

I put it down. Vladimir is never afraid. "Scared of what?"

"Scared that we're fooling ourselves." He reaches for the kaleidoscope, trains it briefly on my face, then sets it down. "I'm scared that we keep wanting to see this country the way it was meant to be, the way it could be, the way it used to be – and not how it is. It's like kids telling themselves a story to keep from getting afraid. We tell ourselves one that makes us feel better, that lets us keep on hoping. But maybe that story is just a lie."

"My parents," I say, "they were like that. What they wanted wasn't what they got. But they wanted it so badly that they never let go of the wanting." I take the kaleidoscope back from him but don't look into it, just worry it in my hand, twisting it back and forth. "*My country.* I hated it when my mother said that. Like she owned it." The cylinder turns in my hands. "But I did choose. I chose this as my country."

"Pavel and Raisa . . . if I talked like this with them, they'd tell me we have to believe, have faith," Vladimir says.

"Faith in what?"

"The future, I guess. The possible. That somewhere, sometime, we'll be able to build the kind of socialism that Lenin and Marx meant for us to have. But I get sick of just sitting around talking."

"Have you and Anatoly had a falling out?"

Vladimir shrugs.

"Vladimir?"

"I'm tired of talk."

"What do you mean? Do you mean you want more than talk or that you want less talk?"

"I'm tired of it."

"That's not an answer."

He smiles, shrugs again. "*What is to be done?*"

"Don't go quoting Lenin on me," I say.

"You know that Lenin got the title from a novel by Chernyshevsky . . ."

"I don't care where he got the title! What we have to do, here and now, is be patient and wait it out."

"You sound like Anatoly," he says. "*You can't fight guns with sticks.*"

"That what he said?"

Vladimir nods. "He also said even talk is dangerous."

"And he's right, Vladimir." At last Anatoly has started to listen to me.

Vladimir smiles again. What is it? What does he want from me?

"Anatoly tells me that at present there's nothing we can do," he says.

"And what did you tell him, Vladimir?"

"I said: *Then let's do the nothing that we can*. A gesture, an act of faith." He's looking straight at me, his eyes clear, stripped of anything but his question.

"Are you asking me for an act of faith? Are you imagining that there's something you can do, something we can do?"

"Annette, don't you get tired of waiting?"

How much of my life has been spent waiting. I know that I can't drift. I can't let the world wash over me. I know that it's what I choose that gives me a life.

But the decision to wait, to endure, survive, after so many losses – it is a decision.

"Vladimir, you're being absurd. It's impossible. We have to pick our fights, decide what's worth fighting for."

"I know." As he does when he worries for me, he's taken my hand, is turning it soft quarter turns, left and then right. "*You can't fight guns with sticks.* Right?" He's smiling, a different smile now, but it makes me uneasy.

"It's true, Vladimir. We can't do anything. Or anything that we do would be useless. We have to admit it, even if we don't want it to be true. We can't tell ourselves a happier story here. It wouldn't do any good."

"I know."

"And besides, you're too clever to do anything foolish. Right?" He doesn't say anything. "Promise?"

"Promise." He says, turning my hand slightly to the right, then the left. "Nothing foolish."

Pavel and Raisa don't get home until after eleven o'clock. Raisa cuts a slice of farmer's cheese for herself, then another, which she holds out to me, smiling. Then, still chewing her mouthful of cheese, she stretches out on the davenport, her feet on Pavel's lap. "Annette, did you see we got a letter from Manya? It's on the desk. Your old school friend, Elena, has had a second baby, another girl. I thought we could send her that baby blanket we found in the market. And I can start a sweater for her." Raisa's taken up crocheting now, evenings, and as she shuttles between work and home on the trolley. "They were afraid Elena would need a Caesarian but everything went fine. The baby was born a week ago Monday."

"Monday's child." I say in English.

"What's that?" Raisa asks.

"There's a rhyme in English:

> *Monday's child is fair of face*
> *Tuesday's child is full of grace . . ."*

"Vladimir was born on a Wednesday – what's the rhyme for Wednesday?"

I can't remember.

"What day of the week were you born?" Raisa asks.

"I don't know."

I have no one to ask.

Did I not see what was at bottom in that conversation? Didn't I understand what Vladimir was asking of me, or, in the end, had decided not to ask of me? In the weeks that followed that day of the kaleidoscope, he was abstracted, even furtive, consumed by the exhilaration and intrigue of what he was doing. Raisa became impatient with his increased absences, his silences. Vladimir had always been so present with us, the core of our little makeshift family. He'd been open with his enthusiasms and ideas, engaged with all the little details of our lives. There was still the odd day when he would come home after school to sit at the table and peel the potatoes, mince the onions while Raisa masterminded dinner. He would have a special tenderness for us those evenings when he was back in family, would linger as Pavel and Raisa talked over their day, quizzing Raisa on some of the details of her cases.

But more often he would come home late, take the leftovers set aside for him in the pantry and head straight to his bed, where his light would be on late into the evening as he laboured over his medical books. For the first time, there was a segment of his life withheld from us. We told ourselves it was natural at his age. Told ourselves he was absorbed in medical school, in love, though no particular girl was mentioned.

The only names mentioned were Solly, and Solly's girl Lena. We could sense there was something special about this young couple by the almost-hidden smile of sly delight when Vladimir spoke of them. But we never met them. Bring your friends by for dinner, Raisa would say, and Vladimir would agree. Yes, they were coming Sunday; they were eager to meet the family. But then Sunday would come, and their plans would have changed. Sincere apologies, excuses, Vladimir's standard gentle regret. Next week, then? Yes, yes, Vladimir would agree. They'd find an evening next week. But as the weeks passed, they never quite managed to come. We never knew them. I never saw them, till that day when we were all to share a room.

Chapter Ten

❄

I'm dressed in the thick flannel nightgown Joseph brought me from Winnipeg, but my feet are bare as I stand in the dark street, my soles freezing, fused to the icy pavement. Papers, the voices are saying, we want your papers. My feet burning with cold.

I sit up in bed, pull the comforter down over my feet, look up. The dream has come into the room.

"Get up. Get dressed." Someone's speaking to me. "Show us your papers." A stranger's in the bedroom, another behind him blocking the doorway. They're wearing heavy overcoats. I can feel the chill coming off the thick cloth.

Now Raisa is in the room, an old suit jacket of Pavel's thrown over her nightgown; it comes almost to her knees. "We'll get dressed together," she says. The man turns silently away. What time is it? Outside the windows there's only darkness.

There are more strangers, tall, broad, crowding the apartment. One is talking to Pavel. What can they want? It has to be a routine documentation check, that's all. They do this, make random checks.

I can't button my blouse properly, my hands are shaking so badly. I pull my sweater over the pale yellow cotton – no one will see whether it's buttoned right or not. Raisa's put on the dark brown skirt, the fine woollen cardigan and white blouse she wears to work. "We're dressed," she says. "You can turn around." The light snaps on.

"Go into the front room." An order. The man is looking through us, as though we were small obstacles in his path; a pair of stones, twigs.

Vladimir, where's Vladimir? I'd forgotten: for the whole week he's been spending nights downstairs at Comrade Yevseyova's. Her niece is away for the week and the poor thing gets nervous when she has to be alone.

Earlier in the evening Vladimir had stood in the doorway of the apartment, his slippers dangling from one hand, an old bathrobe and pyjamas hanging over his arm. *Your toothbrush*, I said, and he grinned. *I've got it.* And kissed me on the forehead. That quizzical, amused look on his face. *It's nice of you to stay with her, Vladimir. You should have been a Boy Scout*, I said, and he'd frowned slightly, not following. *Canadian Pioneers*, I said. *I'm too old for the Pioneers, Annette, too old for the Komsomol.* And I smiled and told him, *Then you can join the Party*, and we both laughed, but I thought, maybe he will, someday. Maybe that would be best.

He's safe downstairs. Best keep him out of the way, keep him out of it.

Among all the men who are making the apartment small there's one who doesn't move: it's Polankov, the caretaker, his normally ruddy face gone white, his hands nervous in his lap. What's he doing here?

"Where is your son?" The man speaking towers over Pavel, my tall uncle; he's three times his breadth.

Pavel opens his mouth, closes it. Raisa puts a hand on his pyjamaed sleeve. "He's gone out with his friends," she says. "They're young people. Sometimes he doesn't come home all night . . ." She smiles, shrugs her shoulders. "Boys. What can you do with them?"

A sound, a low growl almost, from the table. It's Polankov, clearing his throat.

The man beside Pavel turns to Polankov. "What? What was that you said?"

Polankov's words are incoherent.

"Stop muttering. What is it you're trying to say?"

Polankov clears his throat again. "I said, she's lying." Raisa goes stiff. "Earlier in the evening I saw the boy go downstairs to the apartment across the hall."

"Which apartment?"

"Downstairs on the fourth floor," Polankov says. "Number seven. An old woman lives there with her niece: Yevseyova."

"Polankov . . ." As quickly as she says his name, Raisa covers her mouth. He doesn't look up. Bastard. Coward. He won't look at any of us.

Two of the men leave the apartment. We hear a loud knocking, muffled voices, the brief sounds of a scuffle. Raisa starts, moves towards the door just as the two men re-emerge, Vladimir between them, tall, and thin. And afraid. He's never afraid. He's gone white; his eyes are dull, unknowing. They've woken him too, and some part of him is still asleep, still unbelieving. He won't look at Pavel and Raisa, won't look at me, but his gaze scans the men, as if he's measuring them. As if he's measuring what's to come, making some sort of calculation.

"Vladimir Efron?" The tallest, broadest of the men goes over to him. Vladimir nods. "Read and sign."

Black letters on the small page; Vladimir's name and the round, official stamp: Arrest Warrant. MGB, Moscow Region. They're MGB, not local militia, police. MGB the new acronym for the NKVD. Names, signatures, flourishes – the banal insignia of bureaucracy. Vladimir's friend Solly's name is there as well. *Confirmed by the depositions of other arrested members . . .*

"Comrade," Pavel's voice wavers, "my son is a medical student, the top of his class. It must be a mistake."

"It's always a mistake."

"Comrade," Pavel says, touching the man's sleeve lightly, "Comrade."

The man stiffens at Pavel's touch. "If there's a mistake, then we'll sort it out. Read the documentation. It's all legal."

It's so familiar, the process by which he's being taken from us. First with Lev, then Polankov. And then all those whispered stories we've wanted to evade. This is how they come for you. This is how it happens – carefully, deliberately. There are procedures, papers to be signed, red tape.

"Sign."

Vladimir leans over the page. He looks up at me, and for the first time since he was taken into the room, our eyes engage. I can see the dullness of his fear sharpen into something different, some kind of knowledge.

Don't sign. If you don't sign it's just a piece of paper.

But as I'm thinking the words, Vladimir signs. His hand is trembling, though I can see he's holding his body still. His face has gone dull again, obedient. Pavel has his arm around Raisa's shoulder. She's holding herself still as well, though one hand clutches Pavel's arm. None of us moves; none of us says anything, our bodies compliant.

As long as you cooperate, everything will go smoothly. What good would it have done him not to sign? He'd have been beaten, dragged into the Black Raven anyway. The whole family would have been arrested if we'd made any trouble.

"And you," the man says, nodding at Polankov, "you sign here."

Polankov nods back, picks up the pen. That's why they brought him in. It's more procedure: he's the civilian witness protocol requires. He signs, his hand steady. Bastard.

"I'll get dressed," Vladimir says.

"Go with him." The man, the one giving all the orders, who must be the boss, gestures to one of the others to follow Vladimir into the bedroom.

A low mutter – it's Polankov.

"Speak up. I can't hear you."

"May I go now?" Polankov asks. "I want to go back to my apartment."

"You can go. You've done enough." A faint smile passes across the man's face and then, before it can vanish, before his expression can go back to its impassive norm, Polankov is gone.

I hear one of the men shouting. Except for the boss, I can't tell them apart.

"What are these?" He's waving a packet of letters tied with ribbon at Raisa. It's my hoard, the letters from Joseph, from Canada.

The man's face is red, an inch or two from Raisa's. He's shouting. "What are you hiding here?" The English is unintelligible to them. I can hear my old Pioneer leader's, Raya's, voice, when I was learning Cyrillic: *to us the Latin alphabet is foreign.* Us. Raisa's mouth is moving, but she can't seem to find any words. Pavel and Vladimir are also mute. My letters from home. Now the man is shoving the packet right in Raisa's face, shouting, "Tell me!"

"Don't talk to her like that!" I feel my own face go red, step towards him, wrench the packet from the meat of his hand. "It's my cousin who's under arrest, not my aunt. There's no need to shout; there's no need to be so uncultured." The man goes redder, but steps back. I set the letters on the table. They're not touching Joseph.

"Can you explain what these are?" he asks Raisa, his voice quieter now. "And you," he turns to me, his voice even, "you are to sit in that room."

I turn, walk back into the bedroom, put my hands in my lap. I can see Raisa's hands shaking. I've never seen those sturdy doctor's hands tremble. She undoes the ribbon, spreads out the letters, the envelopes. These fragile sheets of paper, the delicate squares of stamps. The stiff, elegant head of George VI, the white or dark military cap too large for his small, fine face. There are larger stamps too, the bigger denominations – size is value – rectangles with their peaceful graven landscapes, the blue and maroon and green dulled, as though the colour had faded, though they're only a few years old. I remember them now, those colours, remember them vivid, the deep green of the line of shelterbelt trees at the horizon, wheat the thick gold of a lion pelt. Taking the Moonlight Special back from the beach with Poppa. The language of home.

Raisa and the man are talking quietly, but I hear my surname spoken over and over again as Raisa counts out the letters, explaining: Gershon, Joseph. Gershon, Avram; Gershon, Anne. A murmur. Gershon, Ben. As though a net were being drawn round us all, though it's only me now, only me.

Pavel has taken a suitcase and set it on the davenport. And I hear it, the knife sharpener's bell, clear, pealing. It's here now. I knew it would come. I let it ring as Raisa comes quietly into the bedroom, her face still, impassive. She doesn't look at me, but I watch as she gathers an armful of heavy sweaters and socks, underwear, and I can see her hands twitch as she tries to control them. She goes into the front room, starts folding them into the suitcase.

The men – how many are there? I can't count them; they keep moving through the apartment. Two are going through every book in the bookcase, through the papers stacked on Pavel's desk, on tables, in corners. What are they expecting to find in books, in papers – razor blades? Bullets? The flattened ghost of a corpse pressed like a leaf between the hard-bound, worn covers of one of Pavel's agronomy textbooks?

Words. They're word hunters. Looking for dangerous, criminal words. These large men are afraid of black marks on white paper.

Now they're putting papers into folders. What are they taking? Vladimir's school essays? His volumes of Lenin? Nothing. There's nothing for them to find. It's madness. He talks with his friends, argues, debates. They're children; they chatter. There's nothing for these men to find.

Vladimir is in the doorway, mechanically putting on his coat. Then he stops, looks at me, looks at his father, his mother, then looks away, stalls.

"No," Raisa says dully, "not that one." And pulls another from the wardrobe. "This one is thicker."

"No, Momma, I can't. It's Poppa's."

"Don't argue with me, Vladimir. Just put it on." She adjusts the collar.

I get up from the bed. I've been sitting here for how long – hours? The sky is paler now, a pale day ahead of us. I've been drifting; I've been everywhere in the room, but now I snap into myself.

"Take leave of your parents now." The massive formality, even here, even now.

Pavel draws Vladimir to him, then Raisa. I'm across the room; in one slight movement I slip by the men. No. I will not let him go. I hold onto the lanky body, so tall, my head against the middle of his chest.

"I have to go." Vladimir says, gently letting me go. "It's all right, Momma, Poppa, Annette. I'll be all right."

And the room is suddenly empty of them, the overcoats, the anonymous men, Vladimir.

I let him go. *Promise.*

I shouldn't have let him go.

Raisa is on the davenport, her hands cupped over her face, rocking back and forth, back and forth the way I remember seeing the men in synagogue at prayer. Maybe she's praying now; maybe we're all at prayer. But to whom? Who would Raisa, the rationalist, the agnostic, address in prayer? God? The devil? Stalin?

The room is empty now, the table. There's only a glass of cold tea, the sugar bowl on the embroidered cloth. The letters. They've taken my letters.

"It's all right, Raisa," Pavel is saying. "He went quietly; no one made any kind of fuss. He's innocent. There's been a mistake. People *are* questioned and released. Vladimir hasn't done anything. He's just a boy."

"A mistake," Raisa echoes, lowering her hands, wiping her face on a sleeve. "They must have made a mistake."

The apartment is back to itself, composed. The books are orderly again in the bookshelves, papers on the desk. But the rooms wear that hunkered-down aspect that I remember from the war: waiting, afraid.

He's done nothing – he can't have done anything. So he and his friends talked; university students and their philosophy. He's done nothing. People *are* questioned and released. Lev was questioned and released. And Polankov – Polankov came back.

Polankov. He came back because Pavel and Raisa helped him, and then – the coward. Bastard. He was the one that told them Vladimir was downstairs. If he hadn't, would they have found Vladimir? Bastard. Traitor. Polankov and his unctuous gratitude; Polankov and his little deals, his arrangements. What did I expect? The bile rises in my throat, the rage. I want to go downstairs and tear his throat out. Bastard.

"Annette?"

Did I say it out loud? Raisa's standing in front of me, a blue striped tea towel in her hands. She's been polishing that same glass for fifteen minutes. I take it from her.

"Raisa, sit down."

Raisa sits, her hands, her mouth, the glass, dry. "I keep remembering," she says. "I keep remembering him as a baby. Why would I be remembering that now?"

"Raisa –" I touch her hand. Cold and dry.

"I keep seeing him as a newborn, that callus on the upper lip when he was born. It was slightly paler than the lip itself. A sucking pad, they call it. He must have sucked his thumb in the womb. Isn't that strange, to think that they have this life even before they're born?"

"Raisa – "

"Did I ever tell you that he never learned to latch onto the breast properly? The nipple cracked on one breast; it didn't heal for months." She looks up at me. "It was very painful. But you bear these things, you know. And the child survives."

"Raisa, it'll be all right. He'll come home. They'll release him."

Raisa draws back from me. "Of course he'll come home! He hasn't done anything! I have to finish the dishes," Raisa picks up the tea towel and is back at the dishes, bone-dry.

I hear something.

A scratching. It's Pavel. He's at the table, sitting, writing. He runs a hand through his hair.

"Pavel, what are you writing?" I ask.

He looks up at me, smiles, pushes the page towards me.

"Comrade Stalin," I read, *"I am appealing to you personally. There has been a mistake. My son has done nothing wrong . . ."*

We didn't know where he was. Lefortovo, Butyrka, Lubyanka – we counted the rosary of names in this city of prisons. We had no news, didn't even know what the charges were. We went from building to building, bureaucrat to bureaucrat, standing in endless, hopeless lines. It was a treasure hunt: one slip of paper with a name, an address, took us to a desk, a face, that in turn gave us another slip of paper that led us to another desk, another face. Forms to be filled out in triplicate. *You'll find out soon enough*, we were told. *You have to be patient, have to understand that certain procedures must be followed.*

And with the evasive answers came averted faces, a reluctance to breathe the air we breathed, as if, despite the barricades of their desks, their counters, their metal wickets, the officials were afraid of us, of contamination.

After three days of this, Pavel and Raisa insisted that I go back to school. Until then I'd been an absence among the many absences – Mikhailov and the others who'd become shadows, disappeared. When I slipped back into the studio in the late afternoon, after lectures were over, the dozen or so students still at work at their drafting boards looked right through me. Polina managed a few polite words and was gone before I could say a word. I'd become bad luck; bad luck or just bad.

I'm standing in the darkness across from Anatoly's apartment building. I need him. I've been leaving messages with the caretaker there and at his faculty office, but I haven't been able to reach him. I can't remember putting on my coat, my mittens; can't remember the walk to the stop, the trolley ride. I pull my scarf tighter against my throat, look up at the window to his room; it's the fifth floor. A light on up there, and a shadow crossing by the window: someone's home. I watch for more movement but can't make anything out. My hands, toes, are going numb.

I cross to the entrance and touch the switch. A pale yellow light trickles in, filling the hallway. Five flights. I knock at the door. There's silence at first, then footsteps. Someone comes to the door, waits. It opens. Misha.

"Annette – hullo." He's rumpled, as usual. There's a heel of rye bread, half chewed, in his hand.

"I'm sorry, Misha – are you in the middle of dinner?"

"Just a snack," he says, wiping his mouth with the back of his hand.

"Is Anatoly home?" Do I hear something, someone else in the room?

"Anatoly? No. No, he's not home."

"I left a couple of messages but I haven't heard from

him." I'll tell Misha what happened, the arrest, and he'll ask me in, make tea, let me wait until Anatoly gets home. But he's standing there, awkward, blocking the doorway. "Do you know when he'll be back?"

"He's um, he's . . ."

"Is he in trouble again? Did he get suspended again?"

He nods. "Yeah. He got suspended." Misha's still got the bread in his hand, a closed grip, as though I'd want to take it from him. "Um, day before yesterday. He was pretty down about it. Drinking. You know. I haven't even seen him for a couple of days. You know what he's like when he gets in trouble."

I hear a muffled scraping from somewhere in the room. "I'm sorry," I say. "Have you got company?"

"Company? No. No, I'm just working."

It must be a girl. He's got Nadya or some new girl visiting and doesn't want me to know. No wonder he's so fidgety.

"Well, I won't keep you then. Thanks," I say. We stand there another moment. "Thanks."

He tries for a smile, closes the door.

I've been in line since eight o'clock. The usual wait: this time it's beef we're hoping for. I'm just another in the stolid line of citizens, impassive, imperturbable. For the last half-hour I've been chatting with the woman in front of me, the routine pleasantries, complaints. It's nine forty. Since nine o'clock the line has been inching along. I exchange a few more comments with the woman, then, at her urging, go to the front of the line to check how empty the shelves look and see whether our wait is going to be worth anything. A few grumbles as I go back to my place, but they subside quickly enough. And then something keeps drawing my gaze forward, something nagging at me.

I look idly at a tall woman a bit ahead of me in line. She must be a good twenty years older than me but she holds her head lightly, gracefully.

And then I see it, three ahead of the woman, the back of *his* head, Anatoly's, the light brown hair curling around his ears, at the nape of his neck. He's not on a drunk; he's here, in line.

How could I have been so stupid as to accept the transparent lie? It was Anatoly who had been skulking at the back of the apartment, hiding from me. He's hiding from me now. He must have seen me when I went to the front. He saw me and said nothing. Didn't reach out his hand, touch my sleeve, call: *it's me*. Hadn't done that, had, instead, must have, let me go. There ahead of me, the sweet back of his head, the straight, strong neck. Anatoly, who saw me, but let me go.

I look at him, and remember that day we met in Moscow, another line, another wait that became our beginning. Will this be how we end, rigid, unthinking, accepting? I look at the back of his head and think how much I love him, how good it is to see the back of his head. What does this mean – that I love him, that it's good to see the back of his head, that some part of me goes, part of me steps forward, touches his neck just where the hair curls against it, part of me rests a hand lightly on his shoulder, calls him, but I stand in line, not moving? I stand in line, something in me going hard, cold. Then I turn around, empty-handed; turn and leave, let him go.

It's after lunch when I get home. As I start up the stairs, the Polankovs' door closes quickly, quietly. When I come round the landing, I can smell beeswax. A rag in a hand is rubbing slow circles into the wooden banister. Round and round and slowly upwards the worn cloth moves, leaving a sheen behind, the tight oak grain of the wood come cleanly into focus. Then the hand stops. A deep breath. I take another step. It's Polankov's wife. She looks briefly up at me and her eyes fill, then her hands continue.

At the next landing Comrade Yevseyova is sorting through her mail. When she sees me, an envelope slips from her hands. I bend to pick it up.

"Comrade Yevseyova, you've dropped this."

She takes it from me and then takes my hand, brings it to her lips. "My dear girl. My dear girl. It's not right." Touches my cheek. A soft noise from below. She goes stiff, then bends towards me, whispers in my ear. "It's not right." And backs into her apartment, closes the door.

That afternoon when I go back to the studio there's a note left on my drafting table. Anatoly has written: Misha told him I'd been by. He's in a bit of trouble and is lying low. He hopes school is going well. He's sorry he hasn't been able to see me. It's not that he doesn't want to be with me. But he doesn't want me to get into trouble. He wants me to focus on my school work. So, for now, we shouldn't be seen together. It's not safe for me. He sends his love to Raisa and Pavel, and of course to Vladimir.

I set the note down. He can't stop lying. He can't stop. Hold on. Let go.

This distance opening all around me, a clearing.

Chapter Eleven

We're outside Lefortovo Prison. I can't imagine a structure more ordinary than this building, its five stories, dull walls, the monotony of its windows. The wind is cold, coils of filthy snow still flung at the base of the walls. Raisa and I are in a long line, mostly of women, waiting outside the gate.

We've asked to see him. He's here in Lefortovo, somewhere; that much we know. So far, we've been refused: *Can't be helped. Not possible. Not allowed. Come back tomorrow and we'll see what can be done.* If we can't see him, maybe we can get a package through. I'm carrying Raisa's carefully prepared bundle of clean clothes, non-perishable food. Each time we've waited two hours, or four, until finally the line of half-frozen women dissolves into the evening.

Suddenly, we're being waved forward. *Efron, Raisa; Gershon, Annette.* A voice summons us brusquely.

We push forward through the line of women, Raisa calling, "Yes, yes, that's us." The gate opens and we walk through into the chilly halls of the prison, follow the man into an anteroom, are told to be seated.

"Annette," Raisa says, her voice soft. Her hands droop at her side; they're so rarely still. As if to find some work, they go through her handbag, take out a clean white handkerchief, snap the clasp shut. "You've got lipstick on your cheek," she says. I scrub at my cheek.

Perhaps an hour goes by. The telephone rings. The official answers it. *Yes. No. Very well then.* He looks up from his desk, examines us distastefully, consults a file, inspects us again and then rises, goes into a backroom. We can hear the sound of muted conversation. Not long after, he emerges, his face dour.

"The girl," he says.

"Pardon?" Raisa asks.

"The girl: Gershon. You're Gershon?"

I nod.

"You can go in."

"Why? Why not me?" Raisa asks, her voice rising, loud.

"The Gershon girl can go in. Or not, if she doesn't want to."

"I'll go," I say, gathering the package, my coat, my handbag. "It's all right, Raisa."

"The handbag," the man says, "leave it where it is."

I pass the bag to Raisa.

"Good," Raisa says. "Tell him –"

"This way." The man points to a door on the right.

"Annette, are you sure you want to go . . . ? Maybe, maybe you shouldn't . . ." She glances at the guard, bites her lip. She's afraid to let me go, afraid not to.

"It's good," I say. "Don't worry. I'll give him the package."

"This way, miss." A guard in uniform is waiting in the corridor.

And then Raisa's standing beside me, pulling at the guard's sleeve. "Comrade, Comrade," she says. "I think it should be me. I have to see him. You'll let me see my son . . ."

He shakes her hand away, takes me by the elbow. "Are you coming, miss?"

I nod, and Raisa steps back. The door closes on her left standing, holding the two bags against her solid little chest, her mouth slightly open, as though there were something more she wanted to say, as though the words took up some small room in her mouth.

I have new shoes, good ones, leather from Czechoslovakia, and they clack clack clack as I walk down the corridor. I feel myself towed along behind the guard. We go down a long narrow corridor to a gate that another guard opens with a set of keys, then down a long flight of stairs that keep turning back on themselves. There's netting across the gap in the stairwell.

"The prisoners," the guard says, the first thing he's said since he told me to follow him, "they like to jump." He points to the netting, grins.

Jump? *The fallen*. Ben. I see them now, the fallen. I have to lean on the railing and stop.

"Come on, miss," his voice is stern. "Don't dawdle."

Another guard unlocks another door, which opens onto a paved courtyard with a few weeds between the cracks in the paving. Though I don't look up, I can feel the height of the building around me, brick and concrete. *Soviet architecture, ideal Soviet architecture.* No curves to calculate here.

Another guard, another door, another staircase and, at yet another locked gate, we stop. The guard's a woman this time, stocky, a bit taller than me. "Raise your hands," she says, no expression on her face. Blue eyes with no particular malice, no interest, no questions for me; she expects nothing from me, has nothing to say.

Those button blue eyes, a red curl straying over one eyebrow.

Tattletale.

She runs her hands down my arms, then my shoulders, my breasts. Along my belly, between my legs. Then down my legs, lightly over the calves.

"Turn around."

"Sonya?" I ask.

The blue eyes give nothing back. Her hands run quickly over my back, my backside, legs. Cursory, now, but she must feel me shaking.

"Go ahead. Go on," she says, nodding to my guard, who has looked away and now looks back.

Is it Sonya, my old playmate, old tormenter? Her eyes gave me nothing. It doesn't matter. It's Sonya, or some other little girl who grew up to this.

My guard is leading me through a narrow corridor, its walls lined with identical anonymous iron doors, a peephole, an opening like a mail slot in every door.

He gestures me to stop. I stand looking at his broad back, slightly stooped shoulders, wondering what his playground games were. A little ways down the corridor two figures go silently by: a prisoner and a guard. Like us. For the first time I notice someone at the far end of the corridor – the traffic guard who's controlling our movements. He gestures with two little flags to signal us to move. My guard and I start forward, then stop again.

I can feel this building with its waiting rooms, its cells, basements, interrogation chambers, functioning around me: doors opening, closing. Gates being locked, windows, gazes pressing against their bars. A factory of some sort, a machine digesting the lives inside. I've been lifted out of my life and set into this machine.

And I don't know any more where I'm going, can't remember deciding to follow this man I don't know. But I did decide; my body decided for me, setting my handbag in Raisa's lap, settling my coat more squarely on my shoulders.

The guard fiddles with a ring of keys, opens one of the doors into a small room empty except for a table, a bench. He points to the bench, tells me to sit down, then closes the door, locks it.

There are tears running down my face. I wipe my face on my sleeve, then notice that Raisa's handkerchief is in my hand. I have to stop shaking.

A sound. I hear it clearly again, that knell. It's here with me in the room again, swaying in my head. Two beats, light and then heavy, and a gap in between. It's come.

I have to settle myself, listen.

Silence except for the distant taut flap of guards' communication flags signalling the prisoners' slow waltz from room to room, cell to cell.

Silence then, except for the flags, the occasional footsteps.

How long have I been sitting here: an hour? a half-hour?

The room is freezing. The walls are a dark green mixed with brown. There's a small window high in the wall, wire mesh soldered over the glass, the bench I'm sitting on, a battered table.

What if they don't let me out? Maybe it's all a ruse: they have no intention of letting me see Vladimir; they just thought up an easy way to trap me, arrest me . . .

Arrest me for what? I haven't done anything.

The door opens. It's the guard who brought me here. He faces me and for the first time I can see him: a lanky, horse-faced man. "A few more minutes, miss. You'll have to wait." He leans against the wall across from me, takes out a paper packet of mints, striped white and green. He puts one in his mouth, then offers the packet. I shake my head.

We wait. Then footsteps. The door opens again. Two new guards, enormous men, enter. Their faces are round, pink, well-fed.

And between them is Vladimir.

I stand up. He doesn't move, a pale smile tugging at his mouth. *I am not who I was.* They've shaved his head, cut off the silky brown hair. His hazel eyes have gone darker, dim. Where has the boy gone? He's been evacuated, and now there's this husk left. He's hunched around his body, stooped, as though he expects at any minute to be hit. As though he's trying to protect what's left of him.

"Vladimir," I whisper.

The door clicks shut, locked. We're alone.

I go to him. He puts his arms around me. I lean my head against his chest, listen. If we're left alone just a little longer, if I'm very quiet, I'll be able to hear the blood moving through him. Just a little more time and I'll be able to hear the electric rustle of his thought.

"You're shaking," he says. "Sit down, Annette. Sit."

We sit together on the bench. I hold his hands, try to warm them. He's shaking too.

I pass him the parcel. "From Raisa. Did you get them – the other parcels we sent, the letters?"

"No. I'm in solitary. We don't get anything." He undoes the brown paper, takes out the loaf of bread, breaks off a piece and starts chewing. "It's good. It's so good."

"There's sausage. Are you all right? Can you sleep any?"

"Not much." He's so thin. "They leave the light on in my cell all night. And then half the time they wake me in the middle of the night to take me for interrogation."

"The middle of the night? Why?"

"All sorts of interesting rules here, Annette." His lips are chapped, cracked. He licks them. My mouth is dry too. "Prisoners are instructed to lay out their socks and towel on the foot of the cot every night. Mugs must be set on the bedside table with their handles towards the door of the cell, aluminum spoons set precisely beside them. Prisoners may have a daily fifteen-minute walk, but it is forbidden to stop, or listen, or watch the sky. It is forbidden to pick the dandelions that grow in the cracks in the pavement. It is forbidden to sleep past the guard's wake-up shout, even though it's still night when he calls us, and all we've got to keep us from the cold and damp is the coarse army blanket they give us. But not me, Annette. I'm lucky. I still have the sweaters Momma packed, and Poppa's coat. I can wrap the blanket around Poppa's coat. I wear it all the time. There's so much I have to do, Annette, and so much I mustn't do."

He stops. He's so thin. I didn't think he could get any thinner. His hand is thinning in mine as I hold it, slipping away.

"And food? Are you getting enough to eat? Have the sausage. There's chocolate. Raisa packed some chocolate."

"It's all right. They give me coffee, black bread. Fish soup of a sort. Sometimes borscht." He bites into the sausage, sighs.

"Have they told you the charges?" My voice is as soft as I can make it.

"The charges?" That smile again. "Article 58. I'm accused of treason against the Motherland, organization, anti-Soviet agitation and terror. I'm accused of being a member of a youth counter-revolutionary terrorist organization –"

"It's nonsense," I say, cutting him off.

"No, it's not. I'm guilty as charged."

I put my hand to his mouth. "Sh! Don't joke!"

"I'm not joking. It's all true."

"Vladimir," I move closer to him, whisper in his ear, "don't say these things. We have to be careful. There may be," I lower my voice further, "some sort of listening device in the room. Why else would they have left us alone together? It has to be a trick."

"It doesn't matter," he says.

"What do you mean?"

"It doesn't matter. I've told them everything. It's the only way. Make a clean breast of it; tell the truth."

"What truth? You haven't done anything."

"We did; we did. All of us."

"All of who?"

"Me. My friend Solly, Solomon. And his girl Lena. We formed a group. And there are others."

"Vladimir, don't . . ."

"I told you Annette. It doesn't matter. They know everything. They've known everything all along. They've kept a file on me since I was nine, since I sent Comrade Stalin that letter about the beggars. We had a group. We called it the Group for the Liberation of the Cause of the Revolution." He smiles miserably. "We argued for two weeks over the name."

"Vladimir, you shouldn't tell me this. You shouldn't say so much."

"I told you, it doesn't matter. I told them everything. They got to Solly first and he told them about me, and about Lena. We have to tell the truth."

"There can't be anything to tell!"

"We talked, Annette. We had counter-revolutionary discussions."

"Counter-revolutionary? What do you mean?"

"You know. Discussions. Criticizing everything. At Solly's or Lena's. We'd talk. At first we just talked about literature and stuff like that. While we were studying. But then everything changed. After all that talk with Anatoly, all that political theory. I started telling Solly about Anatoly, what he'd say. And then, one day early in January, Solly and I went to the movies. We were in the lobby, and Solly suddenly was talking to me, telling me what he really believed, talking openly – about politics, about what he thought of the Soviet Union, what had happened to the Revolution."

"Vladimir, you shouldn't, you shouldn't have . . ."

"We knew that; we knew it was dangerous. So we decided that we would meet again to talk more outdoors, where no one would hear us. We walked and walked, Annette. We walked all over the city. At first we argued about everything. There wasn't a thing we agreed on. But the more we talked, the more we understood what we wanted, what we were hoping for. It was, it was as if I could suddenly see everything, Annette. It was as if everything was suddenly clear. And there was something I could do. Lena would talk with us too. Solly kept asking to meet Anatoly, but it never happened." He looks up at me. "I keep telling them Solly never met with Anatoly, Annette, but they don't believe me. And they're asking about you too, Annette, but I told them you weren't involved, that you never met Solly. They never believe me. They keep asking. They keep asking the same thing over and over and over again. I'm so tired."

He's turning my hand in his, then he raises it to his mouth, touches his lips against the palm. "Annette. Momma, Poppa . . ."

"They're fine. They're all right. You know how strong they are."

"I know. You too. You have to be, don't you? Solly was so strong. A few weeks after that day of walking, Solly told me he'd do it. He was ready to fight to change things. He wanted to know if I was too."

Fighting guns with sticks.

"I didn't agree to anything, not right away. But when I thought about it, I knew it was what I wanted. To fight. So I said yes. And that was when Solly told me that they already had a group, an organized group, and that I should consider myself a member of it. He said he couldn't tell me anything in detail about who belonged, but that he did know that there were more than a dozen of us. They'd already made up an executive committee. Solly and two others were the executive."

"Vladimir, don't tell me this. It can't be true."

"Don't worry, Annette. I keep telling them you and Anatoly didn't know anything about it. And it's not like we did much. We fought about everything." He smiles. "We just couldn't agree. And then we figured that the best thing to do would be to try to open up a discussion. We wanted to have a newspaper. We were trying to get a hectograph, print copies. Lena, Solly and I were going to write articles that would get people talking about what they believed in. Openly. We were going to make twenty copies of the newspaper and distribute them to everyone in the organization. Maybe more, distribute them around the schools."

"That's all you did?"

"Solly and I wanted to write a book. We were going to call it *State Capitalism*. We talked about that for a week, argued about the title, the approach. Then we changed our minds. We figured that what we needed to write was a book on the history of the Party, the direction it had taken.

We were going to call it *Thirty Years*. I would have shown you what we wrote, Annette, but nothing ever came of it. We never finished writing anything. We never got anywhere; we argued too much. So you see? I did everything they say I did. And now I have to tell them the truth. They know everything anyway. They had listening devices in Solly's apartment; they recorded us."

The building bears down on us and I can see it now – section, plan, elevation – this prison, its labyrinth of cells, bars, staircases, corridors. And moving fluidly through the concrete and brick arteries and veins, the life inside: these prisoners yoked to their guards, the monstrous couples they form, half human, half animal. Vladimir's not the one who's guilty.

"What did they record? It's nothing," I say. "Nothing but talk. You didn't do anything wrong."

"It wasn't just talk, Annette. We, we discussed taking action. We had huge arguments. Solly had a gun. He, he even talked once about blowing up a Metro station . . ."

"A gun? What kind of a gun?"

He looks sheepish, chagrined. "From his brother; from the war. It didn't work."

"You promised me, Vladimir. You promised."

"I promised not to do anything foolish. It wasn't foolish."

Not foolish! – toying with rebellion, playing at a revolution! A broken gun. He'd give away his freedom, everything, his whole life, for these childish pranks?

"What do you think you're doing?" I say. "Casting yourself as a hero of the Revolution?" I grab him by both arms, shake him. "A hero! What makes you think revolutions have heroes?" I let go, get up, wanting to walk away, but there's nowhere to go.

He covers his face with his hands, rocking, a dry gasping wracking his narrow chest. He's a child.

They're children, all of them – Vladimir, this Solly, the girl.

Articles he never wrote, newspapers he never printed. Surely the authorities can't seriously be charging him with treason? Maybe they're bluffing; maybe they want to give these naughty children a good scare, give them a year or two in exile for the nothing they've done. And they'll be out, and all right, and everything will start all over again.

But they are: they are charging them with treason. And the sentence for treason – I don't want to think about the sentence. I don't want Vladimir to think about it.

I sit beside him, take his hands from his face, stroke them. "Vladimir?" He looks up, wipes his face on his sleeve.

"Vladimir, I'm sorry."

He's taken my hand now, turning it his quarter turns: to the left, then the right.

The horse-faced guard comes in, an amused sort of smile on his face. "You have fifteen more minutes."

They must be listening.

The guard looks at us and his face suddenly changes. "Fifteen more minutes." Briefly his face seems sad, almost human. He leaves, shutting the door.

We have fifteen minutes. I won't let them take him from me, not this time. "Vladimir," I whisper, pulling him to me, holding him against me. I want what I want. They're not going to take him from me. "Vladimir." I stroke his chest, his face. He's not crying now; he's holding on, pressing his mouth against my hair, breathing me in. I hold on, hold tighter, won't let him go. All my body wants to keep him. It's with my body I'll keep them from taking him away. I kiss his chest, his shoulders. He says nothing, no words any more, just our bodies. Our bodies decide. He puts his mouth against mine. *Have me so you can keep me. Remember me with your body.* His body held against mine, pressed hard now, as if he wanted to erase, just for this moment, the border between us. And we do. There's no time for more than this: my body held against his, legs held around him, him inside me. Where I'll keep him. His eyes are open, looking into mine, steady, holding onto me. In the cold room we're both sweating, our bodies sheeted in sweat. I can feel the bones of his rib cage against my chest, can feel his spine under my hands. I can feel myself both drawing him in and letting him go, letting myself go. The border between us eradicated, so that I can know him and keep him, a part of him. Not just memory. He pulls me tightly against him, releases a small cry.

We hear something.

He lets me go, lets go.

We slip apart, away, quick as we can settle ourselves, our clothes; hear footsteps at the door and then the lock turning, the door opening.

The door opens and everything shifts. It's over. The two men, immense, take his arms, take him away.

But I'm concentrating. More and more I am myself. I'm crouched in a corner of the room, concentrated, shrunk into myself so that I can hold on to what I have of him, of myself. I feel myself gripping down, bearing down on the life I feel approaching, the life I can almost touch, the one I'm giving myself, the one I'll give to the child I know will be born.

Chapter Twelve

I would like to stop here. I would like to stop at this moment when we gave our daughter life, as though we willed her into being. We did. I would like to stop here but I mustn't. I have to go on to what happened next.

They let me go back down the hallways and staircases to the room where Raisa was still waiting, still hanging on to our purses as though that would save us. And they let us both go home, to the apartment, to Pavel. Briefly. Back in the apartment I said as little to Pavel and Raisa as possible, lied as best I could, which is not very well. I had given Vladimir the package; we knew he was alive. We had something to keep us going. But Raisa soon pried the charges out of me – not just treason, but terrorism – and we could not keep from thinking about what the worst might be. I knew that now more than ever I had to protect them, tell them as little as possible of Vladimir's "confession." But I did try to assure them that the charges couldn't possibly stick, that he had done nothing. He had done nothing.

I think they chose to believe me, because it was best to believe. I don't know now what I believed at the time. But what carried me through those days was the certainty that my act of love, of defiance, was right. I remain certain of it, know it a choice I will never recant. All my foolishness before and since, my vanities, my stupidity – none of the evidence against my own good sense keeps me from the conviction that taking Vladimir into me and giving our daughter her life was right.

So our diminished little family held itself together with hope, and disbelief, until, a few weeks later, the MGB came for me too. In daylight this time. I don't think we were surprised to see the men at our door again. Nothing made much sense by then, or perhaps everything made no sense. Like Vladimir, mute, obedient, I signed the arrest warrant. There was less formality this go-round; Raisa had no time to pack me a bag. I was hustled out of the apartment carrying nothing. I remember Pavel holding Raisa in his arms to keep her upright, remember the destroyed look on her face. She'd lost for the moment the stamina that had carried her through Vladimir's arrest.

They shoved me into the Black Raven. The doors closed, and there was no light, and I felt a void invade me, felt hope evacuated. I was alone, or I thought I was alone because I wasn't sure then that my daughter was with me. I clung to the floor of the van, believing I didn't have the strength even to lift my head. I didn't know what strength I would find.

I wonder if that was the moment I was most afraid, the moment that, not knowing for certain that I had my daughter, I felt that I had lost everything. That I could do nothing. In the back of that van, I felt for the first time the full power of the State.

The State apparently feels remorse. My blue file folders prove it. Because the new, improved State has given me back everything it took, at least in the form of documentation. I have everything. Even those pieces of paper that speak straight from the void; the pieces of paper in which I stand accused, in which we all stood accused:

> Arrest Warrant dated 10 April 1951 for Annette Gershon. She is accused of being a member of a counter-revolutionary youth group, based on the testimony of the following other arrested members of the group: Vladimir Efron and Anatoly Trubashnik.

Their names are printed on the warrant, Vladimir and Anatoly. Just as Solly's name was printed on Vladimir's warrant. Did they truly name us? Probably. I can't know, because there were so many lies that the truth is irretrievable. And it doesn't matter. They would have taken me anyway.

And I was taken. Hustled out of Pavel and Raisa's apartment, shoved in the Black Raven, driven to Lefortovo prison, placed, like Vladimir, like the others who were arrested, in solitary. And, like Vladimir, like the others, I was interrogated. Let the State offer its version:

> Record of the Interrogation of Prisoner
>
> 7 May 1951. Gershon, Annette, date of birth: 1926; place of birth: Winnipeg, Canada; nationality: Jewish; citizenship: USSR. Until arrest, student of architecture, Mossovet Architectural Workshops.

Interrogation began at 22:45.

QUESTION: You stand accused under the following sections of the 58th article of the Criminal Code of the Union of Soviet Socialist Republics: 1-a, 8 and 10 of being a member of a youth counter-revolutionary terrorist organization. Do you understand the accusation?

ANSWER: I do. I am accused of being a member of a youth counter-revolutionary organization.

QUESTION: Do you acknowledge your guilt?

ANSWER: No, I do not. I was not a member of any counter-revolutionary organization.

QUESTION: When did you join the counter-revolutionary organization?

ANSWER: I was not a member of any counter-revolutionary organization.

QUESTION: Under whose influence did you join? Did your cousin Vladimir Efron not recruit you as a member of the Group for the Liberation of the Cause of the Revolution?

ANSWER: I was not a member of any counter-revolutionary organization.

QUESTION: You did not become a member of the youth counter-revolutionary organization the Group for the Liberation of the Cause of the Revolution?

ANSWER: No, I did not.
QUESTION: You did not become a member of any other counter-revolutionary organization?
ANSWER: No, I did not.
QUESTION: Vladimir Efron has testified that you had many conversations of an anti-Soviet disposition.
ANSWER: If I am guilty of being of an anti-Soviet disposition, I still did not join any counter-revolutionary organization.
QUESTION: You are not being honest. Tell the truth!
ANSWER: I have told the truth.
QUESTION: You admit to being of an anti-Soviet disposition?
ANSWER: Yes.
QUESTION: Be more specific regarding the nature of these conversations.
ANSWER: My cousin and I had many conversations on many topics.
QUESTION: I ask you again: what was the nature of your discussions?
ANSWER: We shared an interest in Soviet history and political theory.
QUESTION: Did Solomon Koznitsky not recruit you as a member of the Group for the Liberation of the Cause of the Revolution?
ANSWER: I was not a member of any counter-revolutionary organization. I have never met Solomon Koznitsky.

QUESTION: Vladimir Efron has testified that his cell of members included himself, Elena Tarasova and Solomon Koznitsky. Were you also a cell member?
ANSWER: I was not aware of the membership of the cell.
QUESTION: But you were aware of the existence of the cell?
ANSWER: I was not aware of the existence of the cell, or of the counter-revolutionary organization.
QUESTION: Again, I urge you to tell the truth: you were not aware of the counter-revolutionary youth organization?
ANSWER: I was not.
QUESTION: What activities did you undertake as a member of this counter-revolutionary organization?
ANSWER: I was not a member of any counter-revolutionary organization.
QUESTION: Anatoly Trubashnik has testified that you had many conversations of an anti-Soviet disposition.
ANSWER: Anatoly and I shared many interests, including an interest in Soviet history and political theory.
QUESTION: And Trubashnik shared these unhealthy opinions with you?
ANSWER: We were friends who shared many conversations.

QUESTION: Did Trubashnik not supposedly "prove" to you that Trotsky had allegedly been an outstanding historical figure?

ANSWER: I do not recollect any conversations between Anatoly and me regarding Trotsky's historical position.

QUESTION: What is the nature of your relationship with Anatoly Trubashnik?

ANSWER: We had friendly relations. He visited me frequently at our apartment.

QUESTION: Did you have conversations of a political nature with your so-called "cousins" Raisa Efron and Pavel Efron?

ANSWER: No, I did not.

QUESTION: Were you aware of a letter that Pavel Efron wrote to Comrade Stalin dated February 10, 1951?

Answer: Yes I was.

QUESTION: What was the nature of its contents?

ANSWER: I believe Pavel was asking Comrade Stalin to look into my cousin Vladimir Efron's arrest.

QUESTION: Were you aware of the anti-Soviet nature of the contents of the letter written by Pavel Efron dated February 10, 1951?

ANSWER: I did not read the entire contents of the letter.

QUESTION: I ask you again: were you aware of the anti-Soviet contents of this letter?
ANSWER: I did not read the entire letter.
QUESTION: And you never had conversations of a political nature with either Raisa or Pavel Efron?
ANSWER: I did not.

Signature of Prisoner:

____

I sit in the interrogation room on a wooden bench in front of a wooden desk, the only light the watery glimmer of the dim light bulb overhead, going over the official transcript of my interrogation. Bare though the room is, it's crowded with what I remember: my father handing me an orange, my mother stirring cake batter. Why am I here? For no reason. For so many reasons. Because my father wanted a better world, because my mother wanted to go home. Because there is no Poppa, no delicatessen. I'm no one's daughter. Because I have to sign a piece of paper full of lies.

What would my father do?

What would my mother do?

My father wanted to give me the world. My mother held on to herself, kept everything good. She gave me nothing. Or she gave me a gift that wasn't for me – she gave nothing and nothing was wasted. He wanted to give me the world, but would he have given in? He gave in so many times.

She wouldn't have given in. She held on to herself, to everything good.

What is the world my father would have given me? The world isn't good. The world that built the prison that keeps me, keeps Vladimir and the others. But the world is good. And I am holding on. For myself. For the child I'm holding. What can they do to me?

Put me in prison.

All right then, I'm in prison.

So what? So what.

In this moment, waiting to sign or not to sign, it doesn't matter what they do to me. It doesn't matter how I'm punished.

They can't make me do anything. Not if I'm not afraid.

And I'm not afraid.

I won't give them anything.

I've done nothing wrong.

My interrogator takes the transcript, types a furious sentence at the end:

> The interrogation concluded at 5:30. Note that prisoner refused to sign the minutes of the interrogation. Interrogation was concluded by interrogator of the Department on Particularly Important Investigations of the MGB of the USSR.
>
> [Signed] Colonel Yevdokimov

And then I was taken back to my own little room, the cell that sheltered me and the girl who was growing in me. I don't remember ever being sick during my pregnancy, though all the women I know tell stories, tales of morning sickness, of eating only crackers, drinking only soda water, the only thing they could keep down. I ate whatever they fed me. Maybe it was she who sustained me, my girl. I know that she steadied me, gave me the strength I needed to carry us both through. I built the months of my pregnancy and incarceration, the months of waiting for birth and for trial, out of hope, out of stubbornness, determined that this child be born, and born well.

Even inside the machinery of Lefortovo, there were those who still found something human within themselves. An extra blanket appeared on my cot, thick and clean. The prison doctor who checked me over suddenly walked to his desk and handed me an apple. I remember how slowly I ate it, back in my cell; the smallest of bites, to make it last. So I nibbled away the time till my daughter was born, or it nibbled away at me.

And so the State acknowledged my daughter's birth. Maybe it's the light this evening, but these papers seem so bright to me now. I finger the stiff, official paper:

> Birth Certificate dated 10 December, 1951; a female child born to Annette Gershon and Vladimir Efron. Weight: 2.7 kilograms; place of birth: Lefortovo Prison Infirmary, Moscow.

It was an easy birth. And after she was born I built the nights and days out of her breathing.

I'm rocking the baby, my back pressed into the spooled ribs of the stiff wooden rocker they've given me. The locked room in the infirmary is dark except for a pale light that leaks through the square window in the door. Her small body is limp with sleep, but there's no telling for how long, because my daughter's sick again, the fine hair on her forehead damp, her breathing rapid. She was sick and then better, but now she's sick again. The night nurse won't listen to me, refuses to call a doctor. The day nurse doesn't come in until eight. Her touch, the way she'll tuck the corner of the blanket in around the baby – I can tell that she feels something for us. But until she comes, there's nothing for me to do but wait and see this child through the night. In the darkness, in the muddy fear filling my body, time seems to slow, as though my own heart were beating slower, as though I were somehow outside the flow of time.

There's nothing more to do, but I have to do something. I feel that panic, the animal reflex: fight or flight. Tell me, Vladimir, what happens when you can't do either?

I'm holding on. I won't let go, not of my daughter, not of who I am, what the truth is. I'm no one's daughter; I'm my mother's, my father's. I'm holding on to being stubborn. I haven't done anything wrong. I won't give them anything. In daylight, in my right mind, I know I've done nothing, that it can't be that bad. But these nights of sickness, waiting for the fever to break, waiting for trial – they're the worst. This is when I believe anything might happen.

Suddenly the baby stirs. I try to soothe her, try somehow to extend my own body to encompass hers, touching, smoothing. Everything, all my life, has come down to this darkened room and her rapid breathing, the heat her small feverish body is generating even in its uneasy sleep.

She coughs. A charge of adrenaline goes through my body. She coughs again and I feel another surge, my heart jumping. The day nurse told me to count breaths per minute – too fast is bad. But I can barely make out the clock and I can't remember the number: was it thirty-two, thirty-eight breaths per minute? I'm counting, but I'm counting wrong; it's too hard.

Then suddenly there's a sick, miserable cry – she's woken wretched. I get out of the rocking chair and walk up and down the small room, up and down, pacing. And still she won't settle, can't. Whatever I do isn't enough; I can't make it right.

I start to waltz round the room, bracing her head with one hand, my other arm aching, even though she's so light. *There-there.* She twists in my arms; nothing, nothing will help. I try at last deep knee bends, a jounce that sets her small head drooping onto the blanket on my shoulder. *There.* Her body loosens in my arms and I settle slowly into the rocking chair.

This jouncing is what she needed. Is it what my heart did when she was still inside, still a part of me? Can she be any more a part of me than she is now, in this moment? *There.* I wedge my arm against the arm of the chair, look down at her small body, quiet now. And I'm afraid again, wondering what the sudden stillness is. I can see, hear the breath move across her soft lips, but is it easier or worse?

Fine. She's fine. Asleep.

And suddenly in this darkness, listening to the softness of her breath, I feel the love I hold for her flood my body, move – I can swear I feel it move into hers. *I'll give you anything*, I think, *just take it. Take whatever it is you need because it's yours.*

A sturdy little soul, my daughter. She was a mite, only six pounds, but as stubborn as me: she got better. We went back to my cell together, and spent our days skin to skin. I wouldn't put her in the basket they gave me for her. I held her against me, against the moment something might take her away. Let the days spool by as I waited to find out what awaited us, waited for trial and sentence.

Another prisoner and guard move silently down the corridor. Once they've passed, the traffic guard gestures with his little flags to signal us to move forward. There's no sound but the light slap of his flags. My guard and I start forward, then stop again. I can see the construct of this building, section, plan, elevation; feel it function around me. Can imagine the bundled form of my daughter, left in the not uncaring arms of one of the female guards. And now my own guard and I are taking staircases down, past the netting, *they like to jump*, step after step, going down, underground; the workers' palace. Here be monsters. The morning began with an order: *Prepare yourself for trial.* There was no way to prepare, though I tried to pat my hair into place, rubbed a dab of butter into my shoes for polish, smoothed my skirt with damp palms. Gave my daughter to the guard, a thick woman who kept herself from smiling. I should have known my appointment with justice was approaching: for weeks now the food has improved. Only yesterday there was meat in my soup.

At last we've finished descending; the staircase ends. Down another corridor and then the guard pushes open a broad set of doors onto a huge, rectangular room. Four rows of four chairs where at the moment two young women – just girls, they must still be in their late teens, Vladimir's age – sit. I don't know them, my fellow accused. At the other end of the room there's a long table. Two guards stand behind the girls. Otherwise the room is empty. For a brief moment I imagine we're here for some official celebration, that there will be ribbons and state portraits, that the speeches will begin. My guard sets me down beside the girls, takes his position standing against the wall with the other guards. The girls smile, try to speak to me, but a guard shushes them. They seem giddy, little girls ready for a birthday party, though they're wearing anything but party outfits, their dresses threadbare, scarcely holding together. Mine is new. I was given new clothes for my new body after my daughter was born.

More of the accused start to file in, and the strange sense of carnival increases. We nod to each other as each comes in, try to exchange a few words. The girls beside me giggle, whisper behind their hands. And then a face I recognize: Anatoly. He looks at me; looks at the ground. All the swagger gone from his face. He looks at me again, and I shake my head. His face isn't any longer the face of someone I love. And he isn't even heavy in me any more. He isn't there. A distance has opened now between us, a clearing empty of emotion.

And then I see him, escorted by two guards. Vladimir. He risks a nod, a brief gesture of the hand. He's not as thin as last time. I find myself wanting to laugh, just for having seen his face. Vladimir. Vladimir alive. He turns around in his chair to look at me and the guard barks. The room is full of murmurs now; they can't stop us. We're here, together, the accused, and though only two faces are familiar, we're *comrades*, a conspiracy of bewilderment, of pleasure at our own company after our months of solitary, interrogation, uncertainty. The murmur rises; they can't stop us.

And the whisper goes from mouth to ear, mouth to ear. Vladimir is told he is the father of a daughter. I see his face illuminated and then extinguished. For a moment, in the hum of voices, it's as if this circus, this sham trial, is not what's real. All that matters is that we are at last in a room together. And Vladimir knows about his daughter. The guards finally quiet us; the judges are entering the room. Three old men stuffed into their generals' uniforms, the rigid faces of bad actors.

It started then, and didn't stop as the day wore thin. Our "testimonies" were read, lie after lie, and I had only Vladimir's face to hold me to the world. Before the unfathomable judges, one after another the young people stood up, spilled out their confusion, their shame, uttered what they'd been told to utter. And then one of the old men in his general's uniform, that mockery of a judge, stood and read the verdict, and we learned what we had to pay, what we had to lose. We stood not only accused, but convicted. They made Vladimir stand, took him under the arms, and I could see his legs, his will, failing him. He couldn't stop watching me. I couldn't stand his eyes. They took him away and I saw his face broken apart not with what they were doing to him, but with what he'd done to me.

Your father was a hero; your father was a traitor.

My girl never knew her own father. Why was it so difficult to give her stories of him? She needed them, tried to extract them from me. And I gave her so little, scraps, when I could manage. What I could. Who were you, Vladimir, my darling, my daughter's father? How do I fit the real man, the boy, into the changing shapes of this story I've riddled through – for her, for myself – that has come to me now in its portions and shreds? *Your father was a hero; your father was a traitor.* I turn the words in my hands, hold them tight, let them go. And I know my daughter's son, my dear boy –

whose eyes share the hazel of his grandfather's, who is almost grown – he wants the story too.

It's for them I spell this story out to myself, to tell that unimaginable world that I come from and that they come from too.

Vladimir.

I remember, Raisa said, the day he was arrested, *how he looked as a newborn; the pale pink callus he had on his upper lip in those first moments I held him.*

I remember putting a bow cruelly in his hair, and that he looked at me. I remember his head leaning against my shoulder that first cool July in Moscow. I remember him taking my hand, turning it his quarter turns: to the left, then the right.

Your father was a hero. Vladimir was a boy who tried to shed a little light on the story of his country, even if what was spelled out there was too real, even if it left him too little hope. He tried to sift the truth from the lies; he didn't mind that the cause was hopeless.

Your father was a traitor. Not the way the documents tell it, not to his country. He wanted a better country, but I wonder if he might not, in his innocence, have built the same tyranny he wanted to destroy. It's easy, in this new century, to see the foolishness of those children's idealism, their dreams. What are our children's dreams today? *No blood for oil.* A good dream. But there is blood. *Your father was a hero.* I don't believe in heroes.

Your father was a traitor. In this story I've been telling myself, Vladimir comes out pure. Though in his innocence, his misplaced faith, wanting to make a clean breast of it, not understanding the state he was trying to save – he did betray me. His name on my arrest warrant. *Your father was a good*

Soviet citizen. Or perhaps he didn't name me. Or perhaps he was so tired, so hungry, that when they put the piece of paper in his hands, it wasn't him that signed, not his true self. He was so young. He was afraid. And he wasn't used to fear.

I never needed to forgive Vladimir. For me, he never stood accused.

Verdicts dated 20 February 1952.
The decision of the Chief Military Prosecutor on the case of those persons arrested by the Military Collegium of the Supreme Court of the USSR regarding the accused is as follows:

1. Efron, Vladimir, born 1932, native of the city of Moscow, Jew, citizen of the USSR, non-member of the Party, student of Moscow University: the sentence is execution by firing squad.

2. Koznitsky, Solomon, born 1931, native of the city of Moscow, Jew, citizen of the USSR, non-member of the Party, student of philosophy at the correspondence division of the Lenin State Pedagogical Institute: the sentence is execution by firing squad.

3. Tarasova, Elena, born 1932, native of the city of Moscow, citizen of the USSR, non-member of the Party, student at the correspondence division of the

Lenin State Pedagogical Institute: the sentence is twenty-five years of the deprivation of freedom in a Corrective Labour Camp with disenfranchisement for fifteen years.

4. Trubashnik, Anatoly, born 1926, native of the city of Odessa, citizen of the USSR, non-member of the Party, student of Moscow University: the sentence is ten years of the deprivation of freedom in a Corrective Labour Camp with disenfranchisement for five years.

5. Gershon, Annette, born 1926, native of the city of Winnipeg, Canada, Jewess, citizen of the USSR, non-member of the Party, student of the Mossovet Architectural Workshops: the sentence is ten years of the deprivation of freedom in a Corrective Labour Camp with disenfranchisement for five years.

I don't want to feel what I felt then, that's why I wouldn't remember. And in all the not remembering, maybe I have forgotten. *I am not who I was.* Is this what time does to us, dulls us, thickens us? A callus on our souls. But not then. Even with the sentence, I wouldn't stop hoping for Vladimir, believing that Raisa and Lev would appeal, that the state would relent. I didn't know that Raisa and Lev also had been arrested, sentenced to five years in a labour camp for the letter Pavel had written Stalin, for being Vladimir's parents. No show trial for Pavel and Raisa; within three days of their arrest they were sent to Siberia. Not knowing, I continued to hope. I had my daughter.

She's finished nursing. Her eyes close, open, close, open, close, and she's asleep. I button my blouse, pull the blankets around us. Touch my lips to her forehead and she grimaces, then relaxes, though she's still holding onto my sleeve, that starfish grasp of her hand. *You see, Vladimir; you see how beautiful and strong our daughter is?* He's somewhere in this building. I know it. I don't believe the sentence. They just want to scare us. If only he could see her, just once. I close my eyes, let myself rest.

And wake to voices by the door. It opens – a male guard, and a woman who reminds me absurdly of Olga Moiseyevna, our old neighbour, with her painted nails and trim, tailored suit. She goes to the little stack of diapers, nightgowns, at the foot of the bed, starts folding them into a paper sack.

I push myself back against the wall. "What are you doing?"

The woman looks up at me, lets her hands rest on the bundle. "It's all right, miss. She'll be fine."

The male guard is standing in a corner of the room, his hands behind his back. He turns to the window and I can see his wrists crossed, one hand holding the other, as though he's trying to comfort himself.

The baby's still asleep. I touch my cheek against her cheek, feel her breath across my lips.

"You can give her to me now," the woman says. "It's good she's sleeping. I'll just take her in the little blanket you've got her wrapped in."

I look at the woman's face. What's there? What is it I see in her eyes? She's steady, she looks straight at me.

What's happening to the room? I tip my head back, feel

the ceiling open, lift. Close my eyes. Open them, and the woman has her hands out. I pull the baby closer to me. I've never been in a space this large, this small.

"You can give her to me. It's all right."

Something shifts. I snap into myself. No. I won't let her go. My hands tighten around her and she wriggles, sighs. I release the grip a little, put my mouth to the top of her head, smell her. There. That's what I want.

I feel a hand on my elbow, the woman's voice in my ear. "It's better this way, my dear. She'll be fine. She'll be safe; I promise you."

No. I concentrate. Somewhere in the room, the guard is speaking with the woman, but I don't hear. In one slight movement I get up from the bed, holding her, not letting her go.

The guard moves quietly to stand in front of the door. I hear whispers in the hallway. How many of them are there out there? I stand in the middle of the room and suddenly my legs go, I'm on the floor, but I'm holding her, she's fine, she's still asleep.

The guard's lifted me by my elbows; I'm back on the bed.

"Get her a glass of tea," I hear the woman say, and the guard goes.

"Settle yourself down," she says. "You know there's no point making a fuss. Be a good girl, now." My heart is bumping inside me. I won't give my girl up. All my body wants to keep her, and I will. It's with my body that I'll keep them from taking her away. Voices in the hallway again. I pull my knees up, crouch against the rough wall. There are more voices but I'm concentrating, I concentrate, shrink her inside me so that no one can find us.

The door opens.

Two guards this time.

The first one has a glass of tea in his hand.

"Take a sip," the woman says.

I sip. It's sweetened; I think I taste strawberry preserves. My mother used to put strawberry preserves in her tea.

"I won't give her to you."

"I'll tell you what," the woman says. "You behave, and you can go with us. All right? Finish your tea, and bring the baby along with us."

"We've waited long enough," the new guard says.

"Do you see these papers?" The woman stands, waves them at him. "I am the one authorized to transport this child. I am the one in charge. Let the girl finish her tea."

I set the cup down and both men come up, haul me by my elbows. The door opens and we're walking down the hall, past the identical iron doors, their peepholes, their slots. Up and up stairs and if the guards' hands weren't at my elbows my legs would not carry me.

At last we go into a hallway that seems somehow familiar.

"Tell her we're ready," I hear the woman say. The men seat me on a wooden bench. The baby stirs, opens her eyes, closes them. As they go out, the woman catches the door, holds it, just for a moment, open and I see something, someone just beyond the door, a woman. It can't be, the slim figure, little bit of French lace at the collar . . .

"If you give me your daughter now, I'll give her to your aunt."

"Manya?"

"Give me your daughter, miss. She's here from Odessa, your aunt. I told you it was all right. It's better this way. Believe me."

My arms are not my arms. They let her go.

I used myself up in the days that followed, wore myself out, not eating, not sleeping, my breasts, all my body aching. Cored, hollowed, without my girl. What I held on to was that glimpse of Manya, the smell of lavender, hope, the knowledge that Manya would place inside the emptiness of what the war had taken from her a love for my daughter. Manya, who had been barren, who had something now to hold. I held on to that.

The sky bears down on us. It's a steady rain, untiring; my clothes are heavy with it. The truck swerves round a corner and the woman I'm sitting beside is flung against me, her elbows sharp against my ribs. I shiver. The truck's rocking briefly lulled me to sleep and for a moment I don't know where I am, think I am back among the volunteers digging anti-tank ditches on the outskirts of Moscow. I close my eyes. We're being transported, again. The Black Ravens, the Stolypin train cars, now these trucks. I open my eyes. The woman beside me – Lydia, she told me her name was Lydia – touches my hand. She's a lean, tough woman who must be fifty or so. Dark, intelligent eyes, grey hair. She puts her hand in her pocket and takes out two pieces of rye bread, hands me one. Yesterday they did have us digging trenches; that's where the memories come from. Rank upon rank of women with shovels, but we staggered at it, rough, uncoordinated. And Lydia helped me. I was useless, the handle slipping from my hands, just as it had in those first days volunteering during the war. Useless. How have I been used? What have I ever done with my body? Something hard. Something good, my girl: *you*. Think of something else.

"Thank you," I tell Lydia. And suddenly I'm crying.

"Don't," Lydia says. "It'll wear you out. Eat the bread. You'll feel better."

But I can't stop. "What's wrong?" she asks. "Are you sick?"

I shake my head. "My daughter," I tell her. "I'm thinking about my baby."

"You can't," Lydia says. "Once you start thinking like that it won't stop."

I wipe my face with the back of my sleeve. "They took her away after I was sentenced. They gave her to a relative in Odessa."

"Odessa? You said you were from Odessa. I'm from Odessa . . ."

"I lived there before the war. My aunt still lives there."

"Your family is Jewish?"

I look at her before answering, examining her face for the source of the question. "We're Jewish too," she says quickly. I nod.

"So your daughter's with your aunt – she's all right. You see," Lydia's smoothing my sleeve, "she's all right. You don't want her here, do you? I didn't know you were from Odessa." And now it's Lydia who's crying, silently. She turns her face away from me.

"Lydia?"

She leans her head against my shoulder, but without facing me, her eyes looking out into the rain. "I had two sons." I can feel the story coming. This is how we stay human, telling each other our stories. "Our first, Sergei, was adopted." I shiver, remembering my mother's stories of the orphanage. The truck takes another turn, throwing us against each other. "Then we had our own child, just sixteen months later, our son Osip." Lydia's still leaning her head against me, still speaking quietly out into the rain that seems to be gathering now around us. "In the fall of 1941 they were 15 and 16. Your age, I guess?" I nod. "My husband knew Odessa wouldn't last long." She stops. "Your family?"

"My brother and I got out," I tell her. "In June. My father put us on a train to Moscow."

"Your parents?"

I shake my head. It's fog, this rain that's enveloping us now, seeping through our already sodden clothes. Lydia sighs, then continues. "Sergei's natural mother was Christian. He had papers to prove it, so we thought we could save him, send him to stay with a Christian family. He wouldn't go. *I've lived with you and I'll die with you*, he told us." Lydia's looking at her hands. "We couldn't make him go."

I don't need to hear the rest of the story. We're holding on to each other, letting the tears go, our faces against each others' necks, letting the story go.

And then the truck stops. The other women begin to get down. The guards come, order us out.

"Straight ahead," they tell us.

Lydia stumbles as she climbs down. I take her elbow. My breath catches in my chest.

"Straight ahead," the guards shout. "A step to the right or the left will be considered an attempt to escape. We'll fire without warning."

We walk straight ahead.

We want to live.

For twenty months Lydia and I kept each other alive. Hope kept me alive too, the hope that my daughter would come back to me. That Vladimir would be pardoned, that we'd both someday, soon, be released. You can make a diet of hope; you can eat and drink it.

I have everything. Everything. The file is complete. But I won't let the official version take over my story because I have survived the official version – exceeded it. The dates flick by, April 1952, May 1954, but they are pinpoints, pinpricks, and I refuse them.

There was no reason to hope. There was only Manya to appeal.

They shot him.

Vladimir.

April 1952. They did it. Executed him. The fallen. I can see the stammer of his body, the long slow tumble against some prison wall; can see, in slow motion, his body's fall into nothingness. Solly too. Despite the absurdity of the charges, the appeals; despite the mere threads and shreds of evidence against them.

For two years we didn't know. For two years, till May 1954, we went on hoping. It wasn't till my daughter, our daughter, was two and a half, when I'd been released from the Gulag during the Khrushchev thaw, when Pavel and Raisa came back from Siberia, when Manya, who had taken care of the baby all those long months, had handed her back into my arms – it wasn't until then that they told us that he was dead.

This is not a conversation for children. One day, when she was about four or five, my daughter and I were sitting on the concrete steps to our apartment. It was early in spring, and that day it was still chilly, but the sun was warming our little spot. We were eating a bowl of tiny wild strawberries I'd managed to buy at the market, the very first strawberries of spring.

"What do we say, Baby?" I asked her. It was the spell we chanted whenever we were lucky enough to find strawberries.

"Nothing better than this," she answered.

Our little ritual, the sun blessing us on the concrete steps. A family went by on the sidewalk, father, mother, two little boys. The father picked up the littlest and swung him into the air, and suddenly my daughter had brushed the bowl onto the ground. We watched it bounce and then break, pieces of china mixing with the battered strawberries.

"What, Baby? What is it?"

"Tell me! Tell me where he is!" She was pounding on my arm. "I want my poppa!"

I grabbed her hands, held them against my chest. If I hadn't, I think I might have hit her, because it felt as if, with those words, she'd taken away everything I had so carefully built for her.

We sat there, locked in absence, anger.

I dared tell so little about her father – there was so much to hide. You can let secrets ripen till they rot.

And later, when there was no secret, when it was safe to talk and I had no reason to be silent, still I gave her so little.

I think of your brief, unfinished life, Vladimir. If you'd lived, what would you have made of this new century? What would you have made of the end of the old one, the end of the Soviet state our parents laboured for? I never imagined I'd see it end in my lifetime. Perhaps I never imagined it would end. If you'd lived, what would have become of the foolishness that made your life so short and pure? No one should be held accountable for the choices they make when they're eighteen. And yet we are; we are held accountable. We are accused; we are tried; we are sentenced.

What have I made of you, all these years, seeing your mouth in your daughter's mouth, seeing your eyes in your grandson's eyes? You were the boy who was never afraid, who was afraid. The boy who saw through the murk of Stalinism to a truth, though it wasn't the truth. In the story I've recounted of your life, I've made you into a hero, though I don't believe in heroes, never did. I've made you up, perhaps into something simpler than you were, perhaps into something more complicated.

I do know something, about you, and about myself. We have the daughter we deserved, who survived, fatherless, the impossible life we gave her, whose sturdy soul thrived. You would have loved her as I love her; she would have loved you back.

For me, she's been enough.

It's because of Anatoly that I have these folders full of documents, everything. Even the letters they took from me that night Vladimir was arrested. In that brief moment when the Berlin Wall came down and the KGB – NKVD, MGB – files were opened, they all came back to me, all the confiscated material, my entire file, the official record of everything that followed. The papers came to me not by chance or miracle, but because Anatoly rescued them for me. It must have taken some considerable courage to go and get them for me, to send them. At no small risk, even then. As no small gesture of reconciliation.

I spent some time hating him, especially in those first furious nights when my anger battled the numbness of fear. And then I continued to hate him through nights of unbearable loneliness. In the better days that followed, once the fight to survive was past, I started to feel myself going sour with that hatred for him. But I am my mother's daughter, and, tasting that grief, I had to think of who I wanted to be. Sour doesn't suit who I think I am. So, at some point, I decided to forgive Anatoly. Because if I hadn't, it would have made me less myself. And though the grief, and the anger, have gone cold, the love I felt for him, whatever that was – I still keep a piece of it somewhere.

And besides, I don't have any right to judge him. So many good people, good and not so good people, acted the same, did what, in their desperation, they had to.

I have everything. When my daughter was four, we received further fruit of the thaw: a report recording the review of Vladimir's and Solly's verdicts. The report establishes that "certain violations of the law" had taken place during the preliminary investigation, that "measures of coercion" had been applied against these two boys (the nighttime interrogations, the deprivation of parcels, of food), that their declarations had been "taken down prejudicially," records of their interrogations fabricated in their absence, and that, furthermore, the revolver that had been taken from Solly, the reason they were sentenced to death, was "unusable." The report noted without comment that "in view of their deaths," Solly and Vladimir had not been questioned during the review. It made no apology for these deaths, expressed no regret. It concluded that in the light of the investigation, Vladimir and Solly were posthumously sentenced to ten years in a labour camp. They were four years dead.

I have everything. Even the certificates in which Vladimir's and Solly's sentences were rescinded and they were declared "fully rehabilitated." In 1991. Thirty-nine years after their deaths. The new Russian state was cleaning its hands, the wheels of this particular justice grinding slowly but thoroughly.

There. They've said their piece, these yellowing bits of paper, these documents with their dates, their facts and fibs and stories. I knew they were dangerous. Once the past opens its doors, it starts inhabiting you again. But I suppose that's what I wanted, to be inhabited, to inhabit myself more fully. Though nothing is solved. I creak back down onto my knees, gather up the papers, begin to sort them gently back into their folders.

I stood accused. I stand accused still, of having let the story that I had to tell slip for all these years. Who am I now? Where did my story get me? What it got me is this life, a life that is tapering down now, however much I deny it. I think of the truck on that country road that passed me so carefully. Perhaps now it's less than two solemn feet between me and what would end me; perhaps it's more.

I know I sound angry. I am. I am eaten by an anger that kept me silent. Till now.

I was pardoned too. In 1991. But when those papers came, I realized that I didn't want the record wiped clean. I didn't want the story of what Vladimir had chosen to do corrected.

Not in the light of those faces on the television. Not in this world, this new century. Not from my new home in Toronto. That's where they mailed the certificate. My new old home, the home I'll be leaving soon, for another home. We've been here more than twenty-five years, my daughter and I. We got out. I at last got to come back to Canada, to come home. To see Joseph, his family. Home. He's old now, my Joseph, but he's still here, still mine.

I have to eat. I'm going to sit down and eat, put good food in my mouth. And be glad for it. I'm going to turn on more light with the touch of a switch. Maybe put the television back on, watch my young people's faces, listen to their voices and all their certainty and all their hopes. What would Vladimir have to say to those young faces and their protests, their chants? Could we ever have translated for them the unfathomable world we come from? What would Poppa have thought, O brave new world? Capitalism didn't die, Poppa. Every surface gets covered with words intended to make us feel how empty we are so that we'll want something. And my mother, my mother would have been sure about everything as she always was, would have packed everything tight into her suitcase of certainty.

My father gave me an orange, once. I watched my mother make a cake. What they could give me, what they could never give me, resides in me still. There it is; the world. There it is; home.

Acknowledgements

Special thanks to my son, Sasha Tregebov, whose idea this was.

Immense gratitude to Warren Cariou, midwife extraordinaire, splendid editor, friend, and writer. Without his help from beginning to end this wouldn't be much of a book.

Other hands and good eyes also helped: my sincere thanks to Charis Wahl and Lynn Coady. Thanks also to critically encouraging readers Mary Chapman, Nancy Richler, Guillermo Verdecchia and Peter Higdon. How fortunate I was to have Carole Corbeil read this and encourage me very early on.

Thanks to Nik and the whole crew at Coteau for their time, care and generosity with this project.

I am most grateful to Alla Tumanov for the insight her writing has given me not only into the worldview of the young people involved in the Slutsky Rebellion, but into the generosity of spirit that would allow the survivors to emerge from their ordeal with a greater humanity. Alla Tumanov's memoir, *Where We Buried the Sun: One Woman's Gulag Story*, translated by Gust Olson (NeWest Press, 1999) was invaluable to my research. The wording of the interrogation documentation in my novel is drawn from the documents included in Tumanov's book. The names of the officials who signed the documentation are actual. These are the persons responsible during the historical events in which Vladlen Furman was arrested, sentenced and executed.

I hope that my new cousins, Alexander and Danielle Furman, find this story worthy of their family. I am grateful to newlyweds Andreas Schroeder and Sharon Brown for their hospitality and wisdom. My thanks to Prof. Julie Hessler of the Department of History at the University of Oregon for kindly looking over an earlier draft for historical veracity. Thanks also to the amazing Josh Stenberg for consultation on Russian terms and names. And to Diane Caldwell for her research in Moscow.

The following memoirs of the 1930s, 40s and 50s in the Soviet Union provided me with details of everyday civilian life: Seema Rynin Allan's *Comrades and Citizens*; Don Dallas' *Dateline Moscow*; Lydia Kirk's *Postmarked Moscow*; John Lawrence's *Life in Russia*; Deana Levin's *Children in Soviet Russia*; Penelope Sassoon's *Penelope in Moscow*; William A. Wood's *Our Ally The People of Russia.* The excerpt from the Mayakovsky poem "Why Did We Fight" is from the book *The Bedbug and Selected Poetry* (Cleveland, 1960).

Many thanks to the Canada Council for the Arts, the Ontario Arts Council and the Toronto Arts Council for their generous support during the long period in which this book was written.

Author Biography

Photo: Sam Znaimer

Rhea Tregebov is an award-winning poet, author of a half-dozen collections of verse, and also the author of five picture books for young children. Her poetry has won both the *Malahat Review* Long Poem Award and the *Prairie Schooner* Readers' Choice Award as well as honourable mention for the National Magazine Awards. She also acted as editor and co-translator of *Arguing with the Storm: Stories by Yiddish Women Writers*.

Born in Saskatoon, Rhea Tregebov grew up in Winnipeg, and has English degrees from the University of Manitoba and Boston University. She lived in Toronto for many years but now makes her home in Vancouver, where she is an Assistant Professor of Creative Writing at the University of British Columbia.

ENVIRONMENTAL BENEFITS STATEMENT

Coteau Books saved the following resources by printing the pages of this book on chlorine free paper made with 100% post-consumer waste.

TREES	WATER	SOLID WASTE	GREENHOUSE GASES
37 FULLY GROWN	**16,728** GALLONS	**1,016** POUNDS	**3,473** POUNDS

Calculations based on research by Environmental Defense and the Paper Task Force. Manufactured at Friesens Corporation